The
Nightmare
Charade

Tor Teen Books by Mindee Arnett

The Nightmare Affair
The Nightmare Dilemma
The Nightmare Charade

~The~
Nightmare
Charade

MINDEE ARNETT

**TOR®
TEEN**

A Tom Doherty Associates Book

THE NIGHTMARE CHARADE

Copyright © 2015 by Mindee Arnett

A Tor Teen Book
Published by Tom Doherty Associates, LLC
175 Fifth Avenue
New York, NY 10010

www.tor-forge.com

Tor® is a registered trademark of Tom Doherty Associates, LLC.

The Library of Congress Cataloging-in-Publication Data is available upon request.

ISBN 978-0-7653-3335-3 (hardcover)
ISBN 978-1-4668-0070-0 (e-book)

Tor Teen books may be purchased for educational, business, or promotional use. For information on bulk purchases, please contact the Macmillan Corporate and Premium Sales Department at 1-800-221-7945, extension 5442, or write to specialmarkets@macmillan.com.

First Edition: August 2015

Printed in the United States of America

0 9 8 7 6 5 4 3 2 1

To Philip Garybush, for always being there

Acknowledgments

This is it. The end. Of ALL THE THINGS. Just kidding. But it is the end of Dusty and Eli's story and my very first series. It's bittersweet. A part of me wishes this story would go on forever, but another part of me appreciates the closure. I hope you do, too, dear readers.

Firstly, and as always, thanks to God and his Son.

My biggest thanks goes to my editor, Whitney Ross, who saw the potential in Dusty's story and gave her three whole books to have it played out. Thank you also for your infinite patience, your insight, and your ongoing support. Also, thanks to the marvelous team at Tor Teen, the best place a writer could call home—Amy Stapp, assistant editor; Lisa Davis, my production editor; Seth Lerner, the art director; Jane Liddle, the copy editor; Alexis Saarela, my publicist; John Morrone, the proofreader; and, of course, Tom Doherty and Kathleen Doherty.

As always, thanks to my fierce, wonderful agent, Suzie Townsend, and the rest of the crew at New Leaf Literary and Media: Joanna Volpe, Kathleen Ortiz, Pouya Shahbazian, David Caccavo, Mackenzie Brady, Danielle Barthel, and Jaida Temperly.

No book exists without outside help, and I'm fortunate to have awesome friends to call upon. Thanks to my critique partners and beta readers: Lori M. Lee, Amanda Sharritt, and Jason Sharritt. And a special shout-out to my language guru, Junius Johnson. Also, thanks to my family, Adam, Inara, and Tanner—you're my dreams come true.

And, finally, thanks to all the readers who've stuck with me this long. Librarians, teachers, bloggers, teens—you're all special to me; you're all magical beings. I wish I could give you each a hug. Please keep on reading and spreading that magic.

The
Nightmare
Charade

∼ 1 ∼

Last Kiss

J had no idea that the first kiss would be the last.

The last free one that was, the only one Eli and I didn't have to steal or keep hidden like some terrible secret.

No, I had no idea what was coming as I stood in front of the bathroom mirror and reapplied my cherry lip gloss for the fourth time.

"You know, Dusty," Selene said from outside the door where she was hanging posters on the wall of our new dorm room, two floors up from our old one. "Despite what the packaging might claim, I don't think it's actually possible to increase the size of your lips by putting on layers."

Suppressing a nervous laugh, I turned and stepped out into the living room portion of the suite. We were juniors this year, and that meant a larger dorm, complete with a private bathroom. Selene and I had plans to burn our old shower shoes in a celebratory ritual this weekend.

I fixed her with the most serious stare I could manage. "Are you sure? This is magic lip gloss, you know."

Selene snorted. "I don't believe you." She held out her hand, and I set the lipstick canister on her palm. She turned it over in her fingers, and then raised it to eye level to read the label.

"This is in French."

"That's because I bought it in Paris." The memory brought a fleeting grin to my face. Despite the emotional challenges I'd faced during my summer vacation spent touring Europe—being cut off from my friends; stuck with only my mother for company; and most especially, going weeks on end without a single word from the literal boy of my dreams, Eli Booker—the physical experience had been fun. The lip balm was an impromptu purchase at a little shop called the Incantorium Emporium. It was the kind of place that only served magickind. Probably a good thing, given its location inside a secret alcove in the Paris catacombs. Nothing said magical and charming like a bunch of skeletons.

"So I gathered," Selene said with a hint of envy in her voice. Her summer hadn't been quite as exotic, although I would've traded places with her in a hot second. She'd spent the last eleven weeks hanging out with her boyfriend—late-night strolls by the lake, trips to the movies, not to mention hours of kissing, or so I guessed. Even if Selene were the kind of girl to make out and tell, she wouldn't have chosen me as her confidant. Partially because I wasn't thrilled about her reconciliation with my sometimes tormenter and regular jackass Lance Rathbone, but mostly because she knew all too well how little kissing I'd been doing lately.

A situation that was about to change.

A flock of butterflies took flight inside my stomach. I fought to keep the tremor out of my voice, my words coming rapidly. "Yeah, the shop owner told me it has an *amore* charm on it. At least, that's what I thought he said. His accent was pretty thick, and I don't think he liked me at all. He was a Mors demon and you know how they feel about Nightmares. I mean, then again, pretty much everybody hates Night—"

"Dusty." Selene grabbed my shoulders and gave me a shake. "You're babbling."

I gulped, trying to settle the butterflies, but they only increased their frenzy, becoming hummingbirds instead, wings on turbo speed. "Sorry. I can't help it. I'm nervous."

Selene smiled. The gesture was so radiant it made my head spin, and for a second the hummingbirds froze, stunned by an unexpected onslaught of bliss. That was the trouble with having a siren for a best friend—random moments of dazedness. Not that it was her fault. She couldn't help being beautiful and mesmerizing. No more than I could help the way my eyes glow in the dark, an aspect of my Nightmare heritage. At the moment, however, I had a feeling Selene wasn't aware of just how much more dazzling she was being than normal. I suspected it might have something to do with Lance.

"You've no reason to be nervous," Selene said, her smile easing enough to make the radiance tolerable. "You look beautiful."

I shook my head and stepped back. "It's not that. It's . . ." I broke off, searching for the right words. Looks weren't the problem. I didn't feel beautiful, exactly, but I knew I was looking nice, slightly above my average state. My makeup was even and natural, and I'd managed to convince my frizzy red hair to lie flat for once with some help from Magick Madam's Hair Pomade, another purchase from the Incantorium Emporium. Outfit wise, I'd opted for a pair of low-rise designer jeans and a pale pink knit top, the kind that hangs loose around the shoulders, that my mom bought me from a boutique in Italy.

No, looks weren't the problem.

Time was.

Nearly three months had gone by since I'd last seen Eli in person. And though I had no reason to believe his feelings for me had changed, I had no proof they were the same either. We hadn't spoken on the phone at all, and the e-mails had been too few and too brief. I hadn't had access to my cell phone all summer—the moment our plane touched down in London, my mom confiscated it. She claimed it was because of the high international cellular charges. *Yeah right.*

That was the worst of it. None of the adults in our lives wanted us to be together. Everybody from my mother to magickind government officials were trying to keep us apart. It was the primary reason for my impromptu summer vacation abroad. But their rationale for doing so was just a stupid superstition. Eli and I were dream-seers; together we could predict the future and uncover secrets through signs and symbols in Eli's dreams, a gift that made us invaluable to the magickind government. So far we'd stopped a murderous, power-mad warlock who styled himself as the next Hitler, and we'd prevented the magickind island capital of Lyonshold from sinking into the waters of Lake Erie.

The only catch to our ability, the only *price,* came in the form of a curse—if Eli and I were to fall in love we would be doomed to destroy each other.

I don't believe it. I refuse to believe it.

Drawing a deep breath, I let it out slowly. "What if he's changed his mind?"

"About what?" Selene said half-laughing, half-exasperated. "About you? Not a chance."

Relief swept over me at her words and even more at the attitude behind them. She was so certain, so happy and optimistic. Not at all like the best friend that I'd left behind at the beginning of the summer. That Selene would've been careful in her reassurance, logical about the argument. Not so carefree. It was a nice change. A smile broke across my face. "Who are you and what have you done with my best friend?"

Selene blinked. In the low dorm room light, her eyes looked indigo in color. Her glossy black hair hung in a thick braid over her shoulder. "What do you mean?"

"Never mind. I just think we need to have a long talk about your summer vacation. Later." I pulled my cell out of my front pocket and pressed the home button, lighting up the screen: 10:46 P.M. My heart rate quickened, the hummingbirds taking flight again. Eli said to meet him at 11:00. If I left now I would make it right on time, maybe even one or two minutes early. The walk would be easy since I'd opted for flats instead of heels.

But did I want to arrive right on time? Would I appear too eager? Desperate?

With my anticipation wavering toward frustration, I opened the phone to the text screen and reread Eli's message.

> I'm finally on campus. Think you can sneak out? Meet
> me at my dorm at 11:00?

I'd immediately typed back a yes. I didn't have to ask him for his new room number. Selene already knew it. Lance was Eli's roommate again this year, and he'd moved in yesterday.

"Okay," Selene said, still puzzled. One slender dark eyebrow sat higher than the other. "Later then. Shouldn't you be going?"

I bit my lip. "I don't know. Should I?"

Selene cleared her throat. "So who are *you* and what have you done with *my* best friend?"

"What?"

"You're usually not this indecisive. Normally it's all act first, think it over later." Opening my mouth to argue, she cut me off with a raised hand. "Go on. Eli is waiting for you. Don't waste time pretending you feel anything less than what you actually do."

Speaking from experience? I wanted to ask but didn't. I already knew the answer. Returning my cell to my pocket, I headed out the door. I made it five steps, debated whether or not I should brush my teeth again, then forced myself to walk down the hallway to the staircase.

The only drawback to the upperclassman dorms was the longer trek. I trotted down the last two flights of stairs, battling with nerves the whole way. I slowed as I reached the foyer. Two magically animated suits of armor stood guard at the door—Frank and Igor, or so I'd dubbed them freshman year. At the sound of my approach, they turned their faces toward me, blank empty slots inside their helmets where their eyes should have been. Having them look at you like that was creepy on a good night, but in my current nervous state it was downright terrifying. I had no idea if they would let me pass.

Technically speaking, I didn't have permission to be out after hours tonight. But I was hoping Frank and Igor wouldn't know that. I was a Nightmare, after all, and they were used to my late-night schedule. Last year, I'd been allowed out of the dorm three nights a week to dream-feed with Eli. Well, *on* Eli, to be more specific. Even though I was half human I still had to dream-feed to fuel my magic.

"Hey, guys," I said, giving a little wave. "Did you miss me?"

Blank stares.

"I'll take that as a yes."

More blank stares.

"But listen, I'm on my way to a dream-feeding session. Okay if I pass?"

Blank stares to the nth power.

A weak feeling struck my knees and sweat broke out on the back of my neck. If they didn't let me through, I was going to have a meltdown. Nervous or not, I had my heart set on seeing Eli tonight. The skin on my wrist began to warm beneath the silver band I wore there, and it occurred to me I could always force my way through, with magic.

But a second later, they turned their sightless gazes away from me and pulled their spears fully upright. Taking that as a yes, I hurried past them.

Outside the warm day had turned to a cool night. A cloudless sky drenched in stars cast silver light over the campus. The buildings at Arkwell Academy came in an assortment of architectural styles, everything from Gothic to neoclassical to baroque. I never paid much attention to the variation before, but after nearly three months of sightseeing in Europe, I'd developed a keener eye—and vocabulary. Rather than look tacky, the effect of so many styles in one place was to make Arkwell feel like *every* place, the entire world situated in some two thousand acres.

I reached the bell tower at the center of campus without spotting anyone, but as I rounded the corner around Monmouth Tower, my heart lurched at the sight of one of the Will Guard walking down the path toward me. Crap. I didn't think these magickind versions of rent-a-cops would be back this year, not after so many of them had been in on the plan to sink Lyonshold. But it seemed I was wrong. This particular Will Guard wasn't one I'd seen before, but there was no mistaking the red tunic and black pants.

Deciding it was too late to go around, I raised my head, feigning confidence.

"What are you doing out at this hour?" the woman said, coming to a halt in front of me. I saw at once that she was witchkind; she carried a wand made of some dark wood in her right hand. The name Bollinger was embroidered in gold across the left breast of her tunic beneath the Magi Senate crest of the tree, wand, and flame.

"I'm on my way to a dream-feeding session," I said, somehow

managing to sound steady despite the tremble in my muscles. "I'm a Nightmare."

Bollinger stared back at me, unblinking, face expressionless.

"Um." I bit my lower lip. "You know, a Nightmare? I have to dream-feed? Late at night? While people are sleeping?" I hadn't meant every phrase to come out a question, but they had anyway.

The woman's lips twisted into a frown. "I know what a Nightmare is."

That's a relief, I thought, wise enough to keep it to myself. See, Selene was wrong; I could totally think before acting.

The woman's eyes narrowed on my face. "You're the one who broke The Will, aren't you?"

A chill snaked down my spine at the venom in her voice. Her dislike was clear as freshly Windexed glass. It wouldn't be the first time someone disliked me on principle. Nightmares often provoked that reaction in other magickind, thanks to our bloody, evil history, one so violent that there were hardly any more Nightmares around. But this time I had a feeling it was more personal.

The shakiness in my muscles changed to tension—not from nerves but anticipation, like an athlete moments before the start of a competition. The skin around my left wrist began to warm again beneath the silver band, the sensation all too familiar. On the outside it looked like a thick bracelet, but on the inside, hidden beneath a glamour, it wasn't anything so benign. I reached for the band instinctively, twisting it around on my wrist. It was hot to the touch.

"Technically, I didn't break it. I just made it possible for it to be broken." Speaking had been a mistake. A lie would've been better, but it was hard to think with the tension coursing through me, the burning in my wrist. When that happened all I wanted to do was disengage the glamour on the bracelet and reveal the sword hidden beneath it.

Not just any sword, but Bellanax, the sword of legend, sword of power. Ancient and infinitely magical, it had been known by many names over the centuries, including Excalibur and, most recently, The Will sword. Yes, this object around my wrist was what had made The Will possible. It was the power source for the spell that had once controlled and policed all magic use.

But I couldn't reveal Bellanax, no matter how much I wanted to. Few people knew I had possession of the sword, and I needed to keep it that way—if I wanted to stay alive.

Resisting the urge to break the glamour, I focused on the woman in front of me.

Her frown had become a snarl. "I don't care about technicalities. What I care about is having my job reduced to this." She waved her hand through the air as if to indicate the entire expanse of Arkwell.

I wanted to sympathize, I really did—it had to be rough to go from some cushy desk job to foot patrolling a school full of teenagers—but with Bellanax's presence pressing so hard on me at the moment, sympathy was in short supply. The sword wanted to be seen—and used.

"I'm sorry," I said, an alien coolness creeping into my voice. "It's been tough all over."

"You have no idea," Bollinger snapped. Her teeth were startlingly white in the moonlight, the incisors uneven points. She wore her mouse-brown hair in a ponytail at the nape of her neck.

I took a deep breath, let it out, then drew another. "May I go to my session?" Now my voice had a note of daring in it—as in "you don't dare tell me no." I didn't mean for it to come out that way, but it couldn't be helped. When Bellanax decided to make trouble, all bets were off. The last time it had acted out, Mom and I were eating in a seafood bar in Inverness, Scotland, and I overheard the men at the table next to us claiming that if the

Loch Ness monster was real it had to be some long-lost dinosaur. Bellanax had taken offense at the notion, and tried to get me to correct them—the Loch Ness was a wyvern not a dinosaur. It had taken all my energy to resist. The sword was a numen vessel, housing the spirit of a long-dead magickind, and that meant it had a mind and will of its own.

Bollinger swallowed, the veins in her neck working. "Yes," she finally said. "You may go."

"Thank you." I moved past her without another word and without looking back. The farther away I drew from her, the spirit or power or whatever it was that made Bellanax something more than a sword, settled back into a state of dormancy. Which was exactly where I preferred it.

The longer I walked, distancing myself from the run-in, the more the woman's reaction bothered me. I could understand her resentment, but not her hate. She acted like I was an ax murderer on death row, one who'd chopped up her family into little pieces. It wasn't fair. *I didn't*—the thought stopped dead in my mind as I remembered the attack on Lyonshold. We'd kept the island from sinking, but there had been casualties. One of them had even been a friend of mine. Was it really my fault? Was I responsible for breaking The Will and thereby allowing evildoers the chance to do their bad deeds?

There was no answer. Even Bellanax, who often offered opinions on such things, remained quiet.

A new kind of nervousness came over me that not even the anticipation of seeing Eli could shake. At least that was until I actually arrived outside his door. Standing before it, my heart gave a hard lurch inside my chest and then seemed to stop beating all together for a second. I didn't know if I should knock or just go on in. Normally, I did the latter, but nothing felt normal right now.

I stood there for several moments, thinking it over. Unconsciously, I touched my fingers to the silver band, twisting it around and around on my wrist as I tried to muster my courage—knock or enter, knock or enter.

At the sound of a noise coming down the corridor, I reached for the door handle, found it unlocked, and pushed my way inside.

Familiar surroundings greeted me. Except for the larger size and bathroom, Eli's new dorm looked the same as the old one. Expensive stereo equipment and other electronics lined one whole wall, most of it belonging to Lance Rathbone whose dad was a magi senator with all the requisite income included. Band posters and several pieces of sports memorabilia decorated the rest of the walls in and around the two desk units and sofa. I was happy to see that Lance hadn't put up his girls-in-bikinis posters again. I had a feeling I could thank Selene for that one.

All of this I took in with one quick, forgotten glance before my eyes fell on the boy sitting in the chair farthest from the door. Eli's eyes were fixed on me in a penetrating stare, as if he wasn't quite sure who he was seeing. I stared back, my heart beating somewhere near my throat. The hummingbirds still filled my belly, but they seemed to have doubled in size and number.

Eli looked mostly the same as I remembered—only better, because he was here and he was real. His black hair, usually longer, was cut military short, and his skin was tanned to a golden bronze. The lights were turned down low, but even still I could clearly see the blue of his eyes, pale and startling in their color.

Say something! But my voice had gotten lost. And I didn't know what to say. "Hi" seemed inadequate. I had no idea what Eli was thinking, feeling. All the doubt from earlier came crashing back down on me. Here I'd thought his invite tonight was for us to rekindle the first faint sparks we'd left burning weeks ago. But maybe instead he was just going to tell me he'd moved on, found someone else. Or even worse, that he'd decided to believe the curse again, the way he had when he first learned about it last year.

Finally, I mustered my courage and opened my mouth to speak. But then a smile broke across Eli's face. The effect was like sunlight bursting through a wall of storm clouds, sudden, undeniable proof of hope and possibilities and change.

He stood up, his presence seeming to fill the whole room. I'd forgotten how tall he was, how physically imposing. He'd put on muscle over the last few weeks, the evidence clear in the bulging, sinewy shapes visible beneath his well-worn T-shirt. He made me feel small and vulnerable, but also completely safe and protected.

"Dusty," he said, his voice deep and husky. The sound set my pulse to racing.

Two steps later and he stood before me, peering down as he raised his hands to my face, cradling the sides of my jaw, the tips of his fingers slipping into my hair.

And then his lips closed over mine. The world turned sideways for a moment, but in the next it settled into place. Into *rightness*. I kissed him back, wrapping my hands around his waist and holding on. There was no curse. No reason to worry. We were made for this.

Nothing could be more right.

~ 2 ~

Animus Mortem

The smell of him filled my nose—soap and cologne and something earthen like dew-drenched woods at dawn. I breathed him in. His hands fell away from my face, coming to rest on the jut of my hips. His fingers slid beneath the hem of my shirt, his warm skin shooting electric chills over my body.

His lips moved off mine and he kissed a line over my jaw and down my neck. "Dusty," he breathed, his warm breath sending even more chills through me. "God, how I've missed you."

"Me, too," I said. With my eyes closed, his kisses became the only thing in the world, all my senses focused on the sensation. "For a second I thought you'd changed your mind."

"What?" Eli pulled back, and I looked up to find him staring down at me, his mouth slightly open and his eyebrows drawn together. "I will never change my mind about how I feel about you."

Don't say never, a voice whispered in my head. For a second I wasn't sure if it was my own thought or someone else's. The silver band on my wrist was noticeably warm against my skin.

"You're the girl of my dreams," Eli said, his expression softening. "All of them. Every night."

Something about the way he spoke told me he meant this quite literally. Worry started to creep in. Dreams were powerful, dangerous things. My presence in his could mean anything—good or bad.

But then Eli bent his head toward me, and the doubt vanished as his lips touched mine once more.

Neither of us noticed the door opening. We didn't hear the footsteps until it was too late.

"Unless you want a month's worth of detention," a familiar voice said from behind us, "I suggest you desist right this moment."

I froze in Eli's arms even as his body stiffened. Then we both wrenched apart and spun toward the intruders. There were four in all, three I recognized and one stranger. The speaker was Principal Hendershaw, a short, plump woman with Coke-bottle glasses and a prickly temperament. Next to her stood frail, bony Lady Elaine, chief advisor to the Magi Senate. Dwarfing them both was Sheriff Brackenberry, who barked a laugh at our discomfort.

"What are you doing here?" Eli said with a surprising amount of hostility in his voice considering we'd been caught making out in his dorm room. After hours. *By the principal.* Not to mention the head of the local magickind police force.

"We are here for the same reason anyone would call upon dream-seers," said the fourth member of the party. The stranger stepped forward, bringing his face into full view. He was a tall, thin man of indeterminate age. Blond hair so pale it looked white hung in untidy waves tucked behind his ears. Or maybe it was white, a true reflection of his actual age, with his smooth-skinned face the deception. He carried a dark green folder tucked beneath his arm, which he now pulled out and flipped open. "For help with averting a crisis." He dropped the folder on the table next to Eli.

A tremor went through me. Another crisis? Already? I didn't

want to hear it. All I wanted was for these people to leave so we could get back to the kissing and making up for lost time.

Eli put his hands on his hips, but the irreverence was absent in his tone. "What crisis and who are you?"

"This is Detective Valentine," Sheriff Brackenberry said. "Of the D.I.M.S.: The Department of Intelligence for Magickind Secrecy."

An involuntary smile crested my lips. "Dims?" I said. "Like dim-witted? Was that on purpose?" *Darn it, Dusty,* I inwardly cursed. *Open mouth, insert foot.*

But to my surprise, Detective Valentine acknowledged the remark with a wry smile. "You're not the first to make that connection, I'm afraid." His gaze shifted from me to Eli. "Are we free to speak privately? Where is your roommate?"

"In there." Eli motioned toward the doorway into the bedroom section of the suite. "He should have his headphones on with the music turned up loud."

This news made my skin warm. Eli had been looking forward to our reunion enough to make sure Lance gave us some privacy. *Ugh, these people. Go away already.*

"Would you mind taking care of the roommate, Sheriff?" Valentine said.

"Now wait a second—" Eli began.

Valentine cut him off with a raised hand. "He'll be fine. Just a sleeping spell. Everything we say from this moment forward is classified. Is that understood?"

I gulped, sensing the man's seriousness. The D.I.M.S. might be a dumb acronym, but that didn't mean their duty wasn't important. The agency's title made it sound like a combination of the FBI and the CIA.

Eli and I both nodded, not that Valentine had been waiting for our consent. He'd already pulled out two pieces of thick paper from the folder and set them side-by-side on the table. Words in shiny black ink filled it from margin to margin.

Looking up, Valentine said, "Thank you for escorting us, Dr. Hendershaw, but if you wouldn't mind stepping out . . ."

Looking like she'd just swallowed something large and sour, Hendershaw harrumphed. "Very well. I'll wait in the hall."

"That won't be necessary," said Lady Elaine. "I will discuss the new situation with Eli and Dusty when we're finished."

New situation? Dread began to do a slow march inside my head.

Hendershaw made as if to argue, but then she flashed a quick, acidic smile my way and disappeared through the door.

"What new situation?" I said.

"Lady Elaine, if you could please seal the room," said Valentine.

Lady Elaine locked the door. Then she held out her hand, the arm attached to it a thin spindly thing like the leg of a fawn. She began to mutter an incantation, and a tingle of magic filled the air. I didn't know the name of the spell, but I'd seen it used once before. It would soundproof the room, preventing anyone outside from listening in.

"Now, Dusty, Eli," said Valentine. "You two will please sign one of these nondisclosure agreements."

He said it like we had an option of declining, but I knew better. I ran my tongue over my teeth while warning bells sounded inside my head. If he were an ordinary government official, of the human variety, I would've considered a nondisclosure agreement something normal, albeit serious. But this was the magic-kind government and that meant the potential for weird and inexplicable.

"What exactly are we signing?" I paused, eyeing the paper. "And how?" I wasn't about to offer up any blood.

"You'll sign with this." Detective Valentine held out his hand and a sleek gold pen with a razor sharp tip appeared across his palm.

I accepted the pen, but only reluctantly. "What will happen when we sign?"

"Nothing too serious," Valentine said, his expression innocuous. "Your signature will activate a binding spell, which will prevent you from discussing the matter at hand with anyone who has not also signed the nondisclosure."

"What if we try anyway?"

"Your tongue will seal itself to the roof of your mouth until you change your mind."

Beside me, Eli made a sarcastic sound that could've been mistaken for a laugh. "That sounds like fun." He stepped closer to me, his arm pressing against mine. Heat radiated between our bodies.

"Go on and sign it, Destiny," Lady Elaine said, and I winced at the use of my real name. Nope, there wasn't any getting out of this. Real first name meant business. I might not believe in the dream-seer curse, but I definitely believed in the we-are-now-pawns-of-the-government aspect of the job.

Sighing, I set the tip of the pen to the paper and scribbled my name on the line at the bottom of the page: *Destiny Everhart.* The letters glowed ruby red for a second, and the prickle of magic spread down my fingertips, over my hand, and up my arm. The glow on my name disappeared a moment later, leaving nothing behind but black ink.

Eli did the same with his piece of paper and handed the pen back to Valentine. It dematerialized as quickly and soundlessly as it had appeared. I stared at the man, wondering what kind of magickind he was. I didn't see a wand or other magical instrument, and there were no telltale points on his ears to indicate fairykind or some other naturekind. Not that the lack was proof one way or another. All the kinds sometimes used glamour to hide their true appearances.

"I apologize for the late hour and all the protocol," Valentine said, shifting his gaze between Eli and me. "But the situation couldn't wait any longer and the veil of secrecy is absolutely necessary." He exhaled, and I couldn't tell if the gesture was genuine or theatrical. Like his age, everything about him seemed mutable. "We need your help in recovering a lost artifact."

"Lost, as in stolen?" Eli said.

"I'm afraid so," replied Valentine. "This is not the kind of object capable of vanishing on its own, although that would've been a preferable scenario by far."

"Um, does that happen often?" I said.

"More than you would guess." Valentine pointed at Eli and then me. "I need you two to focus your dream-seer skills on finding both the object and who took it."

"Sounds simple enough." Eli folded his arms over his chest, muscles flexing in ways that made me want to forget everything else going on. If I wasn't careful, I would find myself caught up in a random moment of dazedness again, as surely as if Eli were part siren instead of fully human boy. But then my eye caught sight of the leather band on his wrist, and I remembered that wasn't precisely true, not anymore. Yes, Eli was human but he was still magical. He was a Conductor, able to channel the magic contained in the wand hidden beneath the glamoured bracelet. Not that he was hiding his wand like I hid Bellanax. Most people glamoured their wands. Made for easy carrying and access.

"I'm afraid it's anything but simple," said Lady Elaine. "The object in question is—"

"Dangerous?" Eli offered, cocking an eyebrow.

"They wouldn't need us for mostly harmless," I muttered.

"Very dangerous." Valentine ran his thumb over the top of his lip. "And deadly." He turned his attention to the folder, pulling out a blank piece of photograph paper this time. At least it looked blank at first, but as he set it on the table, black inky tendrils began to appear, writhing like smoke across the shiny, slick surface. A moment later, the ink resolved into a full color photograph of a table with a single object resting atop it.

Valentine reached toward the photo and then *through it*. His hand slipped into the paper, fingers and palm disappearing as if it were actually a bowl. He made a cupping gesture, and a moment later he pulled his hand back, carrying the object with him. As it left the photo the two-dimensional object became three.

I stared at it, my mouth suddenly dry as if my tongue were made of cotton.

It was a heart—a real heart, like the kind beating inside my chest. Only instead of red and pink and meaty, this one was charred black and looked as hard as stone.

"This is the Animus Mortem, the Death's Heart. Or, as it is sometimes called, the Soul-Stealer." Valentine held the dead, decaying thing aloft. "What you're looking at is just a photograph, of course, but the real thing is the most powerful object of black magic ever recorded by magickind."

Death's Heart. Soul-Stealer. I didn't like the sound of it. Or the look.

A wary expression colored Eli's face. "Is it a real heart?"

"According to legend, yes," said Valentine. "But no one now alive can say for sure. Here, hold it in your hand, study it so you may recognize its symbolic presence in your dreams." He held the heart out to Eli. Eli hesitated only a second then took it. He turned the thing over, holding it upside down and sideways as he examined every inch.

Swallowing my dread, I asked, "What does it do?"

"It makes corporal animation possible."

I frowned at Valentine, Eli doing the same beside me. Both of the words registered in my mind; *animation* was the particular effect of magic and electromagnetic fields on inanimate objects. Given enough exposure, it brought them to life, like Frank and Igor. And I knew *corporal* meant body or physical. But I wasn't sure what the two of them together meant.

Eli held the heart out toward Valentine. "Are you saying this thing raises the dead? Like a zombie-maker?"

I would've laughed at the idea, but Valentine motioned for Eli to hand the heart to me. I took it, biting my tongue in an attempt to still the squeamish sensation wriggling through my stomach. The thing was surprisingly heavy, tugging my hand toward the ground. The hard exterior felt like wet bone, cold and slippery. At once I wanted to let go of it, but I steeled my courage. If Eli was brave enough to hold it, then I needed to be, too.

"I suppose zombie-maker is an apt name," Valentine said. "But it's a little more nefarious than ordinary horror movies would make it seem."

I glanced at Valentine, relieved for an excuse not to look at the gruesome thing clutched in my fingers. "Have you seen any of those movies lately?"

"I enjoy them immensely." Valentine reached for the Death's Heart, and I handed it over, grateful to be rid of it. "But they still do not reflect the evil of this object. It's known as the Soul-Stealer because that is precisely what it does. In order to return the dead to life—a semblance of life, that is—it drains the soul, the *anima* of someone still living."

Still living. As in not dead yet. At once, an image from a movie I'd watched as a kid rose to my mind. It was an old movie, a childhood favorite of my dad's where all the fantastical characters were played by puppets. In this particular scene, one of the evil characters drained the "living essence" of another innocent character, a process that aged the puppet and turned it into a mindless drone—like a zombie. The scene had terrified me as a child.

I shook the image off. "So you think it was stolen for that purpose? To bring someone back to life by killing someone else?"

"Most likely." Valentine returned the Death's Heart photo to the paper. As before his fingers disappeared into the shiny surface, leaving the heart behind when they reemerged. The ink swirled for a moment, then disappeared again.

"Most?" Eli said, stuffing his hands into his pockets.

"It's always possible the thief will attempt to sell it," said Sheriff Brackenberry. His low grumble of a voice made me jump. I'd almost forgotten he was here, which was saying something, considering the man was the size of a grizzly bear.

"Yes, that's possible," Valentine said, "but for now we must assume the thief intends to use it. We need to recover it before he does."

"Right," Eli said, cracking his knuckles. "But when did it go missing? From where? And how?"

Brackenberry rolled his eyes. "Oh, lord, here we go."

Valentine frowned at Eli, his expression puzzled. "I don't see how that information is relevant."

"That's because it's not. But these two like to fancy themselves as amateur detectives." Brackenberry pointed his thumb at Eli and me. "Call themselves the Dream Team, from what I hear."

I winced. The name did sound a little silly when said like that. Beside me, Eli's expression remained stoic. Silly or not, we were both serious about it, Eli especially. His biggest ambition was to join the FBI.

"Huh." Valentine exhaled loudly through his nose, the sound not quite a laugh but not a huff either. "Well, all I can tell you is that it went missing from a secret vault in Lyonshold. And whoever stole it either works in a high position in the magickind government or has close ties with someone who does."

"Why do you think that?" Eli and I asked in unison. The shared moment made my breath catch, a subtle affirmation of our rightness.

"Well as I said, it was in a *secret* vault. And Death's Hearts like this one aren't even supposed to exist anymore." Valentine grimaced. "They were banned by the Black Magic Purge Act of 1349 and should've been destroyed centuries ago."

"Typical." I folded my arms over my chest. I knew firsthand that the Purge Act wasn't quite as effective as the history books liked to claim.

"Hence the need for those nondisclosure agreements." Valentine motioned toward the table.

"Okay," Eli said, shifting his weight from one foot to the other. "Is there anything else we need to know? Is there any sign of when the heart is being used? There're a lot of ways to detect magic use, right?"

"Normally, yes, but since the Death's Heart hasn't been used in so long we have no idea what those signs might be," Valentine said, once again rubbing his thumb over the top of his lip. "Aside from the obvious ones, of course."

"Obvious?" I asked.

"Missing persons," Lady Elaine answered. A grievous expression twisted her age-lined face. Like Valentine, I had no idea how old she was other than very. I didn't even know what kind she was, witchkind or naturekind or darkkind. I'd never thought to ask. What mattered was that she was an Oracle, the ability to see the future an inborn talent. I didn't like the fear in her eyes, and I wondered what that talent might've shown her recently.

"Yes, that's right," said Valentine. "Fuel for the machine, as it were."

It was a coarse way of putting it, and once again the image of that stupid puppet having its vital essence drained rose up in my mind. I shivered. "Has anyone gone missing yet?"

"No one of importance," said Brackenberry.

My eyes widened. "What is that supposed to mean?"

"It means," Lady Elaine said, "that we've already told you enough to be getting on with. You don't need to concern yourself with missing persons. Focus the dreams on finding the Death's Heart. That is the most important thing."

I recognized the finality in her tone and had to fight back the urge to argue. I glanced at Eli, expecting him to press for more, but to my surprise he seemed content. I decided to take comfort in that, guessing he already had some scheme in mind to get the information we needed.

But that comfort was short lived as a new thought occurred to me, one that made me feel as if I were having my living essence drained right this very second. "If the thief didn't steal it for the money, then why?" I bit my lower lip. "I mean, who's died recently that someone would be willing to go to this length to bring them back?"

As soon as I said it, I knew it was a foolish question. I'd never lost a close loved one, but it wasn't hard to imagine the power of that grief and what it might drive a person to do.

And there certainly had been some significant deaths of late—people who'd held positions of power and who no doubt left behind supporters. There was Consul Vanholt, head of the magickind government, who had died in the attack on Lyonshold. And Senator Titus Kirkwood, of course, the man behind the attack. The magickind police had caught him trying to flee the sinking island, but before he could go to trial, someone had murdered him in his prison cell.

"Anyone with the knowledge of the heart's existence could be guilty," Valentine said.

I shifted my gaze to Lady Elaine, my fear growing by the second. "It's not . . ." I swallowed. "Because of Marrow, is it?"

Marrow. Even saying his name was hard these days, let alone facing the reality that he was still out there. I often called him the Hitler-wannabe, but that was putting it too lightly. Marrow was behind all the recent disasters and upheaval amid magic-kind. It all came back to him. He had broken The Will spell. Titus Kirkwood had been one of his followers. Known as the Red Warlock, Marrow was a man who could be killed but who could not stay dead, and that made him an infinite threat, forever lurking. Thanks to his familiar bond with a black phoenix, whenever Marrow's mortal body died, he would simply be reborn with a new one—same soul, same *anima,* new packaging.

But like the Death's Heart, no one knew exactly how the rebirth worked, whether he would return as a baby or a grown man with a different face, or as a fresh copy of the man he'd been before.

Lady Elaine took several seconds before answering. "We don't believe so. At least not if you're referring to his resurrection. He does not need the Death's Heart for that. The black phoenix is enough."

"Then what then?" Eli said, no doubt catching the hitch in her voice as easily as I had. "Are you saying this is still about Marrow?"

"We don't know," Lady Elaine said, her gaze steely. "But it's possible. If he has returned already, and if he has learned of the Death's Heart's existence, it is most certainly an object he would want in his possession. We might not know much about how the

Death's Heart works, but we do know some of the ways it has been used in the past. In ancient times there were groups of magickind who set themselves up as gods, requiring the primitive ordinaries to make human sacrifices to them. Using the Death's Heart, they transferred the anima of those sacrifices to themselves, ensuring very long lives."

My heart gave a stutter. Eli looked pale beneath his summer-bronze tan. Marrow would definitely be one to set himself up as a god. Only, as Lady Elaine had said, he already had the immortality thing in the bag.

"But there are also accounts of magickind using the Death's Heart to create and sustain armies of the living dead," Lady Elaine continued. "The most famous was Genghis Khan. You can imagine how easy and efficient it was to use the lives of his victims to resurrect his soldiers."

"That sounds like Marrow," I said, breathless. I reached for the silver band on my wrist and began to twist it. If Marrow was back and stealing objects, how long before he came after me? He would want Bellanax back. There was no question of that.

Lady Elaine's gaze shifted toward my wrist, and I stilled my hand, afraid of what conclusions she might draw. A second later, she pulled her gaze away—the pulling obvious, effortful. Eli shifted closer toward me. I leaned into him, drawing comfort.

"I believe that's enough," Valentine said. "As of right now, we have no proof that Marrow is involved. And if I understand how the dream-seer powers work, I think it best that you channel the dreams on the Death's Heart so as not to bend the narrative to a possible suspect instead of the correct one."

Eli nodded. "Makes sense."

"Yes, and with any luck you'll find the person quickly and this will all be over." Lady Elaine smiled. I knew it was meant to comfort us, but it was fragile around the edges, like old paper.

She's afraid. The *Oracle* was afraid. What horrible vision had she seen? What did she know that she wasn't telling us?

Without warning, Bellanax flared into life. For a second the urge to disengage the glamour was so great that starbursts filled my vision from the effort of resisting it. I twisted the band over and over again.

Lady Elaine was afraid.

And it seemed Bellanax thought I should be, too.

~ 3 ~

Death Becomes You

A few minutes later, Valentine gathered up the papers from the table and tucked them back into the folder. "Thank you again for your time, and I'll be looking forward to your dream reports. Oh—" He paused and flashed a diplomatic smile my way. "It goes without saying that your dream journals now fall under the nondisclosure agreements until such time as the Death's Heart is recovered."

And with that, he headed out the door. Sheriff Brackenberry followed after him. I took a deep breath, relieved to be almost alone with Eli again. Now if Lady Elaine would just leave. Only, so far she hadn't moved so much as a pinkie finger. Before I could ask her what the holdup was, Dr. Hendershaw strolled into the room.

New situation.

Someone else came in with her, the red and black uniform sending a jolt through me. But it wasn't just any Will Guard. It was the same woman who'd accosted me on the way over here.

Bollinger scanned the room, distaste clear in her expression. She might've been pretty if she weren't in the habit of screwing up her features that way.

"What's this?" Eli said.

A broad smile, oozing with smugness stretched like warm taffy across Dr. Hendershaw's face. "This is part of a change the school is making to our dream-seer policy. From this moment forward, you two will only be permitted to dream-feed together under the supervision of a designated chaperone."

A full thirty seconds passed before the meaning of her words finally struck me. When they did, it was like a thunderclap, the kind loud enough to shake walls and burst windows.

Eli had gone utterly still, all except for a muscle ticking in his jaw. He inhaled, nostrils flaring. "That's not necessary."

Dr. Hendershaw laughed, the sound close to a cackle. "Very funny, Mr. Booker. Considering what I walked in on earlier."

Eli's hands clenched into fists.

I turned toward Lady Elaine. "Please, don't do this." I spoke low, my voice pleading. Because I knew, I *knew,* that this was about the curse. Again.

To her credit, a pained look flitted across her face.

Before she could answer, Hendershaw cut in. "This is not open for negotiation, Miss Everhart."

Anger heated my skin. "This is bull—"

Lady Elaine snapped her fingers, and something that felt like a hot air balloon filled my mouth. The magic tingled over my tongue. Speaking became impossible.

"Before you say something you'll regret," Lady Elaine said, quietly. Then she let out a small sigh. "I know this is hard for you, but there is no changing it. As long as you are a minor and a student at this school you will abide by whatever rules the school chooses to impose. Do you understand?"

With tears stinging my eyes, I slowly nodded. The pressure eased a moment later, and I drew a deep breath. It did nothing to ease the ache in my chest though, as if the oxygen in my lungs had turned to lead. I sensed Eli shifting his weight beside me, but I couldn't risk looking at him. Not unless I wanted to totally lose it.

"Now, as I was saying," Dr. Hendershaw went on, and I didn't look at her either, for much the same reason. "Miss Bollinger will be your primary chaperone. She will escort Dusty to and from her dorm to Eli's and remain present during the entire duration of the dream session. No exceptions."

The scowl on my face went so deep I thought my skin might split. I made the mistake of looking at Bollinger. Her smugness was tangible, a stick I wanted to grab and smack her with. Bellanax stirred, the feel like a growl inside my head. The skin on my wrist burned. I closed my eyes, pressing against it, trying to remember the risk involved in revealing the sword. Marrow was back. He would be looking for it. The reminder helped, but only a little.

I opened my eyes to see everyone staring at me. Anger pounding through me, I stared back. I was too mad even for sarcasm. I considered telling Lady Elaine about my run-in with Bollinger, but I knew it was pointless. I had no proof that she hated me, just a feeling. And I doubted that Dr. Hendershaw would be overly concerned. My feelings meant nothing to her. To any of them.

Eli looked tense enough to snap. But I wasn't sure if it was from anger. There was some of that, yes, but something else, too. Regret? Relief? But no. That was just my imagination, self-doubt fueled by this latest attack against our happiness.

Dr. Hendershaw brought her hands together in a silent clap. "All right, we shall leave you to your new chaperone. And best of luck with whatever you're searching for."

She sounded so pleasant that an outsider might've mistaken her for nice. As she turned toward the door all I could do was glare at the back of her head.

Lady Elaine followed her out, shutting the door.

Several seconds of painful silence passed, the three of us left eyeing one another like gangland negotiators.

Unsurprisingly, Bollinger spoke first. "All right, you two. Get on with it. I've got patrolling to do once we're finished here."

Now Eli looked fit to be tied. His jaw worked back and forth, making muscles leap and dance on his face and neck. He put his hands on his hip. "You're insane if you think I'm going to be able to fall asleep right now." *With you here.* The unspoken words hung in the air.

Bollinger shrugged. "No matter. I've been authorized to use sleeping spells to help keep things on track. If you would assume the position . . ."

I sensed Eli's silent debate, but what choice did we have? Sure, we could refuse, but she was a Will Guard. She could force us with magic. Or we could fight back, but only at the risk of being expelled or grounded for the rest of our teenage years.

Eli seemed to come to the same conclusion. He stepped over to the sofa and lay down, his head propped on one armrest and his feet hanging over the other. "Get on with it, please," he said.

Bollinger sniffed at the request, but she came forward just the same, holding her wand aloft. *"Hupno-drasi."* Eli's eyes caught mine for a second, his gaze steady, but then the spell took hold, and his eyes slid closed. A moment later he was asleep.

Bollinger smirked, no doubt thrilled that she'd gotten to use the restricted spell. She turned her gaze on me. "Glare all you like, little girl. Won't change a thing." She retreated to the other side of the room and sat down in one of the desk chairs. "Not that I understand the need for me to be babysitting at all. It's absurd, this dream-seer curse. Especially considering the two of you."

"What do you mean?" I said, unable to keep myself from responding even though I sensed a trap.

An overly innocent expression appeared on her face. "Oh, I just mean the vast differences between you two. Him being such a handsome boy and you . . . well . . . being so plain."

I inhaled, her words cutting deeper than I would ever admit. Forcibly, I turned away from her and headed to Eli—my only comfort in all of this.

He was already dreaming. His eyes moved back and forth beneath his eyelids. Seeing him in his dream state, eagerness to join him came over me. We might not be alone in his dorm anymore, but we would be in the dream. Trying to ignore the gaze I felt on my back, I climbed on top of Eli. I positioned my feet on either side of his rib cage and slowly lowered my weight onto his chest. The position was weird—and intimate—but also the most effective for dream-feeding.

The moment I was in place, a burning, aching want swelled up inside me, my Nightmare powers ravenous for the fictus, the magical stuff of Eli's dreams. I had dream-fed on others these past weeks, the need to refuel my magic unavoidable, but those dream subjects were strangers, and their dreams were dull, boring things—black and white and tasteless. Nothing at all like Eli's.

His were powerful—and oh so sweet.

I touched my hands against his forehead and felt my consciousness shuck off the confines of my physical body, trading it for an existence inside Eli's dreams. Colors as bright and pulsating as a super nova filled my vision. The colors were a chaotic blur for a few seconds, until finally transforming into the dream world.

I found myself lying on my back with nothing but blackness overhead. It might've been the sky or a cave or nothing at all. If it weren't for the press of a hard surface beneath my back, I would've thought I was drifting in space.

"Hey, you." Eli's voice seemed to float out of the darkness. "Is that the real you and not the imagined one I've been stuck with these last few weeks?"

I shifted to my side and saw that Eli was lying beside me, our bodies almost touching. Almost, but not quite. We couldn't touch, not in a dream. If we tried I would be ejected out of the dream. Painfully.

I smiled. "Real me."

He smiled back. "I can tell. The real you is way more beautiful than my dream one."

I smiled at the compliment, but Bollinger's insult came back to me. "Are you sure about that? Cause I can do a lot better than this." I closed my eyes for a second, concentrating. When I opened them again, I'd transformed my appearance, trading my red fuzzy hair for sleek platinum. "Do you like this better?"

"No," Eli said. "Not even for a second." He raised his hand and reached toward my face.

I jerked back.

Eli froze. "Damn. I forgot. No touching."

Grimacing, I exhaled. "Stupid dream."

"Stupid chaperone." He sat up.

The reminder brought tears stinging to my eyes again. It was so unfair, so ridiculous.

"Hey," Eli said, staring down at me. "It's not the end of the world. We'll find ways around it. Who's better than us at sneaking around?"

"Nobody."

"It might even be fun."

I laughed and sat up, too, taking my first real look at the dream world, which had slowly come into focus. A gasp lodged in my throat when I saw we were lying in a boat on a dark, fathomless river. The moment I realized it, I became aware of the subtle rock and sway of the water's movement beneath us.

"Well, this is weird," said Eli.

I nodded, my gaze still processing the strange sight. This wasn't a normal ship, but a barge, like the kind Egyptian pharaohs and princesses used to cruise around the Nile on. It was low-sided, the railing no more than a lip, but large, easily the width of a tennis court and twice again as long. We were lying near the rear of the boat, and ahead of us was a raised platform with a canopied roof. The white gauzy curtains hid whatever was inside. Beyond the platform, I could just make out a little of the boat's prow, rising up and in front of the ship like the neck of a dragon.

"Weird is right," I said, getting to my feet. The boat's movement grew even more pronounced as I stood, and I realized that we were moving forward, following some unknown current. I looked out over the boat's edge and spotted what looked like a distant shoreline, although it was hard to tell in the dim light. I glanced up, once again seeing nothing but an endless black overhead—no moon or stars, nothing to light the way. Nevertheless there was light coming from somewhere. It filled the cavernous space around the ship just enough for me to make out shapes, but it had no source, and it made no sense. We shouldn't be able to see anything. And yet as I strained my eyes toward the shore, I could almost make out people standing there, observing our slow, silent passage.

I turned my gaze to the front, wondering where the boat was headed, but there was nothing but an endless black horizon. A sense of absolute isolation, something akin to claustrophobia, came over me, icy fingers clutching at my heart.

"Where are we?" Eli said. The sound of his voice jolted me from the momentary terror, and I rolled my eyes at myself. I was a Nightmare and this was a dream. I wasn't trapped on this barge. I could trade this dark, water-filled landscape for a field of baby unicorns and kittens if I wished.

"I have no idea." I motioned toward the platform ahead. "Have you ever been on a boat like this?"

Eli pushed himself into a standing position. "Nope. I've never even seen a boat like this. Outside of the movies, anyway."

I inhaled, a thrill of excitement going through me. If he'd never seen this before, then that meant we were on the track of something. I didn't know if it was related to the Death's Heart, but it hardly mattered. I'd missed the thrill of dream-seeing.

"Let's look around," Eli said, his gaze focused on the platform.

As we walked forward, I let my eyes wander to my left, out over the water. The glass-smooth surface glistened from that unseen light. Farther away, the bodies now moved on the shoreline, faint and ghostly and humanoid.

"Wait," I said as a new and far closer movement caught my eye. I stopped and turned toward the boat's edge. "There's something in the water." My throat tightened. Anything could be in there. At once I pictured grayish-white corpses floating beneath the surface. "You've seen too many movies, Dusty," I whispered, forcing air back into my lungs.

"What did you say?" Eli asked from behind me. I shook him off and approached the low railing. There was indeed something in the water. Lots of somethings. But not human corpses. They looked like sharks or eels. Long, thin bodies slid beneath the water's surface, moving up and down, sideways, and turning in circles.

"Some kind of fish," Eli said, joining me at the boat's side. "That's normal enough."

"If you say so, but I'm not going for a swim anytime soon."

"Probably wise."

We both turned and resumed our slow march toward the platform. Although there was no breeze, the curtains billowed outward. Seeing it, feeling the wrongness of it, I wanted to turn back, or just leave the dream all together. I didn't want to know what was hidden behind that curtain.

"Eli, wait."

He stopped and looked over his shoulder, frowning. "What is it?"

"I don't want to get taken by surprise." This might be a dream, but we both knew that didn't make it safe. There were things in dreams that could hurt you, and not just psychologically.

Eli nodded, a single up and down of his chin, his expression uncertain.

I closed my eyes and reached out with my Nightmare-keen senses. At once I felt the dream as a physical thing around me, the magic of it like a tightly woven tapestry. But I was a master weaver, capable of pulling it apart and putting it back together again as I chose. With the feel of the dream firmly fixed in my mind, I opened my eyes again and focused on the curtain, willing it to disappear, to *un*-be.

For a second the curtain flickered, like a picture coming in and out of focus, but then I felt the dream push back. It solidified, going from a tapestry to something denser, less easy to break apart, like granite. Frowning, I pressed harder, but the dream's resistance only strengthened in response. It did not want to be vanished away.

"Can't you manipulate it?" Eli said.

I bit my lip. "I'm trying, but it won't go."

He ran a hand over his head, combing his fingers through hair that wasn't there anymore with his new military-short haircut. "Maybe you're out of practice."

"Yeah, maybe." It was possible. I rarely had reason to manipulate the dreams of anybody else—not unless they were dreaming something gross that I didn't want to see. But I'd been fortunate all summer, most of the dreams I visited were pretty tame as dreams go. Only one of them had been a showing-up-naked-to-school dream, but I'd just kept my eyes averted.

Giving it up as a bad job, I disengaged my magic and let the dream settle back into place. It must be something important to resist the manipulation so strongly. I pictured the Death's Heart. Maybe this wasn't an Egyptian pleasure barge at all, but a funeral barge.

A shiver slid over my arms as if from a phantom wind. But again there was no wind. *Then how is the barge moving?* For it certainly was, the floor in a constant, subtle shift beneath our feet. An image of corpses in the water came to my mind once more, only this time they were reanimated. They pushed us along, their dead, water-swollen fingertips pressing into the ship's hull.

I shook the vision off before it could fully materialize. If I wasn't careful, I might end up bending the dream into a nightmare on accident.

"I'll go first," Eli said, and he stepped forward without waiting for a reply.

Chiding myself for being a coward, I hurried up beside him. We would do this together, same as everything else.

When we reached the curtain, Eli grasped the right panel while I took the left. Then in unison we pulled them aside, revealing a narrow room. Same as outside the boat, a strange, impossible light permeated the space beneath the canopy.

Just ahead was another raised structure, this one unmistakably a bed, despite its round shape. There was a mattress or cushion, and beneath it, some kind of dark wood comprised the frame, its side rounded and intricately carved with triangular spoke-like objects sticking out from it. A person lay on top of the mattress, the head nearest us with the feet pointed toward the front of the boat. It was an unmoving person. Perfectly still, as if asleep—or dead.

My bet was on the latter, of course. Because this was a dream, and we were dream-seers, tasked with stopping a great evil once more. Besides, it wasn't the first time we'd come across a dead person in a dream. They had a different kind of stillness, deeper and more solid, like the difference between a still, quiet pond and one covered with ice.

Eli and I exchanged a look and then together we stepped up onto the platform and under the canopy. The curtains whooshed closed behind us. The air was cooler in here, but as before there wasn't any wind.

Moving closer to the bed, I raised my hand toward the lantern hanging from the canopy directly above it, willing it to light. Unlike the curtains, it obeyed at once, a flame sputtering into life in the center of the glass globe. Shadows began to dance across the room.

I blinked once, adjusting to the light, and then I lowered my gaze to the prone figure. The shape looked female, but I couldn't be certain. A sheet covered the face and body. It was some kind of burial shroud, the cloth thick and coarsely woven. I stared at the person's head, checking to see if there was any sign of breathing, just in case. As I'd said to Eli before, I didn't want to be taken by surprise, and this scenario seemed ready made for a horror movie gotcha. To my relief, the cloth and body beneath it remained still.

"Shall we pull back the sheet?" Eli said.

"In a minute." I scanned the bed once more. The person

beneath the sheet was important but there were other details to observe, too. Even the most literal of dreams were still symbolic. Sometimes minute aspects could hold meaning.

I ran my finger along one of the triangular spikes on the bed frame. As soon as I touched it, the design of the thing came into my mind.

"It's a dragon," I said. "This is the neck." I motioned to the pointed triangles, which I now saw were actually spines.

"Huh, you're right." Eli bent toward the bed frame, taking a closer look.

I circled around, wanting to see the rest of the dragon. The neck gave way to shoulders with the short stubby legs reaching toward the top and bottom of the bed, clawed hands wrapped around the edges. The serpentine body continued on, its scales forming ridges in the wood. If a bed like this existed in the real world, it would've taken the artist a long time to craft it. Even in the uneven light I marveled at the intricate, lifelike details. The tail wrapped around the foot of the bed where it met up with the dragon's head. The creature's mouth was opened, swallowing the tip of the tail.

"The dragon is eating itself," I said.

Frowning, Eli stepped nearer to me, observing the sight. "Huh. Now this I have seen before. My aunt has a tattoo like this. It's called an ouroboros."

"An or-ro-what-oh?"

He grinned. "She got it after a motorcycle accident that almost killed her. It's a sign of renewal or something."

"Motorcycle accident? Tattoos? That's some aunt."

"I know. You'd like her."

I smiled up at him, but quickly looked down again, transfixed by the tail-eating dragon. "Renewal," I said, my thoughts churning. "Or maybe rebirth. Like the Death's Heart."

"Or Marrow."

I shivered, gooseflesh rising on my arms.

"There's only one way to be sure." Eli moved around the bed, nearer to the person's head. He glanced back at me. "You ready?"

I nodded, my breathing going shallow. From this angle, I wasn't certain that it was in fact a woman lying there. It might be Marrow instead. I didn't know if I was ready to see him again, even if only inside a dream.

But it was too late to protest as Eli grasped the edge of the shroud and pulled it down, revealing the person's face. All the air in my lungs evacuated at the sight, horror a compressive force against my chest, cutting off oxygen and blood flow.

As I originally thought, the person was female and definitely dead. Her skin was a molten blend of sallow and gray. It sagged over sunken, hollow cheeks. Two silver coins, of a currency I didn't recognize, were set deep inside her eye sockets. The eyes themselves were completely sunken in, hapless victims of gravity and decay.

It was a gruesome visage. Even still, the person's state of death didn't shock me. It wasn't the source of the scream clawing its way up my constricted throat. No. The source of my terror resided in the familiarity of the person lying there. A familiarity that could only be described as *intimate*.

This corpse, this dead thing.

Was me.

4

Nondisclosure

I left the dream a short time later, only to discover that leaving was a mistake, no matter how badly I wanted to escape the vision of my dead body lying there. Eli didn't wake up with me, not even after I gave him a hard shake.

At once I understood why. I turned to find Bollinger kicked back in the desk chair, her eyes half-lidded. "Do you mind taking off the sleeping spell now?"

Bollinger jerked upright. "What?" She glanced around, the look of surprise on her face quickly settling into her usual scowl. "Yes, I mind. The session is over. Let's get you back to your dorm."

"What?" I put my hands on my hips, if only to still the trembling in my limbs. "But Eli and I always discuss things afterward."

Bollinger shook her head. Several strands of mouse-brown hair had worked their way out of the ponytail. "My instructions don't include giving you time to chat afterward. Let's go." She motioned to the door.

Too shaken and defeated to argue, I headed for it. I tried to steal another glance at Eli as I stepped into the hallway, but Bollinger was already swinging the door closed. I glared, hating the finality of that shut door, the certainty that this was how it was going to be—my time with Eli always restricted, always delayed.

I turned around, thoughts roiling in my head. There was so much to process, so much I wanted to discuss. *Needed* to discuss. Eli had reminded me just before I left the dream that they were symbolic, not literal. He wasn't wrong, but I'd gotten the feeling he was trying to convince himself of this truth as much as me.

Symbolic, yes, but I didn't know how many ways you could interpret my dead body in a dream. The dragon—the ouroboros—might have dozens of interpretations. But not me.

To my relief, Bollinger didn't loiter outside my dorm when we arrived. In fact, she didn't even bother coming down the hallway. She just shooed me along like an indecisive house cat and disappeared around the corner the moment I got the door open.

I stepped in, unsurprised to find the place dark and quiet. Of course, Selene would be asleep already. Classes started tomorrow, and it was well past midnight. Still, I was disappointed, enough that I debated waking her for several moments. But with the nondisclosure agreement, I didn't know if I could even talk to her about the dream.

Besides, I needed to write my dream journal before turning in. Only I desperately didn't want to. The presence of my dead body was so weird and scary. Even worse was the worry of how Lady Elaine and the rest might interpret it. They would likely see it as a sign that I was in mortal peril. I could end up with a twenty-four-seven Will Guard chaperone instead of just Bollinger. The idea made my stomach knot.

Sighing, I sank onto the chair beside my desk. My eTab sat in its cradle in front of me. Aside from the rune marks etched around the outside, which were designed to help ward off the animation effect, it looked like an ordinary electronic tablet. I pulled it off the cradle and switched it on, the debate still raging in my head. I was torn between what I ought to do and what I wanted to do, what was right and what was desirable. Why did it always seem like these two things always had to be fundamentally opposed? Why couldn't the universe line up properly so that what I wanted could also be what was right? Like ice cream being good for you. Or French fries. Or sunbathing. What a happy, wonderful world that would be.

Gritting my teeth, I switched the eTab on and navigated to the dream journal app. Then without taking time to fret over it, I began to summarize the dream. When I reached the part about the corpse, I wrote: *I didn't recognize the person.* Guilt made me feel queasy, but I told myself it was all right, that this was just self-preservation. Heck, it was just simple privacy. It was *my* dead body after all. And that made it feel like a secret that shouldn't be shared, my own personal nondisclosure agreement.

Besides, I told myself after I'd saved the journal and sent it off, if my being the dead person was significant, then there would surely be other signs to come along. Often, Eli's most important dreams were repetitive.

If it happens again, I'll tell them.

But even as I thought it, I knew it was a hollow promise.

Predictably, my dreams were bad that night, and I woke the next morning feeling as if I hadn't slept at all. Most of the dreams— when they hadn't featured images of my corpse—had been about Eli. Over and over he told me he didn't want to see me anymore. Just like that. Cold, heartless, and absolute. Then he'd turned away from me and walked right into the waiting, open arms of his ex-girlfriend, Katarina Marcel.

I woke with my heart stuttering in my chest, the hurt of his betrayal refusing to fade even as I lay there awake, eyes closed and wishing those false dream-feelings away. Problem was, they felt so real. As if the dream was some kind of repressed memory. *Or maybe a future one.*

I shook my head. Only Eli's dreams predict the future. Not mine. Except even as I thought it, the silver band on my wrist began to warm, as if to remind me of the recurring dream I'd had about Bellanax last year, months before I'd actually bonded with the sword.

I raised the band to my face, glaring down at the inanimate object. "You shut up."

The sound of a snort startled me. "Huh?" Selene said from the other bed. "What did you say?"

I hid my arm under the covers. "Nothing. Sorry to wake you."

Selene waved a hand at me and rolled over, burying her face in her pillow once more. I got out of bed, trying to ignore my envy that Selene was a siren and therefore able to sleep in an extra half hour because she didn't need to spend a lot of time on hair and makeup. My only consolation was that I didn't have to go far to get to the bathroom anymore. Oh, the perks of being a junior.

I showered quickly, but took awhile getting dressed. This was the first day of school, after all, and no matter how many times I'd done this, no matter how well I knew all of my classmates, I still had the jitters. I hadn't seen most of these people since before the attack on Lyonshold. I'd spent the last few weeks of sophomore year in a coma. Most everyone knew about the part I played in stopping the island from sinking, but as Bollinger proved, I couldn't be certain of a warm welcome.

Thank goodness I would have Eli with me all day. That was one of the best parts of being a dream-seer pair—we'd had matching school schedules last year.

With my thoughts on Eli, eagerness overtook the jitters and I hurried down to the cafeteria. We wouldn't have any privacy for a lot of kissing there, but at least we would be able to talk. We had so much catching up to do. I didn't even know what Eli had been up to over the summer break. Once he realized I didn't have access to my phone, he hadn't bothered sending e-mails.

No, when I finally got my phone back—and charged the months'-long dead battery—the only e-mails waiting for me had been from Paul Kirkwood, my ex-boyfriend. More than a dozen filled my in-box, most with subjects like *I'm sorry* or *Explanations* or *Where are you?*

I still hadn't read them. Even thinking about them made me anxious. My feelings for Paul weren't of the romantic variety, not anymore, but I wasn't emotionally prepared to deal with him. Especially not after his latest, possibly duplicitous, actions at the end of last year. He'd been one of Marrow's supporters when we'd first met, and even though I believed he'd had a change of heart, I couldn't be sure. Thank goodness he was in hiding somewhere. Avoidance was always the easiest tactic.

The cafeteria didn't sound very busy as I approached, the noise nominal instead of the full-on roar it would become at high breakfast. But before I walked in, I paused just outside the doorway to read the posted sign:

**WELCOME BACK, UPPERCLASSMEN!
REMEMBER, STARTING TOMORROW YOU WILL NEED YOUR
CASTERCARD® IN THE CAFETERIA**

I shook my head, recalling the little tidbit about the cards in the welcome back letter. Junior and senior magickind had to start learning about how ordinaries lived, including responsible use of credit cards. Lucky me, I'd learned that lesson early on thanks to my impulse-buyer mother. It was simple—do whatever Mom wouldn't.

I continued on into the large hall, only to come to another halt, this time to deal with the wave of disorientation that had come over me. I'd never been inside the upperclassmen's cafeteria before. It had a similar layout to the underclassmen's, a bunch of tables and chairs scattered in a roughly rectangular pattern. But the lunch line here was completely different. It looked more like a food court in a mall. A row of vendors lined the back wall. I scanned the various names, unable to keep from grinning at all the riffs on ordinary food joints.

Instead of a Pizza Hut, there was a Pizza Tut. It had an Egyptian theme, including a pharaoh mascot chomping down on a big cheesy slice of pizza. Next to it sat a Taco Spell, this one with a wizard in traditional blue robes and a pointy hat holding up a taco that he'd just conjured using the wand in his hand.

Some of the others were less obvious riffs but no less amusing. There was a Fairy Garden that seemed to serve primarily soups and salads, and a Demon Burger that needed no description. My personal favorite was the Unicorn Skewer. It looked like it served pretty much everything so long as it came skewered on a fake unicorn horn.

Once I got over the distraction of the food court, I scanned the tables for Eli. I was almost convinced that he wasn't here yet when I spotted him at a table off to the right. He wasn't alone. A girl stood in front of him with her back to me.

I stared at the figure, recognizing the long blond hair and curvy shape all too easily. I'd just seen it in my dream, after all. Nervous, I headed for them. Why was Katarina talking to Eli? Had they seen each other over break? Was this the reason she'd made an appearance in my dream?

Stop being so paranoid, Dusty. I grasped the silver band on my wrist, responding to the warming sensation there automatically. At once my doubt began to ease.

As I drew nearer the table, Eli's gaze shifted my direction. A bright, broad smile lit up his face. It made my insides turn mushy, but the feeling vanished a second later as Katarina glanced over her shoulder to investigate who was worthy of such a greeting.

When she spotted me, her eyes narrowed. So did her lips, which was saying something considering how fluffy and full they were. She turned back around at once, spoke some final word to Eli, and then sauntered off, catwalk style. I wanted to glare at her, but it was impossible. The sight of her had turned my brain momentarily fuzzy. Katarina was a siren, same as Selene.

Before I could shake the feeling off, Eli was beside me, his arms sliding around my waist. "Good morning," he said, as he captured my mouth with his. As kisses go, it was pretty chaste, hardly more than a brush of lips, but in the middle of the cafeteria, surrounded by our peers, it felt risqué.

Best. First Day. Ever.

"Good morning," I whispered, but Eli stiffened and pulled back. A Will Guard was moving toward us from across the room. We broke apart and sat down across from each other. The Guard, a young man with colorless brown hair, seemed to consider the value of scolding us for a second. Then he decided it wasn't worth it and returned to his station next to the Taco Spell.

I grimaced and turned to Eli.

He reached across the table and took my hand, squeezing my fingers. "You all right?"

"A little tired, but okay."

"Me, too." He motioned toward his food tray. "Are you hungry? I got extra just in case."

Glancing at the tray, I snorted a laugh. A mountain of food covered the entire surface, everything from scrambled eggs to gravy and biscuits to pieces of sausages wrapped in bacon and skewered on a golden unicorn horn. "Um, thanks," I said. "But you know I'm just one person not three, right?" I reached over and pulled a sausage off the horn.

He patted his flat stomach. "Don't worry. It won't go to waste."

I nodded my agreement to this statement, having seen proof of his ability to eat enough for three people.

"So," I said, once I finished chewing, "what did Katarina want?"

"Nothing really." He shrugged. "She just wanted to say hi, and . . . um . . . to thank me for being nice to her little brother."

"Her little brother?" Outwardly, I sounded normal. Inwardly, my stomach was doing backflips and my vision had gone a little hazy around the edges. Great. Now I was being paranoid and jealous.

"Yeah, it's kind of embarrassing, but—" He hesitated, running a hand over his shaved head. "I sorta spent most of the summer at a camp for magickind. A kids' camp, that is. Kat's little brother was one of the campers."

I felt my eyebrows first draw together and then rise up as if pulled by an invisible puppeteer.

A faint pinkish color filled Eli's cheeks. "Dr. Hendershaw suggested I go, to try to catch up on everything I've missed. You know, with the not being able to do magic until a couple of months ago." He tapped a finger against his glamoured wand. It was a numen vessel, same as Bellanax, more powerful than a regular wand but not as much as the sword.

"Huh." Realizing my mouth was open, I closed it, trying to regain my composure. I forced a neutral smile to my lips. "That sounds interesting. How was it?"

Eli made a face. "Awful at first. I didn't even want to go. I'm too old for summer camp. At least to be attending one as a camper. If anything, I should be a counselor."

"No kidding." I cringed inwardly, understanding all too well what it felt like to be so out of place. My whole first year at Arkwell had been that way, and a good portion of the next one, too.

"But after a couple of days, the other counselors started treating me like one of them and it turned out to be fun. The kids were a blast."

"Even Katarina's little bro?" I said, half-joking but mostly just incredulous.

He laughed. "Surprisingly, yes. Tommy's not at all like Kat."

Tommy and Kat? Tom Kat. The thought got me laughing, too, and any worry I might have had about Katarina making a move on Eli vanished. I reached forward and snagged another sausage.

We ate in silence for a few moments. Then Eli glanced around and leaned forward, dropping his voice as he said, "So about the dream last night. I've been thinking it over, and I don't believe the De—" He made a sound like trying to clear his throat.

I frowned at the strange face he was making, as if his mouth were overfull of peanut butter. His eyes began to water.

"Oh," I said. "It's the nondisclosure spell." I started to say more, but an ominous tingle sprouted over my tongue and I stopped. It seemed the spell had deemed the lunchroom too crowded for that topic of conversation. I exhaled. "Well, this sucks."

Eli nodded, his eyes still watering as he tried to force his jaws apart. Several minutes later he finally succeeded. "Holy crap that hurt." He rubbed his chin and cheeks with both hands.

"We're going to have to be careful," I said, not quite unhappy to discover the strictness of the nondisclosure spell. If we couldn't talk about the Death's Heart in here, despite the cover of so much noise and activity, then that meant we would have to wait until we were completely alone to talk about it. The idea of alone time with Eli made my skin warm. "Why don't we plan on meeting up in one-thirteen after classes today and talk about it then?"

"Um . . . I can't. Not today."

"Why not?"

Eli shifted in his seat, his eyes darting across the room as if he were looking for a reason to change the subject. I waited, unaccountably anxious.

Finally, he sighed and his eyes landed on me again. "There's a training session tonight."

"Foooor what?" I said, drawing out the question.

"The gladiator team."

My mouth fell open. "Huh?"

Eli rolled his shoulders, downplaying the monstrosity of this statement. The gladiator team was the only school sport at Arkwell Academy, but joining it required a level of proficiency in combative magic far above Eli's skills. Even if he had been practicing all summer, I doubted he'd be good enough to make it on. Not to mention that Coach Fritz hated ordinaries, stacking the odds even further against him.

"I want to play," he said, his expression hardening.

I winced at the yearning in his voice. A mix of regret and guilt rose up inside me. Before that fateful night a year ago when I first discovered Eli and I were dream-seers, he'd been just an ordinary human boy, handsome and popular, a bit of a rebel, and perfectly content and happy with his life. Now he was low man on the magical totem pole.

"I know it sounds crazy," Eli said, "but I've got to give it a shot."

"You're a lot braver than me," I said.

"Nah." He waved me off. "What's the worst that could happen?"

The worst? Well, firstly, he might fail, and I definitely didn't want that. Just the opposite. I wanted him happy and triumphant. I wanted things to go easy for him just once. And secondly—if I was going to be honest—the worst would be all the time we'd lose together if he made it on the team. The gladiators' training schedule made ordinary football practice look tame. They trained every night and every weekend, sometimes hours at a time, and they competed nearly all year.

But no, I refused to play the part of needy girlfriend, one jealous of extracurricular activities. Besides, I had my own extracurriculars to think about. So far, that mostly consisted of the Dream Team, but that might change. I could join the school newspaper or maybe even the Superheroes of Tomorrow Club, where all the members were aspiring superheroes obsessed with comic books and convincing the magickind government to let them use their magic out in the ordinary world for the greater good. *I could totally rock the superhero thing*, I thought, picturing Bellanax as it looked outside of the glamour. *So long as it doesn't include spandex.*

Yes, there would still be plenty of time for us. Those pesky authority figures would have to try a lot harder before they could stop Eli and me from happening.

Feeling better about the situation, I gave him the biggest, most sincere smile I had in me. "I hope you make it."

Smiling back, Eli reached over and grabbed my hand. "Me, too."

5

Involuntary Separation

My confidence that Eli and I would find time for each other took another hit when we arrived at homeroom a short while later. This was my third year reporting to Mrs. Bar's classroom in Finnegan Hall. Mrs. Bar was a fairy, and one of my favorite teachers at Arkwell. When Eli and I walked in she bestowed on us a smile so wide and jolly that it made her jowls jiggle.

She was still smiling a few minutes later as she handed out our course schedules. I scanned mine at once.

First period, history and English. Those two subjects had been separate freshman and sophomore year, but were now combined to allow room for studying new subjects.

Second period, biology. This was my first entirely new subject. Despite it being a science class I was looking forward to it. Rumor had it we would study magical plants and animals in addition to all that boring ordinary stuff like mitosis and dissecting frogs. Personally, I was hoping for unicorns on the syllabus.

Third period, ordinary living. This, too, was a new subject, one directly related to the CasterCard and the food vendors.

Fourth period, psionics
Fifth period, spell casting
Sixth period, gym
Seventh period . . .

"Math?" I said aloud. "The last class of the day? What kind of cruel and unusual torture is this?"

"What are you talking about?" said Eli, looking up from his examination of his own course schedule.

"We have math seventh period. I'm terrible at math, it's—" I stopped speaking, suddenly aware of the way Eli was looking at me. "What's wrong?"

"I have spell casting seventh period."

A lead ball spiraled down the edges of my stomach and settled into the pit. "Are you sure?"

Eli motioned to my schedule. "Can I see?" I handed it over, and he placed it on the desk next to his. His expression soured as he compared the two.

"Is it bad?" I said, already knowing the answer but still hopeful.

Eli didn't reply, just handed both papers back to me. I didn't want to look, but it was like trying to ignore a wreck on the side of the highway, morbid curiosity a magnetic force. As I'd suspected, our schedules were completely different. Other than lunch and sixth period gym, we wouldn't be seeing each other at all, all day long.

Swallowing anger, I raised my hand. "Mrs. Bar, I think there's a problem with my schedule."

Mrs. Bar, who'd been circulating around the room answering questions, waddled over. "What is it, my dear?"

I handed her my schedule. "I don't think this is right. Eli and I are supposed to have the same schedule. We're dream-seers."

Mrs. Bar's smile, so perky a moment before, drooped. She didn't even bother reading the list of classes before handing me back the schedule. "I'm afraid there is no mistake."

I inhaled, dizzy with outrage.

"Thanks for checking, Mrs. Bar," he said. "We just wanted to make sure."

"You're welcome, Mr. Booker." She patted him on top of his buzzed head, looking relieved. Then she headed off for safer environs.

Huffing, I folded my arms over my chest and fell back against my chair. "Score another one for the establishment."

Eli laughed, although there wasn't any humor in it. "Are you thinking of becoming an anarchist?"

"Yes, if it means we won't have to deal with this forced separation." My voice cracked as I spoke, tears threatening.

Eli reached over and squeezed my shoulder. "It'll be okay, Dusty. We'll make do."

"I know," I said, sighing. "But I wish they'd cut us some slack."

"Me, too. But they just think they're doing what's best for us."

I ran my tongue over my lips, his reasonableness making me feel anxious instead of comforted. Last year, Lady Elaine had shared with him a vision of the future she'd seen—a vision of our future, mine and Eli's. I didn't know what had been in it, but it was bad enough that for a while he'd avoided letting our relationship extend beyond the friend level. I wasn't sure what had changed his mind, although it might've had something to do with how I almost died trying to save Lyonshold. Or maybe he'd decided the same as I had, that our feelings were too strong to deny. So strong that there wasn't any chance the curse could defeat it.

Eli let go of my shoulder. "You could come to the gladiator practice tonight, if you want."

I coughed. "You mean like to train?"

"Sure why not?" he grinned. "You're pretty good at combative magic."

I shot him a crazy look, eyebrows and mouth askew.

"What? It's true. I've seen you do it." Eli's eyes flicked briefly to Bellanax. He knew what it was, of course, although not the sword's name. No one but me knew that. Well, except perhaps for Marrow.

"I think I'd rather watch."

Eli shrugged. "Whatever makes you happy."

Just you, I thought.

We got up as the bell rang and headed out the door. "I'll see you at lunch." Eli leaned in for a quick kiss and whispered against my ear, "Be careful today."

"What do you—" I broke off, remembering the dream from last night.

"I'm sure it was just symbolic, but better safe than sorry." Eli kissed me again and then pulled away. "We'll talk about it soon."

"All right." Clinging to this hope, I headed down the hallway in the opposite direction. My spirits lifted a little when Selene turned out to be in my history and English class.

Taking seats in the middle of the room, we did a quick schedule comparison. We had first, second, third, and sixth period together—a new record for us. Last year I would've been overjoyed about so many classes together, but my happiness was muted by the lingering disappointment with Eli's schedule. But at least Selene was happy—Lance was in this class, too. He sat down on Selene's other side, casting me his signature cocky grin, all teeth and smarm.

"Long time no see, Dusty," he said. "Cause any accidents today? Any scenes of mass destruction yet?"

"Nope," I said. "But it's still early. And now that you're here, I've got more motivation. You do make the best target."

"I make the best everything," he said, sliding his arm around Selene. She seemed to ignore him, but a rosy blush colored her cheeks, making her look more radiant than ever.

Mr. Corvus greeted the class with his usual imperial gaze, the expression inevitable given the eye patch he wore over his missing left eye. Then he proceeded to hand out textbooks that were roughly the size of cinder blocks and stuffed with tissue-paper-thin pages.

"We will be starting this year off with a look at the Old English period, one of my personal favorites in both literature and history," Mr. Corvus said with something like a smile on his face—or as close to it as he ever managed. "First up, *Beowulf.*" He snapped his fingers over his head, and magic filled the air. In front of him, a swirl of dark smoke appeared. It soon took on shape and began to materialize into something solid. Seconds later a giant creature that looked part man, part bear, and mostly monster stood in the classroom. Ten feet tall or better, its massive, bulbous head reached nearly to the ceiling.

I watched transfixed by terror as its lips spread apart, revealing teeth as long as my index fingers and a mouth big enough to swallow a baby goat whole. Or maybe a baby dragon. As its mouth reached its fullest expanse, the creature let out a roar loud enough to make the walls shake. I shrank back from it, along with the rest of the class.

Still roaring, the creature charged forward, spider-quick despite its cumbersome size. It headed in my direction, and I reached for Bellanax, ready to drop the glamour and gut the thing with the sword. But the creature turned toward Lance at the last second. It stretched out its two enormous clawed hands and seized him by the throat. Lance let out a girlish squeal just as the creature dissolved back into vapor and disappeared.

Everyone laughed, including Selene, although she did it with admirable restraint.

"Just be glad it wasn't his mother, Mr. Rathbone," Mr. Corvus said, motioning at Lance. "Female trolls are twice as fierce as males."

Lance rubbed his fingers over his neck and let out a shaky laugh. "That's true of most species, yeah?"

Beside him, a wicked smile flashed across Selene's face.

The rest of class proved much less exciting, but nevertheless it passed by quickly. Mr. Corvus, for all his imperial manner, knew how to give a captivating lecture.

Afterward, Selene and I said good-bye to Lance and then headed for our biology class. It was located in the Menagerie, an area of Arkwell I'd only ever seen—and smelled—from a distance. Located on the north side of campus, a tall stone wall separated the Menagerie from the rest of Arkwell, making the place a campus onto itself. With good reason, I supposed, considering the types of plants and animals that were said to be housed in there.

Selene and I gathered with the rest of the class outside the main gates into the Menagerie, waiting admittance.

"Good morning, class," the teacher called from the other side of the massive gate. She was a trim, muscular woman with short brown hair and skin turned leathery and wrinkled from countless hours spent in the elements. "I'm Ms. Miller, your new biology teacher. Before I open these doors, I will need you to repeat this oath after me. Please hold up your right hand." She demonstrated then waited for the class to comply. Selene and I exchanged a puzzled glance as we raised our hands.

"Very good," Ms. Miller said. "Now repeat after me. I hereby declare, on oath, that I will not touch, tease, or talk to any animal or plant located within these walls—" She paused, allowing us to repeat. "Unless given permission and instruction to do so." Another pause while we repeated. "Furthermore, I will not attempt to open any locked area within the Menagerie. And I acknowledge that failure to follow these rules may result in my death, dismemberment, or involuntary exile."

I repeated the last of the oath, even more puzzled. The death and dismemberment, I got. There might be any manner of magical creatures kept in there, including dragons and trolls, according to rumor, anyway. But involuntary exile? What did that even mean? Better yet, did I really want to find out?

Satisfied by our oaths, Ms. Miller slid a giant skeleton key into the padlock on the gate. A second later, it swung open with a mournful creak and we all shuffled inside. Ms. Miller, looking very un-teacher-like in jeans and a green polo shirt, led us down a narrow passageway and onto a grassy lawn crisscrossed with cobblestone paths. Walls of animal-filled cages surrounded the lawn on all sides. Only a few of the animals were recognizably ordinary, some monkeys, a couple of parrots, various snakes. The rest were clearly magical.

Several Menagerie workers, also in green polo shirts, were walking various leashed animals across the lawn. One of the creatures resembled a salamander, except it was bright red with a steady stream of smoke issuing out from its ears and nostrils. Another looked like a rabbit with antlers. Yet a third was a baby lynx, small, furry, and adorable, but with yellow eyes glowing with magic.

"No need to worry," Ms. Miller said over our excited whispers. "Only class C animals are allowed on the lawn and never without a leash and handler."

"Class C?" someone asked from behind me.

"Those deemed relatively harmless and with only mildly aggressive tendencies," said Ms. Miller.

"That's comforting," I whispered to Selene. She made a strangled noise deep in her throat, half amusement, half dismay.

We crossed the lawn and continued down a wide walkway. On the left was a row of stone stables. On the right were a series of greenhouses, each with thick-paned glass and domed roofs. Signs stood out front of each building, bearing labels of the same classification system Ms. Miller had mentioned.

The stables and greenhouses gave way to a courtyard area. Roughly square in shape, it was surrounded on three sides by zoo-like cages, each containing a unique environment. One held water features, a pool, and several streams running in between grassy banks. Tall trees and climbing structures filled another. The third featured a cave environment. It was completely closed in, gloomy and full of large rocks. Several of those rocks had openings in them, small tunnels barely large enough for a human to crawl inside. Old food and other rubbish lined the floor. Some of it looked like pieces of bone.

To my surprise, there was a human inside the cage, another Menagerie worker in a green polo shirt. He was sweeping the stone floor with a push broom. He glanced up as the class gathered around. For a second, as he swept his gaze over us, he paused on me. A look like recognition crossed his face. I didn't know him, not even a little. He had short brown hair and a long scraggly beard that obscured most of his features, all except for a beaked nose.

I frowned, wondering at that look.

"This area is where we will be spending the first few weeks of class," Ms. Miller said, motioning toward the three cages. Then she pointed to the rocky one. "Can anyone guess what sort of creature lives in this environment?"

No one answered at first, none of us certain what kind of teacher Ms. Miller would prove to be—the kind that would encourage us toward the right answer or make us feel stupid for guessing wrong.

Finally, Oliver Cork raised his hand. We all turned to stare at him as he answered. Oliver was a dryad, tall and thin with light brown skin. "Is it trash trolls?"

Ms. Miller smiled, revealing a set of uneven teeth. "You are correct. This is one of several dens for Arkwell's trash trolls. Every large food waste bin you see in the cafeteria and other places is set over a tunnel that leads back to the Menagerie. We will be studying trash trolls in depth this semester."

I stifled a groan at this news. Trash trolls were tiny, malicious creatures that resembled feral Mr. Potato Heads with pointy teeth and sharp claws. The Arkwell student guide warned to never put your hand in a trash can unless you felt like donating a finger or two.

"But first," Ms. Miller said. "I will show you to the laboratory we will be using for the lecture portion of our classes."

And with that, she led us off to the Menagerie's main building, a tall fortress-like structure, located roughly in the middle of the complex. We spent the rest of the hour getting familiar with the equipment and leafing through our new textbooks before Ms. Miller escorted us out to the main gates once again.

On the way, I spotted that same Menagerie worker with the beard and beaked nose, this time mucking out one of the cages on the main lawn. As before, he seemed to single me out with his gaze. I shivered, the image of my dead body lying on that barge rising up in mind. *It was just symbolic,* I reminded myself, and kept on walking.

Next Selene and I hurried to our ordinary living class where we received our CasterCards, complete with a MasterCard knockoff logo and a unique sixteen-digit number. We then spent a long, boring hour practicing how to swipe them.

Afterward, I said good-bye to Selene before heading to psionics. This was by far my best subject. Not to mention it was taught by the best teacher at Arkwell—and the most handsome. Mr. Deverell flashed his gorgeous smile at me as I came in and sat down. I smiled back.

"How are you doing, Dusty?" he said, in his Southern cowboy accent that had a way of making me want to giggle.

I cleared my throat, trying to stifle the blush rising up my neck. "I'm doing good, thanks. How are you?"

"Fine. Glad that school is back in session." He studied my face for a second, his expression pensive. "We should set aside some time to talk soon. I'd like to hear how you're faring after our private sessions last year."

"Oh," I said, my blush darkening. In all the excitement at Lyonshold and the long vacation afterward, I'd almost forgotten the crucial role Mr. Deverell had played in helping me deal with the mental block I'd developed last year. The cause of that block had turned out to be Bellanax, and it was gone now. But Mr. Deverell didn't know anything about it. Feeling guilty, I said, "I'm sorry. I meant to e-mail but got a little busy."

He smiled again. It didn't make my head fuzzy the way a siren's would've, but almost. "No apologies necessary. Still, I look forward to chatting about it later."

He turned and wandered to the other side of the classroom where Katarina Marcel had just sat down. I groaned at the sight of her and then glanced around the room, hoping for a friend.

Lance appeared in the doorway, a cell phone pressed to his ear. His face was flushed to a dark shade of red, as if he'd just eaten a raw habanero pepper.

"I don't care what you think, Dad," he said taking the seat

next to me. "I'll see and date whoever I want." There was a long pause. "Yeah, you go ahead and do that. See if I care." He lowered the phone from his ear and pressed the end button. "Asshole," he muttered.

I winced, uncertain what to say. It wasn't like I could pretend I hadn't heard. "Is he upset about Selene again?" I asked, gently. Selene had told me that Mr. Rathbone's prejudice against interkind dating was half the reason she and Lance had broken up the first time.

Lance grunted. "If by upset you mean on the verge of disinheriting me, then yes."

I gaped, unsure if he was being serious.

He turned an imploring gaze on me. "Please don't tell Selene. It'll only hurt her."

"I won't." Pity churned in my gut. Or maybe it was more like commiseration. "Looks like both of us are getting a hard time over who we want to date."

A scowl twisted Lance's features until he resembled his pop culture hero, the Joker. "Screw that. We should be free to date anybody we want."

I nodded, but didn't comment. Eli and I had it rough with the dream-seer curse, no doubt, but I had a feeling Lance and Selene might have it harder. There was no "we're just looking out for your best interests" in their case. It was just prejudice, and that seemed a tougher war to fight.

When the bell rang an hour later, I leaped up from my desk and practically ran all the way to the cafeteria. Lance kept pace with me. He was as eager to see Selene as I was to see Eli. I supposed, in light of all this new evidence of how much he adored her, how much strife he was willing to go through to be with her, I would have to cut him some slack. *A lot of it.*

Lunch passed all too quickly, and spell casting afterward way too slowly. So did gym. Eli and I barely got to talk to one another between running laps and doing push-ups.

But he was waiting for me outside the locker room afterward. I hurried over to him, eager for a kiss, but stopped at the sight of several Will Guards loitering nearby.

Eli eyed them dubiously and said to me, "Practice for the gladiator team is at four-thirty if you want to come."

"I'll be there." There wasn't a chance I would miss it.

"Good." Eli said, and then despite the Will Guard watching us, he leaned forward and kissed my cheek.

Sighing, I headed down the hallway in the opposite direction, pulling out my course schedule to double-check the room number for my math class—285 Jupiter Hall.

Spying rain outside the gymnasium windows, I headed down the stairs to the tunnels that ran beneath Arkwell's campus.

As I descended, the murky stench of the canal water filled my nose. The smell teased memories of Eli's dream to the forefront of my mind. The tunnels consisted of a single dirt path of varying width that ran side by side with the canal. There were lots of naturekinds who needed regular access to water. Often, they would slip down here in between classes for a refresher. But right now the surface was dark and undisturbed—far too much like the river in Eli's dream.

With prickles dancing down my back, I glanced behind me and all around, worried by how quiet it was, no signs of anyone anywhere. *Totally normal,* I reminded myself. There were lots of tunnels and Arkwell was huge.

Nevertheless, I quickened my pace, darting around the corner. The tunnel ahead was just as empty as the one before. Except when I passed by an alcove, a hand reached out from the darkness and closed around my arm.

~ 6 ~

New Leads

Shrieking, I spun toward the person. I raised my free arm on instinct.

"*Hypno-soma!*"

The dazing curse burst out from the tips of my fingers and struck my attacker right in the chest. Too late, I saw the familiar face of my mother. She let out a great gasp of air and then stumbled backward.

"Mom!" I dropped my hand and rushed over. "Oh, Mom, I'm sorry. I didn't know it was you."

She pushed me away. Fury and pain lit her expression. Seeing it, I bit my tongue and waited. Speaking now would just make it worse.

Finally, she drew another breath and stood up from her hunched position. "Where are on earth did you learn to cast that hard? You're only sixteen for goodness sake."

I put my hands on my hips. "I'll be seven—" I broke off, finally getting a good look at her. Shock tore through me. This wasn't the Moira Nimue-Everhart I knew. It couldn't be the same woman I'd said good-bye to less than a week ago. This person hardly looked like my mother at all. Her blond hair, normally short and styled to photo-shoot perfection, hung lank around her makeup-less face. She looked so old, like one of those movie puppets after having its vital essence drained. I didn't want to believe that makeup could make that much difference, but apparently it could.

Mom shook her head, refocusing. She grabbed me by the shoulders. "Of all the good luck, Destiny, I'm so glad I found you. I was going to sneak up to your dorm tonight, but this is so much better."

I gaped, still wrestling with shock that was slowly turning toward fear. "What's wrong? Why are you here?"

"They're coming for me."

"Who?" I took a step back and out of her clutches. My shoulders were beginning to throb from her pincer-like grip on them.

"The police."

"What?" I groaned. "Oh, geez, Mom, what did you do this time?"

"Shhhh." She pressed a finger to her mouth and glanced behind us, the direction I'd just come. A second later she spun on her heel and started walking down the tunnel. She grabbed my wrist and hauled me beside her. "How long before your next class starts?"

"Like five minutes." I once again freed myself from her grip, but I kept pace with her. She fell into an easy stride, her movements nonchalant and at complete odds with her anxious expression. She was dressed like a student—another unprecedented event—in jeans, T-shirt, and neon-colored running shoes.

"You can't be late so I'll talk fast."

"Screw that. It's just math class. If you're really in trou—"

She cut me off. "No. The moment you're late they'll come looking for you—and then me."

I gulped, fear starting to bubble up inside me. My mom had

been in trouble with the police before, especially in her younger years. She'd been arrested dozens of times, mostly for social activism stuff like protests and rallies. And back when it was still around, she'd been charged with minor violations of The Will spell. The nature of our Nightmare magic made her immune to the spell, an advantage she liked to flaunt. But none of those run-ins had ever resulted in serious trouble for her.

It seemed things were different this time.

"Mom, what did you *do*?"

She jerked her head at me, her glare hot enough to sear flesh. "I didn't do anything. At least, not what I'm being accused of."

"And what is that?"

She shushed me again and glanced over her shoulder. I mimicked the gesture, spotting nothing following us except the flow of the canal water.

Mom turned back. "They're saying I killed Titus Kirkwood."

I stumbled to a halt, shock making me clumsy. "Are you serious?"

Mom hissed at me. "Come on. Before someone sees us."

I fell back into step, my heart doing a double-time beat in my chest. "Why do they think you killed him?"

Mom hesitated. "I . . . I don't know. There's some new detective on the case. He took over when the trail went cold a few weeks back. He brought me in for questioning right after we got home from our trip. I didn't think it was serious, but it seems he's since found some new evidence."

"A detective?" The weird, weightless sensation of coincidence came over me.

"Yes," Mom said, gritting her teeth hard enough I could hear it. "He's part of D.I.M.S. Detective—"

"Valentine," I finished for her.

Mom stopped so abruptly, it took me several steps to do the same. I turned toward her, seeing concern furrow her brow. "How do you know that?"

I ran a hand over my hair, smoothing the curls for half a moment. "Lucky guess. He came to see me and Eli last night. We're supposed to be finding . . . something for him." I stuck out my tongue, trying to fight off the encroaching spell.

Mom pinned me with her gaze, her mouth a sharp line with its strangely colorless lips. "What something?"

I shook my head. "I can't say. We signed a nondisclosure agreement."

The line of Moira's mouth broke as she began to worry at her bottom lip. "Come on," she said, beckoning me forward. "We need to hurry."

I fell into step with her once again. "I can be a few minutes late without raising any alarm. It is the first day of school."

Mom ignored the comment. "I'm going to have to disappear for a while. I don't know how long it's going to take to get this sorted out. But in the meantime, Destiny, you have to do something for me."

I blinked, wonderstruck. My mom needed something from me? Surely this was a sign of the apocalypse. "What's that?"

"Remember that question you kept asking me all summer?"

I glanced sidelong at her, trying to determine which one she meant. There'd been so many: *When can I have my phone back? When are we going home?* "Do you mean the one about who freed Marrow from his tomb?"

"That's the one."

Curiosity staved off my worry. The mystery of who freed Marrow was one my mom had been trying to solve for months now. It was half the reason for our trip to Europe in the first place. My great grandmother Nimue imprisoned him in a dream centuries ago, the only way she could think of to stop a man who could not stay dead.

Not just any man, but her dream-seer. She and Marrow had once been like Eli and me.

A wrench went through my stomach at the thought. *The curse.*

I pushed it away and turned my attention to my mom, still eager for more. Every time I'd asked her about the search she shut me down right away. Mom didn't want me to get involved. Whoever had freed Marrow was dangerous, his most powerful follower. I couldn't believe she was about to tell me now. Breathless, I asked, "Do you know who it is?"

Mom shook her head, her expression pinched. "I've thought I've had him over and over again, but each time I've been wrong. And now I'm out of time."

We rounded a corner, and I spotted my exit just ahead. My pulse began to pound in my ears. Was this really happening? Was my mom going on the run?

"Here, take this." Mom thrust her hand toward me, and I felt something small and hard press against my palm. I glanced at the object, surprised to see it was a flash drive.

I frowned up at her.

"Everything I've found out about the person is on there. I need you and Eli to take up the search while I'm gone."

My mouth fell open. Not only was my mom trusting me with this information—finally—but she was also giving Eli and me her blessing. At least, that's how it felt, even if she didn't exactly use those words.

"I'm more certain than ever before that the person is at Arkwell," Moira continued, quickening her pace down the tunnel. "I just don't know who. It's most likely a member of staff, a teacher, administration, a lunchroom worker, someone like that."

"That's a pretty big pool of people. . . ."

"There are clues on the flash drive." She stopped and swung toward me, all pretenses of being a student disappearing. This was the mother I'd known all my life. Her nostrils were flared, her eyes blazing—hard and beautiful. "You've got to find him. If we can get to him, we might be able to stop Marrow from coming back for good this time."

I dropped my gaze to the flash drive, doubt churning. "You mean if he isn't back already," I said, remembering the Death's Heart. I inhaled, desperate to tell her about it.

"We have to hope not," Mom said, setting her teeth together in a grimace.

I balled my hands into fists, grappling with frustration. "Are you really going?"

"I have to." Mom started walking again. "There won't be any talking my way out of it this time. From what I've heard of Valentine, the only thing he's going to accept is absolute proof of my innocence. And even then I'm not so sure."

"Are you saying Valentine is out to get you?" I hurried to keep up with her.

"It's possible."

"What did you do to him?"

Mom scowled. "Nothing. Contrary to your belief, I'm not in the habit of making enemies of police officers."

"You mean except for Sheriff Brackenberry."

Mom snorted. "Brackenberry's grudge is personal. He never got over me dumping him."

My eyes widened. My mom and the Sheriff? *Ew.* "Well, that explains a lot."

"Never you mind." Mom waved the subject away. "There's no telling what Valentine's motives are. He could be just one of those cops ego-bound on closing cases no matter what, or he might be one of Marrow's followers trying to stop me from finding out who set him free."

"And arresting you for murder would be a pretty good way," I said, coming to a halt. We'd reached the base of the stairs that led up to Jupiter Hall.

Mom stopped and faced me. "Undoubtedly. I'm just fortunate I had warning before he could."

"From who?"

"A friend in the police department. One of the few people I still trust. Which reminds me . . ." Mom cupped my hands with hers and forcibly closed my fingers around the flash drive. "Don't trust anyone but Eli and Selene with this. Not even Lady Elaine can know I gave it to you."

I arched an eyebrow. "You don't trust Lady Elaine?"

"I don't trust the people around her. Too many of the magic-kind government have turned out to be Marrow supporters. How many more are there? Titus Kirkwood, Bethany Grey—I'm certain they're just the tip of a very deep iceberg."

"Do you really think Val—" I broke off as the bell for seventh period sounded.

Mom flinched. "Hide that flash drive. You've got to go."

"Mom—" I started to protest, but she pulled me in for a quick hug. The gesture was so unexpected, so out of character, that a great whoosh of fear soared through my chest. Mom was in real trouble this time. She was scared. Somehow the reality of that frightened me far deeper than anything else.

Mom let go of me and turned away from the stairs, back to the tunnel. "I'll contact you when I can."

"Wait," I said. "How are you going to get out of Arkwell from down here?"

Mom glanced over her shoulder. "The same way I got in— by boat."

"You boated in here?"

Mom started to answer, but a noise reached us from down the tunnel and we both turned toward it. Heavy footsteps were coming this way. A second later, I spotted three Will Guards. One had a wand at the ready, another a staff. The third was naturekind, his pointed ears and outstretched hand marking him a fairy.

Mom spun the other direction, ready to flee, but she froze as two police offers appeared, blocking the way. There was nowhere to go but into the canal or up the stairs.

"Come on, Mom," I said, choosing the steps. She didn't hesitate but charged after me.

"Don't you do anything to help me, you understand?" she said, panting. "You stay out of the way. I don't want you in trouble, too."

"But, Mom."

"I mean it, Dusty. If Valentine is working for Marrow, we can't give him an excuse to get at you, too. For once in your life think before you act and do what I say."

Her words stung. She was my mother, and the men following us looked set on taking her down. How could I just stand by and watch?

We reached the top of the steps and entered Jupiter Hall.

"You go that way." Mom pointed down the hallway. "Maybe they'll follow."

"Okay." I took off at a run, trying to be as noisy as possible. It wasn't hard with the hallway empty of students. I glanced over my shoulder to see Mom had gone out the door onto the commons.

The men arrived a moment later. I turned back around, doing my best to distract them. It seemed to work for half a second, until I heard one of them shout. "She went outside!"

I skidded to a stop, pivoted, and saw all the men headed after my mom, ignoring me completely. I doubled back. Mom might have commanded me not to interfere, but that didn't mean I had to stay away.

When I arrived on the commons, a half-dozen police officers and Will Guards had surrounded my mom. She stood in the middle of the lawn, both arms ready in front of her as she did a slow circle, waiting for the attack. A steady drizzle of rain was slowly plastering her hair, her bangs falling over her eyes.

One of the policemen called, "It'll be so much better for everyone if you come peaceably, Ms. Everhart."

"Peaceably?" My mother laughed. "It's like you don't know me at all, Matthew." She pointed her arm at him. "*Ceno-crani.*"

The befuddlement spell struck the man in the head, and he stumbled sideways, doing a slow, awkward fall onto the stone pathway.

"Oh, God, Mom, what are you doing?" I said, fingers curled into fists as I fought back the urge to jump in. She couldn't possibly take on all of them.

Or maybe she could. The moment after the first policeman had fallen, one of the Will Guards behind her cast a jab jinx. Mom spun and countered it as easily as if she had eyes in the back of her head.

The other policemen and Will Guards soon followed suit. One after another, they lobbied spells at her. Mom blocked and countered each one. My jaw slowly fell open at the spectacle. It was more like watching a dance than a fight—my mother partnered with all these people. A spell cast here, a block there, pivot, turn, duck, cast again. There was a fluidity to it, I'd never seen before, not even in the gladiator games.

The fight had drawn spectators, students and teachers alike. I turned to the person nearest me. "That's my *mom*." I couldn't help it. My awe refused to be contained. Especially as I realized she was going to get away. One by one the policemen and Will Guards were falling to her magic. The few spells that had managed to get past her defenses hadn't slowed her down at all.

But then more policemen arrived, Sheriff Brackenberry and Detective Valentine among them. The former watched the scene with a look of admiration dawning on his broad face. But the latter's soon twisted into a look of outrage.

"Stop attacking at random!" Valentine shouted. Somehow his voice carried over the noise of the fighting. One by one the policemen ceased their attack.

Fear began to twist in my gut. My mother's haughty, confident stance was giving way to worry as she turned in a slow circle, braced for the next attack.

"On my mark," Valentine shouted, raising his hand.

"You can't!" I screamed. There were more than fifteen of them now. That much magic at once could kill her.

"One, two, three—now!" Valentine's spell reached Mom first, striking her in the chest. More than a dozen followed in the second after. There were too many to block. Even for my superstar mother.

She fell in slow motion, landing on her back in the grass. She did not get up.

7

Guilt Trap

I never made it to math class. Or to gladiator practice. Moments after my mom succumbed to Valentine's coordinated attack, a group of Will Guards surrounded me. They weren't quite as hostile to me as they had been to Mom, but close enough. The flash drive felt as heavy as a stone in my pocket.

"Sir, what do you want done with this one?" the nearest policeman asked.

Valentine glanced at me. His angry expression had been replaced with a look of indifference. "Take her down to the station for questioning."

Oh, crap. Now the flash drive felt as heavy as an anvil. Mom's warning kept echoing in my mind. I needed to get rid of this. I doubted I would have any right to privacy with these guys.

As if to prove this point, one of the policemen ordered me to hand over my schoolbag. I did so, hoping I didn't have any contraband I'd forgotten about inside it.

With the weight of the bag gone from my shoulders, the flash drive grew even heavier. Where to hide it? I scanned around, hoping for a likely place, but there was nothing.

Deciding to bide my time, I glanced over at my mom. They'd placed another spell on her, hoisting her into the air. Her arms were pulled out to her sides with her legs hanging limply together. Her head careened to one side, lank hair haloed around her face. She looked dead.

I turned away from her, unable to bear the sight.

A few minutes later, four of the policemen shepherded me off to the main parking lot. Shepherding was indeed the right word, considering all of them were werewolves and I felt as frightened as a baby lamb. Just before we reached the parking lot, I spotted a single potted plant at the corner of two walkways. This was my last chance to dump the flash drive. I just had to hope that no one else discovered it and that the plant would be enough to shield it from the rain.

I reached into my pocket and waited until we drew near. Then I casually tossed it in. I held my breath, convinced one of the policemen behind me had noticed, but no one called for a halt. By the time we reached the waiting black sedan, I was breathing easy again.

The police station, known as "the Rush" by most of the people who worked there—and the people who made frequent visits—was located a couple of miles west of Arkwell Academy in the abandoned Rush Sanitarium for the Criminally Insane. A sign posted outside the barred gates into the sanitarium read:

UNDER CONSTRUCTION
BY THE IGAM ETANES CORPORATION
NO TRESPASSING

As far as I knew that sign had been there since 1957 when the original sanitarium was shut down by the State Department for unsafe conditions and suspected abuse of patients. The Igam Etanes Corporation was the front used by the Magi Senate to hide magickind-owned businesses and organizations.

This wasn't my first time coming to the Rush, just the first time I was made to feel like a criminal myself. The police officers escorted me inside in the same four-man block formation they'd used at the school. I was asked to turn out my pockets and submit to a pat down. Ironically, I was allowed to keep Bellanax. None of them had a clue how powerful it was.

We walked through the cathedral-like main room of the station, full of desks set in haphazard rows and angles and policemen talking on the phone, plunking away at computer keyboards, and even a couple fielding in-person complaints. Most everyone stopped what they were doing to observe our march through the room and down the hall on the left to the first interrogation room.

A queasy feeling struck my stomach as I stepped inside. The place looked like it had once been the sight of an ax murder. Rust-colored stains covered two of the walls like some kind of weird impressionistic art. A moldy ceiling drooped low in the center, and the tiled floor was cracked and flaking off in places.

"Sit down and don't touch anything," one of the policemen said.

"Like what?" Besides the table and three chairs in the center of the room, the only other object was a camera perched in one corner. I studied it as I sat down, drawn by the way it was moving side to side, as if some drunken operator was messing with the controls on the other end of the feed. Then I heard the faint elevator music playing in the background and realized the camera was swaying to the beat, another victim of the animation effect.

The policemen shuffled out of the room before I could ask how long I was going to be stuck here.

The answer to that question turned out to be hours. Despite the command not to touch anything, I tried the door only to find it was locked. Glowering, I turned and faced the camera. "It's a good thing I don't have to pee or anything."

The camera didn't reply.

Finally, an indeterminate time later, the door opened and Lady Elaine stepped inside.

I stood up, my anxiety spurring me. "This is insane about my mother. She did not kill Titus Kirkwood."

"Insane or not," Lady Elaine said, "Moira is in serious trouble this time. We need to do everything we can to help her, and that includes being careful with your attitude. Understood?"

I swallowed, thoroughly scolded, and nodded. At least she was on Mom's side still. That was good.

Lady Elaine came around the table and sat down in the chair next to mine, like she was my social worker and I some juvenile delinquent. She reached out and patted my shoulder. "We'll get through this. I promise."

I glanced at her, uncertain. "If you don't think she did it, then how come she's being charged? You're advisor to the Consul. Can't you just tell the Magi Senate she's innocent and get her off?"

"It's not that easy, I'm afraid."

"Why not?"

Lady Elaine exhaled, her thin nostrils moving in and out. "Because I have no proof."

I scowled, digging the pads of my fingertips into the table-top. "Since when does that matter among magickind?"

"Since—" She broke off as the door swung open.

Detective Valentine stepped inside. "Hello again, Dusty." Once more, he was carrying a dark green folder tucked beneath his arm.

I sat up from my slouched position, glaring. "I can't believe you're investigating my mother."

"Neither can I." He shut the door behind him, and then sat down directly across from me, placing the folder on the table between us. He acknowledged Lady Elaine with a slight bow of his head, but otherwise his attention remained focused on me. "And before you ask," he continued. "I did not know last night that we would be arresting her today. That would've been bad form not to give you warning."

"No kidding," I said, but I wasn't sure I believed him. That was an awfully quick turnaround. "So what happened in the last fifteen hours to make you think my mom could do something so terrible as commit murder?"

Valentine cocked an eyebrow, the gesture borderline mocking. "You mean so terrible as executing the man who kidnapped her only daughter, tortured her, and then left her to die?"

My stomach gave a hard dip, the sensation like going over a hill too quickly in a car. Not only did they have some kind of "evidence" as Lady Elaine indicated, but they also had motive. A pretty good one, I realized, my mind spinning. Titus had indeed done those awful things to me. When he was being murdered, I was in a coma, the doctors, healers, and everyone else uncertain if I would ever recover from the injuries I'd sustained preventing the island from sinking.

All at once, I was there again, racing across Lyonshold, fire and debris raining down around me from the burning fissure ahead, a deep hole rent through the island by a spell designed to sink it. With Bellanax in my hand, with Bellanax in *control,* I'd jumped headfirst into the last of those fissures, my body falling into the flames. Bellanax had kept me from being burned alive, but it couldn't protect me from all the magic around us that the sword was absorbing into itself to keep the spell from reaching completion. It was so much magic it should've killed me. It almost did.

Mom must've thought it had, I realized, picturing it easily. My mother, so strong, and fierce, and stubborn. I knew she would do anything to keep me safe, but would she also go to any length to avenge my death?

I pushed the thought away, afraid the answer would bite me like a poisonous snake.

Staring over at Valentine, I hardened my resolve. "My mother is innocent."

Valentine pursed his lips. "You are entitled to your opinion. But it has no bearing on why you are here. I simply want to review the events leading up to the attack on Lyonshold." He idly drummed his fingers against the table. "Given the trauma you sustained, you were never asked to provide an official statement. It was an understandable oversight, but it now must be corrected."

"What about Eli and Selene? They were there, too. So was Paul Kirkwood."

"Yes, I know." Valentine opened the folder, revealing a stack of papers inside. The top one bore the title *The Lyonshold Incident*. A picture of the island, post attack, filled most of it. "We will be speaking to all of them, in time. But your statement is the most relevant. Now, if you'd like to start at the beginning, when you first realized that Titus Kirkwood was planning the attack."

I shook my head. "No deal. First I want to know why you think my mom killed him. Then I'll talk."

Beside me, Lady Elaine made a noise. It might've been shock, but it sounded more like amusement. Or perhaps encouragement. Either way, I kept my gaze focused on Valentine. Around my wrist Bellanax heated into life.

"Excuse me?" Valentine sat up straighter. "Are you saying I have to *bargain* for your statement?"

"Yep. Either tell me what I want to know or I plead the fifth."

Valentine cleared his throat. "We are magickind. There is no fifth."

I tapped my foot on the floor. The sharp rap of my boot against the tile would've been a lot more effective if not for the rhythmic *creak, creak, creak* of the camera still swaying along to the song.

"All right," I said, unable to take the silence any longer. "If you don't tell me what I want to know, then you're going to have to force me to talk." With magic at their beck and call, they could do it easily, but I had a feeling that Valentine would want to keep things smooth, especially since I was a minor. At least, I was hoping he did.

With perfect seriousness, Lady Elaine said, "I would be careful here, Detective. She is Moira's daughter, after all."

"So I'm gathering." Valentine rubbed his thumb over his bottom lip. "Very well. I don't see how a little information will cause any harm."

You don't know the Dream Team, buddy. Sometimes being underestimated was the most powerful weapon of all.

"There are three reasons why I am certain your mother is guilty," Valentine continued. "Number one, she had means and motive to commit the crime. The motive, as I already made clear, was you. For means, we need to look no further than the fact that she is a Nightmare."

I bit my lower lip, my heartbeat quickening. For a second, I thought he was referring to the one way of killing only a Nightmare could do—draining a person of all the fictus they possessed. Only, from what I understood, this didn't kill the person in a traditional sense, but left them soulless, neither living nor dead, just . . . done. But that couldn't be what had happened to Titus. I would've heard about it before now.

Carefully, I said, "How do you mean?"

"The prison cell Titus Kirkwood was being held in was a magically restricted ward. All magic is blocked using a spell very similar to The Will." Valentine paused for effect. "And as I know you are aware, The Will spell was completely foolproof against all magical beings except for—"

"Nightmares," I finished for him. It was true, and my mother had loads of experience working magic inside such barriers. Our magic was fueled by fictus, the very stuff of imagination, and imagination could not be controlled or predicted by any force, even a magical one. Acid began to burn its way up my throat, and I swallowed it down. "My mother isn't the only Nightmare in existence."

"True, but of all the known Nightmares in the area, she is the only one with no alibi."

I frowned at the way he said "all of the known," as if there were lots of Nightmares running around our little town of Chickery, Ohio. But that just wasn't true. There were only three—me, my mother, and Bethany Grey. I had been in a coma, and Bethany was locked up in a prison cell right here at the Rush. She'd been here for months prior to the attack on Lyonshold. She was a known Marrow supporter, serving out her time for crimes committed aiding Marrow in his quest to break The Will spell. In both our cases, there was no need for Valentine to confirm an alibi. So who was he talking about? I started to ask him, but he didn't give me a chance.

"However," Valentine said, the condescension in his voice whisper-light, but unmistakably present, "I suppose it's possible that some unknown Nightmare came in from out of town just for the sole purpose of breaking into the magically secured facility and murdering Titus Kirkwood."

I bit down hard on my tongue, fighting back an angry reply.

My insides began to seethe, and Bellanax was so hot around my wrist I thought my skin might scald. But I'd caught the warning in Lady Elaine's quick glance. I needed to do what I could to help my mother, and right now, that meant information and not losing my temper. I had to learn everything I could. The Dream Team would need it for our own investigation. Finding the man who freed Marrow was important, no doubt, but freeing my mother was even more so.

With applause-worthy civility, I said, "What are the other two reasons you think my mother is guilty?"

If Valentine was surprised by my self-control, his expression didn't show it. He continued on, not missing a beat. "We found DNA evidence linking your mother to the crime scene."

I blinked, a weird sense of déjà vu coming over me. Or more like temporal displacement. I felt as if I'd been transported from the magickind police station into a TV police procedural. Words like "DNA evidence" didn't belong here where the emphasis was always on the magical.

Valentine tilted his head. "You do know what I mean by DNA evidence, yes?"

My shock snapped back to anger, and I placed my hand over the silver band on my wrist and began to twist it. "Of course I do. But since when does magickind do things the ordinary way when it comes to police work?"

"Actually, magickind has been mimicking ordinary procedures for years," said Valentine with a flash of teeth. "It's just we very rarely find any at our crime scenes. Most of our bad guys kill people in ways that do not leave physical evidence behind."

"They kill with magic," I murmured, thinking aloud. As horrible as it sounded, I knew that was how my mother would kill, too. Of course, she would. She was a long way from stupid. A little reckless from time to time, but not stupid. And sneaking into the magickind police station to kill a prisoner? That would've taken planning and caution, not some rash in and out where she left behind a bunch of hair and fingerprints, or whatever it was they'd supposedly collected.

I tapped my thumb against the table. "Are you sure you even did it right? I mean, no offense, but magickind aren't exactly awesome at ordinary science."

Valentine snorted. "No argument about that. Oh, don't look so surprised. Regardless of what you might think, I'm not out to get your mother."

You sure about that? He could be a Marrow supporter. There was no way to tell.

"I just want to see the guilty brought to justice." Valentine shrugged. "That said, the evidence was tested and verified by the FBI lab in Cleveland. I have a friend in the agency I often call upon for help in these matters."

He sounded so convincing, so very much like the stoic lead actor of a police procedural that at first I believed him completely—the news crashing down on me like a landslide. But something didn't fit.

I sat up straighter. "Why would an FBI lab have my mom's DNA on file for you to get a match to what you found in Titus's cell? She's never once been in trouble with the ordinary law." I started to smile, certain I had him there.

Valentine sighed, his look one of pity, like I was some dumb kid, a child playing at a grown-up. "Because I sent them a sample of her DNA to compare it to."

"Why would—" I broke off, the truth smacking me in the face. A haze seemed to smear the edges of my vision. "Oh, I see. You already thought she was guilty and so you preemptively had them do an analysis on hers."

Valentine nodded, his lips pressed together in a gesture of regret.

I wasn't buying it. This guy had suspected my mother all along, including last night when he stopped by to enlist my help in finding the Death's Heart. And why did he suspect her? Because she was a Nightmare. I sat back in my chair, folding my arms over my chest. I felt Bellanax's heat through my shirt where the silver band pressed against my side.

Taking a deep breath, I said, "There's no way that's admissible. It's got to be racial profiling or entrapment or something. I don't know for sure, but I'm going to find out."

This time it was Lady Elaine who sighed, feeling sorry for me—although at least hers was genuine. "That's not how the magickind justice system works, Dusty. We have always relied on 'racial profiling' as you call it. With the kinds as different as they are, it's an effective tool."

I gritted my teeth—I had to remember she was on my side in this. "Okay, I get that it can be a good tool for finding the guilty, but it shouldn't be the only tool. Maybe there's some other reason why my mom's DNA was there. And maybe because you've already decided she's guilty, you're overlooking the other possibilities."

"Like what?" Valentine said, and I could tell by the glint in his eye that he was just humoring me.

"I don't know, but I can't believe that *only* a Nightmare could've pulled it off. I know we're awesome and all, but there has to be other magickind out there capable of getting into that ward to kill him." Not that I knew of any. But the Dream Team would figure it out. I just needed to get my hands on the case file. I glanced down at the folder still lying open on the desk.

Valentine tented his fingers below his chin. "Perhaps you

might be right about other ways, but there is the third reason left to consider."

I exhaled, steeling myself for the next blow. "What is it?"

"I have witnessed your mother's guilt on that matter."

"She confessed?" I couldn't believe it. It wasn't possible. Even if my mother was guilty, she would never just admit to it. Not unless she knew she could get away with it.

"Not exactly," Valentine said. "When I say I've witnessed her guilt, I mean that I have felt it, *fed* on it, if you like that word better. And by fed, I mean in the same way that you feed on Eli Booker."

The room spun around me again. "What are you talking about?"

"Detective Valentine," Lady Elaine said, her voice working like a lighthouse beacon, giving my capsized brain a target to focus on, "is a Crimen demon. A guilt demon."

"Correct." A prim little smile came and went on Valentine's face. "My kind feeds on guilt. When I brought your mother in to get her alibi for the night Titus died, her guilt was undeniable."

According to you and you only. My hands clenched into fists. I wanted to hit something. It was so unfair, so much room for deception. "How do you know her guilt is related to the murder? She could be feeling guilty for all sorts of reasons. It doesn't mean crap without a confession."

"That might be true if it weren't for everything else against her." Valentine waved a hand through the air. "But it doesn't matter. It's in the court's hands now."

I sucked in a breath, a helpless feeling coming over me. But no, it wasn't hopeless—I just had to find out who really killed Titus. Clinging to this goal, I said, "I want to talk to my mom."

"I'm afraid that's impossible at the moment." Valentine said. "But I'm sure we can arrange it in a few days."

"How badly hurt is she?" The image of how I'd seen her last flashed through my mind.

"She's fine," Lady Elaine said. "She's just under a sleeping spell for now."

I gaped. "Why?"

Valentine offered me a diplomatic smile. "It's just a precaution until we can get a cell constructed to hold her. It's not easy to contain a Nightmare, since the normal anti-magic spells are so ineffective."

I would've been reassured by the difficulty if the thought of my mother lying unconscious somewhere nearby wasn't so upsetting. "What do you mean construct? You've got Bethany Grey here somewhere, don't you? Why can't she just go in the same kind of cell?"

The two adults in a room exchanged a look, and I could almost hear the silent question pass between them—*should you tell her or should I?*

In the end, Lady Elaine lost the coin toss. "The cell we were using to hold Bethany Grey has been . . . dismantled. Recently."

"Dismantled? Then where are you keeping Bethany now?"

Valentine let out an exaggerated sigh. "This isn't common knowledge yet, and as such it falls under the nondisclosure agreement you signed. But Bethany Grey has been abducted."

"She's gone?" *Nobody important,* I thought, recalling Sheriff Brackenberry's words. I could see his reasoning for saying it now, given Bethany Grey was a criminal. Only . . . "How do you know she didn't just escape? There are still Marrow supporters out there."

"I had a vision of her kidnapping," Lady Elaine said, her expression somber. "But not in time to stop it."

As horrible as this was to hear, a new idea occurred to me, one that sent hope ballooning up inside my chest. "Wait a second.

Was Bethany Grey being held in the same magically restricted ward as Titus Kirkwood?"

Valentine nodded.

I nearly jumped to my feet in excitement. "Then that proves someone else besides my mother has the ability to break into that ward!"

Blank stares greeted my declaration, from both Valentine and Lady Elaine.

"What?" I said, exasperated. "It's so obvious."

"No, Dusty," Valentine said, offering me a sad shake of his head. "It's not. Bethany's disappearance, the Death's Heart. It's all happened since you returned from your trip. Your mother could've easily done it. Right now she's our biggest suspect."

I laughed, feeling on the verge of hysteria. "Wow, my mom's a criminal mastermind, isn't she? I mean, why not blame everything on her. Maybe she even stole a time machine and went back to the sixties just to kill Kennedy."

"Is it really so hard to believe?" Valentine said, his tone annoyingly reasonable. "Bethany and Moira share a long and well-documented history of mutual animosity."

I pressed my lips together, wishing I could deny it. But Bethany and Moira did hate each other. Bethany had even tried to kill her.

Still, I refused to accept anything until I had more proof. "I know she didn't do any of this."

"The judge and jury will determine that," said Valentine.

Swallowing, I asked, "When is the trial?"

"It's set to start at the end of October," Lady Elaine said.

Blood rushed in my ears. "What if she's found guilty?"

"We really shouldn't speculate—" Lady Elaine began.

Valentine cut her off. "If found guilty, she will most certainly be executed."

I swayed on my chair, the image of my dead body in Eli's dream swimming in my mind. *Dreams are symbolic,* Eli had said. Except for our hair, my mother and I looked alike. *Symbolic.*

I closed my eyes and prayed the dream was lying. Just this time.

8

It Bites

The rest of the interview went quickly, painlessly, for the most part. True to the deal we'd made, I told Valentine everything I could remember about Titus Kirkwood and the attack on Lyonshold—including my absolute certainty that my mother had no idea what we'd found out until after it all went down. I hadn't spoken to her at all in the days before Titus Kirkwood abducted me, Eli, Selene, and Paul.

But I also had to admit that since arriving back in the States nearly a week ago, I hadn't had any contact with my mom until today. She could've been up to anything. The day we got home, I went to stay with my dad for the remainder of summer break for some much needed father-daughter time. Up until discovering I was a Nightmare, I'd lived exclusively with my ordinary father, a college professor at the local university.

In other words, I wasn't able to do a thing to help my mother.

It was nearly midnight when I arrived back at campus. Unfortunately, with my Will Guard escort, I wasn't able to retrieve the flash drive from the flowerpot. It would have to wait until the morning. But at least Lady Elaine had made sure I could skip classes tomorrow, a day to mourn as it were.

The moment the bell for first period rang the following morning, I left my dorm room and headed back to the parking lot. To my dismay, the flash drive was completely soaked and covered in dirt. I had no idea if it would work or not. I set it on my desk to dry when I returned to my dorm room and then spent the rest of the day browsing the Internet and watching movies.

Selene brought me back food from the cafeteria during lunch and then later at dinner. I was grateful to avoid the crowds. The rumors were flying high.

"How bad is it?" I asked her as we sat down to enjoy a couple of unicorn skewers of shrimp, chicken, and veggies.

"Boring really." She made a face. "People have no imagination. I mean, if I were going to start a rumor about your mother, it would be that she's a government spy being framed for Titus's murder so that the real criminal can go about his business without worrying that her badass, super-self will arrive just in time to foil his plans." Selene paused, raising a hand to her chin. "But wait, that's mostly true, isn't it?"

I smiled appreciatively, but couldn't muster the will to laugh.

Selene sighed. "If it makes you feel any better, not all the rumors are about your mother. There's one going around that Lance's father has disinherited him because he committed the horrible crime of dating a siren."

I risked a look at her, words escaping me.

"Yep, he's going to be forced out of school now any day."

My mouth fell open. "Are you serious?"

"No," Selene said, a weak smile cresting her lips. "That's just the rumor. Although it is true that his dad hates me. If he's not careful he just might get disinherited."

"I'm sorry," I said.

She shrugged, tossing her long black braid over her shoulder. "It's all right. Maybe there'll be something new for them to make up rumors about tomorrow."

It was a nice idea, but wishful thinking. When Selene and I walked into the cafeteria the next morning, I noticed a definite shift in the noise level. The conversation didn't stop, just changed in pitch, a sudden uptick. There were head turns, pointing, taps on shoulders. It might've been my imagination, but I didn't think so. It wasn't the first time I'd been through something like this. It was just the first time the rumors were about my mother instead of me. For some reason, that bothered me more.

"Just ignore it," Selene said. She swept the room with a hawk-like stare, one fierce enough to make onlookers recoil. Such was the power of a siren. For a second, I imagined her unfurling her hidden wings, taking flight, and then dive-bombing the crowd until they were all prostrate on the ground, too scared to speak a word. She would do it, too, if the situation called for it. My affection for her swelled up inside me, and I resisted the urge to give her a mushy hug.

Eli and Lance weren't there yet, so we went through the line at the Pizza Tut, ordering a couple of breakfast pizzas big enough to share with the boys—roughly half the size of a table. I desperately scanned the food vendors for signs of a caffeinated beverage. After a fitful night's sleep, I would've settled for it in any form, but the hope I'd harbored that caffeine would be an upperclassmen perk soon died. Like sugar and nearly everything else worthy of compulsive consumption, caffeine was a controlled substance at Arkwell.

The boys arrived not long after we sat down. Eli greeted me with a pick-me-up hug hard enough to squeeze all the air from my chest. "I missed you yesterday," he said, then he kissed me, both of us ignoring the Will Guard already closing in.

"Hey, back off, man," Lance said as the Guard reached us. "They're not hurting anything."

Eli set me on my feet, and we pulled apart. I expected the Will

Guard to give us a reprimand, but it was the same one from Monday. He murmured a halfhearted warning and then walked away again.

"Thanks, Lance," I said, a little stunned.

"We'll call it four to three," Lance replied, referring to our ongoing prank competition we'd had most of last year. He winked. "Or you could just concede that I win forever."

"Last I checked, hell is still pretty hot."

We all sat down to eat, and I filled them in on most of what happened in my interview with Valentine. All except for the stuff about Bethany. The second I tried to tell them she'd gone missing, my tongue sealed itself to the roof of my mouth.

Eli clucked annoyance and ran his hand over my back. "Don't fight it. Just think about something else." Then he turned to Selene and Lance. "Dusty and I have to be careful about what we talk about. We signed a nondisclosure agreement a few days ago for our latest dream-seer task."

Selene huffed. "That's going to make things hard for the rest of us."

I nodded, still unable to speak.

"We'll figure a way around it," Eli said. "We can't let it stop us."

By the time the nondisclosure spell gave me back control of my mouth again, breakfast was over. I sighed, dreading the rest of the day without Eli. But at least we had a dream session tonight.

Only, I was dreading that, too, and not just because of Bollinger.

"I'll spend some time coming up with a strategy of how we should start our investigation," Eli said as the four of us exited the cafeteria. "Should we meet after school to really dig into it?"

"What about your gladiator practice?" I asked. "Isn't it every night?"

Eli smiled down at me. "Your mom is way more important."

A flush heated my skin. I studied his gaze and saw he truly meant it, his cool blue eyes unwavering. Only making the team meant so much to him. "Thanks, but I don't want you to skip it."

He cocked his head. "What? Why?"

I squeezed his fingers, interwoven with my own. "Because it's important to you, and I know you'll still manage to help. Besides, the trial's weeks away. We've got a little time."

Eli rubbed his chin. "Tryouts are coming up soon, but are you really sure?"

"Yes," I said, my voice firm. "We should all just brainstorm about it as much as possible so we're ready to get to work when we meet up again."

Everyone agreed to this plan and we made our way to homeroom.

It came and went quickly, the announcements typically long as they always were at the beginning of the school year. When the bell rang, Eli and I shuffled out into the hallway to head to our separate classes. Spotting another Will Guard nearby, I stifled a groan of disappointment. It seemed we'd never catch a break.

I turned to say as much to Eli, but to my surprise, he pulled me against his chest and bent his head toward mine. The kiss was deeper than the last, our mouths opened, tongues touching. Even though it lasted only a second before the Will Guard vulture ordered us apart, I felt the longing in his kiss, the unspoken wish for more time spent doing this.

Ignoring the Will Guard shouting at us, Eli fixed a gaze on me that was more promise than look. *We'll find time together soon.*

I nodded, my whole body tingling from the inside out. *Thank goodness I have Eli,* I thought as I headed to class. Together we could do anything.

Although I was a day behind, I spent most of history and English thinking about how to save my mom. The only way, short of breaking her out, was to find the real killer. We really needed those police files. But getting them would require breaking into the Rush, a place both physically and magically guarded around the clock. As it was, I doubted we'd even be able to break out of school, what with the Will Guard patrolling campus all the time.

Unless we can break into the computer system. It was a good idea, but problematic. The only person I knew capable of pulling off a hack like that was Paul Kirkwood. For the first time in months, I was sorry he wasn't around. It seemed it was time I read all those unopened e-mails.

Later, I decided, catching a stern look from Mr. Corvus.

When first period ended, I tried to scan some of Paul's e-mails on the way to biology, but it proved impossible to read at the fast pace we were walking to get there on time. And when we arrived Ms. Miller kept us busy. Today she had us working with a pack of azbans, raccoon-like creatures with a reputation for being the most clever and mischievous of all magical animals.

"They have a wicked sense of humor," Ms. Miller warned.

More like mean, I decided when ten minutes into the class one of them bit my finger.

"Are you all right, Dusty?" Selene said, spying the blood. "Ms. Miller, we need help."

"I'm fine," I said, pain rippling up my hand into my arm. I glared at the azban, which was staring at me with wide, watery eyes, its little hands covering its mouth like it was either shocked by what it had done—or was laughing about it.

My vote was on the latter.

"Let me see," Ms. Miller said.

I held out my hand. She examined it a moment, pronounced it a flesh wound, and offered me a strip of dirty rag.

"Just wrap that around it. You'll be fine."

"Gee, thanks," I said, staring down at my mutilated finger.

"Karma," someone whispered from behind me.

"Even azbans don't like Nightmares," came the reply.

I resisted the urge to look around. Finding out who had said it wasn't going to make me feel any better.

By the time we got to ordinary living, my finger was hurting too badly for me to hold a pencil. I considered asking Mrs. Bar for a pass to visit the infirmary, but decided to tough it out. Psionics was up next and I didn't want to miss it.

Then again, maybe skipping would've been best. Katarina turned to stare at me the moment I walked in. She leaned toward her best friend Carla Petermeier, whispering behind her hand.

Just ignore them, I thought, reaching for the silver band on my wrist. The extra contact with Bellanax seemed to lessen the pain in my finger, if only by a degree.

A few moments after I sat down, Mr. Deverell approached my desk. "Are you doing all right, Dusty?" He peered down at me, his expression one of open concern.

I gulped, suddenly feeling emotionally fragile. I'd been doing okay all day—rumors easier to deal with than sympathy. "I'm fine. Thanks."

Deverell nodded. "Let me know if you'd rather not participate in today's activities. It could be challenging."

"I like a good challenge."

"I know you do." A smile slid across his face, disappearing a second later. "I'm so sorry to hear about your mother. Please let me know if there's anything I can do."

"Thanks," I said, tight-lipped as I fought back that fragility once again. It was like trying to hold a crumbling wall in place. He made it sound as if my mom had died instead of been arrested and charged with murder.

"Today," Deverell said to the class at large a few minutes later, "we will begin our study of psychometry. Does anyone know what that is?"

Several hands went up in the air.

"Yes, Katarina," Mr. Deverell said.

"Psychometry is the ability to read the history of an object by touching it."

"Very good." Deverell bestowed an appraising glance on her. "Now, this is a very difficult skill as it requires the mind and the body to work as one. But as always, the more open and supple your mind is, the better you will do. So let's start with some focusing exercises and then we will attempt to read some objects."

Deepening my breathing, I closed my eyes and attempted to perform the first exercise—mind-cleaning, as it was called. I pictured a large room cluttered with objects, visual representations of all my thoughts. I imagined myself cleaning out the room, removing the clutter one by one. The goal was to make the room empty and open, an inviting place for the mind-magic to dwell.

After several minutes of trying, I failed to remove so much as a cobweb. Worry about my mom kept pressing in. The image of my dead body in Eli's dream had been replaced with hers. I couldn't shake it.

Giving up, I opened my eyes, inwardly cursing. I supposed if Deverell called on me I would take him up on the offer to pass.

At the front of the room, Deverell was levitating objects from out of the nearby utility closet and placing them on the long table set beside his desk. I spotted a rusted hammer, a skull, a wrench, a knife. I half expected Miss Scarlett and Colonel Mustard to appear next.

Soon, everyone else had given up on the warm-up exercises as well, all of our attention focused on Deverell.

"Okay," he said, clasping his hands. "The objects you see

before you have very long, very powerful histories. They are also very 'loud' as we call it in the business. And by that I mean they are broadcasting a good deal of their histories easily enough for even beginners to detect."

Katarina raised her hand.

"Yes, Miss Marcel," Deverell said, motioning at her.

"Why do they broadcast so clearly, sir?"

Deverell beamed, and it seemed I heard all the females in the room give a collective sigh—myself included. "There are two factors that primarily cause a regular object to both retain and broadcast a history. The first is emotional impact. All mind-magic, be it telepathy or empathy or anything else, comes from living, sentient beings. Inanimate objects will sometimes absorb the emotions of the humans and magickinds that live near them. Objects that have witnessed tragedy or extreme joy are more likely to retain the psychic energy of that history. It makes an impression on them.

"The second factor is the duration of exposure. Objects that have been owned by the same person or even the same family are more likely to retain history. Make sense?"

I nodded along with the rest of the class. It sounded similar to the animation effect, only where magic and electromagnetic fields were replaced with emotions and exposure.

"Now, who would like to volunteer to go first?" Deverell said.

Once again, several hands went in the air.

"Deanna Ackles," he said, waving to the dark-haired, dark-eyed girl sitting at the back of the classroom. Deanna was demon-kind, although I wasn't sure which type.

"You can select any of the objects you wish," Mr. Deverell explained as she arrived at the front of the classroom. "Then all you have to do is place your hands on it, close your eyes, and open your mind to it the same as you would during a telepathy exercise."

After a few seconds contemplation, Deanna selected an antique compass. She picked it up, holding it in one hand and cupping it in the other. She closed her eyes. Several seconds passed with the rest of us watching, silently.

Deanna scrunched up her nose in concentration. "I think I see . . . a . . . a . . . pirate ship."

Several people laughed at this—Deanna had a reputation of being a wiseass—but as her eyes slid opened, I could tell she wasn't joking this time.

Mr. Deverell said, "That is very close to true, Deanna. Good job." He took the compass out of her hand and held it up for the rest of us to see. "This belonged to one of the sailors of the unfortunate *Mary Celeste*."

A murmur of surprise went through the classroom. On a normal day, I would've been utterly captivated by the idea of the ghost ship, but as it was, my head was beginning to ache, the lack of sleep catching up with me. Even worse was the steady throb in my wounded finger. It was starting to make me sick to my stomach.

"Does the compass show what happened to the sailors?" Deanna asked.

A devilish expression crossed Deverell's face. "It just might. We will have to see." He set the compass back on the table then called on Katarina next.

She did her catwalk thing all the way to the front of the classroom, casting her sultry gaze here and there. In seconds, she held everyone captive with her siren bedazzlement. For the first time in perhaps ever, I was grateful for the distraction. It helped me forget the throb in my finger and the pound in my head.

Katarina examined the objects, contemplating the skull before turning toward the knife. A smirk came and went on her face. She picked it up and closed her eyes. The class watched with a collective held breath, all of us enchanted.

"I think," Katarina said, her lips curling. "I *think* . . . that this was used in a . . . in a . . . murder." Her eyes slid open for a moment, long enough to recapture anyone who'd managed to break free of her mesmerizing power. Even with the throb in my finger, I could tell she was deliberately using her siren magic. Dread began to thrum inside me, building low, somewhere deep. *Murder* she had said.

Katarina squeezed her eyes closed again, and now an alarmed look crossed her face—the beautiful horror-flick damsel in distress who just discovered the psycho killer is *in the house.* Like all sirens, she was quite the actress.

"Yes, a murder. Someone important. A politician, I think. And the person who did it was a . . . was a . . . a woman." Katarina's eyes came open once more, and again that smirk ghosted her face. Around me, I heard several snickers, some of the others catching the joke before I did.

The cruel, awful joke.

Throb, throb, throb. My anger coiled inside me like a snake.

"Yes," Katarina said, her snide smile directed at me. "This knife was used to commit murder by a *Nightmare.*"

My anger, coiled one moment, exploded into rage in the next. And it was more than emotion. It became a force. It became power. *Magic.*

I lurched to my feet, my hand reaching for Bellanax. At the same time, I felt the sword reaching for me, calling me to it, compelling me.

"*Luo-dikho!*" I hissed, the spell foreign on my lips and yet familiar, too.

I'd never cast it before.

I'd cast it a thousand times.

The knife in Katarina's hand exploded, the steel spraying outward like shrapnel. Pieces of it struck Katarina in the face, and she screamed.

I started to disengage the glamour on Bellanax, the sword's eagerness to be unleashed like gasoline poured onto the fire of my outrage.

Somewhere nearby, a voice shouted, "*Hupno-drasi!*"

I only had time to see Deverell raise his hand in my direction. Then the spell struck me, and I went under, asleep before my body hit the ground.

9

Motives

I dreamed I was back in the catacombs of Paris. Walls of bone surrounded me on all sides. Skulls stacked in uniform columns stared down at me with black-holed eyes and rictus grins formed by the femur bones set in rows beneath them. I turned in a circle, my gaze fixed on the walls, my heart racing with the sudden certainty that I wasn't alone.

"Dusty!"

I froze. It was my mother's voice, as familiar to me as my own.

"Dusty!"

I raced toward the sound coming from somewhere ahead in this labyrinthine palace of the dead. I turned left then right then left again, chasing it. "Dusty, Dusty, Dusty," she called, her voice strained and growing weaker, even as I drew near.

I rounded a corner into a circular room. More bones filled the place, but they were stacked pell-mell, the dead nothing more than forgotten, inconsequential things. The dark narrow mouth of a pit leered from the center of the room.

My mother's voice rose out from it like a prayer. "Dusty."

"Mom!" I fell to my knees at the edge of the pit and leaned over, staring down into it. It was no wider than a well, and my mother stood at the bottom of it, her face turned up, her eyes wide and terrified, red from crying.

"Dusty!" She raised bruise-painted arms toward me, her nails split and bloody from where she had tried to claw her way up and out. The walls of the pit were lined with more bones, thin and slippery, offering no purchase. "Help me, Dusty," she screamed. "I can't get out. I can't get out."

"Mom!" I reached toward her, on my belly now. She started to climb again, her fingers closing over bones, the veins in her hands and forearms popping out. She rose an inch closer. But then the bones inside the well began to crumble. Soon an avalanche of them was falling down on her. She struggled, trying to get atop of them, but it was no use. The bones were heavy and too many.

I screamed, stretching down toward the pit, but I couldn't get to her. In seconds she was gone, her cries silenced by the weight of the dead. Sobbing, I started to pull back from the pit, but something shoved me from behind and I tumbled forward into it. There shouldn't have been room, not with my mother buried beneath all those bones. But this was a dream, and it accommodated my fear, the pit expanding. It had always been so deep, so capable of holding us both. I hit the bottom, an impossible distance down. Bleeding and crying, I shuffled into a sitting position, the walled bones scraping against my arms. I struggled to my feet and looked up at the opening.

"Help!" I screamed, but I knew it was no good. There was no one to hear it.

Panting now, I grasped at the bones in the wall, trying to find a grip. My fingers ached as I pulled myself up. A face appeared over the edge of the pit.

"Eli!" I shouted, and lost purchase, sliding the meager inches I'd managed to climb. "Help me, Eli!"

He shook his head, his expression inexorably sad, desolate even, like the scarred ground left behind from a forest razed to make room for a parking lot.

"Please, Eli," I said, no longer screaming but begging now. I didn't understand that look on his face. I didn't want it to be there.

He just shook his head again, and then he stood, and I saw a shovel in his hands. He turned away for a moment only to swing back, the shovel now full of discarded bones. He flung them into the pit. They struck me in the face and head and arms, a hundred dull hurts.

In seconds there were a thousand of them, an avalanche of bones coming to swallow me as it had my mother. I screamed and screamed until the bones pressed so tight against my chest I could no longer fill my lungs with air. And then the bones reached my neck and head. Darkness covered me, and I screamed no more.

I woke with my heart pounding, the nightmare emotions chasing me into consciousness. I looked around, trying to will the fear away. I was awake now. It was just a dream. Eli didn't just try to kill me. My mom wasn't dead.

Yet.

I focused on my surroundings, surprised to find myself not in my own bed but in Arkwell's infirmary.

I slowly sat up and peered around, my head feeling like someone had taken a hammer to it, repeatedly. Fragments of the bone dream flitted through my brain, and I tried to ignore them.

I jumped when I saw two people sitting in the chairs across from the hospital bed. Neither was whom I wanted to see at the moment. I wanted my mom, but she was incarcerated. My throat constricted, tears threatening.

"Hello again, Dusty," Lady Elaine said, the smile she offered looking tired and reluctant. The feeling was mutual. I liked Lady Elaine well enough, but never once had her presence in my life meant anything besides trouble.

Beside her sat Mr. Deverell. He, too, was looking tired. He stifled a yawn as he spoke a greeting. Suspecting it was late, I peered out the single large window beside the bed. The curtain was drawn back, the windowpane beyond a screen of darkness.

I looked back at my unusual visitors. "What happened?"

With a hooded gaze, Deverell said, "What do you *remember?*"

I blinked, my mind drawing a blank. Then slowly recollection crept in, of Mr. Deverell's class and Katarina holding the knife, the blade shattering. Choking on a breath, I reached for the silver band on my left wrist, only to discover that it wasn't there. I started to get out of the bed, close to panic, but my knee struck something hard. I knew what it was instantly—Bellanax, unglamoured. I slid my hands beneath the sheet and grasped the sword's pommel. At once, my panic subsided. So did the ache in my head.

"What do you remember, Dusty?" Deverell asked again.

I inhaled, the memory becoming clear in my mind. "I attacked Katarina because she was making fun of my mom. Only, I didn't mean to do it. I just lost my head for a minute." I hesitated, my lower lip quivering. "Is . . . is Katarina all right?"

"She will be," Lady Elaine said. "The wounds are superficial, and given that she's a siren, the nurses anticipate she will heal quickly."

"Is she in the infirmary, too?"

Lady Elaine nodded. "Just next door, but she's most certainly asleep at this hour."

I inhaled, gulping. "I didn't mean to hurt her. Not like that."

"She shouldn't have made those comments about your

mother," Deverell said, his expression darkening. "I regret not putting a stop to it sooner."

"Yes, well." Lady Elaine folded her twiglike arms over her chest. "Dusty here needs to learn how to rise above the silly antics of a petty girl."

I glanced away, ashamed at the scolding. Lady Elaine was right. It wasn't the first time Katarina had taunted me, and it certainly wouldn't be the last. I knew better than to let it get to me.

Lady Elaine sighed. "Not that it was entirely your fault, what happened. Clearly."

I turned back to her. "How so?"

Mr. Deverell cleared his throat. "Do you remember the spell you used to make the blade explode like that?"

I thought about it for several long seconds, my mind racing as I tried to make sense of it. I remembered casting the spell, and I remembered the results clearly—the polka dot array of wounds scattered across Katarina's face—but I couldn't remember the incantation I'd uttered. And I knew without a doubt it wasn't a spell I'd ever learned. I shook my head. "I don't know that spell. I've never even heard it before. But how . . . how did I cast it?"

Beside my leg, I felt Bellanax grow warm, and a sound like a cat's purr filled my head.

"It was the asunder curse," Lady Elaine said.

"What?" My mouth fell open. That definitely wasn't a spell I knew how to perform. The asunder curse was restricted—only law enforcement officers were permitted to learn it. I shook my head. "Are you sure? How did I do it? I don't think I could do it again right now if I tried."

"We believe," Lady Elaine said, "that The Will sword is starting to exert its will."

"No pun intended," said Deverell.

Any surprise I felt that Deverell now knew about the sword was short-lived. He was something of an expert on numen vessels, and to be honest, it was a relief that I no longer had to keep it secret from him. I snorted. "Tell me something new why don't you."

Lady Elaine frowned. "What do you mean?"

I rolled my shoulders, surprised to feel how sore I was, like Deverell had used a dazing spell on me instead of a sleeping spell. Or maybe I'd just injured myself when I fell. "The sword has been like that from day one." It should've been hard not saying Bellanax's name, but it was surprisingly easy, a secret I had no desire to share with anyone.

Lady Elaine crossed one leg over the other, both of her feet swinging more than an inch off the floor. The chair was normalsized, she midget. "Are you saying that the sword has been trying to influence you since the beginning?"

"Well, yeah." I tilted my head. "Why are you so surprised? I mean when I bonded with it the very first thing it did was take over my body and make me jump into that fissure. I never would've done that on my own, you know."

"That was different," Lady Elaine said. "The threat of the island sinking was imminent, and the sword has enough of its own intelligence to have sensed that everyone was in danger, including you, its new master."

"Yes," Deverell added, nodding. "But other than extreme cases like that most numen vessels are quiet. Their masters are barely aware of their existence."

I frowned. That wasn't my experience at all. Right from the beginning, Bellanax had been a constant presence. Sometimes I could even sense it in my sleep. But I'd assumed that was the norm. Not that I'd had anyone else to talk to about it. There was Eli, of course, his wand a numen vessel, too, but thanks to the stupid dream-seer curse, I hadn't been around him long enough to compare notes. Then again, I'd been there when he'd bonded with the wand, but it had been nothing like Bellanax. He'd simply been drawn to the wand and it to him, no possession required.

"What sorts of things has the sword been doing?" Lady Elaine said.

I pursed my lips. "Nothing big, really. I mean until today. Mostly it just wants me to take the glamour off and flash it around. And sometimes it wants to, I don't know, like enforce justice."

Deverell scratched his cheek. "What do you mean enforce justice?"

"Stupid, silly stuff, really." I brushed strands of hair that had fallen free of my ponytail behind my ear. I realized I was still in my school clothes. That was a good sign. I might be in the infirmary, but if the nurses hadn't felt the need to put me in a robe, then it probably wouldn't be for long.

"Like what, Dusty?" Deverell pressed.

I wracked my brain, trying to think of the best example. There were so many to share. "Well, there was one time when Mom and I were visiting Stonehenge over the summer. I saw this little girl being picked on by her older brother and the sword wanted me to stop it. I did, sorta, but not the way the sword wanted. I just got the parents to pay attention to what was happening with their kids."

"What did the sword want you to do?" Lady Elaine asked, her thin eyebrows arching high on her forehead, creating a cavern of wrinkles.

I scrunched up my face. "It wanted me to swat the little boy on the butt with the flat of the blade."

Deverell cleared his throat. "Do you always do what the sword wants in some manner or another?"

A quake went through my chest. I could tell by his tone that this was serious. Deciding it best to downplay the sword's influence, I shook my head. "Some of what it wants me to do is crazy." Then I relayed the story about the incident at Loch Ness and the sword's dislike of the men referring to Bessie as a dinosaur and not a wyvern.

There were other incidents I could've mentioned, but that one seemed the most harmless. Not all of Bellanax's "requests" were so innocent. Like the time Mom and I visited Isla Màgica in Seville, Spain, on one of our rare, nonculturally focused excursions. It had been sun-poisoning hot and miserable while we waited in long lines for rides. At one point, two teenage boys cut in front of us. They did it smirking and victorious, fully aware of their own asshat behavior. I wanted so badly to tell them off. Before I knew it Bellanax was prompting me to throw curses at them, to make them pay for their crime, a warning against anyone else. For a brief moment I almost did it, my mind heady with the thought of exerting such power. They were ordinary boys, not magickind, completely incapable of fending off the attack.

Even now the recollection of that dark impulse made my stomach clench.

Lady Elaine cast a quizzical look at Deverell.

"Should I be worried?" I said.

A few seconds passed with neither adult speaking. Then finally, Deverell exhaled loud enough to be heard. "I don't believe so. Not now that we know what's going on with the sword. We should be able to prevent a repeat of such behavior. In my studies I have come across a couple of stories about numen vessels that needed more than just the naming from their masters. Some of them seemed to require a relationship of sorts. Like a dog wanting the company of its owner. I believe the solution is for us to try to discover what the sword wants from Dusty and then fulfill that need as much as possible."

I felt Bellanax stirring. It didn't like the dog comparison. I couldn't blame it. It was nothing at all like a pet. It was more a wild animal, feral and predatory.

"It's a sword," I said. "What could it possibly want from me?" I had an image of taking Bellanax for a walk, or maybe using it to chop wood so it could feel useful. Then again it was a sword. Would it be satisfied being used for something other than fighting? After all, what was a weapon's purpose but to be used to attack and defend?

"It might want any number of things," Deverell said. He had looked sleepy before but now he appeared wide awake, eager in the way of a scholar faced with a new discovery. "But don't worry. I doubt it will want anything you will be unwilling to give. Clearly, the first thing we can assume is that it wants to be free of the glamour, at least occasionally."

"How do you know?" I asked, even though I had no doubt this was true. It made perfect sense.

"Because the glamour came off on its own," Lady Elaine said. "And that's highly unusual. Although thankfully it didn't happen until after we moved you to the infirmary so no one saw."

"That's a relief," I said, puffing out my cheeks.

"How often do you take the glamour off?" Deverell asked.

"Never," I said. "I mean, it's a sword, and it once belonged to the Red Warlock. I don't want anybody knowing I have it who doesn't have to."

"Yes, that's wise," Deverell said. "But I think moving forward you should take the glamour off each night. The sword needs time to be what it truly is."

Nodding, I said, "I think I can manage it."

"Good." Deverell folded his arms over his chest. "We should also schedule some additional psionics lessons, same as we did last year. You need to develop your rapport with the sword. You must learn how to communicate with it, and most important how to make sure that it is not able to seize control of you again unless you want it to."

"Want it to?" I said, incredulous.

"Well, you might have need to save the world again, right?" Deverell winked. I smiled, feeling better about the idea, but then he added, "I think we should plan on an hour every day after school to start. I have room in my schedule to accommodate it. Then as you progress we can consider cutting it back some."

An extra hour each day? My heart sank. I was already so busy. How was I ever going to find time to work on my mother's case? And what about homework and Eli? Finding the Death's Heart?

I took a deep breath, my chest tight with growing despair. I knew there was no dodging this one. It was too important. I had attacked Katarina with the asunder curse. No, I had attacked the stupid knife, but still, what if the spell had been off? What if it had hit her directly?

She might be dead now.

And I would be a killer.

～ 10 ～

Stranger with Your Face

J spent the night in the infirmary.

"The nurse will discharge you in the morning," Lady Elaine said as she and Deverell prepared to leave. "You will be expected to get to class on time."

I nodded, wondering just how late it was. "What about my dream-session with Eli?"

"Canceled," Lady Elaine said. "Obviously."

"Can we make it up tomorrow?"

She clucked her tongue. "Let's wait for the Friday session. You've had a stressful week. No reason to add to it."

"Okay," I said, even as my heart sank low in my chest. I had a feeling that concern over my stressful week wasn't as big a worry for Lady Elaine as allowing Eli and I the extra time together. I hoped I was wrong, but she had seemed to flinch when I said his name just now.

But my spirits rose a second later when I spotted my cell lying on top of the rolling tray table shoved in the far corner. I said a quick good-bye, eager for them to leave.

Finally, Deverell switched the lights off and closed the door behind him and Lady Elaine. I waited a couple of seconds to make sure no one doubled back and to allow my eyes time to adjust to the dim glow cast by the small emergency light next to the door. I slid from the bed, grabbed my phone off the tray, and then climbed back under the covers, being careful not to bump into Bellanax.

As I suspected, my phone was off. I hoped that the nurses had done it rather than the phone turning itself off by choice. This was a new phone, shiny and fast, but there was no telling how quickly it would succumb to the animation effect. My last cell, a temperamental ancient device that I had despised with the passion of a nuclear bomb, had been destroyed during the Lyonshold incident. It had nothing to do with the island sinking, and everything to do with Paul Kirkwood, who had rigged the phone to explode if anyone tried to access the hidden files he'd loaded onto it—files containing the names of secret Marrow supporters.

Only, the phone never should've exploded the way it had. Not unless Paul had been lying to me about it all along. Suspecting he had lied was the biggest reason I'd been dodging his e-mails. But now, it was time to read them.

First though, I needed to text Eli. Once the phone turned on and found a signal, several waiting message alerts appeared on the screen. I read the ones from Selene but didn't reply. She would certainly be asleep. To Eli, I sent:

> I'm okay. In the infirmary. Lots to talk about soon. I hate that I missed our session.

I pressed send, and then navigated to my e-mails. As before, more than a dozen unread messages waited in my in-box. I decided to start at the bottom and work my way up. But just as I clicked on the oldest message from Paul, my phone buzzed with an incoming text.

I'm coming to see you.

What???

I wrote back, frantically mistyping and relying on autocorrect.

Right now? You'll get in trouble.

I'll be okay. I want to see you. Just don't scream
when I get there and leave the light off. What room?

Giddy, I slid from the bed again and crept to the door. I pushed it open slowly, my hands trembling with a potent mix of fear and excitement. The corridor outside was as dim as my room, but I could just make out the number over the door.

Room 12

I typed to Eli as I climbed into the bed once more.

Got it. See you soon.

Be careful.

I leaned back, resting my head on the pillow while my heart stuttered against my rib cage. Eli was coming here. It was a huge risk, but if he pulled it off we would finally have some alone time together. Warmth spread through me at the thought.

Anxious, I tried to focus on Paul's e-mails again, but it proved impossible. My eyes read the words, but the meaning got lost on the way to my brain. I was able to glean only the basics. He was sorry for what happened at Lyonshold, and he claimed not to be at fault for what happened with the phone. But he didn't offer any explanations about it either. His e-mails seemed vague and cagey. They read like someone afraid they might get intercepted. Could someone be monitoring e-mails? I knew such things happened in the ordinary world with all that homeland security stuff, but my phone was using Arkwell's wireless system. Could the magickind government be reading my e-mails? My text messages?

This last thought had me sitting up again in momentary panic. The magickind government was terrible with ordinary technologies. Paul, a computer genius good enough to be accepted at MIT, had proven that time and time again. But Detective Valentine was using DNA evidence against my mother. Perhaps things were changing.

With my mental state teetering between calm and freak-out, I set my phone on the bed beside Bellanax then forced myself to lie back and close my eyes. I doubted I would be able to sleep any, but pretending couldn't hurt. Yet somehow, I must've drifted off, because the next thing I knew I heard the door into my room open. I peered around, groggy and disoriented for a second, until my eyes fell on the figure walking toward the bed.

"You made it," I said, reaching up.

"Hi, Dusty."

I sucked in a breath, panic bringing me fully awake. *Not Eli.* I opened my mouth and started to scream just as a hand fell over my lips, strangling the noise.

"Shhh, please don't scream, Dusty. It's me. It's Paul."

Thrashing now, I tried to pull out from his grip, but he was too strong. I felt Bellanax lying beside me, and I reached for the sword, ready to fight my way free.

Abruptly, the hand holding my mouth let go.

"Please don't scream. I'm sorry I scared you." He held out his hand and a light appeared in his palm, a faint glowing orb, casting just enough for me to see his face.

"Paul?" I said, my breath coming in quick pants. The voice sounded close to his, but the man standing before me wasn't my ex-boyfriend. The nose was wrong, the shape of the forehead. And he wore a beard, long and scraggly. Recognition struck me. It was the creepy man from the Menagerie who'd stared at me that first day. He was still wearing the green work shirt.

"It's me, Dusty. Here, I'll prove it." He set the orb on the bed, the little ball purely magical and not at risk of catching anything on fire. Then he reached up and unfastened the necklace he wore. It was strangely made, as rigid as a choker with irregularly shaped white beads braided into the hemp-like chain, but long enough that the large green gem at its center had been hidden beneath his shirt collar.

The moment he pulled it off, his face went blurry—the sight making my stomach roil—but then his features righted into something human again. The creepy bearded man became Paul Kirkwood.

I didn't know if I wanted to hug him or hit him. "You scared me to death, and I can't believe you've been at Arkwell all this time."

"Sorry for the scare. I wasn't thinking. But what time?" Paul said, the hint of a grin on his lips. "School's only been back in session three days."

I huffed. He was right, of course, but with everything going on it felt longer. Especially combined with how long it had been since I'd seen him last. "What are you doing here?" I said, finally overcoming my shock. Eli was on his way, and the last thing I wanted was for him to show up and find Paul standing over my bed.

"You never read my e-mails." It came out an accusation draped in a matter-of-fact tone.

"How do you know that?"

Paul shrugged. "I put a read receipt on them."

"Of course you did." I folded my arms over my chest. I was fully dressed, but I felt naked with him in the room, vulnerable. But then I remembered that Bellanax was lying between us and that vulnerability vanished. "You're lucky I didn't stab you." Too late I realized my blunder.

Paul arched an eyebrow. "So it's true. You have The Will sword."

"What . . . what are you talking about?"

"Don't try to deny it." He brushed back a strand of blond hair that had fallen into his eyes. He was wearing it long again, a ponytail at the base of his skull. "But when you've spent all summer being carted around by one magickind policemen after another, you hear rumors."

My shock must've registered on my face. "Nobody is supposed to know I have it."

"Don't worry. It was mostly guesswork on my part." He smiled, reminding me in a very visceral way just how handsome he was. "And I had inside information going in."

Like what? I wanted to ask, but instead I cleared my throat. "Same old Paul. Always angling, aren't you?"

A hurt expression crossed his face, and I regretted my hasty words, no matter that they were true. "I didn't lie to you about the code on the cell phone, Dusty."

"Then why did it explode? I saw your uncle put the code in correctly. There's no reason it should've self-destructed. Not unless you had a time limit for the thing to be secured again." The words came out easy, practiced. Mostly because they were. I'd imagined saying this to him a hundred times before.

Paul sighed. "You're right. There was a timer on it."

"Why did you lie about it?" I was furious that I'd let him trick me again.

"It wasn't an intentional lie. I just . . . forgot to tell you."

"Ha." I kicked the mattress with the heel of my foot. "Well, wasn't that convenient."

Paul crossed his arms. I realized he was no longer wearing the green work shirt but a maroon tee with a MIT logo across the front. The clothes must've changed the same time as his face had. "It's true," he said. "I realized I forgot to tell you right after we said good-bye that day. We were down in the tunnels, in our old spot, remember?"

Against my sincere desire not to, I felt myself blush. Some of the canals dead-ended into reservoirs. There was one such reservoir where Paul and I had always met when we were dating, a secret place where we could have time together in private, unobserved. Exactly the kind of place that Eli and I needed right about now.

Thoughts of Eli chased away my blush. "Of course, I remember. I was there."

"Yeah." Paul started to fidget with the collar of his shirt. "Well, it was a little distracting being down there with you again after . . . after . . . everything. You can understand that, right?"

I reluctantly nodded.

"And when I gave you the code you didn't try to open the data right then. If you had I would've remembered to tell you how to close it properly. And so—" He blew out a breath. "It's gone now, destroyed forever. I can't tell you how sorry I am about that."

I stared at him for several long seconds. The light orb still glowed, but it was starting to flicker, casting dancing shadows over his face. Reluctantly, I decided he was being sincere. Believing the alternative—that he'd intentionally not told me about the timer—felt beyond my ability to deal with at the moment. Besides, what did it matter? Like he said, the data was gone, and I had so many other things to worry about now.

"Okay," I said, "apology accepted. But you've got to go."

"Are you expecting someone?" He said it joking at first, but then understanding dawned on his face. "Eli." The line of his lips went razor thin. "I'll leave in a second, but I didn't come here just to apologize. I've got info about your mother."

My heart seemed to falter for a second, like a car stalling out then surging back to life. "What do you know?"

Paul met my gaze, his expression unwavering. "She didn't kill my uncle."

I held my breath, braced for whatever he would say next. *It was me,* I imagined him saying. Paul hated Titus Kirkwood. I didn't have a single doubt that he would've killed him, given the chance. And deep down, I couldn't really blame him after all the years of abuse he'd suffered at his uncle's hands. No, I certainly wasn't sorry Titus was dead, only that my mother was being blamed for it.

"She was there, on the ward," Paul said, "At least I'm pretty sure it was her. But he was still alive when she left."

My head spun with shock for a moment. "My mom was there?"

"Yeah, I think so. They were keeping me in the same ward as Titus at the time. For my protection, you know. The night he died, someone came onto the ward between the midnight and one o'clock guard check. I didn't see who it was. The person put me under a binding spell."

"Wait." I raised my hand to my forehead. "If you didn't see the person, then how do you know it was her?"

"The magic . . . it felt . . . well . . . a lot like yours."

"Oh." A blush warmed my skin. Magic did have characteristics unique to the person who wielded it, but recognizing them was tricky. It was the sort of thing that required a lot of familiarity with the magic, a kind of intimacy.

"Anyway," Paul continued, a flush rising up his neck, "my uncle wasn't killed until some time between the one and two o'clock guard check, long after I was free of the binding spell. When the one o'clock guard made his rounds, he talked to my uncle briefly. I heard Titus reply. The two o'clock guard is the one that found him dead."

My hope rose, and I reached for Bellanax, wrapping my hand around the hilt as if for a holdfast. If my mom had visited the ward, then that might explain the DNA. It might even explain her guilt, too. "Did you see anyone else come onto the ward during that time?"

"No, but I might have fallen asleep."

I bit my lip. "Did you tell anyone about what you saw?"

He shook his head.

"Why not?"

"I didn't have any proof, for one thing, just a feeling. And I was trying to protect your mom. To protect you. I didn't know what she was doing there, but I knew it would be trouble for her either way. And at the time the detective interviewed me, she wasn't even a suspect yet."

"Okay," I said, grudgingly seeing his point. "But what about now? It was Detective Valentine, right? If you tell him he might let my mom go."

Paul sighed. "It won't work, Dusty. He wouldn't believe me. I already lied once, and . . ."

"And what?"

"He knows how I feel about you. He would just think I was lying now to help you."

I turned away from him, both in frustration and embarrassment. I didn't know how to react. I wasn't sure I even believed him. Paul was so hard to read and so easy to distrust. Mostly because my first inclination was always the opposite—I wanted to believe everything he said wholeheartedly. But that was a bad idea. Paul was a halfkind, like me, but instead of being part human, part Nightmare, he was part wizard, part siren. I knew firsthand how good he was at siren magic. Unlike Katarina, or even Selene, Paul was sly with his siren magic. He could mesmerize without you ever realizing.

Until it was too late.

"Anyway," Paul said into the awkward silence. "I'm really sorry. I wish there was something I could do about it."

"Maybe you can." I bit my lip. Eli would be here soon, but this was too important not to pursue. "I need to get a hold of Valentine's case file on the murder. The Dream Team is going to investigate."

Paul nodded, a polite smile creasing his lips. "I figured. But I don't see how I'm going to get it for you. I'm not supposed to wander far from the Menagerie. This is my witness protection cover." He held up the necklace again, the green gem twinkling as it caught the light from the orb.

"What is it exactly?" I asked, my curiosity getting the better of me.

"It's a shape-change necklace. It allows me to change my appearance without the telltale signs of a normal glamour. No blurring around the edges and stuff."

"It's a good one," I said. "I had no idea it was you in there. But I wasn't suggesting you going to the Rush to get the files."

"Then how?"

"Hacking Valentine's computer. Think you can do it?"

Paul raised his hand to his face and rubbed his chin. He didn't have a beard anymore, not without the shape-change necklace on, but there was a good amount of blond stubble. "I don't know, Dusty. I'm on really thin ice in general. If I get caught it could mean jail time."

I pressed my lips together, angry tears stinging my eyes. My mother was already in jail, and she was innocent. Unlike Paul. I took a breath and then blurted, "Valentine says they'll execute her if she's found guilty."

Paul gaped. "You're kidding. For killing my uncle? That doesn't seem like justice."

"Don't joke about it, Paul," I hissed. "Don't you dare."

He raised his hands as if in surrender. "Wasn't joking. But all right. I'll do it. At least, I'll give it a try. I can't promise I'll be able to get in. This Valentine guy knows his stuff better than any other magickind I've seen."

"So I've noticed," I said. Even still I felt light-headed with relief. "But thank you. I can't tell you how much it means."

"Like I said, no promises." Paul hesitated. "And I'm going to need a couple of things from you."

"Such as?"

"Computer access, mostly. I'm not allowed to connect to the network. I'm not even allowed to look at a computer for longer than a second without my guards stepping in."

"You're being guarded?" It was an all-too familiar scenario.

Paul shrugged. "Sure. Can you blame them? I've got two Will Guards that take turns watching me all day."

"Huh." I frowned. "Then how did you get away from them tonight?"

"With this." Paul held up the necklace again. "I finally figured out how to change the glamour at will. As far as my guards know I can only shift into the Menagerie worker you saw before. The necklace defaults to that, but if I concentrate hard enough,

I can change it to something else. It was enough to let me walk by them tonight without them even knowing it."

"Wow," I said, genuinely impressed. "That's got to be handy."

"Yeah." He grinned. "I was starting to go nuts not having any freedom."

I smiled, utterly sympathetic. "But wait, if you're not allowed computer access then how have you been e-mailing me all summer?"

"Cell phone. But Sheriff Brackenberry gave it to me, so you can bet it's not clean."

"No kidding." That explained the dodgy tone in his e-mails. I was suddenly very glad that I never answered any of them.

"But as I was saying," Paul continued. "I need your username and password. I could also use a good computer, and you'll need to purchase and download some software. Do you have a laptop these days?"

I shook my head. "Just the eTab and my ancient desktop."

"No good."

I thought about it for a couple of seconds, frustrated to meet another roadblock so soon. There was no way I could get my hands on a new laptop. I didn't have any money for it; what little savings I'd had before had taken a hit during my summer abroad. Eli didn't have one either and neither did Selene.

Then the answer dawned on me. "Lance Rathbone might have one. If Selene asks he'd probably let us use it. Actually, if she asks he might go out and get a new one just to make her happy. His dad's rich enough for him to do crazy stuff like that." *So long as he hasn't been disinherited yet,* I reminded myself.

"All right," Paul said. "Talk to him and let me know."

"How can I do that with your phone being monitored?"

"The old-fashioned way." A delighted expression lit Paul's

face. "Write me a note. I'll be sure to be near when you're in biology tomorrow."

I wrinkled my nose. I supposed that would work. With the chaos that was biology, slipping him a note would be simple enough. But it was a slow way to communicate. "We can do that for now, but we should come up with a code so we can use the phones."

"Agreed." He inclined his head. "I'll put something together that Brackenberry, or whoever is watching, won't be able to figure out."

"It's a plan. But you've got to go." I glanced at the door, convinced I'd heard a noise. But several seconds passed, and the door remained shut.

"All right." Paul slid the necklace around his neck, locking it into place. The second he did, the magic in the thing kicked on. That same blurriness obscured his features for a second before clearing again. The creepy bearded man stood in the room with me. I suppressed a shiver.

Paul peered down at me with a stranger's eyes. "I'll talk to you soon. Be careful. Especially with that sword."

I nodded, lacking the nerve to speak. It was just too weird with him in that disguise.

He turned toward the door, but then stopped just short of opening it. He glanced back. "One more thing. Are you going to tell Eli I was here?"

"I . . ." I hesitated, the answer not forthcoming. "I don't know. Probably. Why do you ask?"

"He won't like it," Paul said, a warning look in his eyes. "He hates me."

I scoffed. "Eli doesn't hate you. You're just not his favorite person. Like ever."

Paul chortled. "That's an understatement. Do what you want, but please remember that nobody is supposed to know I'm here."

"Eli wouldn't out you," I said, annoyed.

"No, I suppose not. But please promise to keep it secret. Selene and Lance are okay. But that's it. All right?"

"Sure," I said, understanding all too well. Paul had made a lot of enemies the last few months. He'd been one of Marrow's most important followers once, and now he'd openly turned against him. Every person on that destroyed list might be out to get him.

"Thanks," Paul said. "I'll be seeing you." Then he disappeared out the door, closing it silently behind him.

Alone again, I leaned back on the pillow and closed my eyes, eager for Eli's arrival. Even though having Paul back in my life wasn't something I wanted, I had to admit he'd raised my spirits. The situation with my mom looked less bleak than it had just an hour before. Less bleak enough that I thought I'd be able to enjoy the private time with Eli without too much guilt or worry.

About time, I thought, yawning.

But as the seconds gave way to minutes, and finally an hour, I succumbed to sleep once more.

Eli never showed up.

~ 11 ~

Bad Luck

Where were you?"

Eli chewed the last bit of his bacon and swallowed. Around us the cafeteria was chaotic with breakfast activity, chattering voices, tired laughter, and the click and clack of silverware against plates. Selene and Lance were still going through the food line, giving Eli and me a rare moment to talk in private. Minus the couple dozen of our fellow students, of course.

"I got caught by Bollinger," he said, rubbing his eyes. Two dark circles rimmed his cheeks. "She was patrolling right outside the infirmary. I think I would've made it in to see you if it had been anybody else, but she knew exactly why I was there."

My eyebrows climbed my forehead. "You think she was guarding me?"

"Yeah, maybe. At least she knew you were in there. It was rotten bad luck."

"No kidding." I smiled, ruefully. "That's certainly how it's been running for us lately though, right?"

"So it seems." He pushed his tray to the side, the food half-eaten. I frowned, dismayed by his reaction. I'd expected the opposite. He was usually my bright-side boy.

Deciding it was my turn to take the sunny view, I leaned

toward him, lowering my voice. "In the better news department, I might have a way to get a copy of the case files Valentine has on my mom."

"You do?" Eli sat up straighter. "How?"

"Paul's back. He's here at Arkwell, but it's a secret. He's in disguise for his own protection. But he's willing to try to hack into Valentine's computer for us."

Eli's body went rigid. "When did you start talking to Paul?"

I swallowed, remembering Paul's warning. "He's been e-mailing me all summer. I've been ignoring them, but last night . . . he came to see me in the infirmary. Not long after I texted you."

Eli dug his fingers against the table. "You were alone with him? In the middle of the night?"

I slowly nodded. "I thought it was you at first. You can imagine my shock."

The sound of his teeth grinding sent a shiver down my back. "Not really."

"Well, trust me, I wasn't happy about it. Until he told me that he knows my mother is innocent."

I watched as Eli visibly unclenched his jaw. "What did he say?"

Quickly, I relayed the story. "And so I ended up asking if he could hack into the police computer network for us," I said, as I finished, "and he agreed."

Eli drew a deep breath, and I could see the struggle waging inside him. "That's good news. And I'm . . . I'm glad he's willing to help. We need those files for sure."

"Right," I said, my voice breathless with relief.

Eli reached across the table and took my hand. "Just make sure you don't go anywhere alone with him again. Ever. Okay?"

I pressed my lips together, fighting back a smile at his protectiveness. "I'll try not to."

"I mean it, Dusty." He locked his eyes on my face, his gaze intense. "He can't be trusted, and . . . and I'm worried about you."

I let out a nervous laugh. "Don't be. It's like you said. Dreams are symbolic. It was my dead body but it wasn't me." *Just don't let it be my mother either,* I silently added.

Eli shook his head. "It's not that. Well, not only that."

"Then what?" My pulse quickened as I realized the depth of his concern went far beyond mere protectiveness.

"I'm terrified that you're going to get hurt. And Paul coming back into the picture just makes it worse."

Blood rushed in my ears. One dream containing my dead body couldn't be enough to make him this spooked. "Why are you so worried about me?"

He sighed. "It's stupid. But I keep having a lot of bad dreams about you. Really bad."

The bad dream I'd had about him rose in vivid details inside my mind, all those bones crushing down on me. I stifled a shiver.

"I've always had them since Lady Elaine first told me about the curse, but they faded some over the summer. Now they're back full force. Sometimes I dream about us arguing, you telling me that you don't want to be with me anymore." He laughed, the sound hollow, like the tinny ping of a cheap bell. "Sometimes you even tell me that you'd rather be with Paul. But often, I just dream about you getting hurt." A shudder went through his body.

I didn't press him for details. I knew well enough how vivid and relentless dreams could be and with a thousand ways to die in them.

"And the worst thing is," Eli went on, "I'm the one who keeps doing it. I hurt you over and over again."

The hairs on the back of my neck stood up. It was hard to dismiss his worry when I'd had the same sorts of dreams. There was no such thing as coincidence in the magical world. "Do you think it's the curse?"

"I don't know, but it's definitely something."

My heart did a hard stutter in my chest. Around my wrist, Bellanax felt cold, lifeless. All at once the certainty I'd been harboring that the dream-seer curse was a made-up thing, as powerless to hurt us as the boogeyman in children's stories, came crashing down. There was no denying what happened to Marrow and Nimue, after all. They'd been dream-seers just like Eli and me. By all accounts they had once loved each other, but the feeling had turned to hate. Nimue imprisoned Marrow in a dream, meaning to keep him there for all eternity. And when he awoke, he killed her.

With the very sword glamoured around my wrist.

This truth made me flinch. It was a terrible, wondrous thing to realize that Bellanax had killed people.

No, I thought. *The sword is just a sword. Marrow did the killing.*

Eli squeezed my fingers again. "It's probably nothing. Don't worry about it. Goodness knows we've got enough on our plate right now."

I opened my mouth, ready to tell him about my own dream, but Selene and Lance arrived at the table, trays in hand.

We never have enough time, I thought, my spirits sinking. *Bad luck indeed.*

"Hey," Lance said, sliding into his chair. "And yes." He picked up a unicorn skewer and pulled off the first piece, egg with onion, tomato, and spinach all wrapped in bacon.

I narrowed my gaze at him, immediately suspicious. "Yes what?"

He grinned up at me, forcibly chewing. He gulped the food down and said, "You can borrow my laptop."

"Your laptop?" Eli said, looking puzzled.

"Yeah, she needs it for her ex to hack into the police department's computers."

"Shhh." Selene slapped his arm. "Keep your voice down."

Lance winced. "Opps. Sorry."

I turned to Eli and explained the rest of the plan.

He nodded his agreement, his earlier worry hidden behind an aloof mask—one he wore for my benefit.

We made plans to meet up in room 013 after dinner, then we headed off to class.

Out of respect for Eli, I waited until after homeroom to write the note to Paul—out of sight, out of mind. But it proved challenging to focus on during English and history. We were still studying *Beowulf,* a story I was familiar with thanks to various movies and TV shows. Only, like so many other ordinary myths, *Beowulf* was a true story. And the magickind version was a little more interesting.

"When Beowulf's slave stole the golden cup from the dragon," Mr. Corvus was saying, "the poor fool did not know there was a curse upon the gold. It was this curse that was responsible for all the destruction that came later. The dragon was bound by the laws of the curse to destroy the lives and property of whoever had committed the theft for seven generations on."

I set down my pencil, my note to Paul only half composed. The idea of the curse had caught my attention. Curses came in two types: minor and major. Minor ones were those you could cast with an incantation, like the asunder curse. But major ones were a different beast all together. *A beast like the dream-seer curse.*

I raised my hand.

"Yes, Dusty." Mr. Corvus motioned toward me.

"If the curse was supposed to be for seven generations, does that mean Beowulf broke the curse by slaying the dragon?"

"Yes," Corvus said, scratching his neatly trimmed goatee.

"But only because the dragon had cast the curse to begin with." Corvus paused and swept his one-eyed gaze over the room, making sure he had everyone's attention. "Beowulf was very lucky in this. The dragon was extremely old. If it had died a natural death, the curse would have continued, only instead of the dragon causing the destruction it would've been the elements—storms, earthquakes, famine. That is the nature of major curses. Often, they grow more powerful over time."

I leaned back in my chair, heavy with disappointment, and yet—"Is there no way to break a curse once the creator has died?"

Corvus stared at me a long time before answering. I resisted the urge to squirm beneath the scrutiny. "There are other ways, but none with any guarantee of working."

With that, he turned away from me, the subject at an end.

When I arrived at biology, I spotted Paul right away. His creepy bearded-man disguise was slightly less disturbing in broad daylight, but still weird. Especially when he looked at me with such open familiarity. Ignoring my disquiet, I walked past him, slyly holding out my hand with the note tucked between my fingers. Paul plucked the note from me with an ease that suggested we'd been doing this sort of thing for a long time. I was glad Eli wasn't around to see it.

The rest of the day sped by quickly, mostly thanks to all the homework I was trying to squeeze in between classes. I needed to make some headway, especially with the start of my private lessons with Deverell this afternoon.

Fortunately, when I arrived at Deverell's room after classes, he told me we would keep it short that first day.

"I know you must be tired," he said. "And there's little point in doing a whole lot if your mind isn't rested."

I could've hugged him, but I refrained.

"I figure we will work on some mind-strengthening exercises, but before we do that, would you mind taking a look at this?" Deverell handed me a piece of paper that at first glance I took to be another nondisclosure agreement.

"Student conduct agreement?" I said, reading the title written across the top.

"Yes," Deverell said. "The nondisclosure agreement I had to sign in order to help you with the sword gave me the idea."

I scanned the fine print, which seemed to detail at length all types of bullying. "Does it work the same as the nondisclosure?"

"Indeed, although the range of the spell will be limited to this classroom." He motioned to the room with its auditorium setup and large open space at the front. "But once every student signs one, they will no longer be able to partake in any bullying behaviors during my classes. The magic will quite literally seal their mouths shut."

An image of Katarina looking like a cow chewing cud flashed in my mind. "You're doing this for me?"

Deverell cupped his chin, running long tanned fingers over his angular jaw. "Not just for you, but for all my students. I've had the option of implementing one of these agreements from the beginning. Psionics can be such a delicate area of magic. There are risks involved with opening your mind to other people, as you well know. If you're not skilled at protecting your thoughts, others can glean them."

I nodded, remembering the way he'd taught me to guard my memories and thoughts I didn't want him to see during our sessions last year when we had engaged in *nousdesmos*, a special kind of mind-link.

"And I don't want a repeat of what happened between you and

Katarina," Deverell went on. "This classroom, if nowhere else on campus, will be a safe haven for any student who enters."

Once again the urge to hug him came over me. I beat it back, settling for the hugest smile my face would allow. "Thank you, Mr. Deverell. That sounds wonderful."

He beamed at me. "You're welcome. Now let's get started."

We spent the rest of the time doing basic mind strengthening exercises. By the time we reached the end I was tired, but not nearly as exhausted as I'd been after some of our sessions last year. Before I'd bonded with Bellanax, the sword had haunted my dreams for weeks. But with Mr. Deverell's help, I finally figured out what it wanted—me. I could only hope it was quicker about telling me this time.

"Make sure you leave the sword unglamoured again tonight, Dusty," Mr. Deverell said.

I nodded, picking up Bellanax by the hilt. Deverell had suggested we leave the sword in its natural state during the session.

"Also," Deverell said, "we might want to consider trying some psychometry on it. That is, if you're willing."

I cocked my head, alarmed by the suggestion. The sword had belonged to Marrow for *years*. "Do you think it might tell us something about him? Like what it's like when he resurrects?"

Deverell tented his fingers. "Anything is possible."

The idea was both thrilling and terrifying. I examined the sword, seeing it in a new light. My mom was convinced that finding the person who freed Marrow from the tomb was the best way to stop him, but this could be even better.

As swords go, it wasn't all that impressive, certainly not as ornate as some of the swords you could buy at a Renaissance festival. The cross guard was made of black steel, narrow in width and perfectly straight except for where the ends lifted sharply upward. Bone as pale as ivory formed the hilt, an engraving of a phoenix covering the rounded pommel. I'd always assumed that Marrow had put it there, a symbol of both his familiar and his mastery of Bellanax. I supposed that was something the psychometry might tell us for sure.

Making up my mind, I pulled my gaze away from the sword and reapplied the glamour. "I'm up for it," I said, sliding the silver band onto my wrist. "But maybe you should try it first though, since I'm so new at it."

"That won't be necessary," Deverell said, his expression confident. "We will do it together. Besides, I'm not certain the sword would permit me to probe its secrets without you."

"Permit?" I started to smile, thought better of it, and frowned. "The sword could stop you?"

"Of course. This is not some mere inanimate object. It's alive, in a manner of speaking. If it does not wish to divulge its history to me it won't. I mean to say, that is the point of what we're doing here—for you to learn how to communicate with your numen vessel."

"Right." I hoisted my backpack onto my shoulder. "Together then." It was a more reassuring option than going it alone.

Although Deverell had indeed cut the session short, there wasn't time for me to make it to Eli's practice. Even though I was anxious to see him—if only to quell the doubt that had been plaguing me all day—I returned to my dorm room, deciding to focus on homework instead. I wanted to get as much done before dinner as I could. I also took the time to try my mom's flash drive, which at last seemed to have dried out. To my dismay, an error popped up on the screen when I plugged it into my computer stating the disk was corrupt.

"Damn." I smacked the top of the desk, and my radio gave a

little squawk of surprise. I ejected the drive and slid it into my pants pocket.

When I arrived at the cafeteria, my brain hurting from overload, I said to the group at large, "Do you mind if Eli and I head to room oh-thirteen early? We've got some things to talk about in private."

Lance smirked and then made a kissing sound. Selene smacked him in the back of the head.

I rolled my eyes, embarrassed with good reason—kissing was definitely on the agenda.

"I'll leave first," Eli said as we finished eating. "I'll head around Monmouth and then double back. You leave a few minutes later and go a different way."

I started to ask him why, then understood. We needed to ditch the Will Guard. For a second, I wished we had Paul's shape-change necklace. It would certainly make things easier.

Five minutes later, I left the cafeteria, making a left where Eli had turned right. I arrived at room 013 in the library a short while later. The moment I entered, a chair wheeled out from beneath a desk and charged me.

"Down, Buster!" I screamed, arms braced to defend myself. The chair slid to a stop with a loud squeak. It seemed to stare at me for several seconds—a weird sensation considering it didn't have eyes. Or a face even. Nevertheless the chair was capable of expressing itself—quite clearly. It was another unfortunate victim of the animation effect, which for some reason was particularly virulent in room 013. That was why we'd selected the place for Dream Team meetings. Nobody ever came in here by choice.

"Good boy," I said, leaning forward to give the chair a pat. "Selene will be here to see you in just a few minutes."

Now the chair gave the impression of being delighted. It rolled back and forth several times on its wheels, squeaking them like mechanical peals of laughter. For whatever reason, the chair had taken a fancy to Selene. So much so that she'd been forced to give it its name just in an attempt to keep it under control. The ploy had worked. Some of the time.

Satisfied I was no longer in danger of trampling by chair, I scanned the rest of the room. Eli wasn't here. Frowning, I turned back to the door just in time to see him arrive.

He didn't hesitate, but came in and swept me up in a hug. It was a different kind of hug than all the ones before, as if he were trying to hold on to me while some invisible force attempted to wrench me away.

He's still worried. I was, too, but I wasn't about to let it get to me. Not now, when we finally had a few moments alone. Besides this curse, even if it did exist, wasn't like the dragon's treasure in the story of Beowulf. Our feelings for each other weren't tangible, something we could put in our pocket and carry around. We were people—free-willed and able to make our own choices. *Like choosing to love each other no matter what.*

"I've been thinking about what you said earlier," I said over his shoulder, my voice a little breathless from his arms pressing me against him. "And I've decided that your dreams about me getting hurt don't mean anything. After all, I often dream about showing up to class naked and that never happens."

Eli turned his head toward me, his lips brushing my neck. "That's a little disappointing."

I ignored the comment and the way my skin reacted—all tingling and writhing with pleasure. "The only dreams that matter are the ones we share."

I felt Eli's smile, as if his entire body had just breathed a massive sigh of relief. Sensing it, understanding that my faith in us had the power to make him feel this good, drove all my fear and doubt away, scattering it like sand in a windstorm.

Emboldened, I reached up and grabbed his face, dragging it down to mine. His mouth opened automatically, our lips touching, sliding together like silk on silk. I closed my eyes, the sensations overwhelming, setting every inch of my skin alight. I wanted the moment to last forever, to stretch it out like cotton, soft and willowy, and wrap it around my life as an eternal blanket.

But it seemed that no matter how strong our faith in each other was, we were still victims of bad luck and ill timing.

We never have enough time.

The sound of the door opening reached us, made worse by the sound of a throat clearing.

"Um, sorry you guys," Paul said from the doorway. "Do you want me to wait outside?"

I sighed, and for a second I almost told him yes. But Eli was already pulling away, the moment gone.

Bad luck had struck us once again.

I wondered how long before that bad luck started to feel like fate.

~ 12 ~

The Other Nightmare

Several awkward minutes passed before the others arrived.
Paul recounted his story about Titus's murder for Eli, which
burned a little time. Then he demonstrated the usefulness of the
shape-change necklace, which helped a little more. But still, it
felt like an eternity before Selene and Lance arrived. At least the
latter brought his laptop with him.

"This will work perfectly," Paul said, cracking his knuckles
over the laptop's keyboard. "I just need your username and password for the network access, Dusty."

"Why hers?" Lance said. "Won't that mess up mine?"

Paul shook his head. "It'll be its own unique account, everything separate. And I would prefer to use Dusty's. No offense, but
I know her better." The "I trust her" was implied but everybody
caught it just the same.

"Use mine," Eli said. He was hovering near the desk, his arms
crossed in a way that made the muscles in his chest stand out.

"Why?" Paul said.

Eli's stare spoke louder than words. *Because I don't trust you,*
it said.

"Never mind." Paul lowered his gaze to the computer screen.
"What is it?"

While Eli spoke the information aloud, the rest of us pretended not to listen. Selene was the only one who pulled it off, but only because Buster was giving her such a hard time. In its excitement, the chair kept rolling side to side, bucking a little with each change of direction. She threatened multiple times to remove its wheels if it didn't stop, but so far the chair wasn't buying it.

"Okay, there we are," Paul said. "Now, I've just got to purchase the software I need and we're good to go. Um . . ." He glanced around the room. "Does anybody have a way to pay for this? I would offer, but I'm pretty sure you don't want it traceable back to me. Not to mention ex-cons are notoriously broke."

"Crap, I don't have anything," I said. "Not unless the place takes CasterCard."

"Doubtful," said Paul.

"I don't have anything either," Selene called from the far side of the room where Buster had just whisked her to.

Smirking, Lance pulled his wallet out of his pants pocket. "It's all right. I got it." He slid out a card, seemingly at random. I spotted a half-dozen or more in there. "But you owe me, Everhart." He winked.

Are you sure this is a good idea? I wanted to ask him, not knowing how things stood between him and his father, but Selene was bound to wonder at my concern. I snickered instead. "Would you like that as a personal check or money order?"

Lance tilted his head. "What's a money order?"

"Never mind."

As Paul set to work, I reached into my pocket and wrapped my fingers around the flash drive. It was possible Paul could salvage some of the data, but I doubted my mom would want me to trust him with the information.

"Okay," Paul said a few minutes later. "This will take awhile to download. But as soon as it's done, I'll start working on the hack. But don't expect results right away. It might be a few days, easily."

"Okay," I said, and then taking a deep breath, I pulled the flash drive out of my pocket and held it out to him. No, Mom wouldn't want him trusted with it, but I didn't have anyone else to go to with it. And he was helping us save her. That had to count for something. "Would you mind seeing what you can do with this?"

"What's wrong with it?" Paul said, accepting the flash drive.

"It got rained on." Then I explained what it contained.

Paul looked intrigued and a little shocked at the news, but he slowly nodded. "I'll see what I can do."

"All right." Eli put his hands on his hips. "In the meantime we should start identifying what we know and what we need to figure out." He strode over to the dry-erase board on the far side of the room.

I watched him with hungry eyes. This was how I liked Eli best—in his private detective mode, focused to the point of fervency.

"So," he said, a black marker in hand. "The most important thing we need to do is determine possible suspects." Eli began jotting notes down on the board. "We have to determine who else might've killed Titus."

"Oh, that's not going to be hard at all," said Selene as she forcibly rolled the chair nearer to the rest of us once more. "Every single person who lost a loved one at Lyonshold has a motive for killing Titus Kirkwood."

Eli licked his lips. "I know. Which is why instead we need to figure out just who else is capable of committing the crime. Valentine claims only a Nightmare could do it. So either there's another Nightmare around here we don't know about, or there's some other way the killer could've gotten onto the magically restricted ward."

"What about one of the guards?" I turned to Paul. "You said they did regular floor checks, right?"

"Yeah, they did. I mean they do."

Eli glanced over his shoulder. "Wait. Aren't there security cameras?"

Paul laughed. "Nope. They used to use them, I think, but they've been disconnected. They're too unreliable with the animation effect."

"No kidding," I said, remembering the dancing camera in the interrogation room.

Eli shook his head, bemused. He jotted "no cameras" on the board.

"Well, we know it wasn't one of the guards," Selene said. "Not unless one of them is a Nightmare. No magic on the ward."

"Who says he was killed with magic?" Eli said. "The guards could've killed him like an ordinary would have. A knife, box cutter, even a razor blade would do the trick if applied to the right area."

I shivered, remembering Katarina' taunt about my mother. Had she chosen that knife just because it was the only traditional weapon on the table? Or did she know something about Titus's murder? I wondered what her parents did for a living.

"If it was a guard," I said, turning to Eli, "the killer could've slipped into Titus's cell during the floor check, killed him, and came back out and gave the all clear. Then all he had to do was wait for the next floor check to report the murder. Or let one of the other guards discover the body."

"Yes, that could work," Eli said, biting his lip. He wrote the word *guards* on the board beneath the column *suspects*. He paused, staring at it, his mind working so hard I could almost hear the gears churning. Then to my surprise, he shook his head. "No, it's a good theory, but I bet when we get the case files we're going to find all the guards have been cleared."

"Why do you say that?" I asked. I noticed a fray on my jeans and started picking at it.

"Because Valentine knows what he's doing." Eli exhaled loudly. "The guards would've been the first people he investigated and cleared. If the killing couldn't have been accomplished with magic, then the easiest solution is that it was an inside job. But I bet they all passed the lie detector test or whatever it is magic-kind do in that situation."

"The guilt test," I said, glowering. "Valentine is a guilt demon. A Crimen, I think it's called."

"Wow." Eli snorted. "That sounds really reliable and effective."

"Tell me about it." I rolled my eyes. "But wait. Could someone *disguised* like one of the guards have done it?" I motioned to Paul. "Like with one of those shape-change necklaces? Maybe the killer snuck into the cell pretending to be one of the guards and then snuck out again after it was over without the guard ever knowing he was being impersonated. They would pass the guilt test then, yes?"

Paul ran a hand over his hair. "It's another nice theory, but that's exactly the kind of thing the anti-magic protects against. The second you try to walk in there with a glamour on, even one as powerful as a shape-change necklace, the spell will break and set off the alarms."

"Crap. Why does magic have to make everything more complicated?" Eli rapped his fist on the table. The computer sitting nearby let out a startled beep. Eli pulled his hand away and shoved it into his pocket, making it clear he wouldn't hit anything again.

Violence of any kind was a bad idea in room 013. The animated objects didn't take it very well.

"You're right it does," Paul said. "But if it wasn't a guard, I just can't see somebody else pulling off that killing without magic. The whole ward is restricted, not just the cells themselves. I doubt the killer could've broken in, snuck past all the security, and committed the murder without using magic somewhere along the way."

"It might've been hard to do," Eli said, his expression turning stony, "but we can't rule out the possibility that he was killed by ordinary means. Not until we got a hold of the case files and know for sure. Magickind likes to pretend ordinaries can't do anything at all because they're not magical, but that's not true. Someone clever enough, determined enough, could've found a way."

"Where there's a will," I said, clinging to the thought. Never mind that "clever" and "determined" described my mother perfectly.

"Hang on a minute," Selene said. In her excitement, she stood up, but right away Buster wheeled forward, striking her in the back of the knees. She tumbled onto the chair with a grunt. I waited for the spectacle to ensue, but Selene was so focused she just ignored the misbehaving chair completely. "Paul's right that his glamour necklace wouldn't work, but what if the killer is a real shape-changer?"

"That's impossible, babe," Lance said, giving a little laugh. "There's no such thing. Not anymore."

Selene scowled at him. I wasn't quite sure if it was because he'd dismissed her idea or that he'd called her "babe." My vote was on the latter. "You don't know that for sure. Nobody can prove they ever went extinct. It's impossible to prove considering they can *shift their shape*."

Lance started to argue, but Eli cut him off, raising his hands as well as his voice. "Hold up, you two. What are you talking about?"

Selene tore her gaze off Lance and directed it at Eli. "Shape-changers are, or were, a type of darkkind. They had a reputation for evil—total mayhem and destruction. So much so that their magic was outlawed at the end of the magickind wars. Anyone caught shape-changing was put to death."

"That's a familiar tale," I muttered.

"They did outlaw it," Paul said, "but telling a shape-changer not to shift their shape is like telling a Nightmare not to feed on dreams."

"But Nightmares would die without dream-feeding," I said.

"Exactly."

Selene tapped her toe against the floor. "That was the whole point. Some legends claim all the shape-changers were executed because they refused to stop shifting. Others claim they simply died from magic deprivation."

I shuddered, feeling gut-punched by the idea, by the reality of it. It was the kind of awful truth I wished I could dismiss as mere legend or even exaggeration, but I knew better. The severe lack of Nightmares around was proof enough that such prejudice could happen. Even worse, it was still happening. Everywhere, it seemed. And not just among magickind.

"But other legends say they just went into hiding," Selene continued. "The shape-change isn't detectable like most magic. It's more like a Nightmare's magic. It's part of who they are. A shape-changer could've walked right into that ward without setting off a single magic detector." She hesitated. "I think so, anyway. If the legends about them are true."

I folded my arms over my chest. "I'm not sure that relying on an ancient legend as a possible explanation is going to get us anywhere with Valentine. He's more of a facts-and-evidence kind of guy."

"That's certainly true," Eli said, a sigh in his voice. "But still, we don't have a lot to go on. If we eliminate the impossible, whatever remains, no matter how improbable, must be the truth."

"You know Sherlock Holmes was fictional, right?" Paul said.

"You sure about that?" Eli arched an eyebrow, the sarcastic gesture doing little to disguise the hostility on his face. He might be acting civil with Paul so far, but friendliness would be a long time coming. Like never. "Up until a year ago fairies and sirens and Nightmares were all fictional, too. To me at least."

"Good point," I said, my voice a little higher pitched than normal. I sensed a fight brewing, and I wanted to head it off. "It seems like every other day I discover something I thought was myth is actually true—Atlantis, Beowulf, King Arthur." *Excalibur,* I silently added. Around my wrist, Bellanax tingled against my skin.

Flashing me a commiserating smile, Eli turned back to the board and wrote down *shape-changer.*

"Guys," Lance said, "we don't have to go searching for improbable explanations. Not yet."

All three of us turned to look at Lance. Even Buster seemed to shift toward him, in sync with Selene's gaze.

"What do you mean?" Eli said.

"There's another Nightmare around, besides Dusty and her mom."

"If you're talking about Bethany Grey," I said, "you can forget it. Valentine told me she's gone missing, and it wasn't a jailbreak. Lady Elaine saw a vision that it's connected to the—" I suddenly couldn't speak, my lips sealed together as if with magical cement.

Eli grunted. "That damn nondisclosure thing. What Dusty

is trying to say is that given the reason Bethany has gone missing it makes her a victim, not a suspect."

Selene harrumphed. "I really wish you could tell us what this nondisclosure thing is all about."

Me, too, I thought, unable to say the words aloud.

"Me, too," Eli said.

Lance waved us off. "I'm not talking about Bethany Grey."

"Then who?" Selene fixed a fierce stare on him.

Shifting his weight from side to side, Lance said, "It's Mr. Corvus."

I tried to laugh, couldn't quite do it with my mouth closed, and managed a snorting sound instead like I was trying to breathe through water. *Mr. Corvus? A Nightmare?* No way.

"I don't know," Eli said. "It's hard to picture it."

"Why?" Selene said, her face alight with comprehension. "Because he's male? Trust me, there are male Nightmares around. There has to be. You know, a little thing called survival of the species."

A suggestive grin flashed across Lance's face. Wisely, he made it vanish before Selene noticed.

"Yeah, okay." Eli focused on Lance. "But why do you think Corvus is one? He's never mentioned it in class."

No kidding, I thought, *I would've remembered something like that.*

"His eyes glow in the dark," Lance said.

An awkward silence descended at this announcement. It was true that glow-in-the-dark eyes were the surest sign of a Nightmare, our signature as it were, but how on earth would Lance have ever seen it? It wasn't like Corvus made a habit of turning the lights off to teach. And I knew from experience that Nightmares took measures to keep their glowing eyes hidden.

Lance bared his teeth in a sarcastic smile. "It's not as weird as it sounds, I promise. I snuck out the other night to put some hot sauce in the trash troll feed bins in the Menagerie—"

Selene gaped. "Why on earth would you do that?"

"Wanted to see what would happen to the little bastards. One of them bit my shoe the other day in bio and nearly escaped with a toe." He shrugged. "I figured they might stop being so inclined to bite if they got a taste of something hot."

I snorted. "That has got to be the worst prank you've ever come up with." A half second later, I realized the nondisclosure spell had let go of its hold on my tongue. "Thank goodness," I said, patting my mouth.

"Welcome back," Eli said.

Lance grinned in my direction. "I might have better success with my pranks if you got back in the game."

"Come on, you two," Selene said. "Don't get started."

Lance sniffed. "Fine. The point is, I saw Corvus walking outside the Menagerie. It was really dark, but I'm sure it was him."

"If it was dark, how could you tell?" I asked.

"Are you kidding?" His lips twisted upward in a smirk. "There aren't a lot of people on campus with only one eye. Try none."

"Oh." As soon as he said it, I realized it made perfect sense. It was incontrovertible. Glowing eyes meant Nightmare. Glowing single eye meant Corvus.

"Wow," said Eli. "I can't believe we never figured it out before now."

"Yeah, but do you really think he's involved?" said Paul. "What motive would he have for killing my uncle?"

"Who can say?" said Eli. "There might be any number of reasons."

"Especially if he's connected to Marrow," I added. I stood up, unable to stay still as thoughts tumbled through my mind. "Valentine and Lady Elaine seem to think that all of this might be related to Marrow. Both Titus's murder and the thing that Eli and I aren't allowed to talk about. And with Marrow involved, Corvus might have any number of reasons for killing Titus. Maybe it was a cover-up. Remember how we thought Corvus was involved with the attack on Lyonshold?"

"That's right," Eli said. He looked on the verge of pacing. "Me and Dusty were snooping through Corvus's office when Titus kidnapped us. Titus said he'd bugged our dream-session, but maybe that was a lie. Maybe Corvus knew we'd broken in and tipped him off."

I nodded, scrambling to recall all the details. It hadn't been all that long ago, a little over three months, but so much had happened after Titus captured us. "We suspected Corvus because there were ravens in Eli's dreams," I said, thinking aloud.

"And he owned the *Atlantean Chronicle*," added Eli. "He's an historian. We never did figure out how Titus learned the spell to sink Lyonshold. Maybe Corvus told him."

"That's possible," Selene said, bobbing her head in agreement. "And he might not have known what Titus was planning when he handed over the information at first. But then after the attack, he could have decided to kill him to save his own neck."

I frowned. Was Corvus capable of something so cold and calculating as executing Titus Kirkwood to protect himself? The short answer was—maybe. It wasn't that he was cruel or unkind. He didn't even strike me as vindictive. No, the word that always seemed to come to my mind to describe him was imperialistic. Authoritarian. He ruled his classroom with absolute power, and that sense of dominancy permeated everything about him. He reminded me of a general in a war movie, the kind of man capable of making decisions that he knew would cost lives, but that he calculated would be worth it in the long run.

What kind of a person can do that? I thought, *sacrifice real lives like chess pieces?* Only it happened all the time. Wars were fought among ordinaries across the world every day.

Shaking off the shiver sliding down my spine, I glanced at Eli. "And the third reason we suspected him was because of that symbol. The one with the three rings all connected."

"Oh, yeah, I forgot." Eli turned toward the dry-erase board and drew the symbol. When he finished, he stepped back, giving us all a clear view.

I examined the symbol, a peculiar feeling going through me. Mostly, I suspected, it was because of all the bad memories that came with it. I glanced at Eli. "Didn't you ask Corvus what it meant afterward?"

He ran a hand over his buzzed head, nodding. "He called it the Borromean circle. Said it was an archaic magickind symbol of unity. Each ring represents a kind. One for witchkind, one for naturekind, and one for darkkind." He pointed to each in turn.

"So something less than diabolical, in other words," Paul said.

I nodded, but inside I wasn't so sure.

Only the blood of the twelve can undo the circle.

The odd phrase came sailing at me from out of the blue. For a moment I couldn't remember where I'd heard it, but then it came to me. It was the line Corvus had made me translate out of one of his ancient books as part of my detention with him last year. A depiction of the Borromean circles had been in that book, too. And while the symbolism of the Borromean circles might be positive, that sentence certainly wasn't. It sounded like a way of breaking the circles, shattering that unity—perhaps in the same way Titus Kirkwood had hoped to start a new magickind war by sinking Lyonshold and making the naturekinds look responsible for it.

"Well," said Selene, "the symbol might not be evil, but that doesn't mean Corvus wasn't involved. Does anybody know if he was even at Lyonshold that day? I know I didn't see him. He should've been there though. All the teachers were chaperoning."

Eli twisted the marker through his fingertips, his mouth hanging slightly open as he contemplated the possibility. "We won't know anything for certain until we take a closer look at what he's been up to. But I've got to guess that Valentine knows he's a Nightmare and has gotten his alibi already."

I clucked my tongue in dismay. "He certainly gave me the impression that there was someone other than me, Bethany, and my mom running around here."

"Yes, and I would think he'd have to disclose his kind to school officials, at a minimum," said Lance. We all turned to stare at him, surprised by his sudden contribution. It wasn't that he was dumb, quite the opposite. Lance was absurdly clever—and devious—but he was also perpetually bored and disinterested. It was strange to hear him talk with such enthusiasm.

"Yeah, they probably do," Eli said, recovering first. "But I don't think we should eliminate him as a possible suspect. Not yet. He's our best lead so far."

"And he could've lied about his alibi," Paul said.

"What about the guilt test?" asked Selene.

I scoffed. "Valentine suspected my mother from the beginning. I doubt he tried all that hard to read Corvus's guilt."

"Or maybe Corvus is pathological and doesn't have any guilt about committing murder," Lance said. "He is a Night—" Lance cut himself off before finishing the sentence, but that didn't stop Selene from standing up and punching him hard in the shoulder. Buster followed it up with a full frontal attack, whacking Lance in the knees with its seat.

Lance winced, and cupped his hand over his arm, as if trying to squeeze the hurt away. "Ouch. But yeah, I deserved that." He cast a sheepish smile in my direction. "Sorry, Dusty. Old habits and all." The words were light, but for once he said them straight, no joking or underlying derision.

I clenched my teeth, uncertain how to react, whether to be angry or pleased. On the one hand, it wasn't the first time I'd been faced with the stereotype that Nightmares were born evil. In truth, it was one I'd worried about from time to time myself. I was often haunted by the possibility that there was something fundamentally evil about my nature, especially whenever I screwed up and did something stupid. But on the other hand, Lance had apologized—sincerely. If he could change, well, that was a big enough miracle for me.

"It's all right," I said, and for once I spoke to him straight, too—no snide or sarcasm in sight.

Eli cleared his throat. I had a suspicion he was trying not to grin about the Disney-moment breakthrough Lance and I just had. "Anyway, so it looks like our first order of business is to investigate Corvus."

I nodded. "But we need to be extra careful this time."

"No argument there." Eli wrote Corvus's name on the board.

I stared at it, a weight sinking through my chest and down into my stomach. Corvus was a Nightmare. Like me. Like my mother. Like Bethany. Four of us, the only four I'd ever met or knew anything about. And of those four, Bethany was a condemned criminal and my mother suspected of murder. As much as I was certain she hadn't killed Titus, I couldn't claim that she was entirely innocent either. My mom had skirted the line of the law, the line of *rightness,* her whole life.

And then there was me. Most times I wanted to believe I was good, always inclined to do the right thing. But I'd attacked Katarina. Was that really just because of Bellanax? Or was it because of something in my nature?

There was no answer, not even from the sword, which seemed

to have gone cold and lifeless as it lay in its glamoured form around my wrist.

Please let us be wrong, I thought, looking at Corvus's name on the dry-erase board. *Please let the guilty be anybody else except a Nightmare.*

~ 13 ~

Cell Block B

Bollinger came to get me for my dream session with Eli the following night. She pounded on the door hard enough to make the poster boards on the wall shake and threaten to fall off. I jumped up from my chair, startled by the noise. I must have dozed off. After a fruitless day trying to learn more about Corvus, I'd been researching Nightmares. But as I expected, there were very few ways to determine if a person was one.

Bollinger pounded again. "Come on, Destiny Everhart. You're going to be late."

"Hold on," I shouted back, scrambling to reapply the glamour on Bellanax.

"I would think," Bollinger said as I opened the door, "that someone as into her boyfriend as you claim would be more eager to get there on time."

I folded my arms, Bellanax already going hot against my skin. With an effort, I held back a scathing reply.

"Let's go." Bollinger headed down the hallway not bothering to make sure I was following. Not that I would've considered staying here even for a second. Bollinger or no, Eli was waiting.

On the long walk over there, I made plans of what I would

say and do—namely greeting him with a kiss the moment I stepped through the door. Forget Bollinger. She couldn't stop us from kissing.

Eagerly, I climbed up the stairs to Eli's dorm. When she pushed the door open, I stepped forward, expecting her to wave me inside first, but she went in ahead of me. I had just long enough to spot Eli already stretched out on the sofa, when Bollinger waved her wand and said, "*Hupno-drasi*."

The spell struck him dead center in the chest. His eyes snapped closed, and he slumped against the sofa, his head lolling to one side.

"Why did you do that?" Outrage pulsed so hard through me I started to shake. Bellanax became a hot iron against my wrist. The incantation of a curse rose in my mind. All I had to do was say it.

No, I thought as much to Bellanax as to myself. Beads of sweat broke out on my temple at the struggle to keep the sword glamoured.

"No time to waste," Bollinger said, turning to sit down in the chair nearest the door. "I have duties waiting as soon as this is over. So please, get on with it." She motioned toward Eli's prone body.

I forced my anger to calm. It wasn't wise to bring that into the dream. High emotion on my part could skew the dream—and Eli and I had a lot to explore and discover tonight.

Taking a breath and letting it out slowly, I climbed on top of Eli. He was deeply asleep and already dreaming, his eyes shifting back and forth beneath his lids and the *fictus* coming off him like a sweet, irresistible scent. Still, I held off entering the dream long enough to lean forward and press my lips to his. It was a small intimacy, but it was better than nothing. Once inside the dream, we wouldn't be able to touch at all.

I closed my eyes, sloughed off my mortal body, and descended into the dream. As always, the world swirled around me in an explosion of color and sensations, a thrilling descent into a place of unknown possibilities. I could arrive anywhere, no landscape too farfetched or impossible to be made real by the power of the dream.

But when the world finally formed around me, I found myself in a very familiar place—the school gymnasium. *Well that's just disappointing.* I turned in a circle to take in the scene. Climbing structures and barricades, of the sort that we used regularly in phys ed for combative magic study, were scattered over the yellow wood floor from one wall of bleachers to the other. These same structures were also used in gladiator games.

Which was exactly what was going on around me right now. More than a dozen boys roamed the floor, in between and over the structures. I didn't recognize any of them, thanks to the protective gear they wore, including beetle-like black helmets. But nevertheless, I could tell they were all boys.

"What's the deal?" I said, hands on hips. Did this mean that there weren't *any* girls trying out for the gladiator team? Or was Eli's subconscious a playground for repressed sexism. I voted on the former and resolved to ask him about it once I found him among the chaos of flying spells.

I launched myself into the air, employing my favorite dreamwalking pastime—flying. In seconds I was near the ceiling, the game floor spread out before me like a giant chessboard, each player easily visible now. In seconds, I spotted Eli. He was in the far corner, crouched behind a short square structure. I couldn't exactly say how I knew it was him, given the helmet. It might've been intuition, or perhaps he was just more physically present than the other players. This dream was his party, after all.

I landed a few feet in front of him. "Hey," I said. "Are you ready to get going?"

He didn't reply or even turn his helmeted head in my direction.

"Eli," I said again. "Earth to Eli!"

Again, he ignored me. A second later, he darted around the corner of the structure and threw a dazing curse at an incoming opponent. He passed so close to me that I leaped back, missing a collision by inches.

I shouted his name for a third time. But once again, he ignored me. *No,* I realized, *not ignoring me—he's just too deep in the dream.* It hadn't happened in a long time—normally Eli was aware of my presence the moment I got here—but for whatever reason, his attention was completely captured by this dream.

"I'm really sorry about this," I said, and then I reached out with my Nightmare magic, caught him by the arms like a puppet on strings, and lifted him into the air.

"What the hell?" He twisted around, his legs thrashing for a second. Then finally he turned toward me where I hovered in the air beside him. "Dusty?"

"That's right. Are you ready to get going or what?"

He pulled off his helmet. "Crap, this is a dream, isn't it?"

I nodded and slowly lowered us both to the ground.

"Sorry," he said, a sheepish smile crossing his face. "I must've been distracted."

"No kidding." I grinned and motioned to the gym. "Don't you get enough of this every day already?"

"What?" He winked. "It's fun. And you know I can't control the content of my dreams. That's your job."

"Right you are. I guess I should get on it then. Where should we go first?"

"Let's try the police department," Eli said. "You've been there often enough to re-create it, right? Maybe we'll be able to get a look at the ward where Titus was killed."

"I'll give it a go."

"Good, but do you mind giving me a wardrobe change first?" Eli said, motioning to his gladiator gear.

I raised a suggestive eyebrow. "Would you prefer your birthday suit?"

He grinned back at me and took a step nearer, our bodies only a few dangerous inches away from touching. "I'm game if you are."

A blush heated my skin, burning from the top of my hairline all the way down to my toes. For a second, I almost considered doing it, but no. It would be too great a tease. Besides, I wouldn't be confident enough to show him my true naked body. In this dream world, I would be tempted to present a falsely perfect body—skin tanned and blemish-free, a stomach lean and flat, minus the little pouch just below my belly button.

But I didn't want to give Eli a lie. I wanted to give him me as I truly am, and have him accept me for it, not be disappointed by a dream-world expectation I could never match in real life.

"Maybe next time," I said, giving a little laugh that rang false to my ears. "Like when we're actually able to do more than look." I waved at him, willing his gladiator gear to vanish and his usual jeans and T-shirt to take its place.

"It's a promise," Eli said, smoothing down his new clothes.

His words sent a prickle of anticipation dancing over my skin. I savored the feeling for a moment, and then closed my eyes and concentrated on changing the dream. I pictured the Rush as I'd seen it last, the main cathedral-like room with its haphazard rows of desks and clutter. The dream resisted the change at first, like it always did, but slowly I felt the substance of it give way, bending toward my vision and will.

"Wow, good job," Eli said a few moments later.

I opened my eyes and understood the compliment at once.

Sometimes when I set the scene of a dream, the result was an in-between thing, close to real but not quite, a surreal blend of truth and imagination. This time, however, I was nearly spot-on. The only thing off about the scene was the lack of policemen. I doubted the Rush was ever so empty. Even more strange was all the indicators that people should've been there—a coffee cup with steam still rising from its surface set atop a file cabinet, a half-eaten doughnut on a desk, the red jelly in its middle still wet and oozing. There was even a lit pipe laying on a little wooden stand, smoke trickling up from one end.

Then again, perhaps my magic hadn't worked so perfectly. I doubted any kind of smoking was permitted in the Rush. Too many naturekinds were allergic to the fumes of burning plants.

"Which way should we go?" Eli said, looking around.

"I'm pretty sure the prison is that way." I pointed ahead at a set of double doors. To the left of them ran the hallway with the interrogation room. Offices filled the hallway on the right.

Eli headed that direction, and I stepped into place beside him, being sure to keep an abnormally wide distance between us. The last thing I wanted was to get ejected from the dream early. Bollinger would no doubt call an end to the session.

The double doors led to a wide corridor lined with windows that looked out on a lawn and an artful arrangement of flower beds. They were the kind maintained by naturekinds, the plants large and vibrantly colored, a painting right out of a fairy tale. Bright sunshine poured through the glass, making the air pleasantly warm.

On the other end of the corridor was another set of double doors, these made with iron bars. Eli tried the lock on it, but it wouldn't give.

"Let me," I said. I waved my hand over the lock and willed it to open. The dream obeyed easily, and we stepped through.

We arrived in a short hallway, dim and cramped. Ahead was a glass door and to the left and right two more iron gates. Above the one on the left was a sign that read: WEST CELLBLOCK. To the right was the East Cellblock. Peering through the bars, I saw a wide corridor lined with prison cells on each side. The sight sent a shiver down my arms, and a sense of claustrophobia began to squeeze my chest.

"Let's try in here first," Eli said, striding over to the glass door. He opened it and we stepped inside. A reception desk filled the first half of the room. Behind it was some kind of observation post. TV monitors lined the walls on three sides, stacked from the desks to the ceiling. Microphones, switchboards, and other equipment cluttered the tops of the desks. All the equipment looked ancient, the kind of stuff you saw in old movies from the '60s about the space race. If this really was the type of equipment in the Rush, no wonder the animation effect was so bad. This stuff had been absorbing magic and electromagnetic fields for years.

"This must be central control," Eli said, walking past the reception desk toward the monitors.

I followed him, but stopped as I spotted a massive book sitting open behind the desk. I walked over to it, and in seconds realized it was a prisoner's log.

"Eli, look at this."

He turned and came back. "Huh. Do you think there's real information in there?"

"Maybe." Anything was possible inside a dream, especially if this one held dream-seer power in it. There was no way to tell, but I had a feeling it did. The details so far were too good for there not to be something bigger at work.

"Let's find out." Eli started leafing through the pages. Moments later he tapped his finger against the book. "Got it. It says Titus Kirkwood was being held in cell B-Three."

My pulse quickened at our good fortune, and Eli and I left the control room and headed for the West Cellblock. Once again, I had to will the locks to open. The moment I stepped inside, vertigo struck me and I froze. The cellblock was six tiers high with narrow platforms set at the base of each tier. Stacked in rowed columns, the tiny cells lining the walls reminded me of upright coffins. The place had a cave-like feel, windowless and dark. Through the bars of the nearest cells I saw rust stains on the walls. Chips and cracks marred the concrete floors as if the prisoners had tried to claw their way free. A sick feeling struck my stomach at the thought of my mother spending her days in this place. She would go mad. Anyone would.

"W-One, W-Two," Eli said as he scanned the small plaques on the front of the cells. "Huh, it must be just a straight count." He leaned his head back, trying to get a look at the second tier.

"Hold on. I got it." I flew into the air, rising up high enough to see the labels on the second level. "You're right. It just keeps going up." I lowered myself back down.

"Let's check out the other cellblock."

I nodded, but could already guess that it would be labeled with an "E" not a "B."

My suspicions proved right. The East Cellblock was a mirror image of the west, the only noticeable difference the labeling on the doors.

"There's another cellblock this way, I think," Eli said as we left the East Cellblock. The short hallway in front of the command center wrapped around on both sides of the East and West blocks. We followed the hallway and soon came to a set of iron gates labeled: CENTRAL CELLBLOCK.

"What do you want to bet these are labeled C?" I said as we stepped in.

Eli didn't answer. I was right, of course, which we both saw at once, but it didn't matter. The Central Cellblock was not a mirror match to the others. A few feet down the corridor lay an iron gate set into the floor. Icy fingers stroked the back of my neck. It could be a doorway to hell or an oubliette filled with the dead, decaying bodies of prisoners thrown down into it and forgotten.

"Think B stands for basement?" Eli said.

I swallowed, trying to muster my courage. Even if it didn't, I knew we were going down there.

Wordlessly, Eli strode forward and lifted the gate by the thick handle. Unlike the other iron gates in this place, this one wasn't latched. He headed down first, and I followed after him. A foul, damp stench hung in the air as I descended. I covered my nose with my hand and forced my breathing to go shallow. The walls were damp and slimy. Cool air wrapped around my face and bare arms.

The darkness grew thicker with each step until I could no longer see Eli in front of me. "Hold on a sec," I called.

I heard more than saw him stop and look back at me.

I closed my eyes and willed us two flashlights into existence. The dream handed them over easily, almost as if it was eager for us to see what waited below. I flipped one of the flashlights on, accidentally blinding Eli for a second, and then I handed it over to him.

We continued on for a long time, the descent several stories down, it seemed. Finally, we arrived at the bottom floor. It was true dark down here, no light at all except what we brought with us. All I could see from my vantage point was that the walls were made of a dark redbrick, the color of dried blood.

"You don't really think they keep prisoners down here, do you?" I said, trying to look past Eli.

"I think they certainly do." He stepped farther down the passageway, far enough for me to see the barred door on the left with a plaque on the front that read B1. It opened onto a prison cell so narrow I wouldn't have been able to lie crossways inside it. It was completely empty except for a blackened, ancient pillow and a urinal pot in the far corner. My stomach wrenched at the sight of it, and I pulled my gaze away.

"Looks like we found it," I said.

Eli nodded and moved on. Unlike the cellblock above, down here the cells lined only the one wall, the other nothing but blank redbrick. Except, I realized as we headed farther down, for shackles dangling out from the bricks at intervals. They were set so high that anyone locked into them wouldn't have been able to touch the floor. I supposed that was the point.

"B-Three," Eli announced as we reached the third cell. "Oh, God, Dusty, don't look." He turned his head away.

For a second I almost listened, but my curiosity was too powerful. *Just a dream,* I told myself as I peered in, *nothing here I can't change by—*

A gasp climbed my throat and came out a scream. I choked it off at once, because the *thing* inside the cell had *heard.* It was a giant, slithering thing, scaly in patterned stripes of black, yellow, and red. For a second, my mind resisted the word *snake.* Not because of its size, not because of the too-aware, intelligent look in its black eyes.

But because it was in the process of swallowing a man whole.

~ 14 ~

Doppelgänger

He was dead already at least. That much I could tell. The man's legs and waist were already gone down the snake's gullet, but his head lolled side to side against the brick floor, the movement in perfect harmony with the snake's undulating body.

I turned away, gagging.

"It's Titus," Eli said, a horrified awe making his voice higher pitched than normal. Despite his warning to me, he'd already looked back and was now watching the scene with the same kind of terrified entrancement I felt tugging my gaze back to it as well.

Reminding myself this was just a dream, I focused on the man's face. It was Titus, all right. His was a face I would never forget. "Can you tell how he died?" I said.

"I don't think so." Eli took a step nearer the door. I would've shouted at him to stay put, but the iron bars were too closely knit together for the snake to pass through. Not to mention that it was a little preoccupied at the moment. "There're no visible marks on his neck or chest. He could've died of a heart attack for all I know."

I stared at the snake once more, right into those inky, beaded eyes. They seemed to be watching me with an unsettling keenness, as if it knew just how much it bothered me to be watching this. "He could've died of fright."

Eli looked over at me. "The snake's just a symbol. I doubt it's even supposed to be a magical snake, except for its size."

I pried my eyes away from the creature long enough to shoot Eli a puzzled look. "How do you figure?"

He pointed. "See the colored stripes? That's an Eastern Coral Snake. I've seen some before, on hunting trips with my dad down to Mississippi. They're really poisonous, but not magical."

"Let's move on," I said, turning away from the snake and Titus. I didn't want to see anymore. And dream or not, I wasn't about to open that cell door for a closer look. The idea of snakes and their symbolism was something we could investigate outside of here. Somewhere safe, like the Internet.

"All right." Eli backed away slowly as if the snake might strike if he stopped watching it.

I moved on to the next cell. "I wonder which one they were keeping Bethany in."

As soon as I said it the door to the last cell swung open. I flinched at the loud creak it made. I stopped and waited, braced for whatever was inside to appear. Another snake perhaps—or something worse.

Several seconds later, or it might have been a minute, Eli said, "I think we have to go down there." He stepped past me, once more leading the way. And once again I was okay with letting him. Normally, snakes didn't scare me that much, but I had a feeling that would be different from now on. At least it hadn't been giant bugs. That would've left psychological scars so deep I might never recover.

The second I thought about giant killer bugs, I pushed the idea away before the dream got any ideas.

Eli paused outside the entrance to the last cell. I came to a halt beside him and peered in. Instead of a cell there was a narrow passageway, one deep enough we couldn't see where it led before the darkness closed in. A feeling of déjà vu struck me. The bricks ended right at the edge of the other cells, giving way to stone. From there, the passageway sloped downward.

"It looks like an Arkwell tunnel," Eli said.

"It is an Arkwell tunnel." I stepped through the doorway into it. "At least it feels like one." I concentrated hard, trying to make the connection between my sense of familiarity and a direct memory. "Wait." I reached out and touched the stone wall. "This reminds me of the tunnel that led down to Nimue's tomb."

"You're right, it does." Eli touched the wall, too, grazing his palm over the rough surface. "But I doubt this tunnel exists in the real Rush."

"Me, too." Even if the likelihood wasn't so doubtful, the feel of the dream was indication enough. It had changed the moment I stepped inside the tunnel. The world became less substantial, less real, as if at any moment it might come apart at the seams.

The farther along we walked, the more I began to suspect this was the exact same tunnel that had led us to the tomb of my ancestor Nimue, to Bellanax, and ultimately the showdown with Marrow. Finally, I spotted proof of it when we arrived at a small door.

"We've definitely been here before," Eli said, an ironic note to his voice. "But why would the dream bring us back here? It makes no sense. That chamber was emptied out after we defeated Marrow."

I smirked. "You mean that's what they said they did with it afterward. But I've never been back to check, have you?"

He shook his head.

The only thing I was certain about was that Nimue's tomb as well as her body had been buried in Coleville Cemetery at Arkwell. My mother and I had attended the ceremony.

The small door stood open, inviting us in. I hunched down to avoid scraping my back on the roof and stepped through it. When I reached the other side, I stood up, fully prepared to see a massive chamber lit with torches that burned purple fire. Instead I found myself standing on the shore of a river. Or maybe a lake. It was impossible to tell in the murky darkness, hanging like curtains over the black water. The smell of brine and rot burned my nose.

I looked up and saw we were still underground, in a massive cavern, the roof pierced with stalactites like jutted, misshapen swords. Ahead, a narrow, decrepit dock perched out over the water. Tethered next to it was a boat, the same low-sided pleasure barge from Eli's last dream. *A funeral barge, you mean.* I swallowed as my eyes fixed on the raised platform at the center of the boat with its billowing, gauzy curtains.

"It's the same one," Eli said from beside me. Worry threaded his voice. It wasn't just because of the dead body we'd seen the last time, I knew. No, the worry had to do with the frequency of the thing. This was only our second dream together and already we were seeing the same ominous signs again. Normally, a repeat of dream symbols meant that whatever was coming was coming soon. But never before had it happened so quickly for us.

"They shouldn't have kept us apart all summer." I glanced at him. "I bet your dream has been trying to warn us about the Death's Heart and Bethany's disappearance and all of it for weeks now. We just weren't together to read the signs."

Eli ran a hand over his head, his expression haunted. "Maybe. Which means we better step it up now." He offered me a brave smile. "Ready to go see what's in there this time?"

I inhaled a sharp, quick breath. "Sounds like a blast." But he was right. This was the heart of the dream, the deepest level. I could tell by the way my skin tingled with the subtle presence of magic.

Eli stepped down onto the barge first. I followed after him, holding my hands out at my sides as I adjusted to the feel of the shifting floor. A second later, the barge began to move. I glanced behind me to see the ropes that had moored it to the dock were gone. The boat slid quickly through the black water, and in moments the shoreline grew distant. We were moving impossibly fast. As before there was no wind driving us forward. No visible current. And no oars or ferryman either.

Silently, Eli and I approached the platform and pulled back the curtains.

"Oh," I said, my voice breathless with shock. The strange round bed with the ouroboros frame was gone. In its place stood Nimue's tomb. It was exactly as I remembered it, made of some kind of crystal and engraved on one side with an elaborate battle scene.

I stepped nearer the tomb and peered down on the scene, my flashlight setting the crystal surface aglow. Two armies converged around three larger figures in the center, a woman and two men. One of the men lay on the ground with a sword protruding from his chest. I stooped to take a better look. The sword, I realized, was Bellanax. I hadn't known it the first time I saw this engraving, but I knew it now. As if in confirmation, the silver band around my wrist began to warm.

The other man stood with the woman just behind him, her hands cupped over his eyes, and he seemed to be falling down. *Into sleep,* I realized. Because this was Marrow and Nimue depicted here. Dream-seers, lovers, and ultimately enemies.

"Does it look different than you remember?" Eli said, stooping down beside me.

I shook my head. "Exactly the same." I reached out and touched the figure of Nimue, running my finger over the smooth edges of the carving. "This is the moment Nimue locked Marrow in a dream," I said. For several hundred years, the Red Warlock had slept, trapped in Nimue's spell. It was the only way she could think of to keep him from spreading his evil. With his black phoenix familiar, he couldn't be killed, not permanently. But he could sleep forever.

Until someone broke him out. I stood up. *But who?*

"I wonder how she did it," Eli said.

I blinked and looked over at him. "What do you mean?"

"How she trapped him in a dream. Is it something all Nightmares can do? Could you do that to me?" A humorless smile crested Eli's lips then fell away.

"Don't be absurd," I said, but my tone wavered. The truth was I didn't know if it was absurd or not. Maybe it was something I could do. There was a lot of magic that had been lost after the magickind wars and the Black Magic Purge. Maybe trapping someone inside an eternal sleep was one of those things. I wouldn't know. When it came to being a Nightmare, most of what I knew and understood I had discovered on my own.

"Shall we open it?" Eli said it like a question, but we both knew it wasn't.

Together, we placed our hands against the lid and pushed—hard. Too hard it seemed, as the lid slipped off fast and crashed against the bottom of the boat with a loud, wet thump.

Eli winced. "I thought that was going to be more difficult."

"Me, too." It had been impossible the last time we saw this tomb in a dream.

I peered over the side, feeling my breath catch in my throat and my heart rattle against my rib cage. It wasn't Nimue lying in the tomb this time, but my mother. She didn't look dead, not as my body had in the last dream when it lay in this place. Instead she looked asleep, but also pale and sickly. She was lying on her back with arms folded across her chest. In her hand she held the shaft of a scythe. The long curved blade rested across her right shoulder.

"Why is she holding that?" I said. I didn't expect an answer, but I heard Eli draw breath beside me.

"The scythe is the symbol of the Grim Reaper," he said. "At least in the ordinary version of the myth."

I swallowed. The Grim Reaper. As in the personification of death. Steeling my courage, I stretched my hand toward it. The moment my fingers grazed the metal surface, a surge like electricity pulsed out from the shield. It sent both Eli and I sailing backward, landing in a heap. I groaned, the pain real despite its dream origin.

"What the hell was that?" Eli said, sitting up.

"Magic," I replied. I still felt the tingle of it burning over my skin.

"Let's not do that again." He wiped away blood from where he'd bitten his lip as he fell.

"Agreed," I said.

But there was no need. When we got to our feet and approached the tomb, Moira and the scythe were gone. Eli and I were lying inside it instead, two doppelgänger bodies posed toward each other, forehead to forehead, arms to arms. We looked like a sculptor's rendering of Romeo and Juliet, the final act of tragic romance.

Neither Eli nor I spoke as we took in the sight of us. We looked so real, so entirely like ourselves. I wondered if I could touch this Eli within the dream, but I knew I didn't want to. His skin would be cold, icy, and lifeless. We weren't asleep like Moira. We were dead. The longer I stared, the more I realized it. Our cheeks were colorless and sunken. A deep dark bruise crested my forehead. A line of blood encircled Eli's throat.

"What is that we're holding between us?" Eli said. The tremble in his voice was slight but present. I winced, hearing it. And for an awful moment I considered manipulating the dream, erasing this vision for something better, a future I wanted instead of this ill omen. But I didn't do it. There was too much at stake.

I stared at our cupped hands, fingertips pressed to fingertips. But not palm to palm. Something black and weirdly shaped blocked the way. "It's the Death's Heart," I whispered.

Before my eyes, the skin on my doppelgänger's face began to draw in on itself, creases forming like paper being crumpled by a fist. Her eyes began to sink backward, disappearing into the sockets as the bone of the skull grew more pronounced.

But beside my doppelgänger, Eli's took on flesh and color. His chest began to move up and down as he slowly returned to life.

"No," Eli said from beside me. "This isn't real and it's never going to happen." He leaned forward and grabbed the Death's Heart from between our doppelgängers' fingers. As he started to pull it away, his doppelgänger's eyes flashed open. They were wrong. Jagged yellow slits for irises stood out against all black. His lips spread apart, revealing fanged teeth and a forked tongue.

The doppelgänger grabbed Eli's wrist, its movement as quick as a whip crack. Eli yanked back, but the doppelgänger held fast, fingers pinching. Shaking off my paralysis, I lunged forward, grabbed the doppelgänger's arm and tried to pry him off. Its skin was hot and slick, scaly like a snake's.

"Let go!" I screamed at the wrong Eli. It hadn't even seemed to notice me before, its entire focus centered on the real Eli, but now its head swung my way. Its tongue slid out, and I cringed back, but didn't let go.

Finally, with our combined strength, Eli broke free. He skidded backward, the Death's Heart still clutched in his hand. I backed away, too, resisting the urge to run. There was nowhere to go on this barge, nowhere but out of the dream. But I didn't want to leave. Not yet. Eli and I needed more time.

Side by side we retreated from the doppelgänger Eli as it climbed out of the tomb. Only climbing wasn't the right word—it slithered. Before my eyes, its features turned waxy and began to blur. It was the same as when Paul put on the shape-change necklace. Only the blurriness didn't stop at the doppelgänger's face. It extended outward, obscuring its whole body. The nose, mouth, and eyes of a human boy elongated into the features of a snake. Skin became scales; shoulders and chest became extended rib cage.

As the change completed, the giant coral snake from the basement cellblock was now here on the barge.

"Get out of here, Dusty," Eli said. "Leave the dream and wake me up."

I swallowed, still not ready to leave. A wink of silver caught my eye, and I stared down at Bellanax on my wrist. I could kill the snake, I realized. Taking off its head would be easy. Only, the snake had been Eli a moment before, a version of him if not the real thing. What would happen after I killed it? Would it shape-change back into Eli's doppelgänger? The thought turned my stomach—and made up my mind.

"All right," I said. "I'm going."

Eli nodded, his eyes still fixed on the snake. "Do it fast."

I didn't respond, just shut my eyes and willed myself out of the dream. When I returned to my body and full consciousness, I grabbed Eli by the arms and gave him a shake. "Wake up!"

He didn't respond, his eyes still doing that fast rhythmic sweep from side to side.

The sleeping spell. I wrenched my gaze behind me and onto

Bollinger. She had dozed off and was lying awkwardly to one side. I couldn't believe the noise of my return hadn't woken her yet. I needed her awake, only I couldn't be sure she would undo the sleeping spell. She hadn't last time.

Beneath me, Eli's body clenched and his mouth opened in a sneer of pain and horror.

"Eli," I said, shaking him harder. "Wake up."

But it was no good. The spell lay too heavy on him, and I had no idea how to perform the counter-spell.

What was happening in the dream? Was the snake hurting Eli? If it were a normal dream, I wouldn't worry, but the prophetic ones were different. I'd once been attacked by Marrow's black phoenix inside a dream and the wound it gave me had followed me out of it.

Close to panic now I turned, ready to wake Bollinger and force her to undo the spell. But then pain seared around my wrist— Bellanax awake and pressing for control.

I grabbed the silver band, slid it off my wrist, and disengaged the glamour. Free of the spell, Bellanax was stronger and more present, easier to control. I fought to stay in charge of my mind.

Tell me the spell, I thought, my concentration centered on the sword in my hands. *Teach me. Show me.*

For a moment, Bellanax resisted. It seemed to rear up like a wild horse trying to break free of its lead. But then it settled and the resistance reversed. The words of the spell flowed into my mind.

"*Ou-hupno,*" I said. It was as if I'd cast the counter-spell a thousand times. The magic came easily. It swept over Eli, dragging him awake.

His eyes opened, and he peered up at me, slack jawed. Realizing the picture I must be presenting as I stood over him with naked sword in hand, I stepped back and reapplied the glamour.

"Welcome back," I said, sliding the bracelet onto my wrist once more.

He sat up and wiped his forehead with the back of his hand. "Took you long enough."

"It wasn't easy," I said, and glanced down at the bracelet then back again. "What happened? Did the snake hurt you?"

Eli slowly nodded, and I noticed how green he looked. A tremble went through his body. "It killed me, Dusty. It swallowed me whole."

Alibis

The following Wednesday, Paul finally managed to hack into Deverell's files. I got the text just as I arrived back at the dorm after another dream-session with Eli. The last two had been much less eventful than the snake dream. On Monday we visited the Rush again, only to find it empty—no snake, Titus, or anything else. Tonight we'd visited the barge again, but it, too, was empty. Nimue's tomb had been replaced with the ouroboros bed, but there was no one lying on it this time. I couldn't explain the sudden drop in the dreams' intensity, but I would take it.

It took me a full five minutes to translate the text using the cipher Paul had given me the morning before. It was a code of his own design and so complicated it made my head swim with awe. Sometimes his intelligence was a bit scary. When I finished it read:

> I have the files. Volunteer to get the burn kit tomorrow
> in class. It will be missing.

I frowned down at the screen. Burn kit? Ms. Miller had said that we would start studying fire salamanders tomorrow. I knew the lizards had a habit of randomly bursting into flames, but she assured us we would be fine. Then again, she'd promised that the azbans would prove docile and lovable, too, but my finger still ached from the not-yet-healed bite on my right hand.

Painstakingly using the cipher, I managed to type back:

How do you know we will need a burn kit?

A couple of minutes passed before my phone buzzed again.

Fire salamanders, someone will get burned. Just make sure it isn't you.

I caught myself smiling at that and then went back to sleep.

"Paul has the files," I announced to Eli at breakfast the next morning.

He stopped mid-chew, swallowed, and then smiled. "That's great. When do we get it?"

"I'll get it during bio. He has a plan for me to sneak away for a second and pick it up."

"Oh." Eli's eyes dropped to his plate. "Well, be careful and don't get caught."

Each polite word sounded like it cost him. I sighed, hating to cause him worry. We'd seen Paul a couple of times since that first meeting, but so far Eli's attitude toward him hadn't softened one bit. I had a feeling some of it was because of the anxiety dreams still plaguing him. There hadn't been any sign of either of our dead bodies in the last dream-sessions, but his normal dreams were a different story. I'd started the unfortunate habit of asking him about his dreams every morning, hoping each time he would smile and say they'd been pleasant. But so far no luck.

Even worse was that I was starting to have them more often, too. I was doing my best not to think about it—and I hadn't spoken a word about them to Eli either. What was the point? All it would do was provide fodder to make his worse.

When I arrived at the Menagerie for bio, there was no sign of creepy-bearded Paul. And despite his prediction, the first thirty minutes of class passed without incident. The fire salamanders were caged in a separate area from the trash trolls, a grassy, tree-filled space with several ponds and various water features. Actually, minus the lizards roaming the place, it would've been beautiful. Maybe even with the lizards. Aside from the way their tongues kept shooting in and out of their mouths, they were kind of pretty.

Until one of the smaller ones exploded right in Carla Petermeier's palm. She shrieked and threw the creature halfway across the cage. It crashed into one of the ponds with a loud plop. The fae water lilies nearby immediately closed up, their pink and yellow petals quivering as they scrunched together.

"It burned me!" Carla was holding her hand out in front of her, the thick leather gloves still smoking. For a second, I thought she was just playing drama queen, then I realized it was more overreaction. She had gotten burned, a couple of angry red dots formed on her forearm.

"Stop your shouting," Ms. Miller said, storming over. "Do you want *all* of them to start exploding right now?"

For a second, I thought she was going to smack Carla, and I couldn't help but feel a stab of disappointment when all she did was peel off the glove. Katarina had been back in class since Monday, and she and Carla had started an aggressive taunt-Dusty-every-second campaign. Well, everywhere except for psionics, that was. Mr. Deverell had made us all sign the Student Conduct

Agreement last week. Katarina had been livid—and making up for lost time wherever she could.

"Someone bring me the burn kit off the equipment cart," Ms. Miller said.

Crap, I thought, realizing this was my moment, and stupid me, I hadn't stayed near the cart. Looking like an anxious idiot, I leaped into action and raced over to the cart, bumping at least two of my classmates out of the way. I got there first, examined the cart for half a second, and then announced, "It's not here, Ms. Miller. I can run back to the classroom and get it."

"Yes, all right," Ms. Miller said.

Ignoring the peculiar looks, I turned and bolted out of the cage. Let them think what they wanted. Heck, maybe Carla would assume I was trying to make amends and tell Katarina about it. I wouldn't say no to a cease-fire. Not that it was likely to happen; Katarina never backed down.

A few minutes later, I arrived back in the classroom. "Paul?" I called, not seeing him anywhere. Aside from the closet, there was nowhere for him to hide, not unless he had a spell of invisibility in his arsenal. Where was he? Clenching my teeth in frustration, I went to the closet and searched the shelves for the burn kit, but it wasn't there. Of course, it wasn't. Paul had stolen it at some point to make this work.

I spun on my heel, ready to search the hallway and crashed into Paul as he came through the door. "Ouch. You stepped on my foot."

"Sorry." He wrapped his hand around my arm. "Are you okay?"

"Yes." I pulled away from him. "I was worried you weren't going to show up."

He grimaced, the gesture mostly obscured by his thick beard.

He reached up and pulled off the shape-change necklace. His creepy bearded-man features blurred back into Paul. "I almost wasn't. Problem down in the dragon caves."

"Dragon caves?"

"Yeah, there's a whole network of them beneath the Menagerie."

"There are dragon ca—" I stopped, shook my head. "Never mind. Do you have the files? I've got to get back to class."

"Yeah, I do." Paul reached into his pocket and withdrew a flash drive. I saw at once it was the one my mother had given me. "I'm sorry, Dusty, but nothing on this was salvageable." He handed it over.

"Bummer," I said, unsurprised but still disappointed.

"But there's a lot on this one." Paul pulled a second flash drive out of his pocket and gave it to me as well. "I was up half the night going over it. You're not going to believe this, but . . . I think Corvus might've killed my uncle."

"Wait, what?" I blinked, taken aback by the sudden assertion.

Paul glanced over his shoulder as if to make sure we were still alone. "Detective Valentine interviewed him, and he doesn't have an alibi for the night Titus was killed. Claims he was at home by himself the whole time."

My heartbeat began to quicken, a steady *thump-thump-thump* against my rib cage. I didn't want a Nightmare to be guilty of the crime, but I would take it if it meant getting my mother free. "Valentine said my mom didn't have an alibi. If Corvus didn't either, why did Valentine mark him off the list of suspects?"

"Well, the DNA evidence for one thing." Paul sighed, his tone regretful. "And I hate to say it but it looks pretty convincing. I don't know a lot about that stuff, but it was hard not to be impressed."

I gritted my teeth, hating the doubt in his voice. "If it really was my mom who came onto the ward that night, it's possible that's where the DNA came from. It's just circumstantial."

Paul raised his hands. "I'm with you. I know your mom didn't do this, but I'm just saying the case against her looks bad."

I folded my arms over my chest and stuck out my chin. "What else convinced Valentine that Corvus is innocent?"

"The guilt thing, like you said. Valentine noted that Corvus's guilt didn't spike a single degree. That's a direct quote."

My nostrils flared as I inhaled, my temper on the rise. Bellanax burned against my wrist. "Is that all?"

Paul shook his head. "Valentine couldn't find a motive for him either. There's a background check on Corvus, but it's thin. It's like the guy has done nothing but teach school for the last twenty years. He's never been married, no kids. And no criminal record. He's never even had so much as a speeding ticket"

"Huh . . . I wonder how he lost his eye." It seemed to me the result of some kind of violence, given the scarring around it, visible despite the eye patch.

"I don't know." Paul ran a hand over the stubble on his face. "His records only went back those twenty years. It didn't even have a date of birth or anything."

"That's weird." I looked down and noticed the burn kit tucked beneath Paul's arm. "But I've got to get back to class."

"Right." Paul handed over the kit. "Before you go, I've got an idea on how we can investigate Corvus."

I glanced at the door, getting nervous about my long absence. "How?"

"Well, neither you nor Eli are going to get away with a lot of sneaking around this year, not with the Will Guard tailing your every move."

I scowled, my hands tightening into fists. The two flash drives pressed against my palm. He was right about that. The Will

Guard had dogged us every step, from our evening homework sessions to our Dream Team meetings in the library.

"What if I can get you a shape-change necklace like mine?" Paul said.

My mouth fell open. A hundred questions darted through my mind, but I couldn't seem to snatch one long enough to ask it.

"Eli won't like it, I know," Paul pressed on. "But I think it's our best shot. I can only get my hands on one, but I don't want to give it to him. It wouldn't work. He doesn't trust me enough, and investigating Corvus is going to be a two-man job."

"Why a two-man job?" I asked. "All it takes is a key to get into his office, and I know how to get it." At least, I hoped I did. Last year I'd been able to convince the school janitor, Mr. Culpepper, to let Eli and me in. I'd spotted Culpepper once or twice so far this year, and each time he'd cast me a very faint, hardly there smile. But for Culpepper that was practically a hug.

"I'm not talking about just his office," Paul said. "We need to break into his home. And get this, it's off campus."

"That doesn't make sense."

"I know. Pretty much every other teacher lives on campus, but not Corvus. He's renting a house off Canal Street."

"Weird."

"You mean suspicious."

I frowned.

An exasperated look crossed Paul's face. "Don't you see? By having a house off campus, there's no way of tracing his activity that night. Or any other night for that matter. Every vehicle leaving campus and coming onto it gets recorded, standard security. But he would've left Arkwell at like five that day and could've gone anywhere."

I slowly nodded, catching on. "So if he did live on campus,

the police could've figured out when he left and came back, but not in this case."

"Right," Paul said. "It gives him a lot of anonymity. So long as he comes and goes about the same time each day, nobody would question it." He hesitated then blew out a breath. "Marrow did the same thing when he was teaching here."

I winced at the name, and even more at the reminder that Paul had once been Marrow's supporter. The enormity of what he'd known and had let happen struck me anew, and I shook my head. "I don't know, Paul. I'll have to think about it."

"Oh." Hurt flashed across his face before he hid it behind a falsely pleasant smile. "I understand. Just let me know. I'm still going to get it. If you decide you're in, we'll need to take some time for you to practice wearing it. It's hard to be someone else at first. You don't have your private lessons with Mr. Deverell this week, right?"

"Right," I said automatically. Deverell had been out sick since Tuesday. "How do you know about my lessons with Deverell?"

"You mentioned it to Eli the other day. I overheard." Paul smiled again, this time it wasn't false. "I promise I'm not spying on you if that's what you're thinking."

It was, but I wasn't about to admit it now. "Okay, but so what about my lessons?"

"If he's still out tomorrow, we can meet up and I'll show you how to use it," Paul said.

I nodded. It really was tempting. Even if I didn't go snooping Corvus's off-campus house with Paul, I still could use the necklace. It would make a lot of things a whole lot easier—like secretly meeting up with Eli.

I exhaled, glanced at the clock, and nearly shrieked. "I've got to go. I'll think about it. Probably yes, but I'll text you for sure."

"All right," Paul said, and I could detect the hopeful note in his voice.

Its presence gave me pause. I stopped in the doorway and turned around, narrowing my eyes at him. "Why are you being so helpful with all of this? I mean, if you get caught, it'll be big trouble, right?"

"Yes." His expression turned grave for a moment, then he shook it off. "But it's worth the risk."

"Why?" I pressed, eyes still narrowed.

He glanced away a moment, then met my expression head on. "Because I care about you, Dusty. And I know how hard it will be on you if your mom is found guilty. I'll do whatever I can to protect you from that."

I swallowed, a cocktail of sudden unnamable emotions churning in my stomach. I turned and left the classroom without replying.

I didn't tell Eli at lunch about Paul's offer to get me a shape-change necklace. I decided to wait until I'd made up my mind what to do.

"Did you get it?" Eli said as soon as he arrived at the table.

I tapped my pocket. "Flash drive."

"Good. We need to dive into it right away."

I nodded. "I'm going to go through it while you're at gladiator training. Deverell's out again today."

"Oh." Eli's look was almost comically disappointed, like a puppy being put in its cage for a nap.

"You don't mind, do you?" I said. "I've come to the last two, and you're doing great."

He grinned. It was a true enough statement. He certainly wasn't the best player out there, but he wasn't the worst either.

And considering how much less time and experience he had compared to the others, that was quite an accomplishment. "I don't mind you not being there," he said. "I just wish I could skip and go through it with you."

I smiled, trying not to ignore my own disappointment that he wasn't going to skip. But tryouts were coming a week from Saturday, and I knew he was too anxious to ease off now.

It seemed Lance was getting anxious, too, because he asked Selene not to come to practice tonight either. "You make me distracted," he said, planting a kiss on her forehead.

She rolled her eyes. "How are you going to handle it when I try out for the team then?"

Lance clucked his tongue. "Ha, ha. Very funny."

Selene gave him a look to cut ice. I stared at her, brow furrowed. She wasn't joking. I knew her well enough to see that. Lance clearly didn't—or was choosing willful ignorance—as he planted another kiss on her forehead. "See you at dinner."

I said good-bye to Eli and then made plans to meet up with Selene after classes in room 013. She'd offered to help me go through Valentine's files even before Lance asked her not to come.

"So," I said as we rounded the corner into the room later that day, "you're trying out for the team?" The question had been bugging me since lunch. I couldn't quite accept that she really meant it.

She rolled her shoulders, not meeting my eyes. Mostly this was because Buster had commanded her attention the moment we entered.

I set my backpack on one of the desks. "Why are you? You've never expressed any interest in the team before."

Selene sat down on Buster and crossed one leg over the other. "Actually, I've always wanted to play. I just wasn't motivated to go through with it until I realized there wasn't going to be a single girl on the team this year."

I beamed at her. "You're my hero."

"Heroine," she corrected me. "And you should try out, too. We'll kill them."

I snorted. "I'm not interested in public ridicule and disaster, thank you." I pulled out Paul's flash drive from my pocket and plugged it into the computer.

"I think you're just afraid you might be great at it," Selene said, rolling Buster over to get a better look at the screen.

I sat down and began pulling off some of the files, saving them to the desktop for the time being. Once done, I ejected the flash drive and moved to another computer while Selene took my place behind the first one.

Fortunately, the files on the drive were labeled by subject and not something less convenient like date. I'd given Selene a couple of folders with names I didn't recognize but could guess had been suspects at one point. The three folders I was most interested in, I kept for myself: Moira Everhart, Ian Corvus, and Titus Kirkwood.

I started with the latter one, not quite ready to face the stuff on the other two just yet. In minutes I discovered that Titus had indeed been killed by ordinary means. According to the autopsy report, he died from a single stab wound to the chest that pierced his heart. Death had been instantaneous. *An execution,* according to Valentine's note. The crime scene technicians estimated the knife to be six inches in length with a serrated blade made from a human femur bone.

I read this detail three times before I was finally able to accept it as real. It appeared a small piece of the blade had broken off when the killer wrenched it free of Titus's rib cage. Shivering at the idea of how much it would've hurt and how hard it would've been to do, I resisted an impulse to de-glamour Bellanax and examine the hilt. It too was made of bone, but it was polished smooth, comfortable to touch and hold. But then again I could easily imagine someone carving the material into something sharp.

A knife with a bone blade. My mother owned no such thing. Not that I had ever seen. And how would she even get one? Surely something made from a human femur bone wasn't an object you could order off eBay. It sounded like a black magic item. *She could've gotten it from Culpepper.* The realization increased the chill spreading over my skin. Especially when I read Valentine's note below the knife's description—*finding it is crucial.*

Yes it was. The smoking gun. It would be the key to getting my mom off this. Assuming, that was, Valentine hadn't already found it. It was a guarantee he hadn't told me everything about the case against her in our short interview.

With dread now pulsing in my temples, I opened my mother's file and began to scan through it. In seconds I came across the details of her alibi. Like Mr. Corvus she claimed to have been home all night—*watching my unconscious daughter,* the transcript read. I could almost hear her saying it, face drawn in anger, teeth flashing. My mom was fierce on any given day, but doubly so when it came to me.

I swallowed down guilt. It was my fault she didn't have an alibi. If only I'd been awake by then. But it didn't matter now. What did was the presence of her DNA on Titus's body. How did it get there? I scanned the rest of the transcript and saw that Valentine had asked the same question.

MOIRA: *How should I know? Perhaps those ordinaries who ran the test are idiots and made a mistake. Or perhaps you are the idiot who collected it wrong. Or maybe I just make an easy target for the real killer.*

VALENTINE: *There's no reason to be hostile. This is just an interview.*

MOIRA: *The hell it is. This is a witch hunt.*

I winced as I read it. My mom was usually more clever than this, less prone to emotional outbursts. Beneath the last line of dialogue, Valentine had written a note about Moira's "visible agitation" and her "clearly spiking guilt."

Fighting back a growing sense of despair, I scanned the rest of the files until I came to an inventory of the "items of note" the police had collected from my mother's house. The knife wasn't there.

Satisfied at least by a small degree, I clicked on Mr. Corvus's folder and glimpsed the contents. Paul had been right about the skimpy background check. Actually, the whole thing was skimpy. Aside from transcripts of the one interview, there was little else in there. That was, until I noticed the part of the background check that listed "Distinguishing Physical Characteristics." The missing eye was mentioned, of course, as well as a tree tattoo on his right shoulder. That was a weird idea—a teacher having a tattoo, especially one as old as Mr. Corvus.

But the final characteristics gave me pause and set my teeth on edge. Corvus had a scar over his breastbone that had been "made by a brand" according to the note. *A brand?* At first, I couldn't make sense of it, but then I clicked on a link to a photo and realized they were talking about a brand like the kind used to mark livestock. The picture showed a man's bare chest. On it was a puckered, red scar shaped like the Borromean rings.

Once again those strange words he'd made me translate came to me—*Only the blood of the twelve can undo the circle.* Was it related to the Borromean rings? They'd been pictured on the same page.

I scanned the rest of the file, looking for some clarifying re-mark, something to explain why a man would willingly brand himself with a hot iron. *Unless it was unwilling.* I shuddered.

But the file contained nothing else of note. And I realized that despite Corvus's lack of a verifiable alibi, Valentine hadn't gone through his house the way he had my mother's.

Which meant Paul was right—we needed to go through it.

"What's wrong, Dusty?" Selene called from the other com-puter.

I turned toward her, running my fingers through the loose hair of my ponytail, yanking at the snags just to keep my hands occupied while my mind churned. "Paul thinks Corvus is respon-sible, and I'm starting to agree with him." I motioned toward my computer screen, and then filled her in on Corvus's nonexistent alibi, the house off campus, and finally Paul's offer of the shape-change necklace.

Silence descended as I finished speaking. Selene didn't react outwardly at all while she processed everything I'd just told her. I resisted the urge to break that silence as long as I could—about ten seconds.

"What do you think? Should I do it? Eli will freak out if I say yes. I guess I could always just not tell him but—" I bit my lip before I started babbling in earnest.

Selene cleared her throat. "I think you should do what you decide to do regardless of what anyone else thinks. And yes, you should tell Eli, but don't let him stop you. You are your own boss. No one else."

I inhaled, feeling a thrill of exhilaration at the idea. It seemed so opposite of my reality. Every moment someone else was mak-ing decisions for me—when to eat, where to be, what to do, what not to do. I let my breath out slowly. "What about Paul? Do you think it's safe to trust him?"

There was another long moment of silence, and this time I managed not to break it. Finally Selene said, "I trust you to be able to take care of yourself, no matter what Paul might be up to. Especially with that sword you're carrying. I wasn't kidding that you would make a great gladiator."

I laughed, the sound coming out a snort thanks to my nerves. "Not a chance."

Selene shrugged. "Suit yourself. But they have small team matches you know, two on two. We'd make a great team. The boys wouldn't stand a chance."

Laughing again, I turned back to the screen. My humor quickly faded, giving way to determination. I would take Paul up on the offer. We had to get into that house and look around. I clicked on the Titus folder again, scrolling down until I came across a picture of the knife. I clicked on it, feeling exhilarated once again. We needed to search the house, and I knew exactly what we were looking for.

~ 16 ~

Here Be Dragons

J held off telling Eli about my decision until lunch the next day. He did not take it well.

"Please tell me you're joking, Dusty," he said, a fork gripped tight in his hand. I had a feeling he was thinking about stabbing someone with it. Thank goodness Paul wasn't around.

I took a deep breath, trying not to overreact. I knew he would see reason, once he got past his worry for me. "I'm not. It's a good plan. And we don't have a lot of options with the Will Guard breathing down our necks. Sneaking off campus would be impossible without a shape-change necklace."

"We could get a weekend pass."

I offered him a patient smile. "We don't have time. They don't start approving those until next month."

"What about the tunnels? Isn't that how your mom got on campus?" Eli pressed.

"Well, yeah, but we don't know the way, we don't have a boat, and even if we managed to get out onto the lake, how do we get to Corvus's house without a car? It could be miles and miles, and it's not like there're cabs on every corner. This is Chickery not New York."

Eli's jaw worked back and forth, muscles quivering in his temple, cheek, and neck. "Fine. Then he can give me the shape-change necklace, and I'll go with Paul to investigate Corvus."

I shook my head. "Paul already said no to that."

"He what?" Eli's expression darkened even more.

I shifted in my seat, completely understanding his reaction but being powerless to change anything. "He doesn't think it would be a good idea for it to be you and him. You don't play nice together."

Eli snorted, the sound dangerous, akin to a wild animal growling. "Just because I don't like him doesn't mean I would do something stupid and get us caught."

"I know that, but I can't make Paul do something he doesn't want to."

Eli grunted. "He's just looking for an excuse to be alone with you."

I sighed. "Maybe, but he's the one taking the biggest risk in all of this. If I get caught it'll be a slap on the wrist. If he does . . ."

"I get it." A grim expression crossed his face. Eli glanced to his right, where Lance was listening in on our argument with palpable interest. Next to me, I suspected the same from Selene, although she was doing a better job at hiding it.

Eli ran a hand over his head. "Can we talk about this outside?" He smiled at the others. "No offense, guys."

Lance slapped him on the back. "None taken. Wish I could keep every argument private, too. Makes for better making up options afterward."

Selene shot him a dirty look, but Eli was already standing up, motioning for me to follow.

We dumped our trays and then headed out into the hallway. It was mostly empty, except for a Will Guard standing at the juncture of the nearest hallway. Eli took me by the arm and guided me in the opposite direction, just far enough to let us talk without being overheard, but not so far that the Will Guard felt inclined to move in and push us apart.

Eli faced me. We were standing close enough I had to lean my head back to look up at him.

"Look, Dusty, I know you're inclined to think the best of Paul, and I know you think I'm inclined to always think the worst, but you've got to believe me when I say you need to be careful about him."

I closed my eyes, just long enough to compose myself. I didn't want to sound defensive. "Why do you think so? This time, I mean."

Eli bit his lip, released it again. "It's just, how can we be sure that Paul wasn't involved in what happened to Titus?"

A laugh burst from my chest. "That's absurd."

"Is it?" Eli leaned back, increasing the distance between our gazes. Then he leaned forward and took hold of my shoulders. "Think about it, Dusty. Paul was there, on the basement ward, same time as Titus—by his own admission. And we both know that he had reason to kill his uncle. More than anybody else, after all those years of abuse."

I flinched. The motivation was certainly true, scarily so. I closed my eyes and shook the feeling off. Motive or not that didn't make him the killer. I met Eli's gaze. "Paul was locked up. You saw those cells. How could he have gotten out to do it? We know he's not a Nightmare."

"No, he's a siren," Eli shot back at once, as if he'd had this volley prepared ahead of time. "What if one of the guards took interest? What if one of them was a woman? One willing to leave his cell unlocked for him."

Right away I remembered some of the names in Valentine's files. There had definitely been female names on the list. And similar to a Nightmare's power, the siren's ability to mesmerize couldn't be completely blocked by anti-magic spells.

I jerked my gaze away from Eli, staring at some random spot on the floor. I didn't want to believe it. I wasn't sure I could believe it, but I knew I couldn't discount it either. Not this time.

I turned back to Eli. "Look, I promise I'll be careful. I won't take anything he says at face value. I'm not going to get tricked this time. But—" I raised my hand to his lips, silencing a protest. "I've got to do whatever I can to help my mom. And if Paul is responsible for Titus's death, then spending this time with him will give me a chance to investigate him, too."

My stomach twisted at the idea. Not because I was opposed to spying on him, but because if it turned out to be true, then that meant Paul's offer to help had been about misdirection from the beginning. Just an attempt to keep the guilt from shining on him.

To the detriment of my mother.

I clenched my teeth and breathed in deep. Exhaling, I said, "I know you're worried, but he won't get the upper hand with me ever again." I raised my left arm, showing him Bellanax.

Eli exhaled, and I sensed the fight ease in him. "I am worried, Dusty. About a lot of things." He hesitated and glanced at the Will Guard. The man had moved closer, but was still out of hearing range. Eli turned back to me. "But you're right. This is about your mother and we've got to do what's best for her."

I leaned up on my tippy toes and kissed him. "Thank you."

His answering kiss was just a little bit cold, like the shift toward night at the end of an early summer day.

It left me chilled for hours afterward. So did his warnings about Paul. When I texted Paul last night, agreeing to his plan, he told me to volunteer to help out at the Menagerie after class. I wasn't wild about the idea. Ms. Miller had mentioned volunteer opportunities once or twice in class, but so far those opportunities seemed to consist of shoveling troll manure or removing the cobwebs in the jackalope cages. Fun times.

Fortunately, when I reported for volunteer duty, Ms. Miller sent me to one of the classrooms to clean the dry-erase boards.

"That's all?" I said, arching one eyebrow.

Ms. Miller didn't look up from the sprite she held clutched in one hand. In the other she was preparing to clip its wings with a pair of surgical shears. The sprite was humanoid but with a feline face, sharp pointed teeth like thumbtacks, currently bared in protest at Ms. Miller. Its tiny body was shifting colors, yellow to green to pink to purple. I swallowed a surge of pity for the little creature. I wanted to ask why Ms. Miller was clipping its wings, but I didn't have time for the twenty-minute lecture that would probably accompany the answer.

Finally, Ms. Miller glanced up. "Yes. You have to prove your reliability with simple tasks before you are allowed the responsibility of handling any living creatures, plant or animal, in the Menagerie."

Holding back a reply, I headed to the classroom she'd indicated. I sent Paul a text on the way with just the room number. I didn't have the encoder with me and hoped he would understand by the number alone.

It seemed he did—or maybe he'd known my assignment ahead of time—because he was waiting in the classroom when I arrived. He was wearing his creepy bearded-man disguise, but I was starting to get used to it. When he smiled at me, I could see Paul behind those stranger's eyes.

"Hey, thanks for coming."

"No, thank you," I said, my answering smile already fragile. So much risk he was taking to help me. Why? I pushed the question to the back of my mind—for now. I needed to learn this shape-change stuff.

"Come on," he said. "We need to go somewhere private for this."

"Okay." I managed to sound normal, but my insides were shaking. Going anywhere private with Paul would've made me nervous even before Eli had pointed out the darker possibilities of his sudden reappearance in my life.

We headed out of the classroom, made a left and then another left, toward the rear of the building. When we arrived at the back door, Paul pushed it open and motioned me through. I stepped out onto a narrow walkway running between the administration building and the outer wall of the Menagerie.

Paul joined me a moment later, pulling the door shut behind him. "We shouldn't be seen back here. Hardly anybody comes this way." He started walking, heading deeper into the Menagerie. I followed silently behind him. Although he hadn't told me to stay quiet, there was a clandestine feel to our journey up and down the narrow alleys. Whenever he heard someone nearby, he would stop and wait, making sure the coast was clear before moving on.

Finally, we arrived at a long rectangular building with a low, flat ceiling. The place looked abandoned. It leaned to one side as if it had aspirations toward falling over. A large sign posted over the door read:

WARNING
KEEP OUT
RISK OF DEATH AND DISMEMBERMENT

"What is this place?" I asked as Paul stepped up to the door and slid a key, one of at least a dozen he had on a large chain, into the lock.

He smiled. "Just ignore the signs."

I bit my lip. Ignoring the signs never turned out well in my experience. "But what is it?"

Paul pushed the door open and stepped inside. I hesitated on the threshold, breathing in the strange smell of the place, a mix of ash and rotten egg. Vaguely, the words of the oath Ms. Miller had made us take our first day in the Menagerie passed through my mind, something about not opening any locked areas.

"Come on," Paul said. "Before we get caught. This place is off limits."

"No kidding," I muttered as I followed him in. He shut the door behind me and turned the lock. Inside, the building was one giant room, completely bare of everything except the dirt and leaf litter on the concrete floor. To the left, the floor sloped downward, leading into the tunnels.

Paul reached up and removed his shape-change necklace, his bearded-man persona disappearing. He folded the stiff chain and tucked it into his pocket. "This way," he said, turning toward the tunnel. A lantern hung on the wall next to the tunnel's entrance, and Paul picked it up and whispered a fire incantation. Flames appeared inside the glass frame, casting an impressive amount of light given its size. Holding it out in front of him, he proceeded into the tunnel.

"Where are we going?" I said hurrying after him and half-stumbling over my own feet. "What is this place, Paul?"

He glanced over his shoulder, a mischievous smile twisting his lips. "Why are you so wor—" The smile fell away. He stopped and faced me, his eyes level with mine thanks to his lower vantage point. "It's Eli, isn't it?"

I blinked at him, rocking back on my heels to compensate for the sloping floor. "What are you talking about?"

Paul motioned toward me. "You, acting like I'm an ax murderer luring you away to my favorite chopping block."

I made a face. "That's not funny."

"It is Eli, right?" Paul lowered the lantern as if it were suddenly too heavy to lift. It dangled from his fingers, bumping against his jeans. "I know he's not happy about this, assuming you even told him."

"Of course I told him," I said, my voice dangerously close to a hiss.

"Oh, yeah? What did he have to say about it?"

I opened my mouth and closed it again, gritting my teeth. Paul waited a few seconds, the silence a painful pressure as I searched for a response, one that didn't involve accusing him of killing his uncle.

"Let me guess," Paul continued. "He thinks I'm involved, doesn't he?"

I stared at him, unable to think of a reply.

"Yeah, I thought so." Paul pressed his lips together. Anger glistened in his eyes, which were colorless in the dim cave-like hallway around us, the darkness broken only by the flickering lantern light.

"Don't be silly," I said, a hollow clang in my words. "I mean, yeah, he was mad, but did you really expect anything else from him?"

"Not at all." Paul exhaled then drew in a breath deep enough that I saw his chest expand. "But I also know you're covering for him." He waved off my protest. "It's all right. I don't blame you or him. Not given my history." The timid smile that rose to his face was painful to see.

"I . . . I'm sorry, Paul." I dropped my gaze to the floor, unable to bear his expression a moment longer. I wanted to say something better, but I couldn't think of anything.

"Do you believe in redemption?"

I raised my eyes to find Paul wasn't looking at me, but had

bent his neck to the side, his gaze focused down the tunnel somewhere.

"I don't know." Once more they were hollow words, a hollow answer.

Paul turned back to me, his expression closer to normal, that brokenness I saw in him a moment ago covered by a hard veneer. "All I can do is give you my word that I didn't kill my uncle. I was locked up in that cell with no way out of it for almost three weeks. That makes twice in my life I've been a prisoner inside the Rush. It was the worst thing I've ever endured. And I have no intention of ever ending up back there again."

I stared at him, weighing this answer in my mind. I knew he could still be lying, but then the vivid memory of the Rush's cellblocks rose in my mind. I saw those upright coffin cells, the rust stains on the wall, and the oppressive darkness, the kind made worse by the knowledge of light existing outside of it, like that glass corridor leading to the prison, so warm and beautiful. Even at night it would glow a little with moon and starlight.

I slowly nodded. "I believe you."

The hardness in his expression broke into relief. "Let's get going. We've got lots to do and only a little time. I've got to be at the front gates by five or my watchdogs will get suspicious and come looking for me."

I followed after him, too leery of this underground journey to want to walk beside him. There were more signs down here warning people to stay out or risk being, "impaled, crushed, or incinerated."

The sloping tunnel ended in stairs that circled downward in a dizzying spiral. It was impossible to tell how far down it went, but within seconds I was convinced we would be on it forever. The stone was crumbling around us, bits of gravel and dirt showering down with every step. Even our breath seemed to dislodge it.

"Seriously, Paul, where are we going?" Just as I said it the stairs came to an end, and Paul and I stepped out into a vast cavern, one so tall the lantern stood little chance of illuminating the ceiling. A thousand years of dirt and scree covered the floor.

Paul held the lantern aloft and turned in a circle, as if offering me a view of the place. "No one will discover us down here. It's not as structurally sound as it used to be, but we should be all right for what we're doing."

I didn't like the word *should* but decided not to press. "It looks really old and not manmade. Not this part."

"That's because this is a dragon's nest."

I spun to face him. "A what?"

He grinned. "I knew you'd like it. Once upon a time, a female dragon lived in here and laid her eggs. See." He scooted his foot against the ground, and I heard a faint tinkling.

I looked down to see what I thought had been scree was actually shells. Or mostly shells. There was plenty of scree and other bits of rock and debris mixed in with it. "Wow. This is amazing. So there really are dragons at Arkwell."

"Well, yeah, I told you that, but they're not like the ones that used to live in these caves."

"How so?"

"The dragons that lived here died out a long time ago. Or I guess you could say they evolved into extinction."

Puzzled, I cocked my head. "How are the dragons different now?"

"Size mostly. And viciousness. Our modern dragons are a lot smaller, the size of elephants. But these"—he motioned toward the ceiling—"were the size of dinosaurs."

I gaped, unable to imagine it. I'd once seen a life-sized replica of a blue whale hanging in an entranceway of a museum. It was so large it felt like a cheap gag. My mind couldn't wrap itself around the idea that something that big could also be alive, that it could move and think on its own.

"Our modern dragons are also domesticated." Paul scrunched up his nose. "Sorta. Anyway, come on, there's a clearer spot over here."

He led the way along the nearest wall until we reached a cluster of stalagmites standing up in a rough circle. Inside the circle the floor was clear of dragon shells. An old blanket and several pillows filled the space, along with a couple of additional lanterns.

"I brought some stuff down ahead of time to make this more comfortable," Paul explained when I shot him a quizzical look at the item.

Stepping into the circle, Paul lit the lanterns with a wave of his hand. In the sudden burst of light, I noticed something odd on the nearby wall.

"What's that?" I pointed. Caveman drawings covered the stone. At least, that was what they looked like at first glance. But I soon saw they were more complex, akin to Egyptian hieroglyphs.

"Pretty cool, huh?" Paul said. "There's a lot of this prehistoric artwork in the dragon caves, even in the ones we're still using. Ms. Miller told me they were made by a prehistoric Native American tribe of witchkinds. The Iwatoke, I think they were called."

"The Iwatoke," I repeated, struggling with the strange word.

"They worshiped dragons, apparently. So most of this is about that." Paul stepped closer to the wall, letting the light expand over the surface. He pointed. "See over there, that's the hatching and there's the mating ritual, and so on."

I gawked, in awe of the scene before me. It was the kind of thing that made me want to grow up to be an archeologist, to become the magickind version of Indiana Jones or Lara Croft, minus the guns and killing bad guys. "I would love to go exploring down here."

"Oh, no you wouldn't," Paul said, turning to face me. "This is as safe as it gets. That tunnel over there is almost impassable." He pointed at another sloping tunnel leading downward nearby. "Even I'm not brave enough to go down there."

I considered walking over for a better look but then turned my gaze back to the wall. "Dangerous or not, it would be really—" The rest of my sentence got derailed as my eyes took in a familiar shape. The sight sent a chill slipping down my spine, every hair on my body standing up.

The drawing was of another dragon. This one lying in a perfect circle, its arms and wings drawn close to its serpentine body. The dragon's mouth was open and it was swallowing its own tail.

It was the ouroboros. Right out of Eli's dream.

~ 17 ~

Growing Pains

What's wrong, Dusty?"

Paul's voice broke through my shock, and I turned to stare at him, my mind still whirling. I turned back, walking over to the wall. I had to stretch my hand over my head to reach the ouroboros drawing. I ran my fingers over the rough surface, tracing the twist of the dragon's body.

"I don't get it," Paul said, hands on hips. "What's the big deal? That symbol is all over the place down here." He swung around and pointed at another spot on the wall. "Look, there's another and another." He pointed to two different areas on the wall, and I flinched at the sight of each ouroboros. Every inch of my skin was tingling.

I took a deep breath, trying to regain my composure before Paul became convinced I was having a psychotic break. "It's Eli's dream. We've seen this symbol."

"Oh." Paul's eyebrows drew together. "So you think it has an extra meaning?"

I nodded. "It has to, only I don't think it means quite what we thought it does."

"Huh?"

I glanced at him, uncertain of how much to tell him. Eli's

suspicions about him kept pinging in the back of my mind, tiny warning bells calling for caution. "Well, it's a symbol of rebirth and renewal, according to the Internet." Even the e-net, the magickind version of the Internet, said the same, and not much else. I'd made several searches about it over the last few days.

"You think it represents Marrow then?" Paul said.

Once again, I flinched, inhaling a quick breath. It felt wrong to discuss this with Paul. The contents and meanings in Eli's dreams were something I normally discussed with Eli, but so far we'd had little chance to talk. A lot of what we needed to talk about we couldn't with the Will Guard always around.

I ran a hand through my hair and faced him. The cat was too far out of the bag to try to wrangle it back in now. "Yeah, that's what we thought. I mean, we have reason to believe he's involved in the nondisclosure thing that the magickind Senate has us investigating."

"Oh, I see." He turned back to the wall, his gaze shifting between the various ouroboros symbols. "But I doubt these symbols have anything to do with Marrow. They were here even before his time, I'm sure."

"That's just it," I said, unable to keep the excitement from leaping up in my voice. "What if we were wrong that it represented Marrow? What if the dream's been pointing us toward the dragon caves all this time?"

Paul frowned. "I suppose it's possible."

Suddenly all I wanted was to race upstairs and find the nearest computer connected to the e-net. I wanted to know what a search string combining "ouroboros" with the "Iwatoke" would turn up.

Except, proving my mom's innocence was more important. That had to come first.

With an effort, I pulled my gaze away from the symbols on

the walls and focused on Paul. "I'll look into it later. Show me how to use this necklace."

Paul returned to the circle and I followed him into it. He faced me and withdrew a shape-change necklace from his pocket. It wasn't his, but similar. This one held a blue stone instead of green with the same hemp chain interwoven with oddly shaped opaque beads.

"I just got it last night, but it works pretty well," Paul said, stretching it out so I could see it better. "It defaults to a woman in her mid-thirties, I think. She's tall, easily my height or better. Her eyesight's not great, but otherwise, it's a decent shape."

"Your height?" I looked up at him, cringing. He had me by half a foot at least. "Is this going to hurt?"

Paul hesitated long enough for anxiety to begin churning in my stomach. "Not hurt exactly. It's just really uncomfortable. But you'll get used to it." He held the necklace out to me.

I took it, suddenly aware of how cold my fingers were, practically numb. It was chilly and damp down here, the familiar smell of canal water present as it was everywhere in Arkwell's vast underground, but I knew my current drop in temperature had more to do with what was coming. The necklace was lighter than I expected and undeniably magical. Already I felt its power tingling over my palm, ready to be unleashed.

I raised the necklace for a closer examination, anything to delay the next part a few seconds longer. My breath caught in my throat as I realized the white beads weren't beads at all. "Are these human *teeth*?"

"Yes." Paul winced. "But I try not to dwell on it."

"Gross." I resisted the urge to hand the thing back to him. The knowledge that it was comprised of teeth made it feel dark. Evil. Black magic. "How did you get a second one?" His necklace had come from the police as part of his witness protection gig, but

I doubted they would've given him another one just for kicks, not considering that they wanted to keep tabs on him.

"I got it from Mr. Culpepper," said Paul.

I frowned, my dislike of the thing in my hand increasing tenfold. Although Culpepper was okay, I didn't exactly love his side job. When he wasn't fixing things around the school he ran a black market, one that included black magic items. "So I take it this is illegal?"

Paul scratched his cheek, not quite meeting my gaze. "Kinda, a little."

I closed my eyes and inhaled, reining in my fear. *This is for Mom*. I reminded myself.

"It's all right, Dusty," Paul said. "We're not using it for anything evil, and we're not going to get caught."

He seemed pretty confident, way more than I did. Then again, he'd probably gotten away with a lot more than I'd ever attempted. It was a sobering thought. *Be careful,* I heard a voice like Eli's whisper in my mind. "But how did you get it from Culpepper? I imagine it was expensive."

"I traded him something for it." Paul pulled his cell phone out of his back pocket and checked his watch. "Damn, we need to hurry."

I nodded, my heartbeat picking up. "What do I have to do?"

"Just put it on. The necklace does all the work. You just need to hold still and let it happen. That's the hardest part."

"Why?"

"You'll see. Just don't take the necklace off, no matter what. Let the magic do its job. You'll know when it's done."

Ill at ease with such vague, unhelpful descriptions, I raised the necklace to my neck and fastened it. Magic blazed into life, sweeping over me like a blast of furnace air. My skin began to itch as if a thousand ants were crawling all over me. I looked down at my arms, convinced I would see the bugs. There was nothing there, the magic invisible. I could feel it inside me, burrowing beneath my skin.

In seconds, I understood why Paul said this was the hardest part. Every single instinct I possessed was screaming at me to remove the necklace. My body felt like it was being stretched and poked and pressed a hundred different ways. It was excruciating without being painful. Finally, I couldn't take it anymore. Shrieking, I raised my hands, ready to yank it off. Paul's fingers closed around my wrists, and he wrestled my hands away from the necklace.

"Don't fight it," he shouted over my protests. "You're almost there. And trust me, you don't want to start over again now."

I struggled uselessly against his grip for a moment, and then forced myself to relax. It was like trying to lie still and keep your mouth open with the dentist drilling into your teeth.

An eternity later, it came to an end. I opened my eyes, which I'd held shut the entire time and saw Paul looking at me with an odd expression. He let go of my wrists and stepped back.

"What?" I said, and jumped at the stranger's voice that had spoken my words. It was a deep voice, rough like a smoker's. I looked down and saw hands that didn't belong to me. They were older, the veins more prominent and etched with wrinkles. My clothes had transformed from my usual T-shirt and jeans into a turtleneck and cardigan ensemble over a pair of khakis whose waistband I felt pressing against my navel, several inches above where I normally wore it.

"It's weird looking at you at eye level," Paul said.

I stared at him, suddenly disoriented. It was like I was wearing stilts. I became aware of how much bigger my body was, how alien. I swayed on my feet.

"Whoa." Paul reached out to steady me.

I moved my right leg, widening my stance. "I'm okay. I think."

"This is why we're practicing," Paul said. "You've got to get used to the new dimensions."

"For real." I put my hands on my waist then dropped them away. It was like touching someone else.

Paul smiled encouragement. "That's it. Get used to it. When you're ready, try walking around."

I did as he suggested, first raising my hands to touch the top of my head. The hair was thinner than mine, smooth like silk and ending just above my shoulders. I touched my fingers to my face, feeling the more prominent brow and sharply angular nose. I ran my tongue over my teeth, the sensation of someone else's mouth probably the weirdest part of all.

Finally, I worked up the courage to try moving. It was difficult, especially in the dim light and uneven floor. More than once I had to stop and steady myself.

"You're going to have to be extra careful about any low ceilings," Paul called from inside the circle where he stood watching my progress. "You should wear the necklace on the way back up. That'll be good practice."

"You mean a good way to knock myself out," I said, stumbling over my too-large feet.

"If that happens I'll carry you out. Minus the shape-change necklace, of course."

"Good idea."

A short while later, I came to a stop and said, "I think I'm getting the hang of it."

"Good." Paul smiled and reached into his pocket, pulling out his cell again. He navigated a couple of screens and then held it up, pointed at me.

"What're you doing?"

"I need a picture of you like this."

I arched an eyebrow—at least I tried to, but this face didn't seem capable of the movement. Both eyebrows went up instead.

"For your fake ID," Paul said, making an adjustment on the screen. "You've got to be in the system when we go through the guard gate or there'll be questions."

"Huh." I put my hands on my hips. "They don't check IDs at the gate."

"They didn't used to. But things have changed since Lyonshold." Paul aimed the phone once more. "Smile."

I did, feeling a double dose of awkwardness than at a normal picture. I had no idea if this face would look better open-mouthed or closed, big smile or small, crinkled eyes or wide open.

The phone clicked and the bright flash struck my eyeballs. Paul lowered the camera and examined the result. "Not bad." He handed the phone over to me. I looked at the picture, intrigued by the stranger's face. She was average looking with dark brown hair, the kind of woman that wouldn't draw much notice. *A good disguise,* I decided.

I handed the phone back. "Are you sure you'll be able to make an ID out of that? It's so exposed."

Paul grinned. "Piece of cake with Lance's computer. Printing it will be harder, but there's equipment in the Menagerie. After that, all I've got to do is hack Arkwell's computers and add you to the database."

Bemused, I said, "That's a lot of criminal activity."

The grin slid from Paul's face. "I'm doing it for you."

I inhaled a sharp breath. "I know. Thank you, by the way."

A few seconds passed before he said, "You're welcome."

Smiling, I wracked my brain for a safer subject. "So . . . once we have the ID, how are we getting off campus?"

"I'm going to borrow a friend's car, this guy I work with in the Menagerie. He's the same one whose face I've been borrowing, actually."

I wrinkled my nose. I'd seen his alternate shape just the once, a dark-haired, dark-skinned man in his mid-thirties. "How does that work exactly?"

"It's all about the teeth, I'm afraid." He grimaced. "This one here is different from the rest of the necklace." He pointed to one of the beads that protruded a little further out than the rest on his necklace. "Took me awhile to figure it out, but if I focus hard enough on it, I can change into him."

A quiver went through my stomach. "Do you mean to say that the teeth in this necklace belonged to the woman whose face I'm wearing right now?"

"I'd thought that would've been obvious."

It was, but I'd been hoping the opposite. "But . . ." I raised my hand to the necklace and gingerly touched one of the teeth. "How did they get here?"

"I try not to think about it too hard," Paul said, his gaze on the floor.

I cleared my throat. This woman whose shape I was borrowing wasn't exactly young but she wasn't old either. Was she dead? The thought sent a shudder through my body. "How did you get your friend's tooth?"

Paul blew out a breath. "Pure luck. He got whacked in the face with a dragon tail and it knocked the tooth clean out. I managed to find it."

"Ew." I scrunched up my nose in disgust.

"I was desperate for a little freedom." He checked the time on his phone. "Damn. We need to go."

Paul turned, picked up the lantern, and began leading the way back. I followed after him, anxious not to be left behind. I might be keen on exploring this place, but I didn't like the idea of climbing out of here in the dark. Not in this strange body. Over and over again I bumped into the walls or tripped over my own feet. Paul had been right about the need to practice.

When we emerged from the tunnels, I pulled the necklace off. Undoing the shape-change proved a lot more comfortable than putting it on. In an instant I felt my skin and body snap back into its right form. Relief came over me like kicking off an ill-fitting pair of shoes after hours of walking. Sweet release. I heaved a happy sigh.

"Welcome back," Paul said.

"Thanks." I held up the necklace. "Should I keep this or you?"

"You," Paul answered at once. "And you should keep practicing. Maybe then you'll be ready by the time I've finished your ID."

"All right." I dropped my gaze to the necklace, able to see it more clearly in the light up here. It was hard to believe I ever could've mistaken the teeth for beads. *Teeth. From a dead woman. Black magic.*

I folded the necklace and slid it into my pocket. I thought I could understand why the rest of magickind had come down so hard on shape-changers, at least a little. They could steal your identity, your life, maybe even some of your soul.

Feeling dirty from the outside in, I vowed I would destroy the necklace as soon as this was over.

~ 18 ~

Breakthroughs

My first order of business after leaving the Menagerie was to head to my dorm room and fetch my eTab. Selene wasn't there when I arrived, and I wondered if she'd gone to gladiator practice. She hadn't said she was planning on it, but she might've changed her mind.

I pulled my cell out and examined the screen only to find I'd missed a text from Selene that she'd sent an hour ago. Either I hadn't felt the phone vibrate or the surly thing had chosen not to vibrate. Probably the latter.

In 013 if you want to hang after.

I checked the time and saw it was a little too early for dinner. Tucking the eTab under my arm, I left the dorm again, heading for the library. When I arrived in the hallway outside Room 013, I heard Selene shouting. I broke into a run and skittered around the corner into the room, my hand raised and a dazing curse on the tip of my tongue.

I froze, stunned by the scene that awaited me. Selene was indeed shouting, but it was at Buster and not some enemy. Only a second later, I realized that the chair *was* the enemy. It looked like the two of them were sparring. She was strafing side to side while across from her the chair rolled and darted.

"*Fligere!*" Selene shouted and a stream of blue light shot out from her fingertips. The jab jinx struck Buster right in the headrest. The chair went flying backward, spinning on its axle.

"What are you doing?" I said, completely taken aback. For a second, I considered casting a binding curse at her just to stop the abuse. Sure, Buster was a pain in the butt but this seemed excessive.

Selene spun toward me, a hard, focused look on her face and her hand still held out in front of her, ready to throw another spell.

"Whoa," I said, waving at her. "It's just me."

Selene relaxed at once, lowering her hand. A broad smile split her face. "Sorry, I was just really getting into it."

I shot her a confused look, my eyebrows doing the splits—one of them rising high and the other lowering. "Into it?"

"Practice," Selene said, pushing her long black braid behind her shoulder. "Tryouts are a week from Saturday."

I didn't know whether to laugh or shake her. "You're using Buster for target practice? Really?"

She shrugged. "He volunteered."

"How—never mind. Why didn't you just go to gladiator training with the boys?"

A mischievous glint flashed in Selene's eyes. "I don't want to give up the element of surprise. Plus, sign-ups for the class closed two weeks ago."

I sighed and sat down on the nearest chair, one thankfully not inclined toward animation. "You never cease to amaze me."

Selene waggled a finger at Buster, and the chair came rolling over to her at once, turning to offer its seat. It seemed it really didn't mind being used as target practice. *Dumb chair.*

Selene sat down and crossed one leg over the other. "You really should consider trying out with me. It's good training."

"For what?"

Selene's gaze seemed to pierce me. "Marrow's coming back someday, Dusty. We need to be ready for it." Silence hung heavy around us for a moment, the only noise the click and beep of the two computers in the far corner. It sounded like they were bickering.

I frowned, mostly because I knew she was right. Only— "What good will it really do to be able to fight him?"

Selene scoffed, hands on hips. "How about staying alive?"

"That's just it though." I idly began to twist Bellanax on my wrist. "*He* stays alive. Always. And no matter how good we learn to fight, it won't stop him, not for good."

Selene turned her head to the side, considering the idea. "There has to be some way."

"You think so? My grandmother imprisoned him in a dream, giving up her own life to keep him there and he still came back."

"Well, yes," Selene said, "but we can't know for sure that was the only option she had. Maybe she did know a way to kill him for good, but chose not to do it."

"What makes you say that?" I forced my hand away from Bellanax.

"They were dream-seers," Selene said, matter-of-factly.

"So what?"

"She loved him. Maybe she decided imprisoning him in a dream was more humane than the alternative." Selene leaned back, propping one leg on top of the other. "I don't know much about Nightmare magic, but it seems to me that if he was imprisoned in a dream of her own making maybe she could visit him in the dream."

A weightless feeling came over me at the thought. Was it possible? Powerful Nightmares could enter dreams from afar, but Nimue and Marrow had been on separate continents—she asleep here beneath Arkwell with Bellanax hidden in her dream while Marrow had been in the UK somewhere. Only, did dreams really have boundaries? They didn't seem to. They didn't obey the rules of time, the laws of physics. They could go anywhere, anytime, every dream connected to another in some vast eternal web.

"Wouldn't you do the same?" Selene said. "If Eli turned out evil and you had to stop him, I mean."

The notion of Eli turning evil was absurd, but I could see her point. Would I choose as Nimue had? Would a life spent in a shared dream, able to see and talk to Eli but never touch him, be better than ending it forever? It wasn't a choice I wanted to make—ever.

"Maybe," I said, meeting Selene's gaze. "But we don't know that Nimue could've done something else."

"Exactly."

I touched a finger to the silver band on my wrist. *Do you know?* The sword hummed in my mind but nothing more. If it did know, maybe the psychometry would reveal it. More and more I was ready to give it a try, but the last thing Deverell had said before he went out on sick leave was that I needed to gain more control first.

"Anyway," Selene said. "How'd it go with Paul?"

Relieved at the change in subject, I filled her in. While I did, I sat down and opened my eTab to a search window.

"Teeth?" Selene said, a look of disgust twisting her lips.

"Apparently."

She began to fiddle with the end of her braid. "I suppose that makes sense though. They say the tooth fairy myth was created by shape-changers."

I looked up from the screen. "Really? I figured the tooth fairy would turn out to be real."

Selene laughed. "Not hardly. No more than Santa Claus."

I was strangely bummed by this news.

"Shape-changers made it up as an easy way to get a hold of teeth," Selene continued. "But once they died out, ordinaries just kept on doing it anyway."

I nodded, having heard similar stories before. "But what did they want with baby teeth?"

"Beats me." Selene inclined her head toward the computer. "What are you looking up?"

I faced the screen. "I need to figure out the significance of the Iwatoke and the ouroboros."

"The what and the what?"

I explained the connection between Eli's dreams and the dragon caves. As I talked, I entered the search string and started sifting through the results. Right away the first hit caught my eye—*Iwatoke and the Cult of Resurrection.*

I clicked on it and scanned the first couple of paragraphs before slowing down to read one more carefully:

Perhaps the most intriguing aspect of the Iwatoke culture is their belief in the Great Ouroboros, a legendary dragon who died swallowing its own tail. At the moment of its death, the dragon's body was said to have hardened into stone, creating a walled space set in a perfect circle. The Iwatoke believed the area within the ouroboros circle to be holy, and that it possessed extraordinary restorative powers. They claimed that any person close to death or recently departed could be returned to life if set in the center of the circle. Some accounts state an accompanying spell was needed to activate the magic in the ouroboros, while others say only those blessed by the Great Dragon were granted the power of resurrection.

However, despite the discovery of nearly a dozen ouroboros circles throughout the lands of Ohio, Indiana, West Virginia, and Kentucky, none of them have possessed any magical properties whatsoever. In fact, most appear to be carved of various naturally occurring materials such as limestone, flint, or granite. Although some more determined treasure hunters continue the search for a real ouroboros circle, the magickind historic and scientific communities have determined that the Great Ouroboros was simply a myth perpetuated by the Iwatoke.

I didn't read any further but went back to the search page and clicked on another link. It said much the same thing, although with a little more detail on the supposed ritual as well as speculation on what purpose the myth might have served within the Iwatoke culture.

After exploring a couple of other links, disappointment set in. It seemed the ouroboros simply meant what Eli and I had originally thought—Marrow. Their presence in the dragon caves must be mere coincidence.

"No luck?" Selene said.

"Looks that way." I cracked my knuckles. "But what else is new?"

"Come on, then," Selene said, standing up. "Will you help me train for the gladiator tryouts? You'll make a more interesting opponent than Buster here."

The chair made a disappointed noise.

"Are you sure that's a good idea?" I said, glancing around the room.

Selene waved off my concern. "We'll just pass a few volleys. No big deal."

Ha ha—right.

Selene's few volleys ended up being a spectacle of blood and bruises.

Without protective gear, we could only trade shots back and forth, either blocking with a shield spell or trying to repel them with the counter-curse. Yeah, in hindsight it probably wasn't the best idea we'd ever had. I realized it when Selene failed to repel my dazing curse all the way. I'd thrown it without any real heat or force. Nevertheless, blood burst from her lip as it glanced off her face.

"Oh, God, Selene, I'm sorry." I took a step toward her, just as she threw a dazing curse my way. It was too late to block, too late to do anything except raise my hands in front of my face and hope for the best.

The spell struck me, and then . . . nothing. One moment the magic was there and the next it was gone as if it had never been. Except around my wrist, I sensed Bellanax's presence grow stronger, more physically real somehow.

But the realization mattered for less than a second as pain exploded in my knees. Shrieking, I looked down to see that Buster was in full attack mode. The chair had just careened into my legs and was already backing up to do it again.

"Heel, you stupid thing," I shouted at it. But it only pealed its wheels and charged forward.

A jet of magic struck it just before it crashed into me. Buster careened sideways and tipped over. Its wheels kept spinning wildly, but once it was down there was no way it was getting up on its own.

I glanced at Selene. "Thanks. And wow, I'm really sorry about your face."

She grinned and gently probed her bleeding lip. "Looks like I need to work on that one. And sorry about that spell. It was reaction. But at least you blocked it."

"No problem," I said, and felt Bellanax warming against my skin. I hadn't blocked it, and neither had the sword. Instead, Bellanax had absorbed the magic into itself. I could feel the increased power even now, like a buzz of electricity dancing over my skin. I stared down at it, wondering at this newest development. It had never shielded me from a spell before. Maybe all the mind-magic exercises Deverell had me doing was finally having an effect. The sword did seem more accessible than ever. It was as if there'd been a bad cell phone connection between us before, full of static and nebulous existence. Now it was as clear and steady as a landline.

Deciding we'd done enough damage for one evening, Selene righted Buster, gave the chair a pat, and then we left for the cafeteria.

"What the hell happened to you?" Lance said as we arrived, his eyes fixed on Selene's injured face. His expression turned instantly murderous.

She and I exchanged a look.

Then Selene faced Lance, letting a slow, sultry smile spread over her lips. I wasn't sure how she could do it without wincing from pain, but she did. It was so dazzling it made the injury look weirdly sexy.

"We got to goofing around in room oh-thirteen," she said. "No big deal." She rolled her shoulders, turning up the charm even more, but I could tell she wasn't using her siren magic. She didn't need to. Not with Lance.

His glare turned into a soppy grin. I sat down across from Eli, suddenly very grateful that my injuries from our sparring session weren't visible. I had a feeling a smile and a wink wouldn't cut it with Eli, not considering that I'd spent a good hour alone with Paul earlier today.

But at least when I gave him the recap of my trip down to the dragon caves, he kept his cool. Mostly, I think, because he was so intrigued by the Iwatoke and the ouroboros.

"But the search didn't turn up anything?" he asked.

"Unfortunately, no."

Eli drummed his fingers on the table. "I'd still like to get a look at the cave. Maybe Paul can take us both down there next time."

I nodded, trying to hide my relief that he was relaxing a little about Paul.

"I've found out something new, too," Eli said a few moments later. "But it'll have to wait until we're alone."

After dinner he and I headed back to the library for some studying and a private chat. As usual, a couple of Will Guards trailed behind us. I didn't understand how they could always be so on it. I never caught them following me when I was by myself or with Selene. Only when I was with Eli. They were getting more and more obvious about it. Tonight they were so pursuant that Eli and I had to retreat to the farthest corner of the study room we'd selected—one conveniently devoid of anyone else—and even then he had to whisper before the nondisclosure spell would let him speak.

"Remember when I asked Valentine if the Death's Heart was a real heart?" Eli said.

Slowly, the conversation came back to me. "He wasn't sure, right?"

"Yes, but now I think—" He paused and glanced at the door where we'd both heard a noise. When no one came inside, he turned back to me. "—That it's the heart of a Grim Reaper."

"Like a real Grim Reaper? The personification of death itself?" I couldn't keep the doubt from my voice.

Eli nodded. "I know it sounds crazy, but I guess they were some kind of corporeal spirit. Only none have been seen for centuries."

"Nice," I said, folding my arms over my chest. "So Santa Claus is bogus but Grim Reapers are the genuine article. What does that say about the world?"

Eli smiled ruefully. "I don't know, but are you thinking what I'm thinking?"

I stared at him, uncertain. Then a chill inched down my neck as I remembered the scythe my mom had been holding in the dream. "That my mom is connected to the Death's Heart?"

"It seems that way."

Yes, it did. "But how?"

Eli opened his mouth to answer, but it was no good. The Will Guards chose that moment to come in and drive us out.

"It's getting late," one of them said. "You two should be heading back to your dorms. Alone."

"No kidding," I muttered, my mood suddenly bleak.

That bleakness did not improve. The next few days the Will Guard got worse and worse about breaking Eli and I apart. I tried to keep my spirits up by focusing on freeing my mom, but it was taking Paul longer than expected to finish the ID. Even worse, every time I e-mailed Lady Elaine asking to see my mother, she kept putting me off—*the cell's not ready yet.* Which meant my mom was still under the sleeping spell.

At least training with Selene was helping keep me busy. She and I spent several hours both Saturday and Sunday practicing in Room 013 while the boys were at gladiator training. Selene had managed to borrow a couple of gladiator helmets from the school's storeroom for our use. She'd gotten lucky late Friday night when she snuck into the gym to steal a couple, only to find Culpepper there cleaning up. He liked her almost as much as he liked me, and so had let her borrow two with minimal fuss and grumbling.

The addition of the helmets made gladiator training less perilous, although not incident free. Selene was sporting bruises up and down both arms and along one hip by the time Monday rolled around. For me, I hadn't gotten so much as a broken fingernail. Every time I failed to block a spell, Bellanax was there, ready to absorb it. It was comforting to feel so indestructible.

If only Bellanax was capable of protecting me from emotional attacks, same as magical ones. But no, as Bollinger proved in seconds of arriving at my dorm that night to escort me to the dreamsession with Eli. I tried my best to ignore her mutterings and complaints, the not-so-veiled insults, but by the time we arrived at Flint Hall, I was ready to try the asunder curse again.

Bellanax burned around my wrist. *Shut up, shut up.*

"Then again," Bollinger was saying, "I suppose I shouldn't be that surprised you're the one who broke the Will spell. Especially given your murderess of a mother." Bollinger pushed the door open and stepped inside. "*Hupno-drasi!*"

Eli was just standing up from his desk when the spell struck him in the chest. His eyes slid closed, and he slumped to the floor, whacking his head as he fell.

"You . . . you evil, awful person!" I pushed past her into the dorm.

"That's rich coming from a Nightmare," Bollinger said, completely unconcerned. She pointed her wand at Eli again and muttered a spell I didn't know. His body rose into the air, his limbs jerking awkwardly. She levitated him across the room and dropped him onto the sofa.

Then she turned to face me once more. "Get on with it before I decide to use the same spell on you."

Go ahead and try. My hand rose automatically to my wrist. Bellanax roared inside my head, demanding to be unleashed. The incantations to a half-dozen spells flitted through my mind, each as easy to pluck out and use as selecting a pen from a drawer. *You can destroy her. Silence her forever.*

My vision blurred. I started to slide the silver band from my wrist. In another moment the glamour would be off.

No! I gritted my teeth, wrestling for control. I couldn't do this. Not now, not here with this woman watching. Bollinger had been a Will-Worker, she might recognize Bellanax.

Destroy her! The sword shouted in my mind. It gave up its attempt to be free from the glamour. But it didn't need to be free for me to use the spells it offered. It would be so easy. So satisfying.

No. This time the thought was firm in my mind, and a moment later I felt the fight go out of the sword entirely as it surrendered to my will.

Bollinger watched me with an annoyed expression. "What are you waiting for? Get on with it."

Wiping sweat from my brow, I walked past her over to Eli. Trembles of anger still slid through my body, but there was triumph there, too. I'd come so close to giving up control to Bellanax, but I hadn't. Deverell would be proud when he heard.

You should consider yourself lucky, I thought, glancing back at Bollinger. And that, too, made me feel better, a strange, new sort of power—the power not to act.

Clinging to this victory, I climbed onto Eli and descended into his dreams.

～ 19 ～

Proceed with Caution

We were on the barge again. And this time it wasn't deserted. My dead body was once more lying on the ouroboros bed, but it didn't disturb me quite as much as before. Maybe because of the comfortable weight of Bellanax around my wrist, the sure knowledge that it could hand me spells at will. Nothing could hurt me with the sword around.

Still, I could tell it bothered Eli. I watched as he bent toward my body, his eyes drawn and face shadowed. He studied my corpse as if trying to read some clue of how I died there. I stared, too, ignoring the creep factor. But in seconds, I felt certain we weren't going to learn anything by just looking.

Mustering my courage, I leaned forward, took hold of the burial shroud covering my chest, and pulled it back all the way. Beneath, I was wearing a white gown of a design from a long-gone era, circa the age of King Arthur and my great-great grandmother Nimue. A swath of red as bright as paint stained the gown on the left side of the chest.

Right over the heart. My breath caught in my throat and a wrench went through my rib cage like a phantom pain of the same injury I was seeing below. With my heart starting to pound in my ears, I reached out and tentatively pulled down the collar of the gown, just enough to reveal the open, weeping puncture wound. It was easily the width of three fingers and looked deep enough to have gone all the way through to the other side. Not that I was about to flip the body over to make certain.

Beside me, I heard Eli make a choking noise. I glanced at him and realized it wasn't a sound of revulsion but of despair.

"Cover it up," Eli said, turning away.

I obeyed, as eager to hide it as he was and wishing I hadn't looked in the first place. Absently twisting the silver band on my wrist, I stepped nearer to Eli.

"Are you okay?" I asked. Even though I spoke softly, my words echoed in the cavernous space.

Eli faced me, his gaze hooded. A muscle in his jaw moved in and out. "I've been better." He raised his hands to his temple and pressed for a second. "Seeing you dead or hurting or anything other than happy is really starting to get old."

"I know," I said. I was tired of both seeing myself in his dreams and of seeing him unhappy in my own dreams. The attack was relentless and perpetually cruel. "But the best thing we can do is get this solved. The sooner we find the Death's Heart, the sooner these dreams will stop. I'm sure of it."

Eli's jaw worked back and forth. "Are you?"

I flinched, his doubt a physical blow. "Of course I am. Aren't you? Please tell me you're not starting to buy into all of this." I motioned behind us toward the ouroboros bed. "It's all just symbols, Eli. Nothing means what it appears to on the surface. And we already know my mother is in danger. This is just more of that." My voice broke, tears threatening to make an appearance. Yet again today, I'd been told I couldn't see her.

He didn't reply, and I felt my heart tumble from my chest into my stomach. I couldn't take the idea that he might change his mind about us. Not now, with everything going on. I needed things to be right between us, the possibility of the curse far, far away.

Finally, he drew a breath and said, "I've seen this before. You lying just like that, with just that wound." He pointed to the corpse lying between us. "I've seen it in my own dreams, and I've seen it in—" He broke off at a strange noise. It was a loud moan of wood bending, the sound a tree makes when its bough breaks in the wind.

Eli and I both headed toward it, stepping out from the curtained platform and onto the prow of the ship. The source of the noise became apparent at once. The masthead, which before had been carved into a dragon not much different from the ouroboros bed, was now the likeness of a giant bird. It had the head and neck of a heron, but with the crest of a harpy eagle, two tufts like feathered horns. The bird's wooden façade was beginning to crack and splinter like an eggshell. Real feathers as black as wet ink appeared beneath. Slowly, loudly the masthead was coming to life.

It was becoming the black phoenix—Marrow's familiar.

Eli and I could only watch, horrorstruck and frozen in place. As before there was nowhere to go in the dream but out of it. Not unless we wanted to try our luck with the dark water surrounding the boat, filled with its unknown water creatures.

The cracking and splintering wood continued on until the entire bird was revealed, including the red plumage of its tail. The black phoenix, now free and here and alive, arched its head and spread its wings, the gesture a stretch of pleasure.

Its sharp, hooked beak opened and it let out a shriek. The sound pierced my eardrums, and it was all I could do to cover my ears with my hands. But it was an invasive sound, crawling inside me somehow, making my insides writhe like worms. I felt my body start to crumple, my torso bending toward my knees as if the sound was a down force as well, like gravity.

I fought to keep my head up and my eyes on the black phoenix. It turned toward Eli and me, its red eyes boring into mine with sentient recognition.

Fear seemed to rip me asunder, my heart a quaking, quivering thing in my chest. I was paralyzed with it, unable to think or move, unable to do anything but stare, transfixed by its gaze.

I was barely aware of Eli beside me, his body trembling with the same fear that held me in its grip. But then he reached out and grabbed me by the arm.

Pain seared through my body, and the dream world melted into non-reality as I felt my consciousness being hurled out of it. I rejoined my body with an agonizing jolt, landing so hard I started to tumble sideways. Eli's arms rose up around me, creating a buffer.

He pulled me to him, holding me in place on top of him. "I'm sorry," he said, panting. "But it was the fastest way out."

"You mean the most painful," I said, groaning. At the moment it felt like every nerve ending in my body had been dosed in acid.

"I'm sorry, Dusty." Eli hugged me to him again and then began to run his hands up and down my back. Slowly the pain of being evicted from his dream gave way to pleasant tingles.

I pushed myself up a little, enough to glance behind me at Bollinger. She was asleep in her chair. I turned back to Eli, disbelieving our luck. "You're awake this time," I whispered.

Eli glanced at Bollinger, too, and lowered his voice. "I know. Maybe your painful exit broke the sleeping spell." He paused. "That or fear. I can't believe we saw the black phoenix."

"Me, either." The last time we'd seen it in a dream, it had cut my arm with one of its claws. I still bore the scar.

Worry about the significance of the black phoenix's presence in Eli's dream threatened to distract me, but with an effort I forced it away. The dream, the threat, Marrow, everything else could wait.

I glanced over my shoulder again, making sure of Bollinger's position. She was facing away from us, and deeply asleep judging by the fictus coming off her. I turned back to Eli. For all intents and purposes we were truly, officially alone, unwatched and undeterred, so long as we stayed quiet. I wanted to make the most of this moment, no matter how selfish it might be, no matter that I had to steal it away from more important things.

I inhaled then leaned forward, letting a slow easy smile stretch across my lips. "Did you notice that we've come into some unexpected privacy?"

Eli nodded, a grin forming at the edges of his mouth. It was all the encouragement I needed. Closing my eyes, I pressed my lips to his. My skin heated, an avalanche of tingles spreading over my face. Eli's lips parted and his tongue met mine, sweet and soft and inviting.

His hands moved to my waist and began to climb up my back beneath my shirt. His warm fingers left trails of fire over my skin. My head began to swim with sensation, my thoughts nonsensical like a fever dream. Eli pushed himself into a sitting position, and I shifted down to straddle his lap now. We moved slowly, quietly, afraid of waking Bollinger no matter how heavy a sleeper she seemed to be. His hands left my back and cupped my face, our kiss deepening. I placed my hands on his shoulders, taut muscles flexing beneath my fingers.

Things were escalating quickly. We were like a train with no brakes, headed downhill with a drunken conductor at the controls. Fear and thrill met inside me, blending into a singular feeling: want.

I tried to convey this to Eli through silent communication, kiss and touch, anything but words. I even thought it at him, employing telepathy and empathy both. For a stretch of blissful, soaring moments, I sensed Eli's answer, a resounding yes, more echo than consent.

But then he began to pull back from me, withdrawing both his body and his mind.

"We can't do this, Dusty," he whispered.

I nodded, remembering Bollinger. "Do you want to go in there?" I motioned toward the sleeping quarters.

Eli shook his head.

"Right, Lance." I bit my lip. "I could use a sleeping spell on Bollinger. I know how to do it now." It was true. I could sense Bellanax coiled and ready to guide me. Eager for it.

"How?" Eli said, his arms tensing around me.

I ran my hand down his cheek. "Same as before. I'm learning how to communicate better with the sword."

Eli's expression darkened. "No, I don't want you to use a spell on her. I don't like that sword teaching you things. There's something not right about it."

"Why?" I cocked my head. "My sword is a numen vessel just like your wand. That means there's a living spirit in it, one with thoughts and a personality."

Eli glanced at the leather band on his wrist, his glamoured wand. "But my wand never speaks to me. It's just there, just magic for me to use."

"Maybe it's a difference in the type of vessel or something."

"Or in the spirit it houses," Eli said.

I sighed, caressing his face once more. "There's nothing to worry about from my sword. I promise." I leaned forward and kissed his cheek. "So how about it? She won't even know afterward, and we'll be free to do whatever we want without worry of someone finding out."

"No," Eli said at once. "Not here, not now."

His words felt like a slap, the sharp, certain sting of rejection. I forced my eyes to his, afraid of what I would see there. "Why?"

His expression softened, and he cupped my face again, running a thumb over my bottom lip, swollen from his kisses. "Because this isn't right. It's not how it should be with us."

"What do you mean?" I felt my heart folding in on itself, disappointment a compressive force.

Eli released his hold on my face and reached for my hands instead, squeezing my fingers. "We're dream-seers, Dusty. That's a bond for life. No matter what happens to us in our everyday lives, we'll always be connected by this power. It's an awesome thing, but scary. We gotta make sure we don't screw up by going too fast."

I inhaled, my quivering heart solidifying to awe. No matter how much my body may hate the idea of taking things slow, it did make sense. Reckless wasn't the right approach to forever.

"Okay," I said. "I see your point." But I leaned forward and kissed him again. One last time, while we still could.

Eli seemed to agree, and his hands slid around my waist, pulling me closer.

The dorm room door slammed open hard. Bollinger jerked awake, and fell out of the chair with a muffled thump. Eli and I wrenched our faces apart, but it was too late to hide the position of our bodies from the people now crowding into the room.

There were two Will Guards—of course, who else?—but also Lady Elaine. The look she cast us was one of mingled fury and fear. I gulped and started to disengage myself from Eli, climbing out of his lap.

Lady Elaine swooped down on us. "Have you seen her? Heard from her?"

I stumbled to a standing position. "Who? What are you talking about?"

Lady Elaine grabbed me by the shoulders. "Your mother! Has she texted you, called, anything in the last few hours?"

"What?" I was too stunned to free myself from her grip. "No, of course not. Not for days."

Tears glistened in Lady Elaine's eyes. "Are you sure you're not covering for her? Please, Dusty, tell me the truth."

Fear electrified my skin. "No, I'm not covering, I swear. What's happened?"

"Your mother . . ." Lady Elaine swallowed. "She's gone missing. Just like Bethany Grey."

— 20 —

Three Visions

Lady Elaine turned away from me and sat down on the nearest chair, sagging into it like a warrior in defeat. Her large
purse, bright pink and covered in sunflowers, slid off her frail arm
and landed beside her. The sight of her reaction scared me more
than the news about my mother.

"I'd hoped you were covering for her," Lady Elaine said, dropping her forehead onto her hand. "It's why I came here instead
of calling, but I can tell you're not lying." She looked up, her
expression scornful as she took in Eli and me. "No, not lying.
You two were clearly too busy with your own indulgences for
that."

The accusation slid right by me, my fear too slippery for anything to dislodge it. "How can she be missing?"

"She's just not there. I don't know how. At one check the cell
was full, at the next empty." Lady Elaine turned her gaze onto
Bollinger who was hovering nearby and listening intently. "But
this is a conversation that requires privacy." She stood up and
smoothed the front of her khakis. "Go on, Dusty. We can use the
rec room."

I started toward the door, but froze as Lady Elaine said, "Not you, Mr. Booker. You will stay here. You should be ashamed of yourself after the promise you made me."

I turned back in time to see Eli stiffen and his face go red. My stomach did a backflip. *What promise?* But I could only guess.

"And you"—Lady Elaine swung toward Bollinger—"will no longer be assigned this duty. Clearly, you are unfit for the post."

Bollinger's nostrils flared, and I braced, waiting for the fireworks to start. But Bollinger only pressed her lips together and nodded. So she might be a horrible person, but not a stupid one. *Go figure.*

"Go on, Dusty," Lady Elaine said, shooing me.

"Please," Eli's voice cut through the air. I turned to look at him again, but his eyes were fixed on Lady Elaine. "Please don't do this."

Do what? I thought, wishing he could hear it.

"It's too late," said Lady Elaine. "You knew the consequences."

Then with that, she physically pushed me toward the door. I fought in vain to read some warning in Eli's expression, but he dropped his gaze to the floor, his lips pressed into a tight line.

Fear thrummed inside me with each step I took down the stairs. I had never been inside the rec room of Flint Hall, but I had no trouble finding it. I passed by it every night that I came to a dream-session. When I tried to open the door, I found it locked.

Lady Elaine brushed me aside and then opened the door with a single wave of her hand. I stepped inside first, blinking in the sudden brightness. The room was large and perfectly square, full of armchairs, several ottomans, one careworn sofa, and numerous small tables. A single pinball machine occupied the far corner, its red and blue lights twinkling against the wall. Across from it was a pool table, the green velvet top ratty and faded near to yellow.

"You two can wait out here," Lady Elaine said to the Will Guards who had followed us down from Eli's room. Of Bollinger, there was no sign.

Lady Elaine slammed the door closed and swung to face me. "Sit down," she said.

I dropped into the nearest armchair and waited while she sealed the room against eavesdroppers. When she finished she took the armchair opposite mine. It dwarfed her small body, making her look like a very old doll. Her thin, spindly legs dangled several inches above the floor. Her massive purse sat beside her like some loyal pet.

"Tell me about my mom," I said, before she had a chance to steer the conversation anywhere else.

Lady Elaine folded her arms over her concave chest. "I'm afraid there's little else to say. She has disappeared as mysteriously as Bethany Grey and in much the same circumstances."

I ran my tongue over my teeth. "But Valentine thought my mom had kidnapped Bethany."

Lady Elaine tsked. "We both know that was never true. Just as we both know your mother did not kill Titus."

Relief made me feel weightless for a moment. It didn't last long. My mom's innocence hardly mattered with her missing. A chill inched across my neck as I remembered the scythe. "Her disappearance is about the Death's Heart, isn't it? Whoever stole it plans to use it on her."

"Why do you say that?" Lady Elaine tilted her head. Her silver hair was pulled back in a severe bun, and long, golden earrings hung from her drooping lobes.

"The scythe my mom was holding in Eli's dream," I said, guessing she would remember the description from my dream journal. "It's a symbol of the Grim Reaper, and that ties it to the

Death's Heart, which is made from the heart of a Grim Reaper."

Lady Elaine cleared her throat, and a humorless smile flitted across her lips. "The Dream Team astounds again."

I didn't smile in return, taking no pride in the discovery. I couldn't with my fear worsening by the second. "But why use the Death's Heart on my mother, on Bethany? Is it because they're both Nightmares?"

"Who can say?" Lady Elaine rubbed her temples. "Nightmares are powerful and a rarer form of magickind perhaps, but to my knowledge that makes no difference to the Death's Heart. Maybe they were kidnapped for a more personal reason. Like revenge."

"Against them both?" I gaped. "But they hated each other. How could they have a common enemy?"

"They didn't always hate each other," Lady Elaine said, crossing one leg over the other. "When they were your age, they were friends, as close as you and Selene Rivers are now."

I stared, wide-eyed, unable to imagine it. I wondered briefly what had come between them, but then the contents of Eli's latest dream soared into the forefront of my mind. "This is about Marrow. The Death's Heart, my mother, all of it."

Lady Elaine waved me off. "There's no reason to jump to that conclusion."

"Yes there is." I leaned forward. "The black phoenix was in Eli's dream tonight. We were on the barge again, the same one where we saw my mother with the scythe, and the black phoenix was there."

Lady Elaine visibly paled. "That's . . . that's disturbing news."

Silence descended around us, broken only by the chirp and whirring of the pinball machine.

Drawing a deep breath, Lady Elaine sat up straighter and fixed her gaze on me. "Disturbing yes, but also not your concern."

"Excuse me?" I sat up straighter, too, ready to get to my feet and start pacing. "My mom is missing, kidnapped by either Marrow or someone working for him, most likely. How is that not my concern?"

"Because," Lady Elaine said, "your primary concern needs to be keeping that object around your wrist hidden and safe. If Marrow is back—"

"Yeah, yeah, I know. He'll be coming for it." Wrapping my arms around myself, I fell back against the cushions. "But I don't see how doing nothing is going to help."

"Don't do nothing. Stay focused on the dream and stay safe. Go to classes, do your homework, and don't wander anywhere out of the norm. Not for anything or any*one*."

I braced at her words, fear surging through me again. I didn't have to be psychic to know what was coming next.

"And even more important than that," Lady Elaine continued, her eyes narrowing. "you must stop these romantic interactions with Eli. I thought he would have self-control enough for the both of you, but after what I walked in on tonight, clearly not."

My face heated, but my insides turned cold. "I'm old enough to have romantic interactions with any boy I want. And you're not my mother. You have no right to try to stop me. There's nothing wrong about my relationship with Eli."

Lady Elaine did not react to my outburst, her voice calm, almost a whisper as she said, "There is plenty wrong with it when you're a dream-seer."

Thrusting out my chin, I said, "I don't believe in the curse."

Lady Elaine sighed and shook her head, her expression more

sad than angry. "You don't have to. It's real and coming for you whether you believe or not."

I inhaled, all the bad dreams swimming into my mind. It couldn't be true. It couldn't. Our feelings for each other were in our control, our choice. No curse, no magic could change that.

"But you're right," Lady Elaine continued, her tone now diplomatic. "I can't stop you from pursuing a relationship with Eli."

I stared at her, distrustful of the sudden switch.

She waved a hand at me. "Oh, don't look so shocked. I've known from the beginning all I could do was slow you down. You are Moira's daughter, after all, and nothing can stop you from going after what you want but yourself."

I bit my lip unsure if I should take this as a compliment or not. "Does this mean you're going to call off the Will Guard?"

Lady Elaine scowled. "Of course not. A deterrent is still a deterrent. No—" She stopped and drew a deep breath. "I'm just going to share with you my vision of your future."

The world seemed to pitch sideways for a second. "I don't want to see it."

"Yes, I know. But it's well past time. I've only held off this long because Eli begged me to, and because he swore that he would be the one to keep things distant between you." She made a disgusted noise deep in her throat as she pulled her purse onto her lap and reached inside it.

The purse was so large she could have any number of things stowed in there—the entire contents of her makeup drawer, a portable DVD player, an Uzi. She withdrew a round object wrapped in thick black velvet. She pulled back the cloth to reveal a mirror the size of a dinner plate. Golden filigree framed the edge. For a moment I thought it was elaborate decoration, but then I realized those swirls and hard lines were rune marks, similar to the ones etched onto my eTab.

"What is that?" I said, my voice strangely tremulous. The mirror held undeniable magic. The entire room seemed to vibrate with it.

"It's a scrying mirror. It helps focus my visions." Lady Elaine paused, her gaze penetrating as she turned it on me. "And to share them."

I gulped, fear constricting my throat. Whatever she was about to show me was going to be bad. Eli had seen it already, and it had bothered him enough that he'd spent months trying to deny his feelings for me afterward. Would the same happen to me? I didn't think so. I'd seen visions of the future before, all the time in Eli's dreams.

Not like this.

No, not like this. This was a vision about *my* future. And it wasn't dreams and symbols.

Across from me, Lady Elaine summoned a table with her magic, setting it down right in front of me. Then she gently placed the mirror face up on the table. My gaze was drawn to the glass surface. A faint glow seemed to emanate out of the glass. With an effort I forced my eyes back to Lady Elaine.

"I don't want to see this. I don't care what you show me. It's not going to change my mind."

"Maybe not," Lady Elaine said. "Then again, maybe it will. I can only hope."

My stomach clenched. I could sense the magic growing in the room. The mirror's surface no longer looked solid, but liquid, like I could plunge my hands into it. "This isn't fair. All I want is to be free to kiss my boyfriend without having to hide like some kind of criminal."

"Yes, it's not fair, and yet it is," Lady Elaine said, her voice becoming almost a chant. She laid her palms against the mirror's edge, her fingers splayed. "You have been given a great power. But no power comes without a price. That is how magic works. How the universe works. All things kept in balance."

Hurt squeezed my chest, making my words come out breathless. "I didn't ask for this power. What if I give it up? What if I never visit Eli's dreams again? Then we can be together without anybody caring."

Lady Elaine's eyes flashed. "Is that really what you would choose? A boy over the ability to foresee and stop great evil?"

Shame heated my skin. No, of course I wouldn't. But— "Mr. Corvus says no magic exists within a vacuum. If I give up my dream-seer power it will go to someone else eventually, right?"

Lady Elaine shook her head. "It won't just transfer elsewhere. No, if you give up your power our enemies will gain power. They will grow stronger, the world out of balance."

I clenched my teeth, struggling to resist the pull of the mirror, which was even stronger now.

"Look at it," Lady Elaine commanded. "Your vision awaits."

At her words, my resistance broke, and I leaned forward, gazing fully into the mirror for the first time. For a moment, nothing but my reflection stared back at me.

In the next, I was pulled into the vision as if descending into a dream. Only, it wasn't like a dream at all. It was like watching a movie in 3-D. I could only observe, nothing more. I couldn't act or scream or protest. I could only watch as the horror unfolded.

I saw Eli, and I saw myself. We were standing across from each other, our stances one of anger—of hate. We looked exactly as we did now, no older. This could be tomorrow or the next day.

We were about to fight. Eli had his hand clenched around his wand, raised and pointed at me. Clutched in my hands was Bellanax, free of the glamour—three feet of naked steel, honed and sharp and pulsating with magic.

Just as I saw, I also felt. I was in the head of this future me, sharing her thoughts, her feelings like they were my own. Hatred burned in my guts; my heart quivered with it. I wanted him dead. I wanted it more than I'd ever wanted anything before. That want was a living thing, a will, a force, acting inside me, through me.

Eli felt it, too. I could see it burning in his eyes.

We fought. Spell after spell, curse after curse. He parried and I countered. I struck, and he blocked. But in the end a Conductor was no match for a Nightmare, and his pitiful wand was little more than a twig next to Bellanax.

Finally, one of my spells struck him in the head, and he reeled backward, falling down in a lifeless heap. Only he wasn't dead. Not yet. With rage and hatred burning like lit gasoline inside me, I strode over to him, Bellanax raised.

Don't, I wanted to scream but couldn't. I had no voice here. Even worse, I wanted to do it. I was two people at the same time, my current self and my future self—two wants, two desires so fundamentally opposed, but nevertheless present.

The future-self won, the vision marching onward. I stopped before Eli's prone body. He was lying on his back, his eyes looking up at me, pleading. I raised the sword, turning the blade down as I raised the hilt high. And then with one quick, downward thrust, I drove the blade through Eli's chest.

The vision shifted, the world blurring before my eyes. When it cleared, I saw that the scene had reset. Once again, Eli and I faced each other, our magic ready for the fight. Only this time, it wasn't hatred I felt, but an overwhelming sadness. Tears streamed down my cheeks as I fought him, but once again, he was no match for me and Bellanax. The final spell struck and he fell. I wanted to look away as the vision-me approached. I didn't want to see this again.

But this time, I dropped Bellanax to the ground as I approached. Then I straddled him and knelt on his chest, a Nightmare feeding. Only it was more than that. I wasn't just feeding—I was sending him into a forever sleep, as Nimue had sent Marrow. It was a different ending, yet the same as the first. I was killing him all over again—only more slowly this time, condemning us both to a long life together, but always separate.

Make it stop, I wanted to scream, but as before I could do nothing but watch.

The vision shifted again, the dream resetting for a third time. We faced each other once more, only this time I felt neither hatred nor sadness, but a cold determination. When Eli raised his wand, ready to strike, I lowered Bellanax, opening myself up for the attack. Eli didn't hesitate. His first spell knocked me down. I fell backward, landing on my back. Bellanax flew out of my hand, skidding feet away. Eli went after it at once and picked it up. Then he approached me as I had approached him twice before. He raised the sword high above his head, blade pointed down. He struck. I felt the point touch my chest, the first pangs of pain, and then the world of the vision shattered around me like broken glass.

I found myself once more in the rec room of Flint Hall. Pain filled my chest, and it took me a moment to realize that I was sobbing. Tears wetted my face and chin. I couldn't stop crying.

Lady Elaine watched me, her expression hooded, but not unkind. She waited for me to get a hold of myself.

It had been so real. Even more real than a dream. And unlike a dream, that sense of realness wasn't fading. It was as if those emotions, those thoughts and memories, had been imprinted on my brain. Branded there with a red-hot iron like Corvus and his Borromean brand. I understood more than ever why Eli hadn't wanted me to see. It wasn't that he feared I would believe the vision—it was that he knew how it would make me feel. As he must've felt. As he was still feeling, I realized, remembering our latest shared dream—my body with a puncture wound through the chest—a sword wound.

It wasn't real, I told myself. *It didn't happen.*

Yet.

No! I closed my eyes, fighting to gain control of my emotions. I reached for Bellanax, finding comfort in my indestructible companion.

Slowly, the emotions faded enough for me to open my eyes and draw a breath without sobbing. I wiped the tears from my face with the back of my sleeves, and faced Lady Elaine.

Clearing my throat, I asked, "If what you showed me was the future, then why were there three visions?"

Lady Elaine looked as if she'd been expecting the question. "There are always three. The future is never fixed, but always in flux until the moment it meets the present. One vision is for the first choice and one for the opposite. The third is for the in-between, the hidden, harder path."

I stared at her, not understanding. I considered asking her to explain, but a more important point occurred to me. "If the future is in flux, then all three of them might've been false."

Lady Elaine slowly shook her head. "All three share aspects that are certain. The situation is fixed—you and Eli opposed. Only the outcomes are in flux."

The outcomes. I considered the visions. In the first Eli would die by my hands. In the second I would condemn him to a life imprisoned in a dream, a slow death, once more at my hands.

And in the third, he kills me.

Tears threatened once again. Three outcomes. Three choices. And in the end, which would I choose?

It was a question I never wanted to answer.

~ 21 ~

Sword Dreams

I didn't avoid Eli the next day, but I wanted to. It was an awful feeling, so at odds with the rest of me—the part that wanted to grab hold of him and never let go.

"Are you all right?" he said as I sat down beside him in the cafeteria for breakfast. We both knew he wasn't asking about my mother.

I nodded, but said nothing. I didn't trust my voice not to betray how far from okay I truly was.

Eli touched my shoulder. "It'll get easier. I promise." He hesitated, his fingers pressing into my skin. "And we'll find your mom."

I hoped both were true, but in the meantime, I needed to keep my mind occupied as much as possible, filling every second with something other than the memory of Lady Elaine's visions.

Fortunately, I had plenty to focus on. Knowing without a doubt that Marrow was involved changed things. Finding Titus's killer still mattered, but discovering more about Marrow was now the most pressing. When psionics rolled around, I was relieved to see Mr. Deverell was back. I wasted no time asking him if we could try the psychometry on the sword during our session that afternoon. Deverell agreed at once, despite how tired he looked.

Whatever sickness he'd been dealing with the last few days had taken its toll.

When I arrived at his classroom after class, I immediately removed the glamour and placed the sword on the desk in front of him.

Deverell stared down at it, his expression a mixture of awe and fear. He looked up at me. "Are you sure you want me to help with the psychometry? If what you told me earlier is true, you might not need me for it anymore. Your bond with the sword has grown very strong indeed."

"Yes, I'm sure," I said, trying to make my voice firm. Although there was a strong part of me that didn't want to share anything about Bellanax with anyone, the bigger part of me understood this was too important to risk making a mistake. I knew from class that some objects were sensitive to psychometry. They would close up at the first hint of probing like a touch-me-not plant.

"All right." Deverell's smile looked careworn. His handsome face was tired and drawn, but there was a glint of anticipation in his eyes. I shared the feeling. We were about to embark on a journey no one else had ever taken, to delve into the secrets of the most dangerous magickind of all time.

"How do we do this?" I asked, anxiously shifting my weight from foot to foot.

Deverell motioned to the sword. "We will form a mind-link, the *nousdesmos* we used last year. But we will both need to be touching the sword for the psychometry. Since I will be leading, I will need to have the bigger hold on it. With your permission, I will hold the hilt and then you will place your hands on mine, touching as much of the sword as possible."

"Okay." I waved at Bellanax. "You, uh, have my permission."

Deverell inclined his head, then stretched his hand toward the sword. He moved slowly, carefully, his whole body rigid with wary tension.

"It's not going to bite you," I said.

An eyebrow rose on Deverell's face, but he didn't look up, his gaze focused unblinkingly on Bellanax. "Oh, I wouldn't be so sure. Magical objects like this have a lot in common with wild animals. They can be predatorial, especially about their space and about their masters."

"Huh, well, in that case, you look like you've done this before."

He nodded, just once. "We used to catch snakes barehanded back home, just for fun."

I laughed, nervously. "That's an interesting childhood."

"About as exciting as it gets in the Mississippi bayou." Deverell wrapped his fingers around the bone-handled hilt.

Mine. The thought struck me hard, and I sucked in a breath.

Deverell picked up the sword, both hands on it now.

Mine. Mine. Mine. It was all I could do not to wrench it free of his fingers.

"Are you all right?" Deverell asked. He'd finally moved his gaze off the sword and was now looking at me.

With an effort, I schooled my expression into something other than a scowl. "I'm fine. So I need to put my hands on yours?"

"Yes." He turned toward me, still moving cautiously like before. "Just put them on top, with your fingers on the cross guard."

I did as he asked, trying to ignore the awkward sensation of touching my teacher. My whole educational life I didn't think I'd ever done something like this. But the moment my hands were in place, the awkwardness vanished. Relief that I was in contact with Bellanax again took its place.

"Now," Deverell said, "close your eyes and prepare for the *nousdesmos*. Let me know when you are ready."

I did as he asked, taking a few moments to empty my mind,

to make it open for the mind-link. It was surprisingly easy, given all the worries I had cluttering my thoughts. Then again, Deverell and I had done this before. For the first time in days, I felt at peace, safe.

"I'm ready."

Deverell did not reply with words, but a moment later I felt his mind link to mine. Then leading me, he engaged the sword, prodding it to reveal its history to us, to share its memories. It took awhile, but eventually Bellanax began to project. That was the right word for it. It was as if a movie screen had appeared on the inside of my brain.

I saw an ancient forest, the trees large and the growth thick, completely unmarred by modern intrusion. One of the trees was taller and wider than the others, and it seemed to form the head of a circular clearing. The tree had a dark gaping hole at its base, wide enough for a man to stand inside of, like a wooden cave.

At first, I thought the clearing was empty, but then a woman appeared. She approached the tree, facing the hole. I could see only the back of her, long hair hanging in loose curls down to her waist. She wore a woolen gown of dark blue trimmed in gold silk. I watched her with a growing sense of recognition. But I couldn't be sure, not until she turned around.

She finally did a few seconds later. *Nimue* I thought, and I felt another mind answer, confirming this statement. *Bellanax*, I realized. I scanned the clearing, looking for the sword. It had to be here somewhere. This was its memory, after all. But aside from my great-great grandmother, the only other living thing was the black phoenix perched in the lowest bough of the holy tree. My heart quaked at the sight of it, and for a second, the image went blurry as I felt myself close to breaking away from the mind-link.

But Deverell's mind pressed against mine, strong and affirming. I felt his calm control wash over me.

Feeling more certain, I stared up at the giant bird. For the first time ever it did not look threatening as it sat there, preening itself. It looked younger and smaller than the black phoenix I had fought a year ago. And as it adjusted its position on the tree limb, I noticed that the red and plumage of its tail reached further up its back than I remembered, with a little gold showing underneath as well.

It's beautiful when it's not trying to kill you, I thought, and for some reason the realization made me sad.

A stir of movement drew my eye away from the bird and back to the tree below. A dark shape was moving inside the hole in the tree, a human shape. It stepped forward like a living shadow, until it finally reached the edge of the hole and sunlight shone on a man's face.

Marrow.

He looked exactly the same—black and silver on his head and beard, the same slight but fit build. He was a man both old and young at once, ageless.

"Welcome back, Ambrose," Nimue said, relief shining on her face.

"How long have I been asleep?"

"Nearly eleven months this time." She motioned to the tree. "And that was with the help of the Great Oak's power."

Marrow scowled, his hands clenching to fists. "So long. I need a way to make it faster."

Nimue shook her head. "No. What you need is to stop this madness. Stop fighting and putting yourself in danger. Why must you constantly war? Why must you obsess over this vision of uniting the kinds against ordinaries? There are other ways than violence. This is the third time since I've known that you have needlessly died. Died and been reborn. It's not natural, Ambrose. It's wearing on you." She paused. "It's *changing* you."

His answering glare burned. "You know nothing. No death is needless. With each one I grow stronger, grow closer to all I've worked for." He turned away from her, running hands through his graying hair. He wore a red tunic over black trousers, Bellanax sheathed at his side, The sword had lain next to him the entire time he slept, the entire time his body and soul had required to complete the resurrection.

"I need a way to shorten how long it takes," Marrow said, "but it just keeps getting longer and *harder*." He paused and turned his gaze toward the black phoenix, his expression one of reproach or perhaps disappointment.

We need to see more than this, I thought, sending it out toward Deverell and Bellanax. *This is the Marrow I knew. But what did he look like before?*

Immediately, the scene began to fade away and then blurred into something new. This time we were in a large circular room with thick stone walls. A castle tower, I realized, catching a glimpse of a battlement below through the nearby window, one complete with arrow slits. A single canopied bed stood in the middle of the room, the curtains drawn around it. Nimue sat beside the bed in a plush armchair with an embroidery frame in front of her.

For a moment nothing happened, and then the curtain began to move. Nimue stood up, pushing the frame aside. She reached for the curtain and drew it the rest of the way. Marrow's face peered out at her. A slow warm smile crossed his lips.

He looks exactly the same, I realized, my brain reeling. All those years ago. Hundreds of them, and he'd worn the same face. How was it possible?

Then I remembered a conversation I'd once had with Bethany Grey where she claimed that there were no recorded images of the Red Warlock anywhere. *Some say he cursed his own image,* she had said. It must be true. His face was an Achilles' heel. If his enemies had a way to record his image and pass it down, they and their descendants could target him forever. But since they couldn't, Marrow could always start over again, in another country, in another century, if he waited long enough.

Then I wondered why Bellanax had been able to record his image, but the sword supplied that answer at once—*this is memory.*

"Is the fighting over?" Marrow asked.

Nimue nodded, her expression now troubled. "It is, but you nearly didn't survive it. Your phoenix struggled to find you amid the fighting. I thought it would be too late—"

Marrow waved a hand at the bird, standing on a perch near the window. "He never fails me. . . ."

Show me more, I thought at Bellanax. The memories came faster now, like a movie montage. I watched Marrow's resurrection a dozen times in a dozen different places. One was on a tiny grass- and flower-covered island at the center of a silver lake. Another was in an underground cavern not unlike the one where we had found Nimue's tomb. In all of them he was alone. These were from a time before Nimue.

The more the sword revealed the more exotic the locations became, until finally we witnessed his rebirth inside the newly built Temple of Athena. I didn't think anything could top that, but the next one happened inside an Egyptian pyramid.

Each time Bellanax was beside him. The black phoenix was there, too, only in the oldest memories, its feathers weren't black but scarlet and gold. We were witnessing Marrow's history in reverse time, and it showed that the black phoenix had gradually earned its name, each resurrection darkening its facade, spreading like some kind of cancer.

Once we witnessed his many births, Bellanax showed us his many deaths. Some were normal enough—stabbing with a spear, an arrow to the throat—while others were gruesome—a beheading, pulled apart by chariots, burned at the stake. But all of them were violent. In every one he'd been put to death. Killed by someone's hand or order. It seemed he'd never known a natural death, one from old age or sickness or even tragic accident. The closest he came was the first one, not long after he discovered Bellanax. He'd spent the majority of his first natural life searching for the sword of power. I tried to imagine what it would be like to experience so many different ways to die, to carry those memories forever. It would drive a person insane.

Even worse was when I realized what all this said about Marrow's nature. Here was a man who would never stop. Over and over again he'd made plays for power. Over and over again someone had taken him down, forced him to retreat. But no one ever won. Nimue had come the closest when she imprisoned him in that dream. But she had not beaten him.

And neither will we. I felt a shudder pass through me. *Unless we find a way to kill him forever.*

I started to ask Bellanax if he knew a way, if he could show us, but the scene had changed again, drawing my attention back to it. We seemed to have traveled full circle. Once more I saw the clearing with the Great Oak. Nimue and Marrow were there along with a group of strange men. They were all armed, some with swords or bow and arrow, others with battleaxes and maces. They all wore leather jerkins with no undershirt, their arms and chests bare. Although their clothes were of different colors, there was a uniformity to their appearance that told me clearly that they were a single group.

A hostile group, I realized, as they started to circle around Marrow and Nimue. They did not draw their weapons, but magic swelled in the air around them. These strange men were all magic-kind. But of what type, I didn't know.

Four naturekind, four witchkind. Bellanax provided. *Four Nightmares.*

I stared at them, completely transfixed. All three kinds here at once, and so many Nightmares among them—but why? I kept moving my gaze from them to Nimue to Marrow and back again. Although they were circling around Nimue and Marrow both, it was clear they were only concerned with the Red War-lock. He was the focus of all their hostility.

Slowly and with dawning shock, I realized that all twelve men bore identical scars, visible on their bare chests beneath the sleeveless jerkins. Across their breastbones the Borromean rings had been branded into their skin. They were the exact shape, the exact image, as Mr. Corvus's.

22

Holy Places

Afterward, Deverell and I did not discuss what we'd seen. I started to tell him about Corvus, but he raised a hand, silencing me.

"Lady Elaine has made it clear that the Magi Senate does not want you to discuss anything connected to the sword with anyone," he said.

I frowned as I absentmindedly reapplied the glamour to Bellanax and slid the silver band onto my wrist. "Why not? You already know everything. Or almost everything."

"I was given the impression it was for my own safety." He offered me an apologetic smile.

"Yeah, I guess that's for the best," I said, although it was halfhearted. With so much going on, it would've been nice to have an adult to talk to about all of this—one who wasn't threatening me with visions of the future. Then again, it wasn't as if I could tell him my suspicions about Corvus. I didn't think he would freak out—he'd always been the poster boy of cool, like when he caught me sneaking into the boy's locker room last year—but he would have to wonder how I knew about Corvus's scar in the first place. And short of a potentially disturbing lie about witnessing teacher nakedness, I doubted I could tell him without implicating Paul.

Paul. I needed to talk to him right now. We needed to figure out when it would be safe to go to Corvus's house. I said good-bye to Deverell; then, stepping through the door, I pulled out my cell phone.

"Dusty."

The voice made me jump, and I turned to see Eli leaning against one of the lockers. He wore his gym clothes, his hair dark with sweat and his face flushed. Despite his casual stance, I figured he must have raced here from gladiator practice, his breathing still labored.

"Hey," I said, shouldering my bag. I braced, waiting for him to make the next move.

His hesitation was obvious, even if it lasted only a second before he came forward and crushed me against him. The feelings and images of Lady Elaine's vision reared inside my head, and along with them an urge to push him away. I sucked in a breath, my body shaking. But then I buried the panic deep down inside me. I clung to the realness of him, the feel of his arms around my body, even the smell of his sweat.

Sinking into him, I felt the dizziness retreat.

"How'd it go with Deverell?" Eli pulled back from the hug, but he kept his hands on my waist, as if afraid to break direct physical contact.

"Good. Better than good." I paused, catching sight of a Will Guard who had just stepped into the hallway.

Eli glanced behind him then turned back to me. "Come on. Let's talk in here." He led me to the nearest door and into an empty classroom. He left the door open, but paused long enough to peer out into the hallway. I imagined he was giving the Will

Guard a look that stated—*leave us alone.* I could only hope the man would listen.

A moment later, Eli was next to me again. "Spill."

I plunged into the story, telling him everything Bellanax had shown me. "They had the Borromean brand, Eli," I said, coming to the end. "Just like Corvus, and now I've got to find a way to get to his house. At first I thought we might just be looking for the knife, but now . . ." I stared at Eli, my eyes wide. "What if . . . what if that's where he's keeping them? Like in the basement or something."

Eli ran his tongue over his bottom lip. "I guess it's possible. But either way we need to check it out. We've got to find a time for you to go when we know he won't be home."

"Easy, I'll ditch tomorrow. We know he's in class all day."

"No good." Eli's expression turned stern. "The moment anybody notices that you're missing from class there will be wide-scale panic."

"Crap. This is so impossible." I smacked my fist against my palm.

Eli put his hands on my shoulders, rubbing my arms. "It'll be okay. We'll figure something out."

Peering up at him, I said, "How?"

He thought about it for a couple of seconds. "I'll con him into revealing his schedule. Shouldn't be too hard. I can use the ouroboros and the Iwatoke as a lead in. He is a history teacher. Who knows, maybe I'll even learn something helpful on the way."

This would've sounded like a thin plan from anyone else besides Eli. I had full faith in his ability. He knew how to steer a conversation and he practically oozed charm. "Okay. Can we do it tomorrow?"

"Yes, but I'll do it by myself. It's easier to work a conversation one on one," Eli said. "And I've got the better time for it. Corvus has a free period right after my class. I'll hang back."

I gritted my teeth. I didn't like not being involved, but then again, I couldn't be sure that I would be able to keep my cool around Corvus. Not with all my suspicions about him. "All right. I just hope we get lucky and he spills something."

"If he doesn't, I'll find a way to peek at his day planner." Eli smiled. "One way or another, you'll be heading to check him out soon. I promise."

With all the excitement of the night before and today, I didn't linger with Eli after dinner, but went straight up to my dorm, planning for an early turn-in. At least, that's what I told the little voice in my head nagging me about it.

To my surprise, Selene came up with me.

"For the record," she said as she plopped down on her desk chair, "I hate this nondisclosure thing."

I crossed my eyes for a second. "Ugh, I hate it, too. It sucks not being able to tell you things."

Selene huffed, folding her arms over her chest. "No kidding." She started kicking her leg back and forth. "So, if we can't talk about your secret mission, why don't you tell me what's going on with you and Eli?"

I winced, hating the question, even though her asking it was inevitable. Selene was far too perceptive about people and feelings to have missed the tension between Eli and me tonight. Still, no one could blame me for wanting to avoid the painful subject for as long as possible.

"I'll tell you about Eli if you tell me what you and Lance were arguing about earlier." I'd spotted them having a heated discussion in the cafeteria hallway after school, but the moment they saw me coming, they both put on their play-nice faces.

Anger flashed across Selene's features. "It was about his horrible father, what else."

I swore on her behalf and then started to pick at the fraying end of my shirtsleeve. "What'd he do this time?"

"Nothing," Selene said. "Not yet anyway. But he's threatening to do all sorts of things. Lance wants to just blow him off and keep right on like nothing's wrong."

"What do you want to do?" I said, looking up from the thread that had now doubled in length.

Selene glanced away, a faint blush rising to her cheeks. "I want to break up."

"What?" Shock heightened my voice.

"I mean, I want us to pretend to break up, but keep on seeing each other in secret."

I stared at her, at a loss for words.

"Oh, don't look at me like that," Selene said, finally meeting my gaze. "I know it sounds cowardly, but you've no idea how bad it was last time. Lance started off just ignoring it, but his dad wore him down in the end."

"No, I get it. I really do." I offered her a commiserating smile. "But . . . um . . . don't you think you ought to have a little faith in him?"

Selene shot me a look like I'd said something crazy. "*You* think I should have faith in *Lance*?"

I made a face. It did sound crazy, given our history. "I've decided he can be an okay guy. Besides, he's absolutely nuts about you. Anybody can see that."

She blushed, but waved the comment off. "It's time for you to tell me about Eli."

I took a deep breath to steady myself, and then I spilled on everything I'd seen in Lady Elaine's vision. It was just as awful talking about it as it had been witnessing it—no sense of getting it off my shoulders when I finished.

"That's horrible," Selene said. Her eyes were huge with shock.

I bit my lip. "Yeah, but do you think it's real? Are curses like that real?"

"Some of them," Selene said, her tone far too diplomatic for my comfort.

Fighting back tears, I dropped my gaze to my frayed shirtsleeve once more. "Do you know of any way to break a curse?" I tried to say it jokingly, but it came out pathetic instead.

Selene sighed. "Short of killing the person who cast it, the only way I've heard of is self-sacrifice."

"You mean like dying in the place of someone else?"

She nodded. "But the only trouble with that solution is you end up dead. Which is no solution at all."

I didn't reply, the three visions playing through my mind once again. *One of us is going to die either way.*

If the curse is true.

Eli didn't manage to find out Corvus's schedule the next day.

"But I will tomorrow," he reassured me when we met up after practice. "Corvus had somewhere to be and left in a hurry, but not before I got him to agree to meet with me after classes tomorrow."

"You're skipping practice?"

"Sure."

"But aren't tryouts this Saturday?"

He shrugged. "Missing one won't make a difference at this point, and it's a small price to pay if it means saving your mom."

I kissed him then, but I hated the waiting, hated feeling idle when there was so much on the line.

Not that Eli was the only thing I was waiting on. The last I heard from Paul, he still wasn't quite done with my ID. I had no idea what was taking so long, but I knew better than to ask. It would involve some technical explanation that would make little sense to my technology-challenged brain.

But at least Eli and I had a dream-session that night. With Bollinger sacked, it seemed Lady Elaine would be taking her place as my dream-session escort.

"Temporarily," she said when she greeted me at the door. She waved me out into the hallway. "How are things going with Deverell?"

I glanced sideways at her as we walked along, debating what to share. My mom's warning about not trusting the people around Lady Elaine had come back to me in full force recently. "He didn't tell you?"

"No. He's under instructions not to discuss anything with anyone, including me."

Deciding the risk was worth whatever insight she might be able to share, I said, "We tried psychometry on it yesterday and it worked."

"That's good. What did you find out?" She watched me side-long, her expression anxious.

"Marrow's worn the same face all his life . . . er . . . lives, I mean."

Lady Elaine pursed her lips. "I can't say I'm surprised to hear that. It explains why there are no recorded images of him. Even now the few photos we have of him from his time teaching here show only a blurred form where he should be."

I shuddered, picturing it. It was like some kind of hybrid vampire thing, only with photographs instead of mirrors. Fitting, considering his immortal gig. "And the black phoenix, it wasn't always black. It was all red and gold in the beginning."

"Yes, but what about Marrow's resurrection? How long did it take him to come back? How did he do it?"

By now we'd reached the foyer, and I offered my customary wave at Frank and Igor before answering. "Impossible to tell. The last time took him eleven months, but he had the help of the 'Great Oak' whatever that is."

Lady Elaine came to a full stop and swung to face me. "The Great Oak is like . . ." She paused and glanced around, checking we were alone. She must've decided Frank and Igor didn't count as she continued, "It's like the Death's Heart. It restores life."

I inhaled, taken aback. The idea of a soul-sucking tree seemed too perverse to be true. I liked trees. They were big and old and alive. They shouldn't be evil. "Restores life? Does it steal it in the same way?"

Lady Elaine started walking once more. "No. Its power came from within itself. It gave of its own life to restore it in others. And it couldn't bring back the dead, but it could heal even the most mortal of wounds if the person was brought to it in time."

"That's more like it," I muttered, falling into step beside her.

Lady Elaine nodded, more to herself than me. "If Marrow needed the Great Oak to restore himself to full life back then, maybe he needs the Death's Heart to do the same now."

A tremor went through my stomach. "It makes sense. Only I don't think he needed it. From what I heard, it just helped him recover faster."

"Or perhaps his regenerative power is weakening. You said it was the last time he went through it, yes?"

"Right . . ." I trailed off, thinking hard. "But why go to all the trouble using the Death's Heart? Isn't the Great Oak still out there? Does it still work?"

Lady Elaine's nostrils flared. "It was destroyed during the Second World War. Magickind forces working with the Axis powers cut it down and burned it, roots and all."

I stumbled at this news, shock turning me clumsy. "How . . . why . . . why would they do that?"

Lady Elaine's expression turned grave. "To keep the magickind supporting the Allies from using its power."

Several swearwords went through my mind. Why did the poor tree have to pay for some stupid war? "I didn't think magickind took sides in ordinary wars."

"Magic or ordinary, we're all people. And people always pick sides," Lady Elaine said. "We can't help what's in our nature."

We walked along in silence for a couple of minutes, both of us lost in our own thoughts and worries. I kept picturing the Great Oak, sadness squeezing my chest at the knowledge that it had been destroyed. It was such a waste. So wrong. The Great Oak sounded like the opposite of the Death's Heart—its counterbalancing force. I wondered if another would ever appear. Trees were born, weren't they? It could happen again.

I turned my head toward Lady Elaine. "Are there other places like the Great Oak still around?"

A cool wind blew across the deserted campus toward us, and Lady Elaine quickened her pace, pulling her coat tighter around her body. "Not many, I'm afraid. Most of them have been lost, destroyed, or have gone dry."

"Gone dry?" I hugged myself, wishing I'd thought to bring a jacket.

"Yes. Many of those places are like wells. They store magic, but not necessarily forever. Sometimes they break and the magic seeps out. But more often they go dry. They get used up by magickind and become no more than ordinary objects."

I squeezed my hands into fists, hating the reality of this, even though it was something I saw happening all the time—and not just from magickind. Ordinaries were twice as bad. When I was little there'd been a wood behind my house, but it had been torn down last year to make room for a housing development. They hadn't been magical trees, but it hardly mattered. Especially considering all the empty houses there were around town. Why build new when the old were still good?

With an effort, I pushed the depressing subject away and refocused. "What where some of the other places?"

"Oh, there were healing springs. Mystical caves."

Her words struck a chord inside me. "And all of them are about restoring health and life?"

"Yes, more or less."

My head spun, the memories Bellanax had shared taking on a deeper meeting. So many of the places where Marrow had been resurrected were magical like the Great Oak was magical—restorative, healing places. *Holy places,* in the most fundamental sense. There was the Temple of Athena, the pyramids. It seemed that Marrow had been using these things to help speed up his resurrection from the beginning. I supposed that confirmed that he was behind the Death's Heart theft. Or more accurately, someone working for him was behind it, one of his many followers.

It has to be Corvus. . . . Or at least he was involved somehow—the Borromean brand proved it.

But how to fish for information about him without rousing suspicions? "The last thing the sword showed us," I said, taking a peek at Lady Elaine to gauge how well she was listening, "was a group of men getting ready to attack Marrow. I'm pretty sure it was right before Nimue locked him in a dream. But what was weird about it was that four of the men were Nightmares."

I deliberately stopped speaking, hoping she would offer some insight, but she just kept walking, her gaze focused ahead.

"And even more strange," I continued, "was that all the men were branded with Borromean rings on their chests." I indicated the area, pressing a finger to my breastbone. "Right here. Have you ever seen anything like that?"

Lady Elaine considered the question. "I'm familiar with the Borromean rings, of course, but I don't know of any brands like you're describing."

I frowned at her in surprise. I didn't think she was lying, but why didn't she know about Corvus? Maybe Valentine was keeping secrets. *Don't trust anyone,* my mom's warning came back to me.

We walked on in silence. With the conversation at an apparent end, my mind soon began to wander. Memories of Lady Elaine's vision came pressing in, digging, *clawing* at me.

It only worsened when we arrived at Eli's dorm. He was already asleep on the sofa, on his back, just like in the vision. Seeing him that way, I was afraid even to touch him. It was an automatic fear, like being afraid of a growling animal or a fire burning out of control.

"Go on." Lady Elaine prodded me forward when I just stood there frozen.

I turned my gaze on her. *You did this to me,* I thought. I wanted to say it aloud, to hurl it at her like a curse. But I couldn't. If I did, she would think she'd won, that she'd convinced me to turn my back on my feelings for Eli. She hadn't. I wouldn't. We would fight our way through this like we did everything else.

Despite the quake in my stomach, I turned away from her, climbed on top of Eli, and entered his dreams.

23

Tryouts

His dream quickly became a nightmare. Lady Elaine's vision followed me into it. It was already there, waiting when I arrived. I was on the barge again, drifting along the dark still water. Voices shouted ahead of me, on the other side of the curtained platform. Stepping past it, I saw Eli standing across from another doppelgänger of me. He and the doppelgänger faced each other with wand and sword drawn. My other-self trembled with fear, tears on her cheeks; Eli trembled with fury. The look on his face made the real me want to start crying, too.

"Eli," I said, waving at him. "Eli! I'm over here. This is a dream, Eli. Snap out of it." But he didn't hear me, completely fixated on the fight.

Unable to bear it a moment longer I closed my eyes and willed the dream to change. The dream-seer curse had no place here, no bearing. We had more important things to uncover. *Corvus,* I thought. *The Death's Heart, my mom, the Great Oak, Marrow.* I willed the thoughts to translate into the dream, to manipulate into signs and symbols we could follow.

But when I opened my eyes again, nothing had changed. Eli was still engaged in the fight with his dream version of me. My doppelgänger had lowered the sword, opening herself up for the attack.

"Stop crying. Fight me. Fight me!" Eli's voice seemed to shake the entire ship, the dream vibrating with his anger.

"Eli!" I shouted. I walked over to him as close as I dared without getting ejected from the dream. But it did no good. He was lost to me, caught in the fever grip of the dream emotions.

He raised his wand, pointed. "*Peiran!*" he screamed.

The attack spell struck the other me in the chest, and she fell backward, landing hard. The sword skidded out of her hands. Eli went for it, but the moment he picked it up, the sword transformed into a knife. The blade was made of bone, slick and white and deadly sharp. He turned the knife over, holding it like a cleaver as he knelt over her prone body.

"Eli, stop!"

He plunged the knife down. It sank into the other Dusty's chest hilt deep. My doppelgänger and I screamed at the same time. Terror, hurt, shock, it was a harmony of pain.

The sound of it finally broke the dream's hold over Eli. Or maybe it was the feel of hot sticky blood pooling over his fingers, or the sight of my doppelgänger's face first turning pale and then blank as the life seeped out of her.

"Dusty?" he said, his gaze confused as he peered from her to me. He stood up, wrenching the knife free.

"It's me," I said. "I'm real. She's just a dream thing." I pointed to the doppelgänger, and then summoning all the magic and force of will I possessed, I vanished her from the dream. The only sign of what had happened was the blood still staining Eli's fingers and the knife in his hand. Eli stared down at it for a moment.

When he looked up, tears stood in his eyes. They weren't

falling, but they were there. They made him look broken, defeated. The sight hurt me worse than anything else so far.

"I didn't mean it, Dusty." He shook his head as if trying to convince himself as much as me. "It was just the dream. It had me."

"I know." I tried to smile but failed. "It's not your fault. I was thinking about Lady Elaine's vision when I entered the dream. I think I brought it in with me."

Eli's mouth closed, his jaw clenching. A vein pulsed in his temple. "It's not real. The curse isn't real. This won't ever happen."

I nodded, even though it sounded like he was trying as much to convince himself of this truth as to give me comfort.

He dropped the knife then stepped closer to me. "I will never hurt you."

"I know," I said again, my voice firm and steady. I believed him. He was real and he was here. Lady Elaine's vision was just haze. We would see our way out of it together.

I leaned toward him, wanting to kiss him, overwhelmed with the urge. I stopped myself just in time. We couldn't do that here. And although I knew it was just a limitation of the dream, the separation cut deep. It cut right to the heart.

Things were tense at breakfast the next morning, the dream and vision lingering in both our minds. Eli and I sat side by side, our bodies touching casually here and there, but our inner selves remained distant. I hated it, wishing I could do something to make it better. But only time would help—and getting things back to normal. *As soon as we find my mom, we'll be okay*, I told myself over and over again.

The waiting became more tortuous than ever. I spent every spare moment going over the police files without turning up anything. The day crawled by, seconds imitating minutes, minutes imitating hours. When my session with Deverell finally started, I could barely concentrate, not knowing if Eli could be talking to Corvus right this moment.

Afterward, I rushed out of the psionics classroom, expecting to see Eli waiting for me in the hallway. My heart sank when he wasn't there. I dug my phone out of my back pocket, hurrying off toward Mr. Corvus's classroom.

Where are— I started to type, then froze as I heard Eli calling for me.

I spun around and saw him coming down the hall from the opposite direction. I frowned, wondering why he was approaching from there, but my curiosity vanished at the broad smile stretching across his face.

"You did it?" I said, my voice breathless with hope.

He answered me with a hug, lifting me off my feet. "Sunday morning," he said, setting me back down. "Mr. Corvus attends a ten o'clock yoga session every Sunday. You should have a little over an hour to get in and out before he comes back."

"Yoga?" I said, laughing.

Eli grinned. "Now, now, don't make fun. There's no reason why men can't enjoy that sort of thing."

"Yeah but most men aren't Mr. Corvus," I said, imagining our imperialistic teacher in upward-facing dog or horse pose. It painted an amusing picture. Still, most of my humor was an overspill of delight at this news. I reached up and kissed him. "Thank you."

"What can I say? Anything for you."

His words heated my whole body, and for a moment, not even Lady Elaine's vision could bring me down.

I texted Paul the news about Corvus the moment we sat down in the cafeteria. It took a while as I had to carefully translate each word into the code.

> Corvus will be out of the house on Sunday morning
> from 10:00 to 11:00. We need to go then. Will the ID
> be ready?

Paul's answering text came back a few minutes later. It was short and I decoded it quickly:

> With any luck.

"What does that mean?" Eli asked, reading over my shoulder.

"No idea." I blew out a breath. I wanted to ask for more details, but the coding process was arduous, and as before, I doubted I would understand much of the explanation.

"Remind me to give you the moonwort key and a lockpick kit," Eli said. "You'll need it if Paul manages to pull off his part in time."

"He has to," I said. I couldn't bear the thought of waiting another week. Paul had to come through. Everything depended on it.

Friday came and went much like the day before. I checked my phone over and over again for a message from Paul. I hadn't spotted him during biology, and I was starting to worry that he was avoiding me.

But finally, less than an hour before my dream-session with Eli, his text came in.

We're ready.

I could barely contain my excitement, but I did my best to hide it when Lady Elaine arrived. I didn't want her suspicious of my sudden change in attitude. But as we walked along, each step I took felt light and springy, my hope higher than it had been in ages. Just one more day, and then I would finally get to do something to help my mom. And at least a good portion of tomorrow would be taken up by gladiator tryouts.

Lady Elaine and I spoke only briefly on the way to Eli's dorm. There was little to talk about. In the last two days there'd been no news on my mother, other than that the search for her continued. I didn't place any stock in them finding her, not with Bethany having been missing for so long.

There were no new signs in the dream either. Actually, as dreams went, this one was pretty tame. No doppelgängers showed up, and the dream was supple enough that I was able to shape the landscape to show us the clearing with the Great Oak. Marrow was there and so was Nimue, but the men with the Borromean brands didn't make an appearance. I was disappointed. If only we had some way of connecting the dreams to Corvus. Then the magickind police would have to search his home. But try as I might it didn't make a difference.

When the dream ended, Eli remained asleep, still under Lady Elaine's spell. I didn't bother asking her to take it off. There wasn't any point with her there. Besides, he had gladiator tryouts in the morning and needed the sleep.

"Good luck, tomorrow," I whispered to him before leaving. I probably wouldn't see him before tryouts started. He would need to eat breakfast extra early to get there in time for the warm-up. I had plans to catch up on some sleep myself and then to spend some time wearing the shape-change necklace tomorrow. I needed to make sure the difference in size wouldn't screw me up. With the ID, getting through the gate should be easy, but I didn't want to raise suspicions with any weird behavior—like bumping my head on the car door.

Selene was asleep when I got back to the dorm. There was no need to enter a dream-seer journal tonight—I'd given Lady Elaine the rundown on our walk back here—so I turned in as well. But sleep was a long, long time coming for me.

I woke late the next morning. For several seconds I lay there in bed, my mind groggy and blank. I'd been so deeply asleep that coming out of it was like trying to swim through jelly. I turned over, vaguely aware that Selene wasn't in the bed opposite me. That was weird.

Crap, gladiator tryouts. I glanced at the clock beside my bed, saw it was five minutes to ten, and had a momentary panic attack. I leaped out of bed, grabbed a fresh set of clothes, made a pit stop in the ladies', and then booked it out of the dorm. The campus was as deserted this morning as it had been the night before. It seemed the entire school had turned out for gladiator tryouts. When I arrived at the gymnasium, there was standing room only.

Disappointed, I scanned the bleachers. From down here, I wouldn't be able to see a thing. Then I spotted a single, tiny seat four rows down from the top, close to the aisle. I headed for it, and soon realized the occupants of that row were freshmen.

The one nearest the aisle was a girl clearly here by herself. The sliver of a space next to her was only inches in length, but it might as well have been a mile wide in the way it alienated her from the rest of her classmates. The girl had brown hair, a prominent nose, and round full cheeks. When she saw me coming, her eyes dropped and she seemed to fold in on herself. I could almost hear her thoughts—*please don't talk to me. Please don't notice me. I'm not worth noticing. If you talk to me, I might die of embarrassment.*

I sighed, understanding that feeling all too well. I stopped one level below hers. Then summoning the biggest, friendliest smile I possessed, I said, "Hey, do you mind if I sit there?"

The girl visibly paled then gave a single awkward jerk of her head.

"Thanks," I said, my voice overly bright. "You saved my neck. I overslept this morning."

"Oh, you're welcome," she squeaked.

I beamed at her. "Yeah, some of my friends are trying out today and they would've killed me if I didn't get here to see it."

"Uh-huh. That's great." *Oh God, please stop talking to me,* her expression said, but perversely this just made me want to talk more. I was close to babbling as I told her about Selene, Lance, and Eli, but I didn't care. I wanted to coax her out of her misery. To my triumph, she finally started to relax a little and talk back.

The tryouts started off with the individual evaluation. When the first contender, Nick Jacobi, finally took the field, the crowd whooped and clapped with anticipation. Nick was an Ira demon, the kind that feeds off rage. He put in a strong performance, blasting his way through a line of senior gladiators to capture the flag set at the top of the tallest structure at the opposite end of the court.

Next up was Oliver Cork, a dryad. He fared less well, getting tagged out two minutes into the round. After him came Jarrod Ackles, Deanna's twin brother. He got tagged out four feet from the flag. I didn't know the next two boys, both of them seniors. Both lasted only a couple of minutes before being taken down.

Then finally, it was Selene's turn. She killed it—almost literally. Like Nick, she'd faced an entire line of senior gladiators. But unlike him, she took down everyone with a quick volley of spells. I screamed and leaped to my feet as she grabbed the flag and hoisted it up. Beside me, my new friend Veronica did the same. And when I moved in for a fist bump, she returned it with enough enthusiasm my knuckles stung afterward.

We sat back down and I anxiously waited for Eli and Lance. Only, some twenty minutes later, the announcer said, "And that does it for the individual rounds. We will now move on to the team portion of our tryouts, featuring two-team capture the flag with a mix of senior and hopeful players."

"What?" I said, gaping.

"I thought you said you had three friends trying out," Veronica said.

"I do. There has to be some mistake." With my worry growing by the second, I pulled my cell phone out of my pocket. To my dismay, it was turned off. I switched it on and stared at the screen, certain a text from Eli would appear, some explanation for why he hadn't taken the field for the individual round.

There was no text. No voice mail. No nothing.

Once I accepted this truth, I sent Selene a text—*where are the boys?* I followed it up with a dual text to Eli and Lance—*Where are you two?*

Several minutes went by with no reply from anyone. I soon realized why Selene wasn't answering when she came running out onto the game field with four teammates. The match started, and I watched it unfold, my worry for Eli taking a backseat to the more immediate worry for Selene. I wanted her to succeed, but the team they were up against was good—they'd already taken down two challenging teams. Mere minutes into the match, three of Selene's teammates fell in rapid succession, including Nick Jacobi.

The four players on the opposing team—three seniors and one hopeful—started to surround her. They did it slowly, certain of their victory. I half-suspected they were giving her a chance to surrender, not wanting to hurt the only girl.

But once again, Selene proved that underestimating her was a bad idea. The entire audience gave a gasp of surprise as Selene leaped into the air, her two massive black wings expanding out around her. Somehow she'd managed to modify her uniform to allow for her wings to come through.

Culpepper, I suspected. It seemed maybe she'd borrowed more than a couple of helmets.

With Selene now airborne, the other team didn't stand a chance. She swooped down on her enemies, terrifying them into making mistakes, spells and curses shooting wide as she dodged in between them. Her spells found their mark though, executed with perfect accuracy.

By the time she went for the flag—flying up to it rather than taking the long way over the structures—there were no enemies for her to worry about at all.

The audience erupted into applause when Selene once again held up the flag. She carried it down to the floor, landing gracefully in the middle of the field, her black wings fanned out behind her like billowing royal robes. Then she marched it triumphantly out of the game field, serenaded by the cheering, whooping crowd.

"Wow, she's amazing," said Veronica.

"Tell me about it," I replied. Then standing up, I said a quick good-bye and hurried down the stairs to the gym floor. I pushed and elbowed my way through the crowd and dashed into the girl's locker room.

"Selene!" I shouted.

She stopped and spun around. Her face lit up as she saw me.

"Where's Eli and Lance?" I said, racing over to her.

Her triumphant look blurred into confusion. "What do you mean?"

"They didn't compete for the individual round."

"What?" Selene's eyes widened. "Are you sure?"

"Yes, I'm sure." I resisted the urge to shake her in my panic. "Have you seen them?"

"No. Not once all day. I've been avoiding them on purpose."

I exhaled, fighting back fear. "They're not here at all, Selene."

"Did you try their phones?"

"Both. No answer. Something's wrong."

She nodded and then started pulling off her gladiator gear, her black wings retreating into her body. "I'm finished with my tryouts. Let's go check their dorm."

Five minutes later, we were pounding on the door of their dorm room. Ten seconds after that we were busting our way inside. There was no sign of either of them in the living quarters, and Selene and I got in the way of each other as we both attempted to go through the door into the sleeping quarters at the same time. Selene won, heading in first. Her scream of alarm struck me like a knife to the chest. I gasped without knowing why, my terror multiplying.

Then I managed to peer around her. I didn't scream and I didn't faint at the sight before me, although I wanted to do both. Lance was lying in an awkward heap on his bed, as if he'd fallen backward into it. His head was tilted back, almost out of view, but I could see enough to spot the blood seeping slowly out of a gash on his temple.

With my heart fluttering in my chest, I turned my gaze to the other bed. It was empty. Eli wasn't there.

Eli wasn't anywhere.

～ 24 ～

Hidden Target

Lance's injury was serious enough that they took him to Vejo-
vis, the magickind hospital. Detective Valentine organized
the search efforts for Eli—entire squadrons of police officers,
Will Guards, faculty and staff, even students pitching in to comb
every known inch of Arkwell.

I wanted to search for him, too, but I was sent to the principal's office for my safety, four armed guards posted outside the
door into the conference room. Selene went with Lance to the
hospital. I was worried for her, knowing that Lance's father would
be there sooner or later. But that worry was nothing compared to
what I felt for Eli.

Several hours later there was no sign of him. Deep down, I'd
known there wouldn't be. Even before Lady Elaine came to tell
me her suspicions, I'd known he'd been taken by the same person who had my mother and Bethany Grey, the same person
who had possession of the Death's Heart—a phantom with the
ability to come and go as he chose, leaving behind no trace, nothing but the absence of people I cared about.

The thought of Eli having his vital essence drained made me
feel as if my body were being turned inside out. My heart ached;
my stomach was a leaden ball in my center.

Lady Elaine looked nearly as distraught as I felt when she sat down across from me, the long, narrow conference room table between us. The sight of her distress only worsened my own.

"Don't you have any suspects yet?" I said, my voice pleading rather than accusatory. *Please say you suspect Corvus,* I silently added. It took all my will to keep from telling her my suspicions. I didn't owe Paul much, but I did this—he'd hacked those files for me. If he hadn't, I never would've seen Corvus's brand.

But Eli is more important than Paul, the thought flitted through my mind.

Sorrow filled Lady Elaine's eyes. "No, I'm afraid we don't. You can't understand how clever this person is. There's no trace. Nothing at all."

I slowly nodded. I understood better than she knew. Marrow had made a habit of recruiting clever, powerful people to his cause. The magickind parliament in the UK had never been able to figure out who freed Marrow from his tomb, either, and my mom had spent months trying to, as well.

Something clicked inside my brain—a puzzle piece falling into place. "It must be the same person."

"What?" Lady Elaine said, brow furrowing in confusion.

I leaned toward her. "The man who freed Marrow from his tomb. My mom was tracking him. She was convinced he was here at Arkwell. What if it's the same person behind all of this?"

"It's possible." Lady Elaine grimaced. "But your mother had suspected he was here for weeks and could never pin him down."

No, she couldn't. I bit my lip, hating myself for letting that flash drive get ruined. If only . . . but there was no point dwelling on it now. I needed to stay focused on Mr. Corvus. Once again the urge to tell Lady Elaine what I knew came upon me. This time, I acted on it, seeing a way to shed light on him without implicating Paul.

Clearing my throat, I said, "You don't think it was Mr. Corvus, do you?"

Lady Elaine cast me a suspicious look. "Why on earth would you say that?"

I wriggled in my seat, too aware of the thin ice I was sliding on. "Because he's a . . . a Nightmare. And Valentine thought only a Nightmare could've done it. That's why he suspected my mom. But with her and Bethany missing, that leaves only Corvus."

Lady Elaine narrowed her eyes at me. "How do you know he's a Nightmare?"

I began to fidget with my hair. "I saw him in the dark once. His one eye was glowing." I could tell she wasn't convinced, and growing desperate I plunged on, "And . . . and he has the Borromean rings branded on his chest just like the Nightmares who confronted Marrow. I've seen that, too." I bit my lip and hoped for the best. I hated putting Paul at risk, but if it helped save Eli, it was worth it. *I won't tell even if they torture me,* I thought. I was an investigator, of sorts, and no matter how cheesy it might make me feel to think it, I had a right to protect my sources.

For a moment Lady Elaine didn't react at all, only stared at me like I was some new and strange creature she'd never seen before. "I don't know how you learned these things about Mr. Corvus, but you must swear to me that you won't breathe a word about this to anyone else."

An icy breath seemed to blow against the back of my neck. "Why?"

"Mr. Corvus is working for me. Or with me, I suppose, to be more accurate, and I have vouched for him with Valentine."

My stomach flipped over at this news. Suddenly my mom's warning not to trust the people around Lady Elaine deepened. What if my mom had known about Corvus and Lady Elaine? What if she had suspected him?

Trying to keep my voice steady, I said, "What is he doing for you exactly?"

Lady Elaine shook her head. "I've already told you more than you need to know. But you must swear to keep this to yourself. What Corvus is doing must be kept secret. Even the Magi Senate don't know about him. There are too many people in high places who can't be trusted, Dusty."

You got that right. I nodded, wondering if she was one of those people, inadvertently or not.

"Promise me," Lady Elaine insisted.

"I promise," I said, and my voice sounded steady and sure, as believable as I could make it. "I won't say a word about Corvus."

Lady Elaine smiled, looking relieved. I was glad to see it. The last thing I wanted right now was for her to suspect my true feelings—I was more certain than ever that he was up to no good.

And first thing tomorrow, Paul and I would be on our way to finding out the real truth about Mr. Corvus.

That evening, Paul and I worked out the final details of our mission through a series of short, cryptic text messages. I spent the rest of the day wearing the shape-change necklace around my dorm room, trying to get comfortable in the taller, larger body.

Selene returned from the hospital a few hours after dinner with the news that Lance was still unconscious.

"The doctor's said it was a physical attack and not a magical one." Selene sounded perfectly normal as she spoke, but her eyes were red from crying. "He has swelling on the brain, so they're keeping him asleep for now. They might try to revive him in the morning."

"Do they think he's going to be okay?" I said.

She nodded. Then her expression darkened. "Let's just hope he saw who attacked him."

"Yeah, that would be great," I said, but I doubted it. This guy was too clever for that. I waited, expecting her to tell me more, but when she didn't I quietly asked, "Was Lance's father there?"

Fresh tears blurred Selene's eyes. The wetness made them look more indigo than ever. "Yes, he was there."

"What did he do?"

Selene exhaled, the sound close to a sob. "He demanded I leave." She thrust out her chin, her tear-filled gaze fierce. "But I refused. Not until the doctor's told us what was happening."

"Good for you," I said, trying to smile, but mostly failing.

She nodded. "And I'm going back first thing tomorrow. He can't keep me away."

Her bravery brought me unexpected comfort. Despite my eagerness to investigate Corvus, I was anxious about it, too. So much could go wrong. We might get stopped at the gate, the car could break down, or we might not be able to get into the house. And there was the worst possibility of all—that we might not find anything.

But no, I couldn't dwell on that. We had to find something or Eli and my mom might be gone forever.

I woke early the next morning. Even though I wasn't hungry, I went down to the cafeteria with Selene and forced myself to eat. I could tell she was forcing herself to eat, too. It was as if both of us were preparing to go to battle against enemies unseen and undefeatable.

Finally, an eternity later, it was time to go. Selene and I walked together to the main parking lot outside the front gates. I waited until she'd gotten into the car with her mom, then I headed for my rendezvous point with Paul, just around the corner of the nearest building. Five minutes later he still wasn't there, and I started to pace and fret with worry.

"Hey," someone said from behind me.

I jumped and spun around, startled by the strange voice. I recognized the man as one of the Menagerie workers, Paul's other form. Or at least, I thought it was. "Paul? Is that you?"

He nodded. "Sorry I'm late. Had to get these." He held up a pair of car keys. I was relieved to see them. Mr. Corvus's house was a good fifteen-minute drive from campus.

"Okay," I said, rubbing my sweating hands together. "Are we ready then?"

"As soon as you put on your costume." Paul said, motioning to me.

"Right." I took a deep breath and pulled out the shape-change necklace. The moment I slid it on, I felt that awful stretching feeling come over me, painful without pain. A few seconds later, I stood several inches higher than before—the difference putting me an inch or two shorter than the form Paul was wearing. I turned in a slow circle, adjusting to the new size.

"Looking good," Paul said. He reached out and touched my arm. "I'm sorry about Eli."

I swallowed and managed a nod. I didn't want to talk about it. I was certain that tears would arouse suspicion in the guards at the gate. With an effort, I schooled my stranger's expression into something that I hoped looked calm and innocent.

"Let's go," I said.

Paul headed around the corner and into the parking lot. He held up the keys and double-pressed the lock button. A car alarm squawked once in the distance. A few moments later, I pulled open the passenger door of a blue Ford Focus. The car was small, a fact I was hyper aware of in my bigger, taller body.

As Paul sat down and started the engine, I glanced behind me. "Couldn't I have just ridden in the trunk?" I said, turning back. It seemed like that would've been a whole lot easier than all the business with the ID and hacking Arkwell's computer system.

"Nope," Paul said, backing out of the spot. "There are sensors on the gate that check for that sort of thing. They're magical sensors. They check for any kind of concealment."

I raised a hand, touching the necklace around my neck with the tip of my finger. "Won't it detect this then?"

"No," Paul said, his attitude confident. "These are the best shape-change necklaces around. Nearly impossible to detect. I mean, they're based on shape-changer magic after all."

"I hope you're right," I muttered, but Paul didn't reply. We'd already reached the gate, and he was bringing the car to a stop.

A guard stepped out of the gatehouse and approached the driver's side window. Wordlessly, Paul handed him two IDs, each showing our borrowed faces.

The guard scanned both IDs with some electronic device he held in his other hand. The light on it flashed red to green, red to green. Then he handed both IDs back to Paul. "Have a nice day."

"You, too," Paul said. He wasted no time in driving us through the gates and out onto the street. I inhaled, just now aware of how shallow my breathing had become the last few minutes. My heart felt like a herd of stampeding horses inside my chest.

Paul, oblivious to my distress, gazed sidelong at me and grinned. "Too easy."

"Yep," I managed, and then I sank back against the seat, trying to savor the relief that we'd made it through the first big hurdle.

As we drove along, Paul pulled his cell out of his pocket and brought up the map app. It took us down several main drags and finally onto the side streets of an unremarkable neighborhood, one so ordinary, I found it hard to believe that imperial, eccentric, history-obsessed Mr. Corvus would ever choose to live there.

When I spotted his actual house ahead of us, I was certain there had to be some kind of mistake. It was a perfectly ordinary ranch-style home on a sleepy cul-de-sac. I stared at it, strangely disappointed. It was the least likely house to hold something as sinister as the Death's Heart and its victims inside.

"Where are we going to park the car?" I asked.

"Right in the driveway," Paul said, already slowing us down.

"In the driveway? Are you crazy?"

He laughed. "A little, maybe. But the best way not to get noticed in a place like this is to be obvious. Nothing draws suspicion like suspicious behavior."

I supposed he had a point. I mean, who would believe a couple of prowlers would just park their car outside in broad daylight and knock on the door? They would assume we were relatives, stopping in for a visit. Or maybe we were here to house-sit. I was willing to bet that Mr. Corvus wasn't friendly enough with the neighbors for them to be that concerned about his comings and goings. I'd spent plenty of time in neighborhoods like this, and people generally stayed out of other people's business.

That was American suburbia for you—leave my business alone and I'll ignore yours, too.

Paul pulled the car all the way up to the garage door, and killed the engine. I climbed out, smoothing my hair back and adjusting my pants, which felt strange on my stranger's body.

My anxiety spiked when I spotted the next-door neighbor sitting on his back porch. The guy had a cup of coffee and a book, but to my relief he didn't look our way once.

Tapping my pockets for the contents I'd hid inside them before leaving the dorm, I headed for the front door. Paul followed after me.

"Should we try the moonwort key first?" I asked, reaching into my pocket for it. Eli had given me both it and the lockpick kit late Friday. The moonwort key would be easiest, but there was no guarantee it would work. Mr. Corvus kept his office on campus barred against any kind of magical means for breaking in. I was hoping he wouldn't be so paranoid about his off-campus home.

"Might as well," said Paul.

I pulled the key from my pocket and slid it into the lock. It went in awkwardly, its moonwort consistency making it flexible. Once it was in as far as it would go, I turned it to the right only to be met with resistance.

"Damn," I said, pulling the key out again. "No good." I glanced at Paul, my pulse quickening.

"You've got the lockpick kit, right?" he said, his expression pinched.

I nodded. I knew how to use the tension wrench and the rake, but I wasn't nearly as good at it as Eli, who could jimmy a door in seconds. Still, there was nothing for it. I reached into my opposite pocket, pulled out the kit, and set to work.

Several minutes later I was still at it, the tools slick in my sweaty hands and my frustration building. I was keenly aware of the next-door neighbor. We were out of his line of sight, but that didn't mean there weren't other prying eyes watching us. And it had to be obvious what we were up to now. The sound of the lock rattling while I jiggled the tools back and forth was like an alarm bell.

"This is not working," I said through gritted teeth.

"Here, let me try." Paul's hand descended on my arm and he moved me aside. I barely had time to protest before he'd conquered the lock and was pushing the door open.

"Wow," I said, letting off a low whistle. "Where'd you learn to do that so quickly?"

"I didn't." Stepping into the house, he flashed a grin at me over his shoulder. "I'm just good with my hands."

"If you say so." I couldn't help but be impressed. I'd spent hours practicing with the lockpick and still failed at it.

I stepped in behind him and pulled the door shut, locking it again just in case. Then I turned my attention to the room in front of me. Once more Corvus's house failed to meet my expectations. The living room was perfectly normal, the kind you would see in just about any ordinary house. There was a green sofa, a matching love seat, and a plush leather armchair set around a massive flat-screen TV. The fireplace off to one side looked more like a decoration than anything useful.

"Are you sure this is the right address?" I said, glancing at Paul who was already making his way to the door into the next area.

"I'm as sure as you are. You saw the police files, too."

I sighed, knowing he was right. "Let's check out the rest." But before doing anything else, I reached up and pulled off the shape-change necklace, stuffing it into my pocket.

"What are you doing?" asked Paul.

"I'll have an easier time being my own size. I don't want to break anything." I stretched my arms over my head, shaking off the lingering feel of the shape-change.

"Good point," Paul said, reaching up to remove his own necklace. It was a strange relief to see him in his natural form. Stuffing the necklace into his pocket, he stepped into the doorway to the next room and looked back at me. "I'll go this way. You go that way." He pointed first left then right.

I nodded and followed after him through the door, feeling much more at ease in my own skin. To the left the hallway led to the kitchen. To the right were most likely the bedrooms, although I couldn't tell with all the doors closed. I stopped at the first one and pushed it open.

"Whoa," I said, stepping inside. Now this was more like it. In an ordinary house this would have indeed been a bedroom, but right now it looked like an alchemist's study. A large table occupied most of the room, its surface cluttered with bowls, jars, and various utensils used for making potions. Three of the four walls were filled with books, herbs, and other ingredients. There was no denying a magickind lived in here.

I snooped around, pulling some of the books off the shelves to check the titles and contents. Most of them were printed in languages I didn't even recognize, let alone possess the ability to read. No two volumes appeared to be written in the same language either. How any one person could be knowledgeable enough to read all these books was beyond me.

A few minutes later I decided the room had divulged all the secrets it was going to and moved on to the next. It turned out to be the bathroom, full of the kinds of things you would expect from an old bachelor—aftershave, deodorant, a couple of razors. The next room was another bedroom, currently stocked full of unopened moving boxes. I checked the labels on a couple and saw they'd been shipped here from Scotland. It made sense, given Mr. Corvus's last teaching job.

The final room down the hallway was another bedroom—this one occupied by an actual bed, a dresser, and a nightstand. As with the living room, it appeared to be a perfectly normal room for an ordinary. There wasn't a single magical item anywhere that I could see.

Frowning, I pulled the door shut. There had to be an office of some kind around here, a place where he sat down to grade papers over the weekend or to perform other scholarly duties.

I headed down the hall to the kitchen where I could hear Paul banging around. I stepped in to see him swinging a cabinet door shut.

"Did you find anything?" I said.

He gave a slight jump of surprise then shook his head. "Nothing."

I grimaced. "Did you go through the knife drawer?" I doubted Mr. Corvus would keep the bone-bladed knife in a kitchen drawer but you never knew.

"Yeah, but there are just steak knives in there. Did you find anything?"

I shook my head then ran my fingers over my hair, beginning to fret. "Is this it?" I glanced around the room, looking for another hallway.

"I think so," Paul said. Then he pointed at a door in the far corner. "Unless that isn't a pantry." He walked over to it and turned the handle, only to find it was locked.

"Bingo," I said. I pulled the moonwort key out of my pocket, pushed him aside, and tried the lock. But as with the front door, the moonwort only bended in my hand, the lock holding against the key's magic.

"Try the lockpick," Paul said.

I fetched the tension wrench and rake out of my other pocket and slid them into place. Then I stepped to the left and motioned for Paul to take over. He did so, jimmying the lock in a matter of seconds.

"You're going to have to show me how you do it like that," I said. "Not even Eli is that quick."

Paul shrugged. "It's nice to know I'm better than him at something."

I didn't reply but pulled the door open all the way. A cool draft of air seeped over my face, and I spotted a set of stairs leading down to the basement. There was a light switch just inside the doorway, and I flipped it on. The bright, unfiltered glow of a bare bulb shone up at us.

This is it, I thought, and strangely my heart seemed to slow instead of quicken. It became a hard, steady thump in my chest. I pulled out my cell phone and checked the time. We'd been here for not quite a half hour. I returned the phone to my pocket. Then taking a deep breath, I raised my right hand in front of me, magic at the ready. In my left hand I felt Bellanax pulsating with anticipation. It was ready to help the moment I needed it.

Paul followed after me, his hand at the ready as well.

I wasn't sure what to expect when I reached the bottom, but when I got there, I knew it was anything at all besides what was waiting for us.

The basement, a cool, quiet room with concrete walls, was mostly empty except for a single chair set beneath the bulb.

Mr. Corvus was sitting on it, his one eye fixed on us both. "Hello, Dusty," he said. "So glad you finally made it." Then he raised his hand and uttered a spell. A jet of yellow light shot out from his fingertips and struck Paul in the chest. He fell with a muffled cry of surprise. Then from up above I heard the loud bang of the door shutting.

I was trapped and facing Mr. Corvus all alone.

25

Traps

Except, I wasn't alone. I reached for the silver band on my wrist. Bellanax was with me. But all my sessions with Deverell had taught me that my connection to the sword was stronger with it unglamoured. Thinking only about the danger and not the consequences, I freed it from the disguise.

"Don't you dare try anything," I said, pointing the sword at him. "It won't work while I'm holding this."

Mr. Corvus's narrowed-eyed gaze told me just how impressed he was by this assertion. "I'm quite familiar with The Will sword, young lady." Then as if to prove it, he gave a flick of his hand, and Bellanax was wrenched out of my grip. It went sailing across the room toward him. He caught the sword one-handed.

Terror came over me, squeezing me so hard I couldn't even scream. I couldn't do anything but stare at this man, my body in total paralysis.

"But for the record," Mr. Corvus said, "I won't be trying anything." He lowered the sword and then applied the glamour, transforming it back into a silver band. He tossed it at me.

I barely caught it, clapping my hands around it at the last second. Disbelief pulsed in my temples. Was he toying with me? Or did he really mean it? I glanced down at Bellanax, probing the sword with my mind, worried that he'd messed with it somehow. But the sword felt perfectly normal.

"You can put it back on," Corvus said, a touch of impatience in his voice. "There's nothing wrong with it. No harm can come to that sword from anyone but you."

I frowned, but slid the bracelet back onto my wrist. "What do you mean *but me?*"

"It is a sword of power, imbued with soul magic from its first victim," said Corvus. "It is indestructible except from within. As its master, you control all the power inside it."

I started to ask him what he meant exactly, but he cut me off.

"Don't get me wrong, of course. I'm well within my rights to punish you both for trespassing into my home like this."

Overcoming some of my shock, I said, "What did you do to Paul?"

Corvus glanced at the boy slumped on the floor beside me. "Nothing he won't recover from shortly. No offense to him, but you and I are well past due for a private chat." His gaze flicked back to me. "But I promise that your boyfriend will be fine and you two will leave here without so much as a hair out of place."

"He's not my boyfriend," I said, hands clenching into fists. "My boyfriend has been abducted."

"Oh, yes, of course. But as I'm sure you've figured out by now, it wasn't by me." Corvus motioned around the room. "You've been all through my house and haven't found anything amiss, correct?"

I frowned. "Like that means anything. How did you know we were coming?"

Mr. Corvus made a sound like a growl. "I didn't. As a matter of fact, I was just getting ready to make myself a cup of tea and read for a few hours when I heard you at the door."

"You were supposed to be at yoga." Too late I realized this probably wasn't information I should've divulged.

Corvus didn't miss a beat. "Decided to skip it, after spending half the night looking for your other boyfriend."

"What do you mean other—" I paused, scowling. "Like looking for Eli matters if you're the one who took him."

Corvus shook his head. "So suspicious. And so very much like your mother."

Resisting the urge to pull out Bellanax once more, I said, "What do you know about my mother?"

"A good deal more than you." Mr. Corvus waved his hand again, and from the farthest, darkest corner of the room, another wooden chair floated over to me. "Why don't you have a seat and we'll talk things through."

I considered my options for a couple of seconds. But in the end, there weren't any. Not unless I went for a preemptive strike. Considering how easily he'd disarmed me already that seemed a bad idea. Finally, I exhaled and sat down. But I didn't make myself comfortable. I perched on the edge of the seat, ready to leap into action if this crazy one-eyed man decided to try anything funny.

"Thank you." Corvus tented his hands in front of him. "Now, before I go into details, let me start by reassuring you that I had nothing at all to do with your mother's disappearance or Eli's or even the Death's Heart."

I flinched at his knowledge. "How do you know about the Death's Heart?" It was weird being able to say it aloud to someone new.

"Lady Elaine has kept me informed. And yes, she told me your suspicions about me as well."

I folded my arms over my chest, a feeling of betrayal coming over me. Why did she have to tell him? If he had turned out to be the bad guy—and I hadn't yet decided he wasn't—then she tipped him off to be ready for me. "So you really are working for her?"

"With her would be more accurate. And with your mother." Corvus inclined his head. "I'm here to help Lady Elaine root out Marrow's supporters, and also, most importantly, to discover the man who freed Marrow from his tomb."

I inhaled sharply.

Corvus ran a hand over his goatee. "Yes, that's right. Your mother and I have been after the same thing for a while now. We crossed paths some eight months ago and have since combined our efforts."

I examined his expression, trying to decide if I could believe him, but he was impossible to read, immutable as stone. "If that's true, why didn't she tell me about you?"

"She swore to keep me a secret, same as Lady Elaine. The fewer people who know the truth the better. How else am I supposed to uncover such a man as the one we're hunting?" Corvus pointed his finger. "He's always a step ahead."

"Okay," I said, seeing his point. "But what does that have to do with me?"

"Because we are hunting the same man, Destiny Everhart."

I went very still, even though my heart was now galloping inside my chest. "Are you saying the man who freed Marrow is the same one who stole the Death's Heart?"

"Yes. And I believe he kidnapped Bethany Grey, your mother, and Eli as well."

I slumped against the chair, overwhelmed by this news. It was one thing for me to have suspected it, but quite another to have it confirmed. How were we ever going to capture such a person? "Do you know who it is?" I said, sounding more hopeful than I intended.

Corvus grimaced. "No. But take heart. We are closing in on him, I've never been more certain."

"How?" Despair made my voice breathy.

"First, you must understand how hard this has been," said Corvus. "It's taken me a very long time to learn it, but the person who freed Marrow from his prison is a shape-changer."

For a second the word struck my brain without registering any meaning. When it did I was glad I was sitting down. "Selene was right."

"Excuse me?" Corvus raised his single eyebrow.

I shook my head. "I thought shape-changers were extinct."

Corvus sighed and leaned back in the chair. "That's an impossibility, given their nature."

I stared at him, trying to decide if he was disappointed or relieved to know that an entire group of magickind was incapable of being annihilated. Given that he was a Nightmare, I chose to go with the latter.

"With their ability to steal shapes," Corvus continued, "the man could be anyone at Arkwell. No matter how long that person has been here. The shape-changer could be Dr. Hendershaw and no one would ever have known it."

"But . . . but how?" My mind began to reel. "There's more to being a person than what they look like. Wouldn't somebody have caught him in a goof by now?"

Corvus shook his head. "It all depends on how the shape-changer stole the shape in the first place."

"Don't they just need their teeth?"

Corvus looked surprised by my knowledge, but he only nodded. "Teeth is one way for a shape-changer to shift. But a single touch is all they need to borrow your shape for a limited period of time. In both cases, they only steal the body as you said. But if a shape-changer wants to completely assume another person's life, they can do so by first killing the person and then consuming their heart."

I inhaled and felt my gag reflex kick in. "Do you mean eating them? Like cannibals?"

"Yes, it's both a physical and magical act for them," Corvus said, seemingly oblivious to the way my face was turning green. "It allows them to assume the victim's shape permanently, and it gives the shape-changer access to every memory, mannerism, and emotion that the person possessed. They can quite literally become that person."

I ran my hand over my mouth, willing my stomach to settle. The idea that someone at Arkwell, one of my teachers perhaps, or maybe even someone like Mr. Culpepper was actually a shape-changer in disguise, one dining on hearts like some magickind version of Hannibal Lecter, made my skin crawl.

With an effort, I managed to keep my cool long enough to ask, "Aren't there any distinguishing signs of a shape-changer? Like the way our eyes glow in the dark?"

"There is a sign, but it's very hard to detect." Corvus shifted his weight in the chair, crossing one leg over the other. "They have a strange ridge on the roof of their mouth."

"Oh," I said. "Well that's helpful."

"Indeed. Short of physically assaulting every faculty and staff member at Arkwell long enough for me to probe their mouths, I never stood a chance of simply recognizing the shape-changer. Any time I get close, all he has to do is steal another form."

Frustration began to build inside me. I wasn't sure when I'd decided to believe his story, but I definitely did now. Too much of it made sense, and I'd been alone with him for quite a while; he'd had ample time to do me harm.

"This is impossible," I said. "You've been searching for this guy for months with no luck. How am I ever going to find him in time to rescue my mother and Eli?"

To my surprise Corvus's face brightened. "It just so happens that these recent developments might have given us a way to succeed. And it's why I'm so glad you sought me out today."

I leaned forward, still skeptical but willing to hope. "How do you mean?"

"I don't know why the shape-changer has stolen the Death's Heart," Corvus said. "Marrow does not need it to come to life. At least he has never needed such a thing before."

"Wait." I raised my hand. "How do you know so much about Marrow?"

"I'm surprised you haven't guessed already." Corvus tapped a finger against his breastbone "Once you found out about my Borromean brand, that is."

I stared at him, my mind trying to solve the puzzle. "Those men with the brands . . . they were there when Nimue . . ."

"Trapped Marrow in the dream, yes," Corvus said as I faltered. "There were twelve of them. There are always twelve of us—the Borromean Brotherhood, as we call ourselves. Four darkkind, four naturekind, four witchkind."

"We?" I blinked. "So that means that you—"

"Have dedicated my life to keeping Marrow sealed in his tomb."

I took a moment to process this information, but there were too many questions. Too much I didn't understand. I cleared my throat. "There are twelve of you?"

Color darkened Corvus's cheeks. "There were twelve of us."

"Were?"

Corvus rubbed a thumb over his ring finger, and his voice darkened as he said, "Only the blood of the twelve can undo the circle."

I flinched at the familiar quote.

"The shape-changer killed them," Corvus said a moment later. He drew a breath, and I sensed his struggle to control his emotions. His anger seemed to come off him like waves of heat off a bonfire—anger and hatred. "He murdered us one by one. All but me." Corvus motioned to his missing eye. "I am the only one who survived the attack."

I swallowed a mixture of pity and revulsion. I couldn't imagine what it must've been like for him to go through that. But it made me inclined to trust him. This wasn't just about justice for him. It was about vengeance, too, and that was a powerful motivation. I could only hope it would be enough to save my mom and Eli.

I took a deep breath and let it out slowly. "So you said you had a way to get the shape-changer now. What is it?"

"You," Corvus said at once.

"Me?" A chill slid over my skin.

Corvus nodded, his expression growing even more intense than before. It seemed to glow with a newfound fervor. "Of the people the shape-changer has abducted recently, the only thing they have in common is you."

Eli and my mother, I thought, knowing he was right. "What about Bethany?"

Corvus waved the question off. "I'm not sure why he took her, although he had his reasons, no doubt. But they don't matter now. What does, is that he seems to be targeting the people close to you."

"But why?" I wrung my hands, the reality of this truth hitting me like a blow to the gut. For a moment I wanted to curl into a ball, the fetal position the only way to cope with the guilt. My mom and Eli were both suffering right now—because of me. Assuming they weren't dead yet.

"Again, I don't know why," Corvus said, and I could hear the regret in his voice. It made me feel like crying.

"But what I do know," he continued, "is that you are the key to finding him. I've suspected as much since the moment I found out that you had bonded with The Will sword. Your mother has worried about you being dragged into this from the beginning, which is why she insisted so stridently that we keep you in the dark about the shape-changer for as long as possible. She worried that you might try and go after him yourself."

"Yeah well, she was right." I folded my arms across my chest and began to tap my foot against the concrete floor. "But knowing he's targeting me, what can I do to help find him?"

"The hardest thing of all," Corvus said. "Be patient."

"Huh?"

He bobbed his head, his single eye overly bright. "I need you to wait and let him come for you. He's going to, I know it. And when he does, I'm going to be there to catch him."

I blinked, my mouth sliding open again. "You want to use me as bait?"

"In lieu of a less vulgar expression, yes." Corvus bared his teeth in an almost feral smile. "It will take a significant amount of bravery on your part. But if you're anything like your mother, I know you can do it."

Tears stung my eyes as he said it. I knew he might be manipulating my emotions on purpose, but it worked nevertheless. "I'll do it. But if he comes for me, how am I supposed to let you know?"

"It's simple, actually." Corvus stood up and reached into his pocket, withdrawing a small object I'd never seen before. "And it's something he will never see coming."

Half an hour later, Paul and I left Mr. Corvus's house. Corvus had taken off the spell that had incapacitated Paul only a few minutes before. He'd been livid at first, demanding an explanation of what happened. But I couldn't tell him. Corvus was right about that. Nobody could know the plan we'd just set in motion. In the end, I had to appeal to Paul's better nature.

I took his hand and squeezed his fingers, pleading. "You're going to have to trust me, Paul. All right? Just trust me."

He watched my face for several seconds, not speaking, then he slowly nodded.

After that we'd climbed the steps out of the cellar and headed for the front door. Mr. Corvus watched us go, not speaking a word to either Paul or me. We got into the car and started to make our way back to Arkwell.

When we were less than five minutes from campus, Paul pulled into an alley.

"What are you doing?" I said as the car came to a stop.

"Time to put on our faces again," he said, retrieving his shape-change necklace.

"Right." I reached into my pocket and pulled out mine as well. I stared at the necklace with its smooth, yellowed teeth, an uneasy feeling in my stomach. After what I'd learned from Mr. Corvus about shape-changer magic, I couldn't believe that the magickind police force sanctioned the use of these necklaces. Then again, I supposed maybe it didn't surprise me that much, even now. The Magi Senate wasn't above using black magic to meet its own ends. Still, once we got back to campus I was going to follow through with my vow to destroy it.

"You coming?" Paul said, startling me out of my reverie. I looked up to see that he'd already slid on his necklace and changed back into the Menagerie worker.

"Yeah, just a sec." I put on the necklace and immediately felt the shift into the other woman. "Okay," I said. "Let's go."

Paul pulled the car out of the alley and back onto the main drag. I felt my phone buzz in my back pocket and pulled it out.

"Who's it from?" Paul said, glancing over.

"Selene, she—" I broke off as I read the message. Once. Twice. Three times. Fear closed in around me like collapsing walls.

Lance is awake, Selene had written. *He saw his attacker. It was Paul.*

~ 26 ~

The Shape-Changer

Don't panic, Dusty. Don't panic. Play it cool.

"She what?" Paul said, and I jumped at the sound of his stranger's voice.

"Oh, she, um, Lance is still unconscious but doing better."

"That's good."

I nodded, not trusting myself to say anything more, not if this really was the person who'd attacked Lance and kidnapped Eli sitting beside me. *Maybe Lance made a mistake.* He had taken a blow to the head. But if it was true—the thought was almost too frightening to be allowed. My stomach churned at the idea of Paul being involved in all this Marrow business again. How could he? How was he capable of such deception even now?

Unless this isn't Paul in front of you.

The thought flipped my panic button so hard that for a moment, I almost attacked him. Around my wrist, Bellanax burned, the sword sensing the danger. I held back at the last second. I needed to be careful, needed to be smart. But it was hard to think with the blood rushing in my ears.

"You all right?" Paul said, glancing over at me again.

"Yeah sure. Of course. Why wouldn't I be?" I avoided his

gaze. My knuckles were white around my cell phone, and I forced my hand to relax.

"You sure? Because we're almost at the main gates."

"Oh." I peered out the front window and saw the gate just ahead. *Play it cool, Dusty.* For a second, I contemplated asking the guard for help, only to dismiss the idea. If Paul was behind the attack on Lance—if he was behind *everything*—then I needed to keep it secret long enough to find Eli and my mom. If I tipped him off now, he might run, and I would never find them.

Summoning as much courage as I could muster, I forced my body to relax to its pre-terror state. It was hard, but I managed it. Bellanax helped, its power coiled and waiting, ready to strike the moment I called for it.

Thinking clearly once more, I sent Selene a quick reply:

I'm with him now. Get Corvus to help. We're heading to campus.

I glanced over at Paul as I pressed send, praying I hadn't roused his suspicion, but his gaze remained fixed out the front window.

When we arrived at Arkwell, the same guard from earlier came out of the gatehouse. Paul pulled the car to a stop and handed over our IDs once more.

To my surprise, the guard didn't scan them at once but took his time looking them over.

"Something wrong?" Paul said after a few seconds.

The guard looked up. "We've had a security alert. We're on the lookout for a guy named Alan Early. Six feet tall, dark blond hair. Has a beard. Do you know him?"

I felt more than saw Paul stiffen. "Alan?" he said. "Sure I

know him. We work together in the Menagerie. What's he supposed to have done?"

"Don't know, but the police are on their way here now to look for him. We're putting the campus under lockdown. You got back just in time."

My heart stuttered at this news. I'd never heard of Alan Early, but it didn't take a genius to guess that was the name Paul was using when he wore his creepy bearded-man face.

"Oh, glad we got lucky then," Paul said.

The guard nodded and handed over the IDs. "Say, you haven't seen Early today, have you?"

"No, but if I do, I'll call the authorities right away." Paul's manner as he spoke was a convincing display of innocence and concern. Even I halfway believed him.

"Very good," the guard said.

Realizing the jig was up, I leaned toward the driver's side window, ready to sound the alarm. Paul knew he'd been found out—he would run as soon as he could. But before I could say anything, he touched my wrist, and I felt a sharp prick like an insect bite. Pain lanced through my body, and I froze, unable to move or speak.

"Thanks so much," Paul said to the guard, and then without releasing my wrist, he drove us through the gate and onto campus.

What did you do to me? I tried to shout, but my mouth wasn't working. I had become a prisoner in a frozen body, completely at the mercy of the boy sitting next to me.

If he is a boy. I never knew Paul to have magic like this. My hand felt as if it had been bitten by a snake, and there was something like venom pulsing through my veins, enforcing the paralysis.

But if this wasn't Paul, if it was the shape-changer wearing his skin, then where was the real Paul?

Consume their heart, I heard Corvus saying once more. But no, Paul couldn't be dead. Unexpected tears stung my eyes at the thought. I wanted to wipe them away, but I still couldn't move. I couldn't even blink.

The stranger next to me pulled the car into the same parking spot as before. I waited while he killed the engine, incapable of doing anything else.

"Sorry about the sting," he said, flashing me a chilly smile. "But I had to act quickly once I realized what was going on."

Again, I waited with enforced outward patience, unable to give voice to the curse words screeching in my mind, begging to be shouted.

He finally removed his hand from my wrist, but he didn't let go—not until after he'd pulled Bellanax from my arm and put it in his pocket.

"And now, it seems we have reached a moment of inevitable conflict, you and I," he said, and the sudden strangeness of his speech confirmed for me what I already knew—this wasn't Paul. "I am prepared to counteract the venom's effect if you agree to come along quietly."

Inside my head, I was laughing. Definitely not Paul. He would've known better than to suggest such a thing.

"And I am quite certain," he continued, "that your answer is going to be yes, despite what you might be thinking inside that pretty little head of yours." He reached over and ran a hand over my hair and down the side of my cheek.

The laughter stopped, rage taking its place. I wanted to hit this guy. I wanted to scream and pound my fists into his face.

"Your options are quite simple, Dusty Everhart. I can either kill you right here, or I can undo the paralysis and give you a chance to save your mother and your precious Eli."

Silence filled my head now, the quiet calm of sheer terror.

This man was a killer. He'd done it a hundred times. *And he eats his victims' hearts.*

"You have something I want," the not-Paul said. "And it's important enough that I'm willing to bargain. Let me know your decision in five-four-three-two-one. *Anti-amnes.*"

The spell swept over me, and I felt the paralysis give way, as if I'd been cut free from a spider's web. I opened my mouth, my eyes blinking rapidly to restore the moisture from so many minutes of not blinking.

The shape-changer climbed out of the car and hurried around to my side. He opened the door for me and waited. I got out slowly and faced him, planning my attack.

"*Hypno-soma!*" I screamed, casting the spell with dizzying speed, all those practice sessions with Selene paying off.

But the shape-changer was even faster. "*Alexo,*" he said, seeming to swipe my dazing curse aside with his shield spell. Then he countered with a spell I didn't recognize. I tried to block it and missed. The magic struck me, then nothing, not so much as a tingle of pain.

Shaking it off, I raised my hand for another attack, but when I spoke the incantation my magic didn't come. It was gone. Erased. Cut out. "What did you—" Invisible fingers closed around my throat as the shape-changer raised his hand toward me.

"Don't be hasty here," he said. "I mean what I say. You can save them both. You just have to give me what I want."

"And . . . what . . . is . . . that?" I said between gasping breaths. I had my fingers at my throat, trying to free myself from his magical grip, but there was nothing to grab onto. I'd never met someone with such powerful mind-magic, and without my own magic, I was helpless against him.

"You will find out. And I promise it does not have to involve your death."

"That's . . . re . . . assur . . . ing."

The shape-changer grinned and lowered his hand. The pressure on my neck vanished, and I sucked in choking breaths.

"This way, when you're ready." The shape-changer held out his hand, indicating the direction.

I reached for my magic again, but once more nothing came. "What did you do to me?" Tears burned my eyes, and a sob expanded in my chest. I knew it couldn't be permanent that it was just a spell, some kind of block. I could even sense my magic still waiting inside me, but being separated from it was terrifying. It was like those dreams where you needed to run but couldn't—you knew how to run, knew you were capable of it, but your body refused to obey.

"Convenient little spell, wouldn't you say? One of my specialties. It works so well, even on Nightmares." The shape-changer put his hands on his hips. "Now let's go."

Still I didn't move. I needed to get at the device Corvus had given me, tucked in my left front pocket, some kind of tracking beacon. All I had to do was press the button and it would send an alert to his phone along with my GPS coordinates. The electronic device was new enough that animation wouldn't be an issue. If I could only activate it without the shape-changer seeing.

First though, I needed to ditch this stranger's body. I needed the familiarity of my own skin if I stood any change of activating the device and surviving this. I reached up and pulled off the necklace, half-expecting the shape-changer to stop me, but he said nothing.

Savoring the relief of my own shape, I stepped in front of my captor. He did not remove his necklace or the purloined Menagerie worker's face. He couldn't with all his other covers blown—both Alan Early and Paul Kirkwood were wanted men.

"Where are we going?" I asked, moving in the direction he had indicated.

"The Menagerie."

Nodding, I started to put my hands into my pockets, nonchalant. An invisible force snaked around my wrist and squeezed, restraining me.

"Keep your hands where I can see them, please."

"Oh, sure, since you asked so nicely," I said, scowling back at him. I faced front again, adjusting my course toward the Menagerie. Fighting back dizziness I tried to formulate a plan, some way out of this. Then I realized that I might not need to. I'd thought this shape-changer was supposed to be clever, but heading for the Menagerie was the epitome of stupid, given what the guard had just told us.

Then again, I should've known better than to hope it would be so easy.

Just before we rounded the corner toward the Menagerie's main gates, the shape-changer said from behind me, "Now, be sure to play your part well, my dear."

"What?" As I started to turn around he grabbed my arm. Magic crawled over my skin, followed by the familiar squeeze and stretching sensation of trading my face and body for someone else's.

When the shape-change ended, I looked down and saw fingers lined with age and thick blue veins—the hands of an old woman instead of my own. Somehow he'd shifted my shape without the necklace. "How are you doing this?" I said, and I gasped at the familiar voice of Lady Elaine issuing from my mouth.

"Just one of my many talents," the shape-changer answered, only his voice was different now, too. I didn't have to look back to know who it was, but I did anyway. Instead of the Menagerie worker, the shape-changer now wore the face and body of Detective Valentine.

"Are you really Valentine or is that shape stolen?"

"Borrowed, my dear, borrowed. And no, this is the first time I've worn him."

The brilliance of his power filled me with both awe and terror, and I understood more than ever before why these creatures had been so hunted. If they were all like this one, maybe that persecution was even deserved. The thought sickened me, and I hated myself for thinking it.

This is only one shape-changer, I remembered. Condemning them all based on his behavior would be like condemning all witchkind based on the things that Titus Kirkwood had done. Still, I couldn't deny my revulsion at such unrestrained power.

When we arrived at the gates into the Menagerie, the shape-changer pulled a D.I.M.S. badge out of his pocket and ordered the workers and Will Guards assembled there to let us inside.

They didn't even consider refusing. Why would they? The shape-changer was convincing. For my part, he'd ordered me to be silent. I was okay with obeying. It gave me a chance to slip my hand into my pocket and activate the beacon. At least, I hoped it was active. I'd pressed the button once and then yanked my hand out, convinced for a second that the shape-changer had noticed.

But he was busy giving false instructions to the Menagerie workers. "We have an idea of where to look for Alan Early. You all stay put and wait for the rest of the police force. Sheriff Brackenberry will be here shortly."

Again, no one questioned, no one doubted. I wanted to scream the truth at them, but that desire warred with my need to get to my mother and Eli. I didn't trust the shape-changer for an instant, no matter what he said about not killing me. But I believed completely that he had my loved ones hidden somewhere in this place. He was my only way of finding them.

The shape-changer directed me further into the Menagerie and around a corner, heading out of sight of the guards. He touched my arm briefly, and I felt my body return to its true shape with a relief. Then we double backed to the long low building that Paul had taken me to once before. Fear rose up in me at the sight of it—and doubt. The abandoned dragon caves below would be the perfect hiding place. Had that been the real Paul who took me there that day? Or had it been the shape-changer all along? I couldn't decide. Before, when I'd been here, Paul had seemed so much like Paul. But how could he have been coming here and not have known about the shape-changer? Was it just coincidence?

My insides clenched—I didn't believe in coincidence.

We entered the building and the shape-changer closed and locked the door behind us. I headed for the tunnel without being asked, but he called for me to stop. I swung to face him. He was still wearing the Valentine disguise.

"Turn out your pockets, please," he said.

I felt my heart pulsing in my throat. "What?"

"You heard me." The shape-changer folded his arms across his chest.

Glowering to hide my fear, I shoved my hands into my pockets and withdrew my cell phone from the right one and the tension wrench and rake from the left.

The shape-changer took a step closer to me and examined the objects. He picked up the tension wrench and rake and slid them into his own pocket. Then he picked up my phone. Before I could protest he smashed it against the floor and stomped on it for good measure.

"You didn't have to do that," I said, wincing. "You could've just turned it off."

"Destruction is always the safest option."

I started to argue, but he grabbed my arm and wrenched it behind my back.

"What are you doing?" I tried to pull free, but he only increased the pressure. I had no choice but to bend forward at the waist. With me now immobilized, the shape-changer slid his free hand into my left pocket. I wanted to squirm, the feel of his hand there sickeningly intimate, but before I could react, he let go of me.

I spun toward him to see the beacon in his hand.

"Oh, poor, poor Corvus." A look of mock pity appeared on the shape-changer's borrowed face, but I saw the delight of victory twinkling in his eyes. "*Cine-aphan,*" he said. There was a loud crack as the beacon vanished.

I trembled, my knees threatening to buckle. My best chance of help had just been obliterated.

"Go on." The shape-changer motioned me toward the sloping floor ahead. "I believe you know the way."

Swallowing, I headed down the tunnel. In seconds, the darkness grew too thick for me to see the ground in front of me, and I stopped and faced him. "You got a flashlight or something?" Once again I felt the painful absence of my magic.

The shape-changer raised his hand and a ball of light appeared over his head. It hung there for a moment and then flew forward like a giant, round firefly.

I followed after it. We reached the spiral stairs and headed down, eventually arriving at the dragon cave where I'd come with Paul just a few days before.

I slowed down, but the shape-changer pushed me forward. "Head for the next tunnel."

Inwardly cursing, I made my way toward it. Whether it had been Paul here with me the last time or not, I soon found out it was no lie about the tunnel being dangerous. I had to hold one hand pressed against the wall to keep from sliding with every step. But no matter where I put my hand, the rock wall crumbled, adding more scree to the already treacherous floor.

I walked on, uncomplaining. Deeper and deeper we went. Soon the main tunnel branched off into several smaller tunnels. The shape-changer pointed to the one on the left. I headed down it only to be confronted with more branching tunnels not far ahead. Once again, the shape-changer indicated the way. Over and over we reached branching tunnels until I was so hopelessly lost I doubted I would ever find my way back.

"Do you want to tell me where we're headed?" I said, giving into my nerves.

"I don't think so," came his quick reply. "You'll see soon enough."

I rolled my eyes, the gesture wasted with my back to him.

A few seconds later, I tried again. "So who are you for real?"

Silence answered the question, and I glanced over my shoulder, nearly losing my balance in the process. The shape-changer was still wearing Valentine's form.

"That's an interesting question," he said, motioning for me to continue down the slope. "I have so many shapes that belong to me. And to be honest, my first shape is so old I barely remember what it feels like to wear it any longer. Not that I would ever want to."

I gave a sharp intake of breath. "What do you mean old?"

"Oh, I take it Corvus did not fill you in on everything about shape-changers, did he?"

I shrugged. "How am I supposed to know if I don't already know?"

"Good point." The shape-changer sniffed. "But surely he told you how we claim the body and mind of others."

"If you mean the bit about eating hearts, then yes."

The shape-changer tsked. "It's not as disgusting or unfathomable as you make it sound. The true shift, as it's called, prolongs our life. It's the ability that got my kindred in trouble all those years ago. I mean, what would you do if you were sick and dying of old age and had the ability to take someone's life so you could continue living?"

I suppressed a shiver of horror. "You really want me to answer that?"

"No," he said. "What value would your opinion have? You can't judge if you've never been in the situation, now can you? You are young and healthy, full of hopes and dreams about long life. You have no idea what it will be like for you in the end. But I have been there, and suffice it to say it's a decision I have never regretted."

"Really?" I said shooting him a look over my shoulder. "I'm so surprised that you don't regret murdering people." We'd been traveling ever downward, but the steepness of the slope seemed to be lessening. The smell of water had been growing steadily stronger. "But what you're really saying," I continued when my sarcastic comment failed to get a response, "is that you've stolen so many lives that you don't remember your own?"

"Oh, I remember it," he said. "I just don't choose to wear it anymore. It's like casting aside a pair of shoes. They served you well, and now you're ready for something new. But don't fret, Dusty Everhart. I do have a current true form, and it's one you're very familiar with."

As he spoke, I felt icy fingers slide down my back. It was a voice I recognized. The voice of someone I trusted enough to have let him into my head over and over again in the *nousdesmos*. With my heart in my throat and my stomach drawing in on itself, I stopped and slowly turned around to face the shape-changer.

Mr. Deverell's handsome face grinned back at me. For a second, I refused to believe it. This had to be another trick.

But then I felt the brush of his mind against mine, the touch of it unmistakable.

The shape-changer, the man who'd freed Marrow from his tomb, was Mr. Deverell. It had been him all along.

~ 27 ~

Will of Its Own

I couldn't stop the tears. They came of their own will. I turned around and wiped them away before he could see. His betrayal stung deep, making each breath shaky and painful. I didn't understand it—he could've kidnapped me easily before this. So why had he waited? What did he want from me? I was afraid to find out.

Fortunately, our walk continued on for several more minutes, giving me a chance to regain my composure. I buried the hurt of his betrayal as deeply as I could. I told myself there had been a real Deverell once, the man whose memories and mannerisms had created the teacher I cared about so much. That man, that first Deverell, deserved vengeance against the creature that had stolen his life.

Hatred began to build steam inside of me. It gave me focus, driving away the fear. I needed to rescue my mom and Eli, and I needed to destroy this monster behind me.

Finally, the passageway we'd been following came to an end. Deverell's ball of light flew into the room ahead of us, and once it got there, it multiplied. Soon dozens of such lights hung over our heads, revealing a vast cavernous space. The ceiling was so tall that all I could see of it were the tips of stalactites pointed down at us like clawed, accusatory fingers.

Ahead stood a circular structure some four feet tall that at first appeared to be made of stone. I would've called it a wall but the description didn't fit. It wasn't made of sharp angles, but was perfectly round in shape, a cylinder lying on its side. I blinked, trying to make sense of it. But as I drew closer to it I realized that what I had taken for stone blocks were actually carvings in the wall . . . of *scales*.

"The Great Ouroboros," I said, the words involuntary in the force of my astonishment.

Deverell made a noise of approval from behind me. "Yes, very good. It took me months to find it. But I knew it was down here somewhere. All the historical documents on the Iwatoke said so. I had to find it, of course. After you killed my master."

I snorted, unable to help myself. "Your master? What is this, a *Star Wars* movie?"

Deverell narrowed his cool blue eyes on my face. He might be a monster, but he was no less handsome than before, a scary kind of handsome. "I am proud to call the Red Warlock master. He is worthy to be served."

"Whoa, somebody's been drinking the Marrow Kool-Aid real hard."

To my surprise Deverell smiled. "Soon the whole world will feel as I do." His smile widened, revealing perfectly white, straight teeth. "And those who don't will be silenced forever."

I gulped, the idea of his brainwashing no longer funny. Not when it had such real consequences. I pulled my gaze away from him and surveyed the rest of the area. My breath hitched as I spotted a distant shoreline. Black water glistened beneath the balls of light overhead. Floating in the water was an ancient-looking boat. It wasn't the same as the barge in Eli's dreams, but close enough to set my heart to racing.

I turned back to Deverell. "Where's my mom? Where's Eli?" I kept glancing at the boat, fearing his answer would involve a trip down that black river.

To my relief Deverell turned toward the Great Ouroboros and pointed. "In there, along with the Red Warlock."

I turned my gaze to the dragon statue again, wondering what horrors awaited me inside.

"Go on," Deverell prodded. "I'll help you climb over."

Dread began to beat a steady tattoo against my skull. True to its mythology, the Great Ouroboros was a singular object, with no beginning or end. There was no secret door through it, no passageway beneath it. The only way inside was to climb over, it seemed.

As Deverell had guessed, I needed help. It was too tall for me to jump and the top too high and round for me to hoist myself up. If only I'd been born a siren like Selene. Then it would've been easy.

For a moment, after Deverell helped me up and over it, I was alone. It would've been the perfect time to prepare an attack—if I'd had access to my magic, and if I hadn't been completely shocked by the scene inside the large stone ring.

There were five low stone altars—one in the middle with the others set around it like the four points of a compass. A body lay on top of each one. On the center stone, which sat higher than the others, was Marrow. I recognized him easily—his face the same as it had ever been, the only difference the longer, unkempt beard. He was lying on his back, his eyes closed and his arms crossed over his chest. The Death's Heart had been placed between his hands. It gave off a faint red glow that pulsated like a real heart. Sitting on the wall directly across from the altar was the black phoenix. Its red eyes were fixed on me, but it made no move to attack.

With terror twisting in my gut, I pulled my eyes away to look at the other altars. My spirits lifted as I saw Eli on the nearest one. He appeared to be asleep, but otherwise okay. Not at all like my mother lying on the next one. She was noticeably thinner and sickly pale. I rushed over to her. Dark bruises rimmed her cheekbones and the blue-black lines of veins were visible in her forehead.

I put my hand on her bare arm and flinched at the iciness of her skin. "Mom!" I shook her.

"Don't waste the effort," Deverell said, walking over to me. "She will not wake up so long as she is under the spell of the Death's Heart."

I glared up at him, tears hot in my eyes. "Take it off." It was a stupid demand, but desperation clouded my reason.

"All in good time," Deverell said. "And assuming you do your part."

I dropped my gaze back to my mother. If I only knew how to break the spell myself. I tried to reach out to Bellanax with my mind, but it was hopeless without my magic. Somehow I needed to break free of Deverell's spell and get the sword back.

With despair pressing down on me, I turned away from my mother. My eyes fell on the next altar, the one directly above Marrow. For a moment, I had no idea who was lying there, but then slowly I realized it was Bethany Grey.

She was utterly changed. The woman I'd known before had been large and strong, with mounds of extra flesh on her body, the kind of woman who would've looked at home in a powerlifting contest. But now, Bethany Grey had been reduced to a shell of a person. There was still extra flesh, but it hung off her bones in loose folds, as if all the muscle and fat beneath had been sucked out. Wrinkles covered her ashen skin in a thousand spiderweb cracks. Like the vision of my dead body in Eli's dream, her eyes were sunken into her head, her face skeletal.

I covered my mouth against my revolting stomach.

Seeing my alarm, Deverell turned his attention to Bethany. He let out a long, low sigh. "It's tragic, isn't it? She was once such a fearsome creature."

"You're disgusting. You did this to her." Bethany Grey had been a horrible person, who'd done horrible things, but she didn't deserve this. No one did. This was the very worst suffering I'd ever seen anyone endure. She'd been wasted away to nothing by the Death's Heart.

"Wrong," Deverell said, placing his hands on his hips. "Bethany did this to herself. Oh, I put the spell on her, to be sure, but she earned her place. In fact, when I helped her escape the Rush, she surrendered to the Death's Heart's magic willingly. She failed the Red Warlock. You and your mother should never have been able to defeat him. Bethany understood she was the weak link. She failed him in life, but has repaid him in her death. She has made the ultimate sacrifice to our master."

"That's sick." I pointed at Marrow. "He's already lived dozens of lives. He didn't even deserve the first one."

"You're wrong. He deserves all we have to give him."

I shook my head. "So is that why you killed Titus? Did he fail Marrow in some way?"

"Not exactly. Titus's sin was that he presumed himself to be as great as Marrow. I couldn't allow him to continue." Deverell turned and motioned to the fourth altar. "But like Bethany, Paul was also there when you defeated my master. He, too, owes a death, but he is so young still. I decided to give him a second chance, but sadly he failed once more."

My head buzzed with alarm, and I jerked my gaze toward the last altar. Paul was lying there in the same unconscious pose as the others. I hurried over to him, afraid that he wouldn't be far behind Bethany. But when my eyes fell on him fully, I saw that he was hardly more drained than Eli.

"How long has he been like this?" I turned to Deverell.

He thought about it a moment, doing a mental calculation. "Six days. He's been working for me all along, you know. From the moment he first revealed himself to you in the infirmary. I needed your help, you see. Or more specifically, what you call the Dream Team's help. I'd been trying to take out Corvus for months now. I've been able to stay ahead of him, but he was closing in. I couldn't risk going to his house on my own. If he'd discovered me, I would've had to find a new disguise, and that takes planning and more time than I could afford. But the investigation you launched against him proved the perfect cover."

I felt the color leach from my face. Paul had been involved in all the evidence we discovered. He'd hacked Valentine's files. He could have altered the contents before handing them over. It was Paul's idea for us to go to Corvus's house. It was Paul who gave me the shape-change necklace and insisted only I could go to Corvus's house with him.

But no, I refused to just take this man's word on it. Deverell was a master of deception. "Why would Paul have helped you? He turned his back on Marrow after he learned that Titus was one of his supporters."

"Did he now?" Deverell arched a single eyebrow. "Are you sure?"

I wanted to rip the mocking expression from his face.

"The thing about Paul," Deverell said, crossing his arms over his chest, "is that he craves freedom and acceptance above all else. These are the two things his uncle denied him for so long. But

Paul is not stupid. He knows that given his history the only way he will ever be free is when Marrow is in control. The Magi Senate will never trust him enough to leave him unattended. He found that out quite well in the months after Marrow's defeat."

The room seemed to spin around me. I remembered how sincere Paul had been when he told me he would do anything to avoid being imprisoned once more. At the time, I'd thought he meant that he was on the straight and narrow path. Except with his Will Guard monitors and the need for the shape-change necklace, he was more a prisoner than ever.

The realization turned my blood to ice water. "If Paul is working for you, then why is he like this?" I motioned to his unconscious body, tears threatening again, angry ones this time.

"He had a last minute change of heart," Deverell said. "He started questioning me at every turn, doubting my decisions. I knew it was only a matter of time before he weakened. It all started when he and I brought your mother down here. I think it was because the two of you look so much alike."

"What does that have to do with anything?"

Deverell rolled his eyes. "As if you don't know. Paul is in love with you. You might be the one thing he wants almost as much as his freedom and autonomy. Of course, again, he's not stupid. He knows you don't love him in return, but feelings like that are a sort of sickness. The heart has a way of corrupting the mind. I knew it was just a matter of time before he was tempted to tell you the truth, so I took the option away from him."

I gritted my teeth. "So now you are the one denying him his freedom."

Deverell shrugged. "I could've just killed him instead. Would that have been better? It certainly would've been easier than having to pretend I was him all day, if I had done the true shift on him."

"No kidding," I said. "You sucked at being him." Outwardly,

I sounded brave, but inside my fear was spreading like an epidemic. He could've killed Paul—and eaten his heart. He could've done it to Eli or my mom.

He could do it to me and no one would ever know. They'll never find me down here.

Deverell laughed. "It was good enough to fool you for a while. The mission to Corvus's house was a success." He reached into his pocket and withdrew a silver ring.

"You stole that?"

"Oh, yes. This ring was the main reason I've had Paul working so hard to get you there. Corvus kept it in a safe in the kitchen. Took us a long time to figure out the location and combination."

"What is it?"

"Invincibility." Deverell reached into his other pocket and withdrew two more rings, one golden and the other the dark dull color of iron. He placed the silver ring with the other two. Then he closed his fingers around them.

Magic stirred in the air. There was a faint tinkling sound, and then Deverell opened his hand once more. The three rings were now linked into one. He held it up, and I saw that together they made the Borromean rings—the symbol of magickind united. If the silver ring belonged to Marrow, I wondered if the other two had once belonged to his Borromean brothers, now dead.

I shivered, sensing the power in the rings the same way that I sensed it in Bellanax. "That makes someone invincible?"

"As near as it is possible to be." Deverell aligned the three rings into one and then slid it onto his right index finger. With a look of triumph he clasped his hands together and turned his attention fully to me. "It's now time for your part." Deverell reached into his pocket once more and this time he pulled out my silver bracelet.

I inhaled, jealousy and fear warring for dominance inside of me. I wanted Bellanax back. Right now. For a second I wanted it more than anything else, even saving my mother and Eli.

Unaware of my inner struggle, Deverell took off the glamour on the sword. Bellanax appeared in his hand, the runes on the blade winking in the lights floating overhead.

He turned the sword over, examining it from all sides. "Do you know much about sword lore, Dusty?"

I shook my head. "Lady Elaine says most of the lore has been lost."

Deverell clucked his tongue. "So it has, like so many things. I didn't know much about it myself, either, but I've since learned. It appears that some swords, the most powerful ones, have the ability to steal the souls of those they kill. A bit like the Death's Heart, actually."

Mr. Corvus's words came back to me—*soul magic.* A deeper, darker fear began to spread through me now.

"Only for most swords, the soul-stealing happens only during the first kill," Deverell continued, turning Bellanax over to examine the other side. "It was for this reason that a young swordsman in possession of a newly made sword would often seek out the most powerful being he could find to kill first. That's how this sword became a numen vessel in the first place. The very first person to possess the sword all those centuries ago sought out the most powerful magickind of the age, and killed him with it."

Bellanax, I thought. Had it been a person once? A magickind, slain by the sword's first owner and trapped inside it forever?

"Marrow became its owner not long after," Deverell said, walking over to the center altar. I followed him, reluctantly. "He made it what it is now. He possessed the sword up until the time you killed him."

I flinched. It was true—I had killed him, stabbed him with his own sword; I'd done it to save my mom, Eli, Selene, myself.

But I suddenly felt unclean, soiled by the sword and its blood-thirsty history.

"But a strange thing happened then." Deverell shifted the sword in his hands, turning it sideways where he cupped the blade with his other hand. "The sword had never been used against Marrow before, never on a man who can be killed but who cannot die. All the other times Marrow had been killed before, the sword remained safe from his attackers, the bond unbroken. But when you used his own sword on him, you trapped him in it. His soul—his vital essence—should have stayed tethered to his body long enough for the phoenix to reclaim him. Instead, you sliced it free and the sword pulled him in. Marrow has been trying to get out ever since."

I felt my knees go weak and I started to sway on my feet. Memories raced through my mind of all the times the sword had spoken to me, of the way it had shared spells with me. It's intelligence and liveliness had been so far above other numen bonds, nothing at all like Eli and his wand.

Marrow, I thought. It had been Marrow all along. *Or had it?* Bellanax was in there, too. Wasn't it?

"It took me a very long time to figure it out," Deverell said, drawing my attention back to him. "I'd done everything right to revive Marrow. He trained me well what to do if he was killed. I sought out the Great Ouroboros, knowing he would need its power to speed up the process, and the black phoenix performed its part—resurrecting his body with its magic. Everything seemed to be working, but Marrow would not wake up. I performed *nous-desmos* with him and there was nothing there. He was an empty shell."

Deverell paused, his gaze dropping to Marrow for a moment. Then he looked back at me again. "I'd started to believe he might really be gone this time—that you had done the impossible and defeated him. But then you came to me for help, and I noticed the block on your mind. Marrow told me once it had been the same for him when he first claimed the sword. He did not know its name, but oh how he wanted to."

Just like me. My muscles clenched.

"At first, I thought you bonding with the sword was evidence that Marrow was truly gone," Deverell continued. "But I refused to give up hope. Not until I had a chance to see the sword myself. The Magi Senate had hidden it away. I knew I had to help you get past the block and complete the bond. After you saved Lyonshold, while you were lying unconscious, I convinced Lady Elaine to let me examine you and the sword. It was easy once she learned all I'd done to help you." He paused, drawing a deep breath. "But the moment I touched it, I knew my master was not dead. I felt him there, dormant but no less powerful. It was then I realized what I needed to do to bring him back."

I thought I might be sick, shame burning in my belly. I'd fallen for it, fallen for everything. I'd been so easy to manipulate, so willing to trust.

"But all this had taken a long time," Deverell said. "Without its spirit, my master's body began to decay. I had no choice but to steal the Death's Heart to keep that part of him alive. And now, it's time for you to make him whole again." Deverell held the sword out to me.

"What am I supposed to do?" I didn't make a move toward the sword, even though every instinct I possessed was telling me to take it back. It belonged to me; we belonged together.

"It's simple." Deverell motioned toward Marrow. "I want you to kill him with it again."

Kill him? My stomach clenched. I shifted my gaze to Marrow. Asleep he didn't look at all scary, not how I knew he would be once restored to full life. This was a man bent on dominating the world. How could I willingly set him free? Assuming it would even work. The very notion that death would bring life seemed ludicrous.

"Come on now, Dusty. A deal is a deal," Deverell said, taking a step closer to me. "Once I restore Marrow to his full self, I will let you, your mother, and Eli go."

I clenched my teeth, knowing against all hope that he was lying. The last time I'd faced Marrow he'd made it quite clear that he couldn't let a pair of dream-seers live, not if we weren't using our powers for him. Deverell wouldn't be any different.

I looked away from him, down at Marrow. There had to be some way. There was always a way, wasn't there?

Bellanax. My eyes fixed on the sword. It was The Will sword, the most powerful magical object in existence. And Deverell was offering it back to me. He believed I would do it, that I would use the sword on Marrow to save my loved ones. But he was forgetting something crucial. While Marrow might have corrupted the sword's magic from the inside, on the outside, it was still a sword—a weapon designed for killing.

Oh, I would use it all right.

On him.

I closed my eyes for a moment, summoning all my courage. I would have to be quick. No hesitation. We were standing close enough I could reach him easily with that three feet of steel.

"Okay," I said. "Give it to me."

A confident smile snaked across Deverell's face as he handed the sword over.

My fingers closed around the hilt, and something clicked inside me, the reassurance of my bond with Bellanax. The sword surged to life, and its power began to flow into me. My own trapped magic didn't matter. With this sword in my hands, I was invincible once more. All my fears drained away. Bellanax was here with me. To serve me, to defend and protect.

But then another power reared up in the sword, something dark and equally strong—*Marrow*.

The two powers struggled for dominance. For a moment, I was certain Bellanax would win, but in the next I sensed the dark power expanding, forcing out the light. I started to let go of the hilt, but I wasn't fast enough. In an instant, the sword's power turned against me—and took over. It was a feeling I'd experienced before. Once on Lyonshold and once in Deverell's classroom. *Possession.*

No. I fought against it, eyes squeezed shut. But it was like trying to stand in a rushing river. Without my own magic to cling to, my mind and will bent toward Marrow's. Inch by inch the sword turned me away from Deverell and toward Marrow's body, lying prone just ahead.

I shifted the sword in my hand, pointing the blade downward. My gaze fell on the Red Warlock. His face was waxy in his long sleep, his body close to lifeless.

I raised the hilt of the sword above my head, and then with one mighty thrust, I drove it down, burying the blade in Marrow's chest.

There was a loud burst of power as the sword connected with the Red Warlock. Magic exploded outward, making the ground shake and the walls tremble. Bits of rocks sprayed down from the ancient ceiling in a haze of dust. The black phoenix launched into the air, seeking a safer perch.

I barely noticed. The sword was vibrating in my hands, making my whole body shake. Something was wrong. I could sense the sword's fear—the real Bellanax, the true heart of the sword and numen vessel.

I tried to pull the sword out, to save it, but the blade shattered.

There was another explosion of magic, and Bellanax's presence in my mind vanished. I held the hilt in my hand, but several inches above the cross guard, the blade ended in a jagged, diagonal line of shorn steel. The Will sword, the sword of power and ancient magic, indestructible and infallible, was broken.

My eyes dropped to the body beneath me. One moment my heart pounded painfully against my breastbone, as if it were trying to force its way out, and in the next it stopped beating all together. The air in my lungs left me in a scream loud enough to make the walls tremble again.

It wasn't Marrow lying on the altar beneath me.

It was Eli.

He was awake, eyes open, and mouth twisted in a grimace of pain. Blood was spreading over his chest where the sword had pierced him, where even now half of Bellanax's blade remained.

28

The Curse

The world ended.

I could feel it happening, a single moment stretching on into eternity. There would never be anything good again, nothing but this—Eli dying.

By my hands.

My knees gave way, and I collapsed beside him, dropping what remained of the sword. "Eli!" I screamed. "Eli!"

It couldn't be him. It couldn't. Marrow had been lying here, so real and solid. But then I saw the necklace around Eli's throat—stiff like a choker, a green gem at its center, in between smooth, opaque teeth. It had all been an illusion, a horrible deadly charade. Even the Death's Heart was gone. But if Eli had been here the whole time, where was Marrow?

I turned to the altar across the way, the one where Eli had lain when I first arrived. Marrow occupied it now. He was slowly rising to his feet, the real Death's Heart in his hand. It no longer glowed, but was a black lifeless thing once more.

"Master," Deverell said, stepping forward to help steady the older man. "Here, you'll want this now that the sword is broken."

Marrow turned his clouded gaze onto the object Deverell was

holding out to him. "The Borromean rings?" Marrow's voice creaked like too-dry leather.

"Yes, the true one. I have finally united them again."

Marrow dropped the Death's Heart, tossing it aside like it held no more significance than a child's toy. He extended his right hand and allowed Deverell to slide the ring into place on his index finger.

"What did you do?" I screamed at Deverell, the sound choked by tears. My mind was beyond thinking, beyond anything but the horror expanding in my chest, threatening to suffocate the life from me.

"There was one final piece of the sword lore I forgot to mention," Deverell said, his voice mockingly casual. "The only way to free a spirit trapped in a blooded sword is to break the blade." He paused, and the smile that crossed his lips might've been mistaken for sympathy if not for the cold glint in his eyes. "And the only way to break a sword of power is through an act of betrayal by its master."

Betrayal.

"But . . . but I didn't do it. It wasn't me. You made me do it. I didn't know!"

Deverell laughed. "You think intent matters in such things? That the magic can distinguish between what's you and what's the sword? It does not and it cannot. A physical act is a physical act. Murder is murder."

I looked back at Eli, flashes of Lady Elaine's vision playing in my mind. *The curse.* "Oh, God, Eli." I touched his face, fingers trembling. I didn't know what to do. He was bleeding out. He was going to die.

But he was still awake. A moan escaped his lips, and he reached for the blade in his chest, trying to wrench it out. He only succeeded in slicing his hands.

"Stop it, Eli!" I grabbed his arms and forced him down. If he pulled the blade free he would only bleed out faster. I looked at Deverell and then Marrow. The latter was fully awake now, fully alive and returned.

Thanks to me.

"Help me," I said.

There was no pity in Marrow's gaze as he turned it on me. No mercy. He no longer seemed confused by what was happening. Perhaps he wasn't. He'd been present for the whole thing, trapped inside Bellanax.

"Help me," I said, pleading now. "I saved you. You owe me."

"I owe you nothing," Marrow said. The creak in his voice was gone, replaced with the cold, firm surety of a man who'd lived and died a thousand times before. A man who feared nothing. Immortal and inhuman. "I gave you the chance to serve me once. Now you will serve no one."

I braced, waiting for him to kill me. Tremors rolled through my body in chaotic waves. But Marrow only stared at me a moment longer before turning his attention to Deverell. "You have done well."

Shock tore through me. He was going to let me live? It didn't make sense. Only . . . without my dream-seer power, I was no threat to him—and Eli was already dying.

A sob bubbled up in my chest, and I choked it off. I searched for my mother, hoping she could help now that the Death's Heart spell was broken, but she was unmoving atop the altar. Asleep or dead, I couldn't tell.

I turned to Paul. He was awake and sitting up, his eyes dazed—until they met mine. Understanding crossed his face, but his reaction was unreadable. It might have been triumph or regret or cold indifference. I didn't care. A fierce and primal desire to attack him came over me.

Belatedly, I realized that I *could* attack him—with magic. The shock wave of Bellanax breaking must've undone the block Deverell had put on me. With the knowledge came new hope. Not that I would survive this; I wasn't delusional. But that I didn't have to go quietly. I would rather die fighting than live without Eli. Than to live knowing I had killed him.

Marrow and Deverell both had noticed Paul now, and I took advantage of their distraction to retrieve what remained of Bellanax, the hilt with its broken blade lying at the base of the altar. The moment I picked it up, I sensed the magic in it still; some small remnant of Bellanax remained. It would have to be enough.

"What shall we do with the boy?" Deverell said, directing the question at Marrow.

The Red Warlock rubbed a hand over his long beard, smoothing the ragged strands straight for a moment. "Stand up, Paul Kirkwood," Marrow finally said.

Paul did so, visibly trembling from either weakness or fear or both.

Marrow walked closer to him, his long red tunic billowing behind him. From its perch atop the wall, the black phoenix gave a loud, long screech. The sound made Paul flinch, but he did not retreat.

Marrow halted a few feet from him. "You have betrayed me in your heart, Paul Kirkwood. You claim to serve me, to want my will to be done, but in your heart it is your own will that holds sway."

Paul swallowed, the cords in his throat flexing.

"If you would have me spare you, if you would commit yourself to me, then you must prove your loyalty." Marrow stopped speaking, and the black phoenix shrieked again.

"How?" Paul said.

Marrow's gaze slid to me then back to Paul. "You already know."

Kill her.

I gritted my teeth, my fingers clenched around Bellanax. So it would be Paul first. First him, then Deverell. If I could take down those two, it would be enough to make a difference—to have made my life matter.

I was still kneeling beside Eli, the sword out of sight for the moment. I touched what remained of Bellanax's spirit with my mind, asking it for help one last time. Sluggishly it gave me its answer.

"Dusty," Eli said.

I looked down to find his eyes on my face. He was more aware than before, fear and pain etched around his mouth. "Shhhh," I said. Then I leaned forward and kissed him on the lips. At the same time, I raised my hand and gave him the sword, forcing it into his palm. "Its name is Bellanax," I whispered. "It will keep you safe." *It will spare you more pain,* I silently added. It was all I could give him now.

Then not allowing him a chance to respond, I stood up and walked around the altar toward Paul. He approached me slowly, meeting my gaze. I saw hatred in his eyes and determination in the hard line of his mouth. I braced for the attack, turning the word of the spell over in my mind. But I needed to wait for the right opening. If I attacked too soon, he might block, and I would lose the element of surprise.

And my nerve.

My skin turned to ice, my body to stone. Every muscle clenched, every nerve ending firing with adrenaline.

Paul drew a deep, steady breath and let it out slowly. "I'm sorry, Dusty."

I didn't respond, only stared at him. My rage was beyond words, my hurt beyond argument.

"Did you . . ." He hesitated, his expression softening. For a moment, he looked like the Paul I first met—handsome, sweet, and incapable of duplicity, the Paul I always wanted him to be. "Did you ever love me?"

I could tell the question cost him, and some of my anger gave way to pity. I evaluated my answer carefully. This was the end, my last moments. I didn't want to lie. "Yes," I said, and my answer cost me, too.

Paul's lips twisted in disbelief.

"It's true. Do I feel for you what I feel for Eli?" My voice caught on his name, and I paused, wrestling for control. "No. But love . . . the kind that matters, the kind that lasts . . . that's not a feeling. It's a choice. I chose to believe the best of you, Paul. I chose to forgive you despite everything. I would never have been able to do that if I didn't care about you. Hatred? It's a whole lot easier."

"I know," Paul said at once, and there seemed to be a deeper meaning in his words. I wasn't sure if he believed me, or just that he wanted to. Or maybe some truth resonated inside him.

"Get on with it, Paul," Deverell said. "Before we make the choice for you."

"I'm sorry, Dusty," Paul said again, but his voice was different this time.

I braced, my magic at the ready, humming beneath my skin.

Paul raised his hand, and his mouth parted with the words of an incantation. "*Temno!*" he shouted, spinning around. I ducked, but there was no need. The spell burst from Paul's fingertips in a flash of white light and struck Deverell in the face. Deep, red gashes appeared across his cheek.

Deverell shrieked, but the pain didn't slow him down. "*Hypno-soma!*"

"*Alexo!*" Paul's shield spell went up just in time to deflect the dazing curse. It ricocheted, zipping over our heads and up toward the cavernous ceiling. A shower of rocks came falling down a second later.

Recovering from my shock, I cast the jab spell, aiming for Deverell's head. "*Fligere*."

He parried the spell and countered. I dove to the right, just out of the way. The black phoenix launched into the air, letting off another screech.

I rolled and jumped up. With Paul already engaging Deverell, I took aim at Marrow. "*Peiran*."

The spell soared right toward him, and Marrow made no move to defend. He didn't have to. When it came within a foot of him, the spell struck an invisible barrier and bounced off. Around Marrow's finger the Borromean ring glowed with a pure, white light.

A horrible sense of déjà vu came over me. The last time I faced Marrow he had been protected by Bellanax, the sword absorbing every combative spell we aimed at him. Nothing had gotten through, not until I'd used my mind-magic on the sword, making the attack physical instead of magical.

I searched the ground for a weapon, soon spotting a jagged rock the size of a baseball lying a few feet behind Marrow. With my mind-magic, I lifted it into the air then I flung it toward the back of his head, putting all the force into it that I could. It cut through the air with a sharp hiss followed by a loud crack. The rock bounced off the invisible shield same as the spell.

Marrow raised his right hand toward me, the glow of the Borromean ring painting his gaunt face a ghastly white with deep black shadows over his eye sockets. "*Ana-acro!*"

I flung my hand up. "*Alex*—"

Screeching, the black phoenix dove at me, talons extended. I fumbled the spell, and the bird swerved at the last second, dodging Marrow's incoming spell. The magic slammed into me.

Silver ropes appeared around my wrists and ankles, pinning my limbs together. I lost my balance and fell forward, striking the ground hard with no way to brace myself.

Marrow strode forward, his face lit with a sinister grin. "*Kaiodontia.*"

Pain exploded over my skin like being jabbed with a million tiny needles all at once. I screamed, convulsing against the silver ropes. Marrow took off the spell, giving me a few seconds of relief, only to cast it again. It was worse the second time, knife points instead of needles.

I forced my eyes opened and onto Paul, onto anything that might distract me from the pain. But my screams had distracted him. He turned a quick glance on me, just long enough for Deverell's spell to strike him in the leg. There was a sharp snap, like the sound of someone breaking a tree branch over a knee, and Paul collapsed.

Once more, Marrow removed his spell, and the feel of those fiery fangs chewing up my skin dissipated. I sucked air through my teeth, my body raw and throbbing.

"What shall we do with them now?" Deverell said, his gaze fixed on Marrow. There was something hungry in his expression. Gooseflesh broke out over my already tender skin.

I looked away from him, my stomach roiling as my mind provided a gruesome image of him eating a human heart. Movement in the distance caught my eye. My breath hitched when I saw that my mother had rolled over onto her stomach. She was awake and positioned behind Marrow and Deverell.

I pulled my gaze away from her, afraid Marrow would notice. At the moment he was staring at Paul, his expression evaluative. I could hear Paul's labored breathing as he held his broken leg between his hands. He wouldn't be able to attack with magic, not with the pain of a broken leg getting in the way.

Marrow shook his head. "Neither shape would be worth much to you after—"

"*Hupno-soma!*" My mom's voice cut across the room, shrill and tremulous.

Marrow and Deverell both turned. I watched the spell reach Deverell, but nothing happened. He didn't even flinch. The magic in it had been weak, almost nonexistent. With a sinking heart, I realized my mom had been under the Death's Heart spell too long. She hadn't dream-fed in weeks, her fictus all but gone.

"Now that one," Marrow said, extending his hand toward my mother. "Has a heart worth taking. *Ana-agra!*" The same silver ropes around my wrists and ankles appeared around my mother's. The next moment, Marrow lifted her into the air by those ropes and levitated her closer to where Paul and I lay. She landed in an awkward heap and let out a whimper. I tried to shut the sound out, tears stinging my eyes. At least from this position I couldn't see Eli. I didn't have to watch him dying.

"It will be my pleasure to take it," Deverell said. He stepped up to my mother, stretched out before him. Long, curved claws had appeared on the tips of his fingers. They looked sharp enough to shred raw meat, to tear through the bones of her rib cage and yank the heart from her body.

"Don't!" I jerked against the ropes, ignoring the way they burned my skin from the movement. The sweet, repugnant stench of singed flesh and hair reached my nose. "Don't!"

"Hold on," Marrow said, and Deverell paused, his predator's hands hovering inches above my mother's prone form. "Let's see to the daughter first."

My mom started to scream, but Deverell slapped her, open-palmed. His claws left red ribbons of blood across her face, and she fell silent.

Marrow took a step closer to me. "Do you have your knife?" he said, motioning to Deverell.

A moment later, Deverell handed him a knife with a serrated blade made of bone.

Marrow gripped the knife overhand like an ice pick. "It's only fitting that the dream-seers should die together, slowly and painfully. But don't worry, my dear Dusty. In the end, dying is so much like sleeping. For you, it might even be like dreaming."

I could only hope. My thoughts turned to Eli, the fear inside me smaller than it might've been. There was no point in fighting anymore. There was no way out of this. With the silver ropes around my wrists I was as helpless as a newborn kitten, completely at the mercy of the man standing over me. My life, as short and insignificant as it had been, meant nothing to the Red Warlock. I was just one more victim in a long slaughter line.

Marrow raised the dagger over his head, and I craned my neck toward Eli. I could just see him still lying on the altar. His eyes were closed, but his chest rose and fell. Asleep then, or so I hoped. I would join him in his dreams, and we would die together. In the end, there was no other way I would've chosen.

~ 29 ~

The Fallen

My eyes slid closed, and I waited for the blow to fall.

It never came.

A strange thumping sound filled the air—no it *beat* the air.

I opened my eyes, my heart climbing into my throat, hope filling my lungs. A second later, I spotted her. Somehow, someway, Selene had found her way here. She soared through the air, her black wings like rallying banners. She wasn't alone. Impossibly, Corvus was dangling from her arms. The weight of him dragged her down, each vertical inch a struggle, but it didn't matter. As soon as they cleared the Great Ouroboros, she let go. Corvus hit the ground, rolled, then sprang to his feet with the agility and grace of a much younger man. He let fly with a spell, aiming low.

The magic struck the ground a few feet from Marrow. The rock floor exploded, pieces spraying up like shrapnel. Marrow and Deverell both dove for cover, while I rolled around, trying to protect my face and head.

"*Ou-agra*," a voice spoke from behind me. A second later, I felt the silver ropes around my limbs falling away. Gaping, I looked toward Eli. He was leaned toward me with Bellanax pointed like a wand. I lurched to my feet and raced over to him.

"Eli, you shouldn't—"

He silenced me with a hard, fierce look, one that belied the weakness I sensed in him. Blood still flowed from the wound in his chest.

"Fight," he said. "Stop them."

It took all my will to turn away from him. But he was right. The odds had tipped, and there might still be time to save Eli. Real life wasn't like the movies. Death wasn't always so quick, but sometimes a slow, creeping thing like a snake stalking its prey through tall grass. *Hurry, hurry, hurry,* the need pulsed through me, adrenaline sharpening my focus and reflexes.

Corvus was taking on Marrow and Deverell at once, lobbying spells and countering them. His skill made the best of the gladiator team look like beginners. I cast the unbinding spell at my mother, freeing her from the silver robes.

"Help, Eli," I told her. Then I joined Corvus in the attack.

Overhead, Selene was busy with the black phoenix. The moment the bird had spotted a moving target it had zeroed in on her. Now they were engaged in a kind of aerial war dance. They dove and soared, spun and twirled—the phoenix chasing while Selene aimed spells at it over her shoulder.

With Marrow protected by the Borromean ring, the best Corvus and I could do was keep him and Deverell too preoccupied to escape. Marrow spent as much time protecting Deverell as he did attacking us. We were lucky that Marrow seemed to be at half strength. As it was, we could barely match him.

But the scales tipped once again as Selene dove toward us, heading for Marrow. She was covered in dirt and blood, her wings ripped in places, but she flew straight and fast, more missile than girl. Marrow only had time to duck, but Selene caught him easily, one hand taking hold of his long beard and the other his arm. Then using the momentum of her dive, she hoisted him up, flew a few dozen feet, and hurled him at the wall.

He hit it back first, skull whacking against the stone. He dropped to the ground and lay there, motionless. The black phoenix screamed outrage and went after Selene with renewed fervor. She tried to stay ahead of it, but she was tiring and the attack on Marrow had slowed her down. When the black phoenix reached her, it sank its talons into her left wing and yanked, shredding feather and cartilage both. The phoenix didn't let go until it had torn all the way down the length of the wing. Selene tried to stay in the air, but her injured wing failed. She began to fall in quick, awkward spirals, half-gliding with her uninjured wing.

"Selene!" I reached out to her with my mind-magic. I couldn't stop her falling; I wasn't strong enough for that, but I helped steady her descent. She landed on her feet hard then tumbled forward. Her wings were stretched out behind her, one black and whole, the other a bloody ruin.

The black phoenix wasn't satisfied. Already it was swooping down for another pass at her. Leaving Corvus to deal with Deverell, I raced over to Selene, arm extended over my head as I let off a barrage of spells at the bird. Despite its massive size, it was impossible to hit, but I was able to keep it from getting close enough to strike again. It helped that Selene had fallen near the wall, giving us partial cover.

"Are you okay?" I asked, when I reached Selene. She was slowly struggling to her feet.

"I will be," she replied, although I could hear agony in her voice. But the pain didn't keep her from shooting a dazing spell at the black phoenix circling above us. In seconds she had things under control enough that I could turn my attention back to the fight between Corvus and Deverell. Marrow was still lying next to the wall, unconscious it seemed.

"So you finally found me," Deverell said, flashing a malicious grin at Corvus. "Took you long enough."

"It was easy," Corvus replied. "Once you entered my house and stole my ring. *Fligere!*"

The spell soared to Deverell, but he blocked it. "How did you find your way down here though? That was impressive, even from you. *Ceno-crani!*"

Corvus parried the magic with a casual flick of his arm. "I put a tracer spell on my safe. Although I never believed you would be stupid enough to fall for it."

Deverell's expression darkened, and he cast another curse at Corvus, anger threading his voice.

I turned back to Selene. "You got this?"

She nodded, biting her lip as she concentrated on the black phoenix. Wishing her good luck, I darted across the circle, meaning to run behind Deverell to get to Marrow. If Selene had been able to pick him up that way, then maybe the Borromean ring didn't protect him from a close, direct physical attack. If I could get the ring from him, we might succeed.

The moment I drew near, Deverell launched a spell at me. "*Fligere!*"

"*Alexo.*" My shield spell went up just as Deverell's jab spell crashed into it. The shield shattered on impact, but it still deflected Deverell's spell, shooting it right back at him. He saw it too late, and the magic glanced his shoulder, knocking him backward a step.

It was the opening Corvus had been waiting for. With hatred burning in his eyes, he ran forward, seized Deverell by the throat, and hoisted the shape-changer into the air with brute strength. Deverell grabbed Corvus's wrists and tried to pull him off, but Corvus was bigger and his rage lent him power.

Abruptly, Deverell stopped struggling. His face began to blur as he shifted his shape. Lean, wiry Deverell disappeared, replaced by a hulking, mountain of a man I'd never seen before. Corvus wasn't strong enough to hold up this new form, and a second later the shape-changer broke free. He let out a booming, gleeful laugh and threw a punch. The meaty fist connected with Corvus's jaw. The older man's head snapped sideways, and he stumbled, nearly falling from the blow.

"*Frangere!*" I said. The breaking spell struck the shape-changer in the chest, but he only grunted, the thick, tough hide of his new shape protecting him.

Corvus recovered enough to throw a dazing curse at him, but like my breaking spell, it had little effect. Deverell was slower in this body, but his size and strength made up for it. He lunged for Corvus with a bearlike movement. Corvus shuffled back, just escaping the assault.

"*Ana-agra!*" I heard Paul cry from behind me. I turned to see that he struggled to a standing position, all the weight on his un-injured leg. The spell hit the shape-changer, but as the silver ropes began to appear, he widened his arms and legs, using sheer physical will to keep the magic from binding him.

"No you don't!" I shouted. "*Ana-agra!*" A second set of binding ropes appeared around Deverell. Half a breath later, Corvus cast the spell as well. Beneath the power of the three spells, the shape-changer's strength finally gave way. The magic drew his hands and feet together, and it was all he could do to stay upright.

Corvus strode toward him, once again seizing him by the throat. The shape-changer's form blurred for a second time. I half-expected him to turn into Corvus and make a twisted play for mercy, but instead he reverted to his Deverell shape. Fear sparkled in his eyes. He opened his mouth, trying to speak, but Corvus only tightened his grip. For a moment, I thought he meant to strangle Deverell to death.

But then Corvus drew back his right hand, still holding

Deverell's neck with the other. He pointed at the shape-changer's face. "This is for my brothers, you son of a bitch. *Luo-dikho!*"

Strangling would've been better, cleaner.

The asunder curse struck Deverell dead center. His body ripped apart in a spray of blood, tissue, and bone. Then the two halves of him crumbled to the floor with wet, meaty thumps.

All the light in the cave vanished, and darkness descended like curtains. But it was too late to block out what I'd seen. My gorge rose, and I choked it down.

Corvus spoke an incantation into the darkness, and light reappeared, the same glowing orbs that Deverell had used. With the shape-changer's mangled body once more in view, I turned away, my arms and legs trembling. I was too sickened to be relieved about Deverell's demise. I almost forgot where I was, what I should be doing. Then I spotted Marrow lying in the distance, and I forced my feet to propel me forward.

"Dusty, look out!" Selene shouted.

Too late I saw the massive form of the black phoenix diving my way. Several spells struck it, one from Selene, one from Corvus. Even Paul had taken aim at it from where he stood, leaning against one of the altars. It didn't matter. The black phoenix was either immune or too focused on its goal to care. Its talons closed around my shoulders, piercing flesh and muscle. I shrieked as it pulled me into the air. Agony shot down my arms and back.

"Dusty!" This time it was Paul shouting.

The black phoenix carried me across the circle toward Marrow then let go. The fall wasn't far but I landed hard enough to knock the wind out of me. Panicking with the need to breathe, I couldn't fight the hands that closed around my arms, hoisting me to my feet. The renewed pain in my shoulder drove off the haze from the fall, and I let out an involuntary scream.

"Don't struggle," Marrow spoke into my ear. His familiar had delivered me to him like a cat with a dead mouse. A shudder passed through my body.

Suddenly aware of the serrated knife at my throat, I forced myself to still.

Everyone else had frozen as well, all except for the black phoenix, flying in calm, sweeping circles above us now.

"You all understand how this works," Marrow said, pushing me forward. "I will be leaving, and so long as you stay there and don't try to stop me, Dusty will live. If you try to stop me, she will die and the rest of you will follow."

It wasn't a hollow threat. He might be weaker than the last time I faced him, but he remained impossibly strong, his magic coming off him like an electrical current. Combined with the Borromean ring's protection he was as formidable as ever.

"Do what he says," I said, fixing my gaze on Corvus. Of all of them, he remained the biggest threat to Marrow. My mother was standing next to him, and although her face spoke of murder, she didn't have the strength to back it up. She looked ready to collapse at a single puff of wind.

I shifted my gaze to Eli. He was still sitting up, leaning heavily on one hand, the other clutching Bellanax. There was something odd in his expression. He looked far away. *Fading away.* Terror clawed at my thoughts.

"Please let him go," I said, once again addressing Corvus. *And hurry,* I silently added, tears burning my eyes. Eli was still alive, but each second, each desperate beat of his heart, only drove him closer to the end. The life was seeping out of him in visceral display. Blood soaked his chest and the altar beneath him.

"Okay," Corvus said. "Go."

"There's a good Nightmare," Marrow said, and then grabbing me by the shoulder, he pulled me back with him, edging us toward the wall. I kept my eyes on Eli. I didn't care if Marrow escaped so long as Eli lived. My heartbeat counted out the seconds. How much longer did he have?

"Dusty," Eli called, and his voice was so weak I barely heard him.

"Don't talk, Eli. Please don't talk."

He raised his hand, the one holding Bellanax. "This is still yours," he said, and then with all the strength he had left in him, he hurled the sword into the air.

It was an impossible throw, an impossible distance. But this was no ordinary sword, and Eli no ordinary boy. The sword flew through the air, spinning hilt over jagged blade. Time seemed to slow around me, around everything except the sword that flew with a singular purpose. I raised my hand, fingers outstretched, and Bellanax soared into it, the hilt landing in my palm like it had always been there.

The moment my skin brushed it, the bond between girl and sword, between magickind and numen vessel, knitted into place, like ligaments binding two bones into a single joint. The spirit in the sword was weak, only half-present, but our connection remained strong. Bellanax reached for control and I gave into it, lending the sword strength. This was the Bellanax from Lyonshold, the one who had saved the island and everyone on it. And now it would save me.

With the sword guiding my movements, I spun toward Marrow. His hand still held the knife, but he didn't have the same skill with a traditional weapon that he did with magic. I knocked the knife aside with Bellanax's jagged blade. The Borromean ring couldn't protect him now. I was too close, within its sphere of magic. I plunged the sword straight into Marrow's heart.

His eyes widened, and his lips spread as if he meant to laugh like he had the last time I'd stabbed him with this sword. But he didn't laugh. Death was too quick. With one, mighty shudder, the muscles in his body seized, then let go. He dropped to the floor. I kept hold of Bellanax, pulling the blade free as he fell. I didn't want his spirit trapped this time.

I looked down at Marrow's dead body, any thrill I'd felt vanishing at once. Already smoke billowed up around the corpse. The resurrection process had begun. The black phoenix screeched from on high. I looked up, my hope extinguishing.

This had to end. He had to die once and for all. But how? The bird was infallible. It had been hit with spells a half-dozen times, but it looked as sure and steady as ever. Maybe we could keep it away, never allow it to reclaim Marrow's spirit. But for how long? Eli didn't have time.

Screeching again, the black phoenix dove toward me. I knew it wouldn't stop, not until it had driven me away. I could either run or die. I stood my ground, Bellanax hot in my hand.

Something collided with the bird midflight, a human-like object. For a second, I thought it was Selene, then I saw it was a boy with white, underdeveloped wings, thin and malformed rising out of his shoulder blades.

Paul, I realized, bewildered. Paul, who was half wizard, half *siren*. Like Selene. Only unlike her, he had never learned to use his wings. He couldn't really fly, not much more than that first initial launch that had brought him soaring into the black phoenix's path. But it had been enough. He latched onto the bird's back as if he were trying to ride it like a dragon. The black phoenix was big, but not big enough to bear his weight. It had flown all the way to the ceiling, hundreds of feet above in its attempt to dislodge him, but now they were falling back to the ground.

Paul didn't even try to fly, his wings limp things streaming behind him. Instead he shifted his grip until both hands held the thin, hollow bone at the top of the black phoenix's wing. He gripped it—then yanked up, forcing the bone to bend in a way it was never meant to.

The black phoenix's cry drowned out the sound of the wing snapping. The bird twisted hard, body jerking convulsively. Paul's grip loosened. He started to slide, only to have the bird catch him as it turned. It wrapped its talons around his waist in a perverse sort of a hug. Paul hugged it back, his hands around its neck. He twisted as hard as he had with the wing. The black phoenix's body went rigid, and what had been a restrained descent turned into a straight plummet.

I tried to slow them down, but they were too heavy and the velocity too great. They struck the ground together in one deafening crack. They lay as they landed, boy and bird entwined, and did not move.

"Paul!" I rushed over to him but slowed as I drew near. The black phoenix was clearly dead, its head thrown back on its broken neck, its lifeless eyes like dull, black stones.

And Paul . . .

I turned away from his limp, shattered form, gasping. Hopeless despair pressed down on me. He'd died saving me from the black phoenix. He'd killed the mythical bird, but what did it matter? The creature was eternal. It would resurrect. So would Marrow. Only his foes truly died, never him. He would—

The thought halted in my mind, overtaken by the sudden realization that something had changed. Marrow's body was no longer smoking. There was no sign of fire, no sign of life.

I turned and looked back at the black phoenix. It, too, showed no sign of life, no hint of the magical flames that would resurrect it.

My mother staggered toward me. "Is it possible?" Her voice rose in shock, hopeful but afraid.

I glanced at Corvus. His gaze shifted between Marrow and the black phoenix over and over again. Then finally, he gave a single, slow nod. In my hand, I felt Bellanax's answering agreement.

"He's gone," Moira said. She turned to me. "He's gone."

I didn't reply. I wanted to be happy, to be relieved, but I couldn't. Paul was dead, and Eli—

My heart lurched into my throat. *Eli.* I spun around and raced over to him. "Eli!" He lay motionless on the altar, on his back once more, eyes closed. The broken blade still rose out of his chest. There was so much blood it looked as if the stone was bleeding along with him. But that was just an illusion. The blood was all his, all him—his life leaking out with every precious red drop.

It had leaked and leaked until he finally ran dry. I knew it without checking for a pulse or a breath. I could feel the absence of him as if a piece of myself had been ripped away. I collapsed next to him, cupping his head in my arms.

We had beaten Marrow, but the price was too high. Unbearable.

Eli Booker was dead.

~ 30 ~

Death Like Sleep

I cried.

Every fiber of my being wept, every muscle clenching and unclenching, spasms of despair and heartbreak. It was pointless, an empty gesture, but it was all I had left.

Eli was dead. I would never hear his voice again or feel his fingers on my skin. I would never taste his dreams, so sweet and perfect. He was lying on his back, eyes closed, death a masquerade of sleep on his face. But he wasn't dreaming. There was no fictus. There was nothing but the absence of everything.

"Dusty." A gentle hand touched the top of my head. "Come on, Dusty. We have to get out of here."

"No." I didn't look at my mother. I couldn't bear to take my gaze off Eli, knowing that this was the last time I would ever see him. Despite the ashen color of his skin and the caked blood around his mouth, he was still beautiful. I wished I could see his eyes, if only to memorize forever their unique shade of blue.

"He's gone, Dusty," my mother said, her fingers at my shoulder now. "You've got to let him go."

"No!" I shook her off, fury bubbling up inside me like acid.

"Your mother is hurt, Dusty," Corvus said from somewhere behind me. "So is Selene. They need your help to get out of here."

Guilt squeezed my chest, and I looked up at my mother. Her face was nearly as ashen as Eli's, deep black divots beneath her eyes. The Death's Heart had nearly killed her.

The Death's Heart.

Blood began to pound in my ears. I still held Bellanax in my hand, the hilt warm in my palm. A tiny thread of the sword's spirit remained, more echo than voice, but I touched it with my mind, seeking reassurance—and knowledge.

Once again, and for the last time, Bellanax told me what I needed to know. I stood up, summoning all the strength I had left. I was tired and sore, my shoulders aching from where the black phoenix had wounded me, but I had to push past that just long enough to accomplish this task. The others would try to stop me. I had to take care of them before they could.

"*Hupno-drasi!*" I aimed the sleeping spell at Corvus. The attack took him by surprise. His eyes widened with shock, but he was asleep before his body struck the ground.

"What are you doing?" my mom asked, taking a step back from me.

I pointed Bellanax at her. "What I have to. You need to dreamfeed. Selene and Corvus will need your magic to help them get out of here."

"Dusty, what are you saying?" Selene ambled toward me. Her wings trailed behind her. I doubted she could retract them with the damage to the left one. She was pale, like my mother, but still strong enough to put up a fight if she had to. And I knew she would, once she realized what I intended to do.

"I'm sorry, Selene, but I've got to do this. *Hupno-drasi!*" As with Corvus, she hadn't anticipated the attack, not from me, her best friend. She crumpled to the ground, deeply asleep and already dreaming. I hated the betrayal, but she would understand if the situation were reversed, if it had been Lance lying on that altar instead of Eli and she had been responsible.

"Stop this, Destiny," my mom shrieked. I'd never heard her sound like that, as if she were being rent apart from the inside out. For a second it was almost enough to stop me.

"I can't, Mom." Then turning my back to her, I walked over to the altar where Marrow disguised as Eli had lain when I first arrived. It seemed like years ago, an eternity. The Death's Heart had fallen behind the altar, nearly invisible in the shadows. I picked it up, my skin crawling at the slick, dense feel of it.

"You drop that now," my mom said, one hand pointed at me. It was an empty threat. She didn't have enough magic or physical strength to stop me—and we both knew it. But that didn't keep her from trying. "You can't do this. I won't let you." Her voice broke on a sob.

I closed my eyes and drew a breath, fighting back my own tears. I didn't want to hurt her, but—"I have to do this, Mom. I can't . . . I can't live knowing I killed him. And I can't live knowing I could've saved him."

My mom was crying in earnest now, her breathing jagged and her expression broken.

I didn't relent. I had to make her understand. "If you want to stop me, you'll have to kill me yourself. Either way I die, but at least this way, Eli will get to live."

She wasn't convinced—I could read it in her face—but I saw the fight slowly slipping out of her. She glanced at Corvus. As with Selene, fictus was coming off of him in waves, and she was hungry. Without a word, she turned toward Corvus. For a second, I was shocked by her compliance, but then I realized her plan. She would recharge her magic and stop me.

I was willing to let her try. It didn't matter. Only Eli mattered, and this heavy, gruesome object in my hand. With Bellanax's help, I would turn its evil power for good.

As my mom got in position over Corvus, I hurried over to Eli. I climbed on top of the altar, settling my knees on either side of his waist. I held the Death's Heart in my left hand and Bellanax in my right. Closing my eyes, I listened as the sword showed me how to turn on the Death's Heart, and how to channel its power the way I needed it to flow—my life for Eli's. Instead of draining his vital essence, I would pour mine into him.

The Death's Heart began to glow, red light oozing out of it like liquid blood. At once I felt the pull of it. It was like the pull of a dream, only deeper and heavier, a descent into darkness instead of the multicolor explosion of light and fictus. Terror, like in the split second before a car crash, came over me. But it was too late to change my mind, too late to let go.

And I didn't want to. I was a fire being snuffed out by the wind. I could feel it happening, my limbs growing heavy as my heart slowed. I became terribly aware of my breathing. It, too, was slowing down, each in-and-out of my lungs a greater effort than it had ever been before. I didn't fight it; I couldn't. It was like falling asleep, inescapable and welcome. Darkness swept over me. My vision dimmed. My muscles relaxed, and I fell forward.

I fell down . . . down . . . down into oblivion.

The cave was dark, the only light a scattering of glowing orbs, the magic inside them weakening by the second. But the two apparitions hovering above the stone altar could see easily, their spirits' eyes possessing a greater spectral range than their physical bodies had ever known.

"Is this a dream?" the girl asked, turning her gaze on the boy.

She was young and slender with red hair and eyes mirror-bright in the darkness.

The boy returned her gaze, an uncertain expression crossing his face. "I don't know," he said after a while. "It feels like a dream. . . ."

"But it doesn't," the girl finished for him.

He turned to her very slowly, unsure of himself, unsure of everything. "There's only one way to test it." He held out his hand palm up.

The girl studied him a moment, equally unsure.

Then making up her mind, she raised her own hand and pressed it to his, fingertips to fingertips, palm to palm. They were spirit, but their bodies inhabited the same plane of existence, giving them substance, one next to the other.

Nothing happened.

"Not a dream," they said together in eerie unison. But they did not break the touch. Instead they wove their fingers together. They drew closer, shoulder to shoulder. She leaned against him, sighing.

"What happened here?" the boy said. He swept his gaze over the room. It was a strange place, comprised of several low stone altars surrounded by a circular wall shaped like a dragon. They weren't alone, the boy realized. Some of the people were asleep, some were dead. At least two were dreaming. The boy glanced at the girl once more. "Are we dead?"

The girl opened her mouth to speak, but closed it as her eyes were drawn to the altar nearest them. Two figures lay on top of it—a boy and a girl just like them. "I don't know," she answered truthfully.

The boy reached for her with his other hand. He pulled her close. "I know what you did. I remember now." It sounded almost like an accusation, but not quite. The way his voice broke spoke of something different—awe or maybe despair.

"I had to," the girl said. "It was the only way to save you."

He cupped her face, fingers splayed. "But how do I save you?"

Tears appeared in the girl's eyes, glistening like diamonds. "You already did."

She leaned forward and kissed him. He kissed her back. It was a kiss full of unspoken words and affections, full of everything they couldn't say—*I love you . . . I need you . . .*

Good-bye.

A strange noise pulled them apart. They turned toward it, but they didn't break their embrace, arms folded around each other. He held her close, ready to die again to keep her safe. She did the same.

In the center of the circle they saw the carcass of a dead animal. Smoke was billowing up all around it. Flames quickly followed. Soon the fire was so large it filled the room with both heat and light. The flames licked and writhed, looking like something alive, a ravenous beast consuming the body of the bird at its center. It burned and ate and burned until there was nothing left but ashes and the fire went out.

The girl and boy watched it all, still locked in their embrace. They knew they should be afraid, but wonder prevented the feeling from reaching them. They were ghosts, after all, what did they have to fear from flame and ashes?

But then the ashes began to move, like the ground in an earthquake. Some of it gave way, while some of it bulged up in smoky upheavals. Slowly, a form began to take shape, rising out of the ashes like an animal burrowing out from the ground. First a beak appeared, and then a long, thin neck, like a heron's. The phoenix emerged fully grown, as large as a man. Black from beak to tail, it stretched its neck and then its wings. It gave a great shake as if it were covered with water instead of ash.

The girl covered her mouth, stifling a giggle. It was strange to see the formidable bird doing something so ungainly, so utterly normal. But the giggle soon turned into a gasp. The ash was falling away from the bird in a cloud of gray dust. When it cleared, the boy and girl saw the phoenix was no longer black as it had been in death. In this new life it was yellow and red, gold and rubies. Red feathers covered its back, head, and the top of its tail, while golden feathers formed its chest and the underside of its wings.

Tears filled the girl's eyes as she looked at the phoenix. It was so beautiful, indescribable in the way it made her heart feel light. She thought she could go on looking at it forever and never want for a different view.

"It needs a new name," the boy said, and the wonder in his voice gave sound to what the girl felt.

The phoenix opened its mouth. They both expected a screech, like the one they remembered—the kind that would pierce their hearts with terror. Instead it made a soft, cooing sound, sweet and almost musical. It was a lullaby sound, designed to soothe. Now the girl laughed openly.

The bird's head cocked toward the sound of her laughter. It stared at her with wide, curious eyes, a newborn exploring a new world. The girl told herself she should be afraid, but she couldn't manage the feeling. When the phoenix took a step forward, neither the boy nor the girl backed away. Just the opposite. The girl had a wild urge to rush forward and throw her arms around the bird's neck.

But then doubt sunk in. She was spirit. How could she touch it? She could touch the boy, yes, but he was spirit, too. The phoenix was real. And yet, when it reached them, it stretched out its long neck, bringing its head close to hers. The girl gave into desire and raised her hand, running her palm over the bird's head. Her fingers were solid against it, and she stroked its warm, silken feathers. The lightness in her heart suddenly grew lighter still, until she almost couldn't bear it.

The boy reached out and touched the phoenix as well. It permitted the touch, standing perfectly still. But only for a moment. Then it raised its head and breathed out, making that cooing sound again. It spread its wings and launched into the air. It was even more beautiful in flight. The girl openly cried now. The boy pulled her close, kissing the top of her head.

She turned toward him as the phoenix soared above them, its golden wings lighting the darkness like flames. Her lips found his, but the moment they touched a force began to pull them apart. The girl tensed, fear reaching her at last.

"Don't go," the boy said. He felt the pull, too. They were being drawn back to their physical bodies still lying on the altar. It was like ascending out of a dream. But to what?

"I love you," the boy said.

"Forever," the girl replied, and then the two spirits disappeared, vanishing back into the vessels where they belonged.

～ 31 ～

The After

Sunshine warmed my face, my eyelids awash in golden light. I was pleasantly hot, a heat that spread over my body like a blanket. A breeze teased across my skin, and strange sounds filled my ears. I spent several moments trying to identify them—flowing water, rustling leaves, chirping birds.

Was this heaven?

I didn't want to open my eyes. I was dead. I remembered dying, the way it felt to have my body surrender, all my vital processes giving out. One moment I was here, alive, and the next I was just gone. It was as simple as a light going out. On then off. Light then dark. Here then not here.

Only . . . I hadn't been completely gone, had I? I remembered Eli and me standing side by side, hand in hand, as we watched the black phoenix resurrect. No, as we watched the black phoenix reborn into something new—the golden phoenix. Then again, maybe that had been my imagination.

"Dusty, are you awake?" The voice didn't startle me. Instead it was a caress to my ears. *Eli.* I would know him anywhere. Definitely heaven then. Or more than heaven. It was paradise, a dream come true.

I opened my eyes and saw him peering down at me, blue eyes aglow in the sunshine. He was sitting on the ground next to me. I sucked in a breath. "Are we dead?"

He laughed, but winced right away, clutching his chest. "Not dead. I'm pretty sure I wouldn't hurt this bad if we were."

I sat up, the pleasant warmth switching to cold so fast I shivered. I started to ask if he was okay, but it came out as a gasp. A fierce ache throbbed through my entire body. Both of my shoulders felt like they were on fire.

"Are you okay?" Eli said, touching my arm.

I shook my head. "I feel like I've been run over by a truck."

"I know the feeling. But take it easy. You've been through a lot. We both have."

I looked up at him, ignoring the pain. "So we're really not dead?"

Eli didn't laugh this time, and he kept a hand pressed to his chest. He was wearing a green tunic and loose-fitting brown pants. It looked like a cross between a medieval Halloween costume and a hospital robe. "Not anymore."

Not anymore. So we had been. Dead. Memories crept into my mind—of the fight with Deverell and Marrow, of Paul and Eli dying, and of me using the Death's Heart on Eli. No, that wasn't right. I used it on myself. Bellanax had shown me how. The sword's absence gnawed at me. It was like knowing you've forgotten something important but being unable to remember what it was other than that it was important.

The memories were too much to think about. I turned away from Eli, taking in our surroundings. We might not be dead, but this place did indeed look like heaven, or at least heaven as I wanted it to be. We were in a glade hemmed by woods on one side and a stream on the other. Grass as green as AstroTurf and dotted with cartoon-bright wildflowers filled the glade, wrapping around ancient trees the width of cars and stretching along the bank with its short, steep drop-off into the water.

I turned back to Eli. "This isn't a dream, is it?"

"No." Then to prove the point, he took my hand and squeezed. My skin tingled at his touch. "This is fairyland."

"Excuse me?"

He grinned. "It's an otherworld, a realm for naturekind only."

I arched an eyebrow at him. I'd heard about otherworlds and fairy realms, like Mag Mell and Avalon, the legendary resting place of King Arthur. I knew enough about them to know that two people like us—human and Nightmare—weren't permitted to be here. "How is that possible?"

"Well," Eli said, cracking his knuckles, "when the naturekind senators found out we defeated Marrow, they insisted on sending us here to recover from our ordeal. There's healing magic here, apparently."

I dropped my gaze to his chest, the worst of the memories coming back to me—Eli with two feet of steel sheathed in his rib cage. "Do you . . . is it . . . is it bad?"

He shrugged, although the gesture wasn't as casual as it might have been. I could tell he was being cautious with each movement. "It's not pretty, but I survived, and that's what matters."

I nodded, swallowing back tears. "I'm sorry, Eli."

"What?" He grabbed my shoulders. "Are you kidding? It's not your fault. You didn't know it was me, Dusty. And then after." He hesitated, his eyes suddenly brighter than before, and glistening with unshed tears. "What you did with the Death's Heart— you saved my life, and you almost died doing it. You did die, but the phoenix brought you back. At least, that's what Lady Elaine thinks happened."

"That was real?" My heart fluttered in my chest, remembering what it had been like to see it.

"Yes, it was real. It seems that when Marrow and the black phoenix died at the same time, the familiar bond broke. Marrow stayed dead this time, but the phoenix was reborn back into its natural state, before Marrow corrupted it. I think . . . I think we freed it."

I didn't reply, my chest was too tight with emotions for speaking. But in my heart, I knew Eli was right. We had freed it. How many hundreds of years had the phoenix been chained to Marrow? How long had it been polluted by his constant, unnatural resurrections, his obsession with power? In some ways it had suffered more than anyone else.

But the idea that Marrow was really truly dead, that the threat of him was over for good was almost more than I could wrap my mind around. My relief wasn't as great as it should've been. Maybe in time.

"What about Paul?" I said, my voice quiet.

Eli looked away. "He didn't make it."

I nodded, already guessing as much. The truth cut deep, and I pushed it away. For now I wanted to focus on the good—Eli and I being here together, alive. And he didn't hate me or even blame me for what happened.

I leaned toward him and kissed him. He wrapped his arms around my back, pulling me closer. I savored the taste of him, but only for a moment. My heart began to ache as I realized this couldn't last. We couldn't keep doing this. Marrow was dead, but there was still the dream-seer curse. The phoenix was free, but we weren't.

"Are you two supposed to be doing that?"

Eli and I broke apart at the sound of the intruder. Lance and

Selene had just emerged from the trees across from us, walking hand in hand. Selene's wings were visible, the left one bound in white bandages. When her gaze met mine, she rushed forward.

"You're awake!" she said with a very un-Selene-like shriek of glee. She dropped down beside me and threw her arms around my neck.

I laughed, hugging her back, despite how much my body hurt at the gesture. "How long have I been asleep?"

"A year."

The laughter died on my lips. "What?"

"I'm kidding," Selene said, her expression impish. "It's just been two days, but it feels like a year. Time runs weird in this place."

"Yeah, but the scenery is like wow," Lance said, plopping down beside us.

I snorted. "You? Enjoying the scenery?"

He shrugged. "There's not much else to do. Besides kissing, of course."

Selene giggled.

"But what are you two doing here?" I said.

"Same thing as you," Selene replied. "Recovering. Every morning the fairykind send us to a different area to hang out. They claim all the nature around here speeds up healing. They've been taking you out of the castle every day and have you lie in the grass and stuff. Good thing it never rains."

It was so strange to think of my body going places without me being aware of it. But I had no memory of anything beyond using the Death's Heart. Watching the phoenix being reborn had felt more like a dream than anything real.

"But your wing," I said, shaking the weirdness off. "Are you going to be okay?"

"Yep, I should be flying again in no time." She flexed the good one in emphasis, the black feathers glistening like oil.

I beamed at her, relieved by this news. "But what about my mom and Mr. Corvus?"

"All fine," said Eli.

"Your mom is here with us," Selene added. "She needed the healing, and she insisted on coming, besides. I think she was afraid you weren't going to wake up."

I couldn't blame her for that. Not after Lyonshold. That time I'd been unconscious for weeks. Two days was a huge improvement, although the ache in my body disagreed.

"Actually," Selene said, standing up. "I'd better go get her. She's liable to hurt me for not telling her you're awake right away."

"We can save the hurt for later," a newcomer said.

We all turned toward the voice, and I saw my mom emerging from the woods now, following the same path Selene and Lance had. She looked good, or at least better. The ashen paleness in her skin had been replaced by a light tan, and only a shadow of bruising remained beneath her eyes. Still, I barely recognized her. She wasn't dressed in one of her usual snazzy outfits, the kind that belonged in a fashion magazine for young professionals, but in a silken gown with a scoop bodice and long, drooping sleeves. She looked more like Nimue than Moira Everhart. I sort of liked it.

"Stand up, Destiny," my mom said, striding over to me. "Prove to me you're really on the mend."

I frowned up at her. I couldn't see how standing up proved anything more than talking and sitting here. But then I tried to get up and saw her point. My muscles didn't want to obey. Gritting my teeth, I pushed through it, finally managing a vertical position.

My mom wasn't fooled. She folded her arms across her chest. "Well, alive but not better yet."

I flinched at her anger, not understanding it.

She pointed a finger at me. "I'm only going to say this once, but if you ever do something like that again, I'll . . . I'll . . ."

"Kill me?" I offered.

She scowled. "That's not funny, although it's a relief to see your inappropriate humor remains intact. But if you ever try that again, I'll ground you for the rest of your life. And trust me. I will ensure that it is a very long life. Full of absolutely zero danger."

She still sounded angry, but I saw the brokenness beneath her expression.

"I'm sorry, Mom."

Her anger vanished, and she swept forward, hugging me hard enough that I groaned. "I love you, Dusty," she whispered against my ear. "And I'm proud of you."

"I love you, too."

We spent another three days in the fairy realm. I asked my fairykind chaperones several times if the place had a name, but none were willing to say. I had a feeling that they wanted to keep it secret from outsiders like us. We might be welcome at the moment, but it was a temporary hospitality.

I spent most of my time walking the grounds outside the castle and exploring the woods with Eli. I avoided the bedroom I'd been given for the duration of my stay as much as possible. There were too many mirrors in there, and I couldn't quite stomach my appearance these days. I'd survived the ordeal with Marrow and the Death's Heart, but it hadn't been without a price.

I had aged, as if the Death's Heart had quite literally sucked away years of my life. I didn't look old exactly, but certainly not as young as before. Faint white hairs now streaked through the red. It wasn't anything a visit to the salon wouldn't fix—my mom had already volunteered to take me—but there was no disguising the changes in my face. I looked thinner, gaunt almost, but I hadn't lost any weight. In fact, I was eating more than ever before. This fairy realm encouraged indulgence of every kind. Although I never ate the fairy food. Normal food was being imported for us daily.

But the damage went deeper than my looks. None of the magickind doctors who came to examine me could say how bad it was, but they suspected that my organs, joints, and vital systems might have suffered partial degradation.

"But don't fret, my dear," one of the doctors said. "It's nothing too severe, I'm sure. Nothing worse than what happens to us all as we age."

I hadn't replied. The "effects of old age" wasn't something that should've been in my vocabulary for at least another decade or two. There was nothing to say about it though, nothing to make it better. Not that I regretted the price. Eli was alive and that was worth a hundred years of my life. Besides, the only time I noticed the changes in my body was if I sat too long in one position or if I exerted myself too hard. If I did, a weakness came over me, and I had to sit down until it passed.

Eli wasn't much better with his injury. The stab wound was healing quickly, thanks to the fairy realm magic, but he would never be the same physically again, according to the doctors. His hopes of being on the gladiator team were over, for this year definitely. Even once he recovered, he might not be capable of the demanding activity. Only time would tell.

But Eli never once complained. Instead, one day he sat down beside me after a long walk, both of us breathing too hard from the exertion. He wrapped his arm around my shoulder and pulled me close. "We might be a little broken these days," he said, "but I wouldn't trade it for anything."

My heart throbbed inside my chest, the feeling of both joy and pain. I didn't know I was capable of loving one person this much, as if my insides were bigger than my outsides, love an expansive force. It made the truth of our pending separation all the worse. But it had to happen. Once our stay here was over and we returned to the real world and our real lives, we would have to put an end to this. The risk of staying together was too great. I never wanted to be there again—watching Eli die, living one of Lady Elaine's visions. I understood that now.

Eli did, too, although we never spoke of it.

There were other things to talk about. My mother came to us on the third day with news that the Magi Senate was planning an awards ceremony in our honor.

"No way," Eli and I said together.

My mom sighed. "I told Lady Elaine you weren't going to like it."

I hated the idea. We'd been through one of those ceremonies last year when we saved Lyonshold from sinking. I understood why they wanted to do it, but it didn't feel right this time. There'd been too much death, too much loss. I just wanted to put it all behind me.

"Can't we just say no then?" Eli said, rubbing his jaw.

Mom put her hands on her hips. "I'm afraid not. We have to give them something. This is too momentous an event for there not to be some kind of official closure."

I bit my lip. It wasn't the response I would've expected from my mom, the queen of bucking the establishment. But that just drove home how serious the situation was. *Closure.* I supposed I needed it, too.

"What about Paul?" I said.

My mom turned to look at me, her mouth a thin line. "What about him?"

"Has he been buried yet?" The words felt alien in my mouth, an impossible language with impossible meaning. I'd seen him die, but I couldn't accept it. He might come walking around the corner any moment.

"I don't think so," my mom replied, a suspicious eyebrow climbing her forehead.

I drew a deep breath. "Then let the Magi Senate hold their ceremony at his funeral." I glanced at Eli, trying to gauge his reaction. He met my eyes, and I read understanding in his, if not agreement.

I turned to my mother, who needed the most convincing. "Paul deserves the honor as much as the rest of us, if not more. He died stopping Marrow. He sacrificed himself to save us."

"Yes," my mom said, her voice surprisingly gentle, "but he betrayed you first. If he hadn't have been helping Deverell he might—"

I cut her off. "That doesn't matter. All that does is what he did in the end." I paused, waiting for my mom and Eli to make their arguments, but my heart was set on this. Paul had done a lot of bad things, but he chose good in the end.

When neither of them spoke, I pressed on. "With his uncle dead and his mother who knows where and his father who knows who, it's up to us to see he has a proper send-off."

My mom's jaw worked back and forth, for a second. Then she relaxed. "I'll talk to Lady Elaine and see what we can do."

"Thank you," I said. The decision eased the ache in my heart, just a little.

Do you believe in redemption? I remembered Paul asking me. I hadn't had an answer then, but I did now.

Yes, I thought, hoping Paul would hear it wherever he was now. He had earned his redemption.

⁓ 32 ⁓

Dream's End

It took a while, and a great deal of cajoling according to my mother, but the Magi Senate finally agreed to the plan. Paul was set to be buried in his family's mausoleum in Coleville Cemetery, located on the north side of Arkwell.

Eli, Selene, Lance, and I arrived back at campus the day before. We'd been placed under sleeping spells for the journey back to the human world. I had no idea how that journey worked, but I suspected it involved boats. There'd been several moored at the dock by the river that ran in front of the castle. I didn't ask for confirmation though. After all of Eli's dreams with the funeral barge, I didn't want to know.

Selene and I spent the next twenty-four hours confined to our dorm room by choice. Reporters of all types and shades had infested Arkwell like so many rats—everyone eager to gnaw at us with their questions. I didn't understand why the school had allowed them on campus in the first place. Even worse was the separation from Eli, but I told myself it was for the best. We both needed to get used to the distance.

The funeral started at sunset the next day. Selene and I met up with Lance and Eli, and we walked to Coleville escorted by a troop of police officers. The reporters hurled questions at us the entire way, but all except a select few were barred from entering the cemetery.

Eli took my hand as we stepped inside. As always, the heavy scent of flowers filled the air. Coleville was kept in bloom year-round by the fairy gardeners. I'd never before appreciated it as much as I did now. It reminded me of the fairy realm. I wished we could go back—Eli and me, spending the rest of our lives there. Surely, the curse wouldn't be able to touch us in such a magical place.

But it was wishful dreaming.

The entire school had turned out for the funeral, it seemed, along with the entire Magi Senate and their entourage. Magickind filled every inch of the area around the Kirkwood's mausoleum. There were people leaning on gravestones, standing in the flower beds. Several had even climbed trees to get a better view.

We were escorted to the front where the coffin sat just before the door into the mausoleum. The moment I spotted it, the tears I'd been holding back broke. I didn't try to stop them. Eli wrapped his arm around me, his silent support all the comfort I needed.

Chairs had been provided for the honored guests, and we took ours right up front. To my surprise Lance's father, Senator Rathbone, appeared on the other side of Lance. I watched as his gaze took in Selene sitting beside his son. Her wings were still out, although some of the bandages had been removed from the left one. He stared at her for several long seconds. She raised her head and met his stare head-on, unflinching. Lance was holding her hand with both of his, knuckles white.

Finally, Mr. Rathbone sighed and stretched out his hand to Selene. "I want to thank you for what you did in stopping that monster. And I couldn't be prouder of my son's wise choice of girlfriend."

Selene's jaw came unhinged for half a second. Then she recovered and stood up, accepting his handshake. "Thank you," she said, very stiff and formal.

Mr. Rathbone nodded then let go of her hand and took the seat next to his son. I exchanged a quick glance with Selene. It had been a very diplomatic statement, the kind to save face in a public arena, but even a false gesture might become true with enough practice. A smile ghosted the edges of her lips, and her eyes sparkled. I squeezed her hand, happy for her.

But the good feeling didn't last long. Sadness pressed down on me as Lady Elaine stood up to officiate. It was a solemn affair, no music, no pomp. Consul Borgman gave a speech, thanking Paul for his service, as well as the rest of us. Every pair of eyes in the place turned toward Eli, Selene, and me when she pointed us out. I hated the scrutiny, wanting to keep my despair private. Fortunately, Borgman soon turned her attention to my mother and Mr. Corvus, giving the assembled a cleaned-up version of the events in the dragon caves, as well as exonerating my mother for any wrongdoing.

I wept again as Lady Elaine delivered the eulogy. I wept both for Paul's death and the tragedy of his life. His pretender of a mother hadn't bothered to come to her own son's funeral. It seemed I was the only person to truly mourn him.

When the ceremony ended, the four Magi Senators who'd volunteered to be pallbearers stood up and took their places around the coffin. As they hoisted it up and carried it into the mausoleum I realized that Paul had finally gotten his wish. He was free. The thought might've seemed glib, but it wasn't to me. Not after what I'd been through. I knew beyond doubt that death wasn't the end. Paul would find freedom on the other side.

Afterward, Eli and I escaped deeper into Coleville, dodging the Magi Senators and the rest looking to ply us with questions. It was surprisingly easy to disappear.

"Do you remember that this was the first dream we ever shared, right here in this cemetery," I said as we walked along.

A sad smile crossed Eli's lips. "Of course I remember. I'll never forget it."

My heart did a slow steady thump against my chest. The end was coming. It was almost here. I supposed this first dreaming place was a fitting sight for the end of our relationship.

Eli came to a halt and faced me. "Dusty," he began.

I raised a finger to his lips, silencing him. "We don't need to say it out loud. Just say it with a kiss."

Something broke in Eli's expression, and when he reached for me, he did it with both hands cupping my face, holding me like something fragile that he desperately wanted to hold on to but didn't want to shatter. His lips captured mine with a ferocity that said he was never letting go, even though he was.

The kiss lasted an eternity, even as it ended all too soon.

A strange noise broke us apart sometime later. We both turned to see we weren't alone anymore. Lady Elaine and Mr. Corvus were standing a few feet away.

I sighed. "You don't have to lecture us. We know, and we will."

"Will what?" Lady Elaine said, folding her broomstick-thin arms over her narrow chest.

I scowled at her, hating that she was making me say it aloud. "We won't be together anymore."

Lady Elaine pursed her lips. "It just so happens that is what I'm here to talk about."

"I mean it. It's really not nec—"

She raised a hand, silencing me. "I don't know how or why, but my vision about the two of you and your future is gone."

I frowned. "Gone how?"

Lady Elaine drummed her fingers against her arm. "Just gone. There is no vision about you anymore. I've tried scrying about it over and over again these last few days, but there's nothing."

"What does that mean?" Eli said. He slid his hand into mine, intertwining our fingers.

"I'm not entirely sure, Mr. Booker," she said, and it seemed to me that there was a twinkle in her eyes. "But my guess is that the dream-seer curse has been broken."

A tremble slid through my body, and I sagged into Eli. That couldn't be right. Dreams didn't come true in real life. Not like this.

"I don't know if it was the self-sacrifice," Lady Elaine continued, far too nonchalant than the subject warranted, "or if it was the work of the phoenix, but the curse is no more. As far as my sight can tell, you two are free to be however you want."

I froze, unable to move, unable to react at all. But not Eli. He turned me toward him, hands on my shoulders, and kissed me once again. It wasn't a chaste kiss either. But we didn't care. Our joy couldn't be held back by such trivial things as appropriate public displays of affection. Not breaking the kiss, Eli dropped his hands to my arms and hoisted me into the air. I wrapped my legs around his waist. I was both laughing and crying at the same time.

Lady Elaine let it go on far longer than I would've guessed, but eventually she said, "That's enough you two. I might have given you my blessing about the curse, but this is still school."

Eli set me down, his grin so wide his face seemed to be all lips and teeth.

"Well now that you've gotten that out of your system," Mr. Corvus said, "I have more good news. At least, I believe you'll be happy about it, Dusty."

I faced him, barely listening. There couldn't be anything better than the news Lady Elaine had just given us.

But I was almost wrong about that. Mr. Corvus slid his hand into his pocket and withdrew a silver bracelet. I gaped, my heart now fluttering in my chest.

"Is that . . ." I began, but the words died in my mouth. Corvus had removed the glamour, revealing the sword beneath. It was Bellanax, whole once more.

"Not everything about sword lore has been lost," Mr. Corvus said, and he held the sword out to me.

I hesitated, glancing at Eli. "Are you okay with this?" The sword had been the means of his death, after all.

He smiled, the expression genuine. "Of course. That sword saved us, didn't it?"

And he knows its name now, I remembered. I nodded. Bellanax had saved us. But the sword had been broken. Was the spirit still there or was it just a sword?

Bracing myself for the worst, I took the sword from Corvus. At first, I felt nothing but the hard, slick bone of the hilt against my skin. Disappointment set in at once, a despair nearly as deep as what I felt for Paul.

But then the hilt began to warm in my hand. Bellanax slowly stirred to life. The sword seemed to purr inside my mind, the feeling one of welcome and relief. It had missed me, and I had missed it.

Swallowing the emotions rising up my throat, I fixed my eyes on Mr. Corvus. "Thank you."

He bowed his head, and for the first time I noticed the Borromean ring on his finger. "You're welcome. It was the least I could do. You stopped Marrow and you helped me bring justice to my brothers. I would give you the world to show my gratitude if I could."

For the first time ever, the reality of Marrow's death hit me. It was like a massive weight being pulled off my soul. I felt so light I half-expected my feet to leave the ground. It was over. Truly over.

I applied the glamour to Bellanax and then slid the silver bracelet onto my wrist where it belonged. Where it would always stay, for as long as I lived.

"Come on then," Lady Elaine said, flashing a quick smile at Mr. Corvus. "Let's leave these two alone."

Leave us alone. Three words had never been more beautiful.

And they made good on the statement, walking away from us and not looking back once.

Eli kissed me again. It was shorter this time, but no less sweet. "I think I'm going to have to do that about once every five minutes. That okay with you?"

I laughed. "I don't know. Five minutes seems like an awfully long time."

He grinned, and the two of us started walking again.

"I wonder what our dreams will be like now," Eli said after a few moments of silence.

"Better than they've ever been?" I ventured.

"Oh, that's a given, but there will still be trouble, sooner or later. I mean, we are still the dream-seers."

"I suppose so." I paused. "And Marrow is gone, but he still has supporters out there. Some in the senate even."

Eli nodded.

"Is it weird that I'm kind of glad? I mean, all the death and destruction aside, the mystery-solving, hero stuff is pretty fun."

Now it was Eli's turn to laugh. He stopped and kissed me again. "I wouldn't want you any other way. That's why we're the Dream Team."

The Dream Team come true, I thought. But I didn't say it

aloud. There was no need. We walked on, exploring new paths as we went, heading deeper and deeper into the cemetery. With Bellanax on my wrist and Eli by my side, I realized the real world had now become the dream. And I wanted to stay in it forever.